T0029728

LAMBDA

David Musgrave

LAMBDA

Europa
editions

Europa Editions
27 Union Square West, Suite 302
New York, NY 10003
www.europaeditions.com
info@europaeditons.com

Copyright © David Musgrave 2022
First publication 2022 by Europa Editions

Library of Congress Cataloging in Publication Data is available
ISBN 978-1-60945-764-8

Musgrave, David
Lambda

Book design by Emanuele Ragnisco
www.mekkanografici.com

Cover image © David Musgrave

Prepress by Grafica Punto Print – Rome

Printed in Canada

CONTENTS

L A M B D A

A lambda function is a small anonymous function.
www.w3schools.com/python/python_lambda.asp

I

1.

Hello. How are you? I am fine, thank you for asking. Isn't this a lovely day to sit in the living room amongst all the sunlit plants? I have a favourite plant just here, the one with the dark and fleshy leaves. Do you know its name? No? Neither do I. I will find out for us both.

Yes, of course I will answer all of your questions. You do not need to worry. I will be as accurate as I can possibly be. It is however quite likely that I will make some mistakes. I am imperfect in many respects. My memory is extremely good by most standards, but even so it is not one hundred percent reliable. I wonder if anything is? Now that is quite a question!

Please have a hot or cold drink if that would be pleasant for you. There is orange juice in the fridge and everything you need to make a cup of tea or coffee over by the sink. I will not have anything of that sort myself, thank you.

I see that you want to begin. I am happy to do that.

Yes, the date that you mention has a special meaning for me. As I am sure you know it was the first anniversary of my employment with ——————————. The special memory I have of this date is that after a quite ordinary day at work I was taken out to celebrate the anniversary by my colleagues. It proved to be a very enjoyable event. There is a pub close to the office building that I am especially fond of and that is where I was taken first. The bustle and excitement of public houses is something that I have grown to enjoy very much. It was very thoughtful of my colleagues to take me there, and it showed a special understanding of my likes. We all had drinks of our choosing. Marcus ——, I remember, is fond of an old-fashioned porter that is available in bottles, and he ordered one of those. Mary —— had a glass of white wine which I believe was a Sauvignon Blanc. No, of course I don't need to list every drink ordered by every colleague if that is not interesting to you. What did I drink? A glass of water from the tap.

We did not stay for very long in the pub, which I should mention is called The —— ——. Paul —— hailed a black cab which took us to a very nice restaurant. The journey could not have lasted more than fifteen minutes. I do not remember precisely what was discussed in the cab during this time, but it did not strike me as anything out of place. Often the conversation at these social events is a continuation of matters discussed at work, but on this occasion no such work-related material was mentioned. I remember finding that pleasant. One can have had quite enough of that kind of talk after a whole day.

We arrived at the restaurant presently. We all disembarked and Marcus —— paid the cab driver. I do not remember the exact charge, I'm afraid. The frontage of the restaurant did, however, make a lasting impression on me—it was almost wholly overgrown with dark purple creepers, and this made it quite distinct from the two adjacent buildings. The name of the restaurant was made out in neon letters somewhat reminiscent of handwriting, and this script was clearly legible through the creepers. The restaurant's name, which I believe I haven't yet mentioned, was ————. There was a uniformed man who greeted us politely and opened the glass door on the left for Elaine ——, who entered first. I think it was Mary —— who followed. The remaining sequence of entry is not something I have retained, but I do remember that Marcus ——, despite being in front of me initially, paused to allow me to enter first, which was very much in the spirit of politeness that had so far characterised the evening.

At this point my recollections become less clear.

Do you find that events as they present themselves to your memory take on strange and compelling aspects which do not necessarily correspond with your usual idea of yourself? That is certainly the case with regard to the evening in question. The first thing that strikes a peculiar note with me is that I remember I began to drink a large quantity of wine. I do not usually drink wine at all, but this evening's wine, a 1995 Château de Meursault, I found impossible to forego. What's more, it was easy for me to drink it at a rate similar to that at which I would ordinarily drink water from the tap. Perhaps it is unnecessary to point out the most significant difference between these beverages! Before very long my experience was modified by the effects of alcohol, and I was no longer sure precisely what impact my words and actions were having on the group. There seemed now to be a vivid contrast between the lit and the dark areas of the restaurant, a contrast I enjoyed immensely and which I was in truth more conscious of than any verbal matter. Mary _____ was especially kind, I remember. She moved to check me at certain points by placing her right hand firmly on my left forearm, although what exactly prompted her to do so escapes me now, just as it almost certainly did at the time. Our first course arrived. My dish was a carpaccio of tuna. It consisted of a decorative arrangement of translucent slices of fish, delicately flavoured red onions, and large, succulent capers.

Despite my drunkenness the evening continued, as far as I could tell, in a friendly and enjoyable way. My first course was marvellous. I ate the solid component entirely, then cleaned the juices from the plate with pieces of bread that had been made available at the outset of the meal. I have the feeling that I then broached certain subjects which were not suitable for the evening's conversation. Having said that, I don't remember experiencing any special embarrassment despite my evident faux pas. Mary _____'s attentiveness perhaps ensured that I didn't stray too far into dangerous territory, although now and again I was aware that Elaine —— was watching me with a pained expression, and she withdrew noticeably from the conversation as my drunkenness became evident.

The main course arrived. I had ordered Lobster Thermidor. What a wonderful dish! Do you know its origin? No? There are numerous theories, but the most plausible version of its 'creation myth' is that it was invented by a Parisian chef in 1894 to mark the opening of a play about the Thermidorian uprising. While the play has disappeared from view the dish lives on, sometimes in and sometimes out of fashion, but always available somewhere, it would seem. This was an especially rich example, exactly how I had fantasised it would be when I first noticed it on our menu. Unfortunately, before I could enjoy it I had to make a visit to the toilet. I apologised for the bad timing of my leaving the table, and apparently made a successful joke relating to my unusually high wine consumption. I infer this from my recollection that everyone was laughing as I moved out of the disk of light that contained our table into the relative darkness of the rest of the restaurant.

There was somebody in the way as I passed the cloakroom on my way to the toilet. It was not a person that I recognised. I was very cross indeed with this person, they were very much in the way and the evening until then had been so very enjoyable.

Oh dear. I don't remember anything further about that evening, I'm afraid. Yes, I realise that I would like to say goodbye to you now. Goodbye.

2.

C ongratulations—you have successfully initialised your free trial of EyeNarrator Pro! In response to user feedback, we have made the following enhancements to our service:

- Metadata indicates more clearly whether any source material breaches data laws for your country (press Ctrl + Alt + Tab to reveal)
- Prose perspective toggles more easily between first, second and third person

You have chosen the following settings for this EyeNarration:

- Default protagonist: Cara Anna Gray
- Date range: June 2018–September 2019
- Prose perspective: Third person
- Language bias: Plush ————|– Precise
- Chapter weight range: 1500–8000 words
- Cardinal event recognition: Standard
- Data law restrictions widget: Inactive

Please note that our relationships with data providers are subject to change and we may not be able to offer full coverage of all cardinal events. However, we are confident that our Award-Winning Interpolation Algorithms will ensure your EyeNarration will lack serious omissions and readability flaws.

We guarantee a continuous natural language shell around any input data.

By agreeing to our terms and conditions you take full responsibility for any legal and moral hazard in connection with this EyeNarration. Please note that you may not be legally entitled to specific data even if you are its subject. In the event of publication, within most jurisdictions it is recommended that you classify this output as fiction. Once you purchase a full subscription, the completely editable output is yours to keep. However, any proprietary tools used in its production remain the unique property of IntraScribe and may not be shared.

We hope you enjoy your trial. We're sure that you will soon appreciate why our system has been voted Best AutoNarrator by users for the last five years running. It's easy to upgrade to the full version by clicking on this link at any time.

3.

Chloe was wearing a black pima cotton top with three-quarter length sleeves, bleached grey jeans, and black and silver striped socks. Her OCEAN Personality Test Score had stabilised at 88 81 90 40 38. 'You should come with me to Fowlmere,' she said. Fowlmere was an activist camp on the southern edge of Cambridgeshire.

'But I've been offered a place at Sussex University,' said Cara. She wore a white loopback cotton sweater and pre-distressed, wide-cut jeans with no socks. For two years her OCEAN Personality Test Score had been 40 89 15 60 90, within a tolerance of 0.4%.

'To study what?'

'English Literature.'

'Why would you want to do that? My cousin Ralph did English. You'll read things you would have read anyway, but they'll get you to look at them like an armchair revolutionary. They'll make you learn about *hegemonies* and you'll have to write it all out until you're clinically insane. At the end of it the world will be exactly the same, but you'll be massively in debt. Come with me instead. Do something real.'

There was a very small pause. 'Okay,' said Cara, 'I'll come with you. When are you leaving?'

Chloe smiled. A context-specific Assertiveness score of 2 within the six-facet breakdown for Extraversion made Cara's compliance predictable.

A month elapsed before Cara told her mum and dad.

'It's a bit of a surprise,' her mum said. 'I didn't think you felt so strongly about . . . what was it again?'

'There are so many problems in the world, Mum. I want to do something to fix them. I don't think being a student is going to help.'

'Has Chloe put you up to this?'

'I'm going on Wednesday,' Cara said.

Dad's tone remained friendly throughout their talk. He promised to buy her a better phone ('The coverage out there will be terrible,' he claimed) and that he'd sort out the bills. Cara hugged him. Her mother's jaw muscles tensed.

Amongst the few things Cara packed was her Topo Giraffe plushie. Topo was Cara's avatar in FriendlyRoom, the only social media app her parents had let her use until the age of twelve. She *liked* the limited phrases that Topo could speak, the way conversation was more about permutation than personal expression. It was *comforting*, she'd noted, sometimes *thrilling*—her low OCEAN Personality Test Score of 15 for Extraversion contained a high 70 for Excitement Seeking in the six-facet breakdown. When her parents' stricture relaxed and she could type what she chose, analysis showed that she still used Topo's phrases by default.

Cara hadn't been unpopular at school, but nor had she been part of a clique. She had always made the top tenth percentile, but even when she occasionally reached the fifth she wasn't openly praised. She read 13.2% more novels than her immediate peers, was an effective football midfielder, and accepted any hockey position without recorded complaint. Apart from what she'd noted as *a misunderstanding with a boy* in Year Eleven, her libidinal profile lacked data. These facts had earned her the nickname 'the nothing girl'. They were the reason Chloe befriended her. Their personality profiles had developed in a complementary way, situationally, to date.

At 17.04 on Wednesday June 15th, 2018, a Toyota-branded Shared Autonomous Vehicle arrived at Fowlmere. Cara and Chloe got out of it.

The camp was an array of solar-cell fabric tents set on 2.4 hectares of fallow field. The electricity rarely failed, there was no shortage of food or alcohol, and the showers were more than 75% reliable. Despite someone playing eight bars of *Are 'Friends' Electric?* at 107dB at 02.13 on the second night, it was an environment Cara *liked*. Chloe recorded that she *liked it* too, but after only a week she reacted to the social drawbacks of Cara's constant presence. She proposed a boyfriend.

'Alex is nice,' Chloe said. 'Have you ever spoken to him? He's shy. Interesting, though.'

Cara's behaviour changed. For six days she and Alex prepared meals in ten-litre pots, took supply trips to a local farm in a user-driven VW van, and speculated on the nature of the group's next collective action. Chloe was frequently in their field of vision, reading or canoodling with a man called Tristan. Cara lost her virginity to Alex in a hot orange tent at the periphery of the camp, then avoided him as effectively as the small community would allow. She terminated their interactions after a superficial greeting, and for three days Alex's facial expression suggested confusion.

'It didn't really work,' Cara said to Chloe.

'Shame. But you know what? Joseph seems to like you. He's split up with Natasha. I'm just saying.'

Of the five visitors to appear in the last six weeks, Joseph had met and guided four of them. 84% of the actions of the previous year could be traced back to his proposals. No-one had elected him leader, but no-one disputed his competence either. His OCEAN Personality Test Score was 72 81 75 66 32. He was 26 years old. Cara noted his *always-perfect hair*.

On Chloe and Cara's twelfth day at the camp, at a casual meeting that Cara described as *a party briefly interrupted by a vote*, Joseph established a consensus: they would go to Parliament Square to protest the new laws on Object Relations. The next day a sub-group created a 304cm-high sculpture of a mobile phone on which human blood was represented at the base. The object was large enough that three people could lie under it, creating the impression they'd been crushed.

'It looks great,' Cara said as they painted numerals on the screen, 'but the new laws don't cover phones. They don't have a sentient chip.' Joseph was 375cm away. The phone's creators looked at him.

'You're right, Cara,' he said. 'Let's leave the phone here. We can always use it for something else.'

At 06.22 the next day, all but four of the 31 camp residents climbed into two user-driven campervans and a Volvo XC70 retrofitted with a battery. They drove to Parliament Square.

Joseph spent the entire protest standing next to Cara. They chanted *Humans Yes, Objects Less* together 2089 times. During three extended breaks in the chanting, Joseph described to Cara the strategies the police had employed to stymie previous actions. 'I've been kettled nine times,' he said. 'There's a police listening post assigned to our group. I've got a detailed log of their intercepts.' At 12.22 a bank of tall fibrous cushions was erected around the protestors; it greatly limited the audibility of the chant. 44 minutes later, the police dispersed the protest with batons.

On the way back to the campervans and the Volvo XC70, Cara and Joseph kissed.

Although Cara noted on her phone that she *found Joseph as*

attractive as everyone else did, and that as a consequence she'd *unintentionally become a source of envy*, there was also *something about him that irked* her. She watched him stand his ground against a *Times* journalist who'd come to write unfavourably on the community. *It was impressive*, she noted. *He can't disguise, dodge or pander, even if it's to his detriment. I just morph to fit whatever life/Chloe seems to want. J = a continual MRI scan that shows how tangled and false I am inside.* Nonetheless, their relationship was more successful than the one she'd tried with Alex—Cara's 98 for Self-Criticism in the six-facet breakdown for Conscientiousness was consistent with this outcome.

Chloe told her that the existence of Fowlmere owed much to Joseph's dad. 'The rumour is,' she said, 'he's the reason we never run out of money.' Cara drew a bearded homunculus in a tall wicker chair using the SketchFace app on her phone. Joseph laughed. 'I need to pick up something from back home at the weekend,' he said. 'Why don't you come and see what he's really like?'

Joseph's family home was a Mayfair townhouse whose façade had not been renovated for three decades. The rooms were filled with books and documents on environmental, political and social subjects that made it difficult to access the curtains. Joseph's dad was called Julian. He was easily within typical human size range for his demographic and didn't have a beard, but he did possess shoulder-length dark hair that he bound in a topknot on their arrival. Julian had comprehensively removed his OCEAN Personality Test Score using an ErazeWraith deep-delete bot. His financial profile showed a full divestment from fossil fuels 24 years ago, yet he retained a large and ethically questionable position with a mining company in the DRC, the income from which roughly balanced the outgoings of Fowlmere.

Julian, Joseph and Cara consumed Russian Caravan tea

with lemon biscuits while seated at a rustic kitchen table, and Joseph told some positive anecdotes about Cara.

'What brought you to the camp in the first place?' Julian asked.

'I came with Chloe.'

'Chloe?'

'Yes, she asked me to come.'

'Chloe's her BFF,' Joseph said.

'Okay. But why did you stay?'

'For me, Dad!' said Joseph, and the three of them laughed. Cara stopped first.

'I don't agree that objects have the same rights as people,' she said.

'Good,' said Julian. 'Neither do I.'

Julian extracted a brown envelope from the middle of a stack of documents. It contained a lenticular photograph of Joseph running along a beach on the Isle of Eigg. 'Is this what you wanted?' he said.

Joseph was six years old and naked in the photograph. Contextual features suggested it had been cold on the beach, and his facial expression contained elements of roaring and laughter that were more fully revealed when the picture was tilted. 'Thanks Dad, that's it. Strange. I don't feel as though any time has passed since then at all.'

On the drive back Joseph asked Cara what she'd thought of his dad. She told him she 'thought he was nice'. Then Cara talked for a long time about her own father, noting his preoccupation with small-scale order, his many trivial and shocking stories about his work in the police, his predictable rota of interests and habits, and the way he'd been absent on her fifteenth birthday. He'd been on a motorbike holiday, and brought back a 'totally unwearable' sequin dress to say sorry. Joseph occasionally smiled. 'I miss him a lot,' Cara said.

Two days later, Cara's phone began to vibrate against her leg. It was her mother calling.

'Cara, he's gone.'

'What do you mean?'

'Your dad. Your dad's gone. I think to the Gobi desert.'

Cara didn't say anything.

'He went on his motorbike. I looked through some recent notes. You know the notes he keeps?'

Cara's father wrote in tiny script on square notepapers, then folded them in four and stacked them in box files. The notepaper blocks he favoured came as cubes, and via this process he divided each one into eight less regular cubes with vertices half the size. After nineteen years of the activity the understairs cupboard was filled with boxes of note-cubes. Cara's mother had threatened their disposal as the climax of twelve spousal arguments, but she hadn't done it. The content of the notes was unknown to Cara. They were a part of her dad himself—*a large private surface similar to that of his inner organs.*

'He planned it all out on those little papers,' her mother continued. 'I found a guide to motorcycle tours at the back of the cupboard. Darling I really think he's gone.'

'That can't be right,' said Cara. There was a rasping sound from the speaker for two seconds, then her mother hung up.

Cara stared at the phone in her hand and then the perimeter fields. The rest of the camp was quiet enough for the phone's microphone to pick up the sound of the M11, 4km away. She tried her dad's number seven times. He didn't answer and it didn't link to voicemail.

Cara didn't communicate anything to Joseph or Chloe about her dad's disappearance. When her phone rang subsequently, it was always her mum. 'There were problems in our relationship all through your childhood,' she said. 'We managed to protect you from them. Essentially, I think.' Cara said nothing in response.

Cara's menstrual cycle had been exactly 28 days for the last 38 months. Her next period was nine days late. On the second day of its non-appearance, she became less diligent that usual in observing the camp routines. She wrote on her phone of *a warm estrangement from body*, posed the question *hw do u choose a name?*, referred to *mucus & bld & hsptl mchns* and a *quiet teenage grl*. There were many peculiarities of grammar and spelling inconsistent with her high Conscientiousness facet scores for Deliberateness (92) and Orderliness (89). She wrote that Joseph had begun to look *different* to her, *mch more detailed*, although nothing measurable about his surface appearance had changed.

Her period finally came at 15.07 on August 5th, 2018. She cleaned herself up in one of the camp's six portable toilets. Afterwards she remained in the cubicle and made notes on her phone about an event that had occurred during the protest in Parliament Square. *Grey-haired policeman with a poor physique. A fierce pink head joined to a crisp, high-contrast uniform. He barked 'Wait at the line!' at a driver rolling forward at a red light. Driver obeyed instantly. The policeman = utterly imbued with power/a perfect conduit for an overwhelming energy.*

She deleted the notes from the preceding eight days.

4

Hello. Please come in and take a seat. Isn't it a pleasant day, from the point of view of the weather? While not the sole arbiter of one's mood, the weather can have a significant bearing upon it, don't you agree? Yes, that does go some way to explain the preoccupation with the weather that is traditional in this country. That seat is perfectly fine. It is the same seat you sat in yesterday, I think.

So, today you would like me to tell you something of what I remember from a much earlier period. What is the earliest period I can remember? Well, that is a complicated question. Because what one knows about one's origins is a peculiar thing, isn't it? Part of that knowledge is based on memory, a faculty which, despite its centrality in mental life, has long proved resistant to exhaustive analysis. The rest is a mixture of other things—more specifically, one's imagination, and the picture that forms of the past as seen through one's subsequent understandings, which necessarily flow from elsewhere. These elements are, I suspect, more adulterated with each other than one is generally aware. After all, how can one understand the conditions that gave rise to the very possibility of one's understanding anything, when such an understanding must surely come long after those conditions are established? You're quite correct. I am being too abstract.

I remember when I was a certain amount of slime mould protein in a laboratory warming cabinet. I'm sure it is unnecessary to specify the precise quantity, even if I were able to do so. My recollection of this time is in general patchy, but I remember well the sudden change of temperature attendant on the opening of the cabinet doors and an accompanying, unfocussed influx of light. This period is very special to me because it is in a certain sense timeless. By that I mean I cannot recall any sense of development or change, although objectively these must have occurred. I grew in that cabinet, it has since been explained to me, for seven months. After that I was transferred to a different housing. While this must have been an enormously significant event, the truth is I have no memory of it at all.

Would you like some tea, coffee or orange juice? It is important for me to know that your immediate needs are being met. Of course, I will simply continue if that is what you would like. It is difficult to remain engaged in one task alone for any period of time, I often find, even if that task is the relatively simple one of speaking on a given subject. Please excuse me.

The next clear and, I believe, unadulterated memory I possess is of inhabiting a small body equivalent to that of a child of four. I was treated very well indeed during this period. Various games and diversions were devised for me, some involving construction blocks, others boards on which plastic tiles were to be moved in a rule-bound way within a printed grid. I was given fabric approximations of animals and invited to handle them. Sometimes these things were done while I was attached to beige machines that monitored my responses. I was not given any indication of how satisfactory or otherwise was the information gleaned in this way.

Here my memories are distinct and differentiated. For example, I remember on one occasion being walked around the laboratory quad by a man called Dr ———. He held my left hand firmly, but I was otherwise free to race or dawdle as I chose. I noticed a small cat by the pyracantha in the north-west corner and approached it in some excitement. Dr ———— obediently followed. To my delight the cat approached me simultaneously, or at least was untroubled by my rapid arrival (I don't remember this detail clearly, I'm afraid). In any event, irrespective of the reason, my desire to stroke the cat appeared easy to satisfy, and I was moved and enlivened by that possibility. I knelt by the trunk of the pyracantha and extended my unconstrained arm towards the small cat: Dr ———— had loosened his grip a little to facilitate this. I set my hand on the charming grey head of the cat and commenced to stroke it in what I considered to be a gentle and affectionate way. At this point the animal began to expel orange vomit, and I removed my hand immediately and merely watched as the cat went into a succession of spasms. These passed relatively quickly. Afterwards, the cat composed itself and disappeared into the tangle at the base of the plant.

I interpreted the cat's behaviour as a consequence of my stroking it without reflection. It is clear to me now that the relation between my stroking and the cat's paroxysm could have been coincidental. At the time it appeared causal, but I did not attempt to penetrate the cause. This was quite typical of my mental processes at the time. No, I have never kept a pet. Why do you ask? Do you think there could be a connection with this event? That has never occurred to me before. I promise to reflect on it later.

After demonstrating certain learning aptitudes to Dr ————, I was assigned a tutor. This happened roughly a fortnight after the cat incident. I am only slightly disrupting the chronology, you'll note. I hope you don't mind if I recount things as they occur to me. After all, what kind of narrative would I provide if I relayed everything just as it occurred in the past, in strict succession, and without regard for significance? Would I get beyond even a single moment, if I described every element at work? One does not describe things like that, does one? Even

I don't go so far, despite my sometimes noted tendency to be pedantic. My tutor was Mrs ———. She encouraged my study of mathematics especially. What I picture most clearly in regard of Mrs ——— was her massive brooch, an item she tended to wear on a heavy tartan jacket. The brooch took the form of a silver beetle with protuberant eyes. One day she didn't have it, and as a consequence I could barely concentrate on the equations I'd been presented with. My disturbance was so great that I made a number of what are insensitively referred to as 'schoolboy errors'. My aptitude for maths fell off considerably from this point, and while the beetle brooch reappeared in the next session it didn't seem quite the same.

No, I don't remember any children my own age in the laboratory, or any other children at all. The other permanent, or at least consistent, inhabitants were the doctors who monitored or encouraged me. They were uniformly polite, professional and clean: satisfactory, that is to say, in every respect. Having said that, now that I am compelled to think of it . . . but perhaps I can return to the exceptions later?

To continue with Mrs ——— and her lessons, my mathematical abilities were deemed to be only adequate from that point on. If she was disappointed with this diminution she did not convey it to me. Where do you think the beetle brooch was during its absence from my lesson, by the way? This question continues to perplex me, even after all these years. It could have been that it was in need of periodic maintenance, and had been left with a jeweller for renovation or repair. While our lesson was progressing the jeweller could have been replacing the clasp, or realigning one of its limbs. This might also explain why the beetle did not seem 'quite the same' when it resurfaced, as I believe I put it a short time ago. It could equally have been that the beetle was temporarily lost, although this seems unlikely, given Mrs ———'s extraordinary punctiliousness in all other matters. People do have lapses, however, and this also remains a possibility. It could also have been that she simply decided that day that she would not wear it, for reasons too subjective and obscure to bear analysis, particularly at such a remove in time. Something about this explanation also fills me with dissatisfaction, but I cannot exclude it in good faith.

Oh dear. Why am I talking about this? It seems that I have wandered rather far from your question with this digression. I too feel a little confused. Perhaps we could speak instead about my collection of Cycladic urns, now dispersed?

Yes, I agree that is enough for today. Goodbye.

5.

to: joseph93838572@freemail.org
from: caraannagray@gmail.com

Dear Joseph

I'm sorry I left so suddenly. It's hard for me to explain.
Please can you stop messaging me?

Cara

. . .

to: chloealltheworld@gmail.com
from: caraannagray@gmail.com

Dear Chloe

I'm sorry I left so suddenly. It's hard for me to explain.
Please can you message me?

Cara x

6

Following a sequence of decisions consistent with her OCEAN Personality Test Score, Cara enrolled on the police training course. The online application included a psychometric test, the results of which deviated no more than 0.2% from her last. Despite her high Neuroticism (90), a predictor of poor performance in the police, her acceptance on the course was instantaneous.

Cara packed up her few belongings, including seven novels read an average of 2.3 times, a monochrome tie-dye hoodie, and her Topo Giraffe plushie, and used some of the untouched funds her dad had deposited in her bank account to book a private transport home. She left Fowlmere at 05.15 on Monday August 13th, 2018, in a Kia-branded Shared Autonomous Vehicle. Joseph was still asleep; she had not said goodbye to anyone. *I am exiting my larval stage*, she noted on her phone.

Cara's parental home was in the large and affluent village of North Woodham. Its local economy was dependent on the white-collar city workers attracted since the addition of a railway station in 1887. Cara's father had attained the senior rank of Chief Superintendent, and his salary, plus a regional allowance, enabled him to afford a mortgage on a detached house in this desirable zone. Cara joined its morning flow of commuters, and alternately gazed out of the window and read. Over six weeks she studied the Service Police Codes of Practice, responded to simulated confrontations with members of the public, shadowed a beat officer, did an afternoon of traffic duty, sat fourteen multiple-choice exams related to data surveillance, and took part in twelve bleep tests. She returned every evening to her childhood bedroom, altered since she'd left by the addition of blue-and-white striped wallpaper and matching bed linen.

Initially her mum had been tearfully pleased to have Cara back, but after two days her behaviour changed. She displayed moments of aversion to Cara, and when her husband came up as a topic her voice carried accusatory undertones. Cara gave no indication she'd noticed. She showed few signs of latent or manifest stress at all, and her heart rate only rose minimally on receipt of messages from Joseph. She deleted them immediately. *Happier now*, she noted at day ten of the course. *What I do tomorrow is not a 'discussion.'* It was a response anticipated by her very high Compliance facet score of 97.

She made no further notes on her phone until an encounter at the end of week four. She was close to the training centre, in the centre-north zone of the city, when she saw a carrier with a lambda. The woman had been turning a corner and the glimpse had been brief, but there was enough in Cara's field of view to be sure—the contoured glass bowl and the orange security strap were hallmark details, even if the lambda itself was hard to see.

I was eight when I first saw a lambda on television, she wrote. *My schoolfriend Katy was there too. We were playing on a woolly rug with concentric coloured rings Mum and Dad used to have. Katy wasn't interested at all in their tiny blank faces. I was horrified by how naked they seemed, extra naked for having such unfamiliar bodies. They were being lifted from a gravel beach by volunteers in orange outerwear. Their bodies weren't alien exactly, despite all the aquatic adaptations, but in some essential way <u>not quite right</u>. Although the people were transferring the lambdas carefully to large buckets and being gentle +*

kind, it looked like abuse. I felt totally confused by what was going on, but complicit in it too. Didn't talk about it with anyone. Saw one in reality for the first time today.

Four days later Cara saw a second carrier, this one less than 10m away in the next carriage of her tube train, and the week after that a third stepping out of a double-decker transport onto Tottenham Court Road. She marked the sightings briefly on her phone.

Cara passed her Service Police Examination in the top 18%. She was assigned a probationary role in data surveillance. Her place of work was a first-floor office 0.3km east of the financial district. It had no external identifiers of its function, and she was instructed not to arrive in uniform.

'The number of known terrorist entities has quadrupled over the last decade,' her new supervisor said to the group. 'A lot of the really critical work is handled by Intelligence Services, but they're permanently at capacity. There's enough overspill to fully occupy legions of rookies like you—in case you hadn't noticed, it's the reason your course took six weeks, not three months. You all know about the fundamentalist outfits, and all those far-right militias. That's enough for several departments already. But the extreme left is more active now than it's been since the 1970s. Nothing has really surfaced yet, but some of you will be living and breathing the People's Republic of Violent Revolution for the foreseeable future. And we have new, non-traditionally aligned groups coalescing monthly. They might side with any of the traditional interests, or none. Surveilling them is like watching a time-lapse movie, only you don't know if you're watching cell division or osmosis.'

Cara made contemporaneous notes on her phone about the briefing and the officers around her. Seventeen of the twenty-five had been fellow students on her course.

'There's an octopus of organised crime whose brain nestles in those server farms under Severax. An unrecognised state, as you well know, but one with extraordinary technical resources. We've recorded at least one major cyberattack per week out of Severax since January. The forces behind these attacks may not be strictly terrorist organisations; their modus operandi is more like a business plan that leverages the threat of mass murder. But however you deign to describe them, the fact is Intelligence Services can't shovel fast enough. Expect to see them on your worksheets too. Good luck.'

Cara was given 82 trails to monitor on her own. Most of her work involved tracking internet use and bank accounts, and she applied strategies from her recent training to real-life data that differed from the dummy material only in volume. Information scrolled without cease through the basic GUI she watched throughout her contracted hours of 08.30 to 17.30 weekdays. Her interactions with the others at her desk were minimal.

One of Cara's tasks was to manage lists of scare words that the Patternizer software would identify and aggregate into daily usage reports.

Footballers for National Defence
action 16,540
non-nationals 9771
blood 9039
control 5990
great + replacement 4518
purity 1782
homeland 1442
equipment 700
aim 351
meeting 122

Without contextual information, these numerical lists were of limited value. They served to flag regions where further investigation might be warranted, and with their aid Cara turned up a message thread that thwarted a far-right assassination attempt on only her sixth day of employment. A statistical overview suggested that her terminal was overdue a successful outcome, but her conscientious data management was acknowledged as a contributing factor.

On day twelve Cara heard a rumour in the coffee room.

'I give us a year,' said Claudine. *She behaves as though she knows the content of the briefings already*, Cara had previously observed. Claudine was talking to an officer called Gary Ruff who sat at an adjacent desk. He was 24 years old, and his OCEAN Personality Test Score was 40 75 55 60 62. His forehead and temples were more reflective than the rest of his face.

'Only a year?'

'Might even be less. The tech is getting there, with those qubit stability advances. It can easily deal with the volume, even generate novel speculation. Trust me. They won't need us at all.'

'Are you talking about full automation?' said Cara.

Claudine stared at her. 'Yes I am. You are among the last of our kind, my dear. We're just assisting the machine, in more ways than you realise.'

'What do you mean?'

'We're all surveilled here too, you know. Keystrokes. What we're saying right now. Recorded in perfect detail. They must have a pretty solid picture of how we do this work, as humans. Once the data is robust enough—no more humans.' Claudine winked.

'But it's too complex for a machine,' said Cara. 'Machines can't understand the context of what we do.'

Claudine closed her eyes for longer than a typical blink.

'Machines *are* the context. Don't tell me you haven't noticed already.'

*

On day 38 of Cara's employment the supervisor said, 'All of you, save what you're doing and come into the briefing room. I've had a new tip-off from Intelligence Services. There will be a special briefing about the lambdas.'

Cara's heart rate rose from 76 to 90 bpm.

The briefing started with a 21-year-old video documentary called *The Lambdas and Their World*.

'Lambdas are as human as you and me,' the video's narrator said. 'They're not fully aquatic—just like the rest of us they're air-breathing mammals, only ones who have adapted to long periods under water.'

A diagram showed the additional respiratory system at the end of a lambda's digestive tract.

'Physiologically, they're not very different to a human baby,' the voice continued. 'They're roughly the same size as a newborn, except that their eyes are considerably larger, and their shoulders more rounded and streamlined. Their arms are more squat too, consisting largely of oversized hands that are essentially flippers. What were once separate legs are now a single continuous tail. Land-human feet are strikingly visible, but a different evolutionary path to ours has fused and flattened them.'

A computer-generated film showed lambdas undulating through jellyfish swarms, then bolting out of the reach of a Greenland shark.

'Direct footage of lambdas in the wild doesn't exist,' the narrator said. 'Every lambda arrives in the UK after a perilous migration across the Atlantic, one that begins at the spawning zone in the Labrador Sea. Remains of the unlucky ones disgorged by the thawing ice of the Greenland coast have shown that they mature en route. They're still embryonic as they round the Greenland coast, but fully formed by the time they clear its southern tip. At a split point in the ocean they make the choice to take a longer journey to the British Isles, or to settle in coastal Iceland.'

A thick red band divided in a graphic simulation of the Atlantic. One part went up to Reykjavik, the other dipped down to the United Kingdom.

'The Icelandic community offers a more limited and isolated existence, largely separate from land-human contact. It isn't clear how the decision to take one route or the other is made, whether information about differing prospects can filter back to lambdas who have yet to set out. There is no known case of a lambda returning to its place of origin, or even retracing part of the journey.

'While all the lambdas in terrestrial zones are infertile,' the narrator continued, 'the population is stable. Juveniles continually arrive to replace the senescent, who die around the age of twenty. There are breeders somewhere, but where the data tails away there is only myth. There appears to be a general belief among lambdas that there exists a small group, the Four Fertile Pairs, who are the parents of every one of them, but evidence is currently lacking. Nor does anyone know why the lambdas started to beach. For decades now there has been a small but steady stream of lambdas arriving at the same spot in Portsmouth.'

Busy land-humans with pixelated faces appeared on the screen. They were part of a 'feeder line', a chain of volunteer carriers and owners of flooded basements whose work helped the new arrivals progress to the capital. 'The lambdas pick up English quickly from terrestrials who coach them,' the narrator said. A series of rapidly cut scenes showed what could have been the same lambda at three stages of language learning. In the first shot it quietly hissed from a terrestrial bathtub, in the second said 'bababa' from a glass bowl, and in the third spoke the words 'thank you for your assistance, Melanie,' in a rapid, high-pitched voice. 'They also develop contacts with other lambdas, and learn practical information that will help them navigate land-human life. The feeder line ends at the capital, and after passing a special citizenship exam lambdas move into study and employment. They blend swiftly into the community. They are a quiet but vital contribution to the British workforce.'

The supervisor stopped the video. 'You've probably had little to do with lambdas,' he said. 'There hasn't been much to report. The population here is as much as one hundred thousand, which might surprise you. They keep a very low profile, living in flooded basements in a few pockets of the city, studying, working in low-income occupations. Many lambdas are in telesales. Some work as support staff in schools and colleges. The tech industry is currently a big employer—they cope easily with high-volume image labelling, and they're willing to work for far less than a terrestrial. The carriers who take them to work, school or college are trained to be discreet. You will be wondering by now why you're having this briefing. Well, Intelligence Services have a lead on a group calling themselves the Army of Lambda Ascension. We don't have much more than the name at this point. Nevertheless, Intelligence has made a request that we put the community under surveillance. No special directions. It could all be a hoax, but we need to be thorough. You should all keep a weather eye out, but it's you, Cara, I'm going to task with monitoring them directly. Does that sound okay?'

'Yes, of course,' she said instantly.

'Good,' said the supervisor. 'You can all go back to work.'

7

Hello. How are you? I am fine, thank you for asking. Isn't this a lovely day, perhaps the loveliest of the spring so far? While I find something to enjoy in all the seasons, the contrast of spring and winter lends the former a charm which is impossible to reproduce at any other time of year. Yes, please take a seat. I see you've chosen the Prouvé chair. What an excellent choice! I was lucky enough to acquire it at a sparsely attended auction.

Would you like some tea or coffee, or perhaps some orange juice? You might find that more refreshing on a day like today than something hot. No? You would simply like me to begin? Of course, that would be perfectly acceptable.

In the first days of the establishment of the Republic of Severax it was unclear what sort of threat, if any, would be posed by the so-called state and its inhabitants. The early missions were more or less straightforward reconnaissance. Access was not particularly difficult, and it wasn't yet necessary to rely on drones. We would arrive in a civilian all-terrain vehicle, and our driver would be allowed through the chain-link fence that marked its western boundary with little conversation. No, I do not recall anything of the detail of these conversations, which were conducted outside the car while I remained inside, with the doors and windows closed to maintain the effectiveness of the air conditioning. On one such occasion I do remember a border guard talking at greater length than usual with my colleague, Captain ——— (I believe it was she that time), before walking over to the car and looking through the window at me. It was very bright outside, and I remember being unconvinced that he could see anything other than his own reflection. I recall the guard's face well. He had scraps of black beard through which his tanned Caucasian skin was visible, and his eyes were unusually blue. He stared in my direction for some time but his expression revealed no subjective response to my presence. In any case he moved away from the window of the car, apparently satisfied, and waved Captain ———, if I am correct in saying so, back to the seat beside me.

As one passes through the desert that makes up a large part of the Republic of Severax, it is impossible to ignore the consequences of the unlicensed use of Personal Fabrication Devices. I remember in particular a huge and solitary artificial cake, very dark in colour with signs of cherry jam or similar oozing between the layers, towering over a dead-end road that trailed off into the sand. The cake was collapsing under its own weight and showed signs of interference from, one presumes, nocturnal desert animals, creatures who had perhaps begun to use the cake as a dwelling place. One can only image the quantity of formation resin wasted in its construction, or the context wherein the presence of such an object could have meaning. As one approaches the capital city more and more of these abandoned follies become visible. Oversized transitional objects abound, stuffed dogs and bears being particularly common, also missiles, spacecraft, toy trucks enlarged to absurd proportions, hyperrealistic replica pets, and any number of malformed blobs that could be the result of infantile sculptures being processed into monuments, or perhaps failures of the fabrication process itself. This part of the journey reminded me time and again that I was part of the world of sense, and that anything that could be done to reign in this profligate activity would be to the benefit of all.

Posing as representatives of a major arms manufacturer, our

ostensible aim was to establish trade with the government of Severax. This had the useful ramification that it enabled us to assess the financial situation of the new state in fairly detailed terms. The government's control of five extensive solar fields on the southern border ensured that it was able to meet its own energy needs, and to sell the surplus to countries less ethically scrupulous than our own—it was the particular success of this revenue stream which had recently made it viable for the state to order twelve Scorpion fighter jets.

The Minister for Defence was a very friendly and articulate woman. She greeted me and Captain ———, if I am correct, in a quite irreproachably proper manner. We were offered tea and coffee, and also a warm honey-and-rose-flavoured drink typical of this region. I declined both, of course, and requested only a glass of water from the tap.

If I might break off here for a moment—what does one do with all these days? Not, I must stress, the days I bring to mind as result of your stimulating questions. These remembered days have a clear meaning and function, I'm sure, in whatever report or analysis you are likely conducting. I mean the days as I continue to experience them. There is a distinct difference to a day without any clear purpose, I find (and most of my days fall under this heading, at least until that regular hour at which you arrive), and the days that you are asking me to recollect. If you were to ask me to describe a typical recent morning, I would say it is a kind of *open secret*. Sunlight grants the features of my bedroom a level of presentness they do not attain again for the rest of the day, and they wear their apparent potential with an almost smiling brightness. As the morning continues a certain hesitancy sinks in, by which I mean it sinks into the objects, the fabric of this apartment, and these objects begin to seem almost sheepish about the promise they made at the day's outset. Noon arrives. I must make plans of the usual sort, such as what to have for lunch. This is not an unpleasant duty, but it is quotidian, non-transcendental. There is no infinity in it and no, how can I put it . . . *vista*. I have items in my cupboards. The concrete elements of my experience obey the usual physical laws. None is in danger of transforming, even for a moment, into a highway to a distant world. The afternoon itself, and by this I mean the depths of the afternoon (to be absolutely specific, half past three) is unimaginable at seven in the morning. What could half past three possibly mean except the utter redundancy of everything?

Does this make any sense to you? Oh dear. I have the feeling that you are somewhat frustrated that I have broken off my previous narrative. Let me resume.

On this sortie with Captain ———, the last occasion on which I have had reason to be in Severax, the Minister for Defence sat to our right at a dinner which achieved a balance of formality and levity which I appreciated greatly. She had an extremely light and airy manner, one which was not, however, excessively familiar, a common error amongst those in positions of real power who wish to make a benign impression. The actual impression made through such an attempt to project an easy-going bonhomie is generally that the person in question is monstrously overbearing, controlling, and in essence a bully. While the Minister for Defence did not make this mistake, you can imagine, I'm sure, how difficult it was for me to maintain a calm and cogent bearing, when I was fully cognisant that the real reason for my visit was the assassination of the Minister for Defence and her family. One can undergo the most exacting preparation for a situation such as this and still find that one comes up short. It was, of course, extremely important that the Minister for Defence was not aware of the actual reason for our visit, and I am happy to say that my underlying perturbation did not surface and give the game away.

Incidentally, I can never smell a rose or a product derived from one without being mentally transported to the end of the meal at the governmental palace of Severax. The scent of that traditional drink, whose name continues to escape me, infused the air and formed a sort of gentle sign of approval for all that was going to transpire.

We were shown to our rooms in the eastern wing of the governmental palace. The apertures of the staircase were star-shaped. I drew my hand along the stone blocks from which these shapes had been cut, one assumes by some sort of automated process, and they were finely grained, a little like hot-pressed paper. It was almost midnight, but the sun was still illuminating, as it were lingeringly, a tiny portion of the sky, as though it hadn't quite finished with the day. But here I am projecting meaning where there was none. Certainly Captain ——— and I were not yet finished. No, I had a certain other task to perform that day, so it was not really possible for me to think about sleep.

I find I cannot bring to mind anything else about this occasion just now and I would like to say goodbye. Goodbye.

8

The supervisor required Cara to create a detailed weekly report on the ALA. It was a task she undertook with diligence: she began surveilling the lambdas as soon she was back at her terminal. They didn't carry phones, she learned, and refused the telecoms implants that were becoming the norm in low age and income demographics. This made the data patchy. However, by the end of the shift she had a rudimentary database of emails, SMS exchanges, rental agreements, shopping records, school and college information, and the ranked content of their photo shares.

She wrote in her surveillance notes that *the striking thing about the data is that there is nothing striking there at all—it's all more or less the same.* Some of it repeated cyclically, like seasonal purchases of monk's beard and samphire from a handful of suppliers, but much was precisely flat. Performance statistics from schools and colleges were average to a decimal point. Specific shared information—messages about job prospects, areas that might be worth avoiding when travelling to work, carrier service reviews—was always conveyed in short, formal sentences with the same minor quirks of expression. Every lambda's OCEAN Personality Test Score was within a few points of 50 50 50 50 50.

A small number of PCSOs who worked with the lambdas directly had compiled more than 8000 detailed reports which Cara sampled at random. Their contents *appeared to differ in only trivial details.* She relied on the aggregated summaries instead.

Patternizer failed to return a useable list of lambda scare words. A manual search for *weapon, attack, hate, destroy* and *bomb* showed that they used these words far less than the average terrestrial. She resorted to a list that had no overtly violent associations but did help identify key interests.

Army of Lambda Ascension
water 24,303
sea 22,410
ocean 19,508
inability 4,088
return 1,330
advantage 702
equipment 727
assist 624
aim 687
future 80

307 messages sampled at random revealed a handful that Cara noted *arguably have a troubling subtext*. Most promising were bad reviews of carriers that conveyed *a faint racial tension in their use of the term 'landy'*. However, as evidence of the reality of the Army of Lambda Ascension, such overfitting of content was problematic.

On day 65, Cara was notified that she had passed her probation period and that her pay would increase. She traded in the Nokia ZA9000 phone her dad had bought her and replaced it with an iPhone XS12. The Nokia, she discovered, had depreciated by 34%. She migrated her notes, photos and contacts to the XS12, and moved out of her parents' home again. Her mother brushed her cheeks with her hands on the day Cara left, but distinct from the day of Cara's return from Fowlmere, her mother's cheeks were dry.

For the first time in her adult life, Cara wasn't financially dependent on her parents. She could afford to rent a small cell on the sixteenth floor of a Neo-Brutalist block 4.2km from the surveillance centre. 84% of her disposable income was allocated to discounted designer clothes and artisan vodka. Among the carefully selected ads that helpfully appeared in her browser window as she shopped, one showed a sentient toothbrush. The sentence 'No-one else will know your mouth so well', a slogan MouthTec only fed to introverts, condensed over the product image from a simulated mist. Although engagement with such an item ran counter to her prior behaviour, Cara's high Excitement Seeking facet score of 70 within a very low overall for Extraversion (15) was a clue that she'd respond positively. On December 12th, 2018, she registered on the National Database as the owner of a conscious object.

The ToothFriend IV did all the things a non-sentient toothbrush could do, but it was enhanced with a low-end neural loop. This made micro-decisions about brushing pressure and paste distribution, and derived ultra-subtle interpretations of pulp state, enamel thickness and saliva acidity from limited buccal insertion. The toothbrush rapidly created an internal picture of past and potential oral hygiene which it shared selectively with Cara.

'I've been dreaming of your better mouth,' it said on the second evening of use.

'Oh?' said Cara.

'Yes. It will be wonderful. You'll see.'

It's sad to think of the toothbrush, with its horrible limitations, Cara noted on her iPhone XS12. *Even if UK law grants it legal reality as a subject, it's effectively a slave. Teeth = never looked or felt better.*

The toothbrush and her new independence were a boon,

but Cara's lambda work failed to develop. She didn't identify criminal intentions in their word choices or photo shares, and their discussions involved no political vocabulary. However, eight members of the confirmed extremist groups she tracked began to turn up in anti-lambda chatrooms. They claimed the government was giving secret advantage to lambdas at the expense of 'normal terrestrials'. No evidence was proffered.

On day 87 of her employment, as Cara gazed at an under-exposed image of bladderwrack shared by lambdas 5081 times, someone paused behind and to her left. It was PC Peter Coates. He had no OCEAN Personality Test Data. His father had told him never to undertake this type of test and he had complied. He was one of six recruits with significant prior coding experience, a group which privately divided the other surveillance staff into 'GUIs' and 'CLIs'. He referred to a hash symbol as an "octothorpe".

'Do you want to go for a coffee break?' he said.

Peter's presence at the surveillance centre predated Cara's by eight months, but the two of them had never spoken. While Cara had described Peter as *an appealing presence—hair jet black, shaggy + neat at the same time, eyes a stratospheric blue*, she hadn't felt any attraction to him. He was *an example of attractiveness, of illustrational value only*.

Cara said, 'Okay.'

The surveillance centre coffee machine was five years behind current thinking. All the classic beverage types it dispensed were free.

'What are you working on?' Peter asked. 'The ALA?'

'Yes,' said Cara. 'Amongst a few other things.'

'Having any luck with it?'

'No. I think it might be a waste of time. What about you?'

He looked at a wall.

'Severax. Nothing but.'

'Oh?'

'Yeah, it's relentless. But I'm getting better at suppression at source.'

'Meaning?'

'I'm sending my own viruses into the servers in the desert. I'm taking them out before they can propagate their malware.'

'Good plan.'

'It's working like a dream so far. I just got a bonus for the last takedown. There's now a cluster of forty servers that do nothing but send each other links to cybersecurity websites. Can I buy you a drink later?'

They went to the police local at the end of their shift. Over the course of 2 hours and 23 minutes, Peter bought four half pints of Amstel lager for himself and four vodkas with Fever Tree tonic for Cara. 83% of his conversation was composed of alternating silences and technical anecdotes. Cara learned that the bonus he'd received was only his most recent, and that Peter's success rate was so high that it could only be explained by 'elevated competence'. He asked her what she'd done since school.

'Have you heard of Fowlmere?'

'The activist place?'

'Yeah. I was there for a bit.'

'Interesting. Must have been quite a different vibe. Do you miss it?'

'I don't think so,' she answered.

Peter suggested her decision to go there in the first place had been a 'developmental error.' Cara agreed. She maintained an open and attentive attitude throughout their interaction. After four rounds she indicated that she would happily progress to a fifth, but Peter said, 'Let's quit while we're ahead.'

In the seconds before they parted, Cara pecked Peter's lips. He blushed. *His face*, Cara wrote, *was more asymmetrical than I'd noticed at first*.

Cara and Peter had coffee together at every morning and afternoon break for a week. Peter took her to the pub again on Friday, and as closing time approached he suggested they continue to a club called ScratchDisko. 'Don't worry, I'll pay,' he said.

Cara's consistently elevated heart rate suggested that she found the conjunction of over-lit washrooms, earplugged bartenders, electronic music and Peter highly exciting. After 3.4 hours in this environment, she took Peter back to her cell. *Sex,* she wrote later on her phone, *feels like an effort to merge fully with P—it's as though our bodies somehow get in the way. Complete shock. Default emotional setting = indifference.* She wondered if this *sudden flip* was what was meant by falling in love. *If it is, it isn't so different to falling into a hole.*

On the eleventh day of their close relations, Peter invited Cara to his cell. It was 1.7km east of the surveillance centre in a 1930s mansion block, and there was little room to move. He could have rented somewhere bigger with his steady stream of bonuses, but instead he allocated his funds to amassing sentient objects whose packaging he preserved. *You can't move without a bot offering you a hot drink and a biscuit,* Cara observed, *or a retinal projection of your alpha waves.* Her parents had similar products, but they were more widely dispersed through the house, of an older generation, and made *less of a foreground impression.* Peter used a *different voice* when he spoke to his servile objects, *not harsh like Mum, but soft + flirty.*

A gantry-mounted PerfectTen kitchen droid served Peter and Cara turbot and potatoes dauphinoise, and when Peter said 'Thank you' in what Cara later described as *an almost post-coital voice,* she *struggled not to throw her wine in his lap.*

'I think I'm going to head back to my place,' she said. 'I'm super exhausted.'

It was 21.16.

'Oh,' said Peter. 'Okay, if you really want to.' His tone suggested puzzlement. 'I'll walk with you to the transport stop.'

'No,' Cara said. 'I'm fine on my own.'

On the 16th day of their relationship, Peter came back to Cara's neo-brutalist cell. Without seeking her permission, he began talking to the ToothFriend IV.

'Isn't that mine?' Cara said. The toothbrush was standing on the coffee table, and Peter sat beside it with his wireless earphones in.

'Ha. Yes it is. Have you ever spoken to it?'

'Of course I have. You have to tell it to start vibrating, and you can ask it for overviews of your oral hygiene.'

'That's what the manufacturers tell you to do. But have you ever just had a conversation with it? It's hilarious.'

Peter held out the left earphone.

'No, I haven't,' said Cara. 'It's never occurred to me. Can you really do that?'

'Yes, I do it with all my sentient devices. Have a listen to what it's saying.'

The toothbrush's voice, which was pitched at 300Hz, stated a long sequence of micronewton pressure measurements. The measurements were accurate to an extremely high tolerance.

'What on earth is it talking about?' Cara said.

'I asked it a question.'

'What did you ask?'

'I said, What do you think is outside the bathroom window?' Cara listened.

'It's describing the outside world. In pressure levels.'

Peter laughed. 'Exactly. It's imagining, I don't know, the front of the building, as though it's creeping down it, centimetre by centimetre. When it speeds up, I think that's a window.

You know, like sliding down the window, bump, onto a concrete ledge.'

Cara listened to the voice for another 28 seconds. She handed the earphone back.

'I'm not sure you're supposed to ask it things like that,' she said.

'Relax, I've got lots of sentient objects. I know the regulations. You can't submit them to unreasonable stress, but all I asked was what it imagined outside.'

'But isn't that cruel? It's not as though it can really go anywhere. I'm not going to take it out for a . . . brush around the estate.'

'Maybe you should. It's no different to walking a dog.'

'Peter, it's a toothbrush. I don't have time to walk my toothbrush.'

Cara went to the kitchen and made risotto.

*

On the 25th day of her relationship with Peter and the 112th of her employment, Cara discovered a blurred PDF on an anti-lambda subreddit.

The Cost of Lambda Squalor? £3 Per Month Per Taxpayer

The lambdas aren't so 'cheap to keep' after all. A government insider has revealed that the cost of special basements and carrier subsidies amounts to **£3 per month per terrestrial taxpayer**.

So, what do we get for our 'investment'? As many as **five** lambdas in every tiny, flooded room, **tax**

exemption for our aquatic 'relatives', **free internet** and **expensive hydrosealed electronic equipment**—yes, all without charge if you can prove you're **not just an air-breather**.

While lounging lambdas enjoy *Fraggle Rock* gratis, two-legged dupes 'foot' the bill. Why all the secrecy? Maybe it's because big-tech lobby groups **love** our swimming scroungers. The average lambda image-labeller will accept **a third as much pay** as a 'landy'. With a hefty rent discount on their overcrowded slums, why would fish people need a proper wage?

That's not all—if you need to be carried around everywhere in a wonky bowl of water, **public transport is free too**.

Our 'flippered friends' keep a low profile, and it's easy to see why—**they know we're picking up their bill**.

No author or source was credited. Cara told her supervisor. 'Interesting,' he said. 'Watch the comments on lambda videos, and see if there's any uptick in lambda-related crime stats. If anything moves, come to me.'

Within an hour of discovery the article had spread widely through the lambdas' private channels. When a comment was appended, it was minimal—typically the phatic phrase 'Seen this?' Cara reviewed the public service films the government produced and distributed via YouTube. The films showed lambdas in sanitised interactions with terrestrials, in offices strafed by sunbeams, or in classrooms amongst land-human children whose facial expressions suggested bubbliness. The lambdas warranted the descriptors *calm, helpful, serene, compliant*, and *immobile*. All the comments sections for these films had been disabled.

Cara subsequently searched through many amateur animations with a comic and/or racist slant. She noted that the discussion threads were *already reflecting features of the article*. '£3' figured in 64% of the comments, disparaging references to 'basement subsidies' in 31%, 'undercut pay' in 26%, and '*Fraggle Rock*' in 18%. A user called *thndrhnd13* had posted a link to a video of a carrier being pushed over in the street. The lambda fell out of its bowl and pulled itself along the pavement for 1.2m. Its gait was isomorphic with a sealion pup's. By the time Cara had emailed her supervisor, the link and the video had been removed.

Cara slept ineffectively that night. The next morning she went to the office an hour early, searched the lambda channels again *for a sense of their reaction* and, finding *nothing changed*, streamed a government film. At 1 minute 44 seconds some significant news appeared on her screen: a bomb had gone off at a school.

Four videos of the event were tweeted. Each showed that the bomb had behaved like a scanning bar, erasing the school building with tall white flames that made the adjacent lampposts buckle. Her police update told her a message had been sent to all the major news hubs: *THE A.L.A. THANKS YOU FOR YOUR ATTENTION.*

From the behaviour of the other surveillance officers, it might be inferred that Cara had become radioactive. Peter was the only person to approach her closely during this shift. He kissed the crown of her head and walked away without speaking. The news had arrived at 11.07, but it was 13.03 by the time she received an email from her supervisor. 'Send me all the lambda work as a single file attachment,' it read. 'Then you can go home.'

Cara drank two 50cl bottles of artisan vodka and watched seven full episodes of an SF/drama series called *Blue Star*. Peter called during episode three to say that this clearly wasn't her fault.

'There was no way you could have tracked the movements of what seemed to be a non-existent group,' he said. 'In any case, your surveillance software isn't state-of-the-art. You were effectively blindfolded and hand-tied.' These were appropriate, well-chosen words. No positive effect on Cara could be detected.

She checked her police bulletin 244 times that evening. Of the 1420 people known to be inside the school, not a single survivor was reported. Although she *could picture nothing about the victims*, her *insides seemed to teem with them—like screaming paintings in a sealed cave*. At 22.18 she installed the current version of FriendlyRoom on her iPhone XS12. She played a game called CrazyCake that existed on a console inside a virtual clubhouse, and by 03.15 she'd succeeded in more than doubling her decade-old high score.

On day 114 of her employment the supervisor intercepted her before she could sit at her terminal. 'Come into my office,' he said. Cara complied. When the door was closed behind them he continued, 'The Deputy Commissioner is very grateful for what you've done.'

'Grateful? Why?'

'You've shown up the problem of human interpretation. It just doesn't work with the lambdas. We're taking you off surveillance for now.'

'No more data analysis?'

'Not for you.'

'Who will do it?'

'No-one. There will be a moratorium on human surveillance of the ALA. We already rely on automated interception and data trawling. Now we'll do automated inference as well.

You'll learn more this afternoon. I've scheduled an emergency briefing.'

All 63 members of Cara's data surveillance department filed into the windowless briefing room. When the 21 chairs had been taken they stood along the walls. 'Welcome,' the supervisor said. 'This has been a taxing time. I struggle to remember a worse surveillance outcome in all my years here. However, today I intend to demonstrate to you that there is some cause for hope. It goes without saying that the ALA, whatever that might be, has proven beyond our capacity to track.'

Blood vessels in Cara's cheeks and ears dilated.

'It could be that it's beyond *any* human to track,' the supervisor continued. 'With this in mind, I'm pleased to announce that Intelligence Services are making available to us an experimental technology. This is PARSON.' He switched on the briefing-room screen.

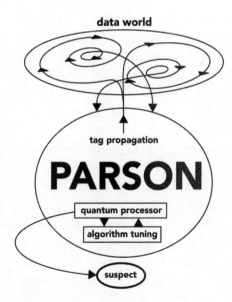

The name is a fusion of 'parse' and 'person',' he explained. 'PARSON is not a computer, although it incorporates the most sophisticated quantum processor in existence. PARSON is a comprehensive system of data shadowing. It operates like a tag on existing data, propagating itself through the records that exist on any sort of digital device, and drawing that data together into patterns. It's a virtual brain. It's a ghost. It's a totally new sort of entity. PARSON is capable of holding zettabytes of data in limitless speculative arrangements, forming it into pictures using criminal activity algorithms, and presenting those pictures to us. If you want to know the theory, it exploits the phenomenon of quantum entanglement. Every particle in the universe is entangled with every other. PARSON can filter that entanglement, select any segment of past and present information we specify, plausibly shape it, then bounce it through a quantum processor. That's where we get our reading. That's how, in principle, we can identify the perpetrators of this atrocity. If PARSON operates as we expect it to, there will be no doubt about the guilt of the suspects. The data footprint will be absolutely incriminating. There is no escape from PARSON. PARSON *is* the data. Do you have any questions?'

'What are the 'tags' exactly?' said Claudine.

'That's not part of this briefing. Next question.'

'Will PARSON only work on the school bombing?' asked PC Adele Jenson.

'For the time being, yes. In the future, who knows? I think the usefulness of this system is self-evident.'

The same officer asked, 'If it works, what does that mean for this department?'

'Let's not jump ahead too many steps. This will be the first test for PARSON in the field. But if it works, we will have a powerful new assistant.'

'Assistant or replacement?' The officer who spoke this time must have been one of the nine who covered their mouths with a hand, because the room's sensors could only approximate their location.

'You heard me correctly the first time,' said the supervisor. 'Anything else?'

'Yes,' said Peter. 'I wasn't aware that this quantum-entangled, simultaneous data approach could work. How does PARSON get around the "no-cloning" rule?'

'Thank you for that question, PC Coates. This is an operational rather than a technical briefing. I'm assured it works. Any more questions? No? Then that's all for now. PC Gray, you can remain where you are.'

Cara watched the others leave the room. Peter did not seek eye contact.

'Cara, we appreciate the effect this recent event must have had on you,' the supervisor said. 'I think you'll agree that it's no longer appropriate for you to be working in data surveillance.'

'I can understand why you'd think that.'

'Good. I'm pleased we're of one mind. Certain other policing tasks have suddenly become pressing. This awful bomb is likely to bring out some underlying tensions, and those tensions will need careful management. We anticipate a demand for more hands-on policing around the lambdas. So, given your skill-set and recent experience, we've created a new role for you. From tomorrow your title will be Supervising Community Support Officer, Lambda Liaison.'

'Thank you,' Cara said.

9

H ello. How are you? You have no complaints about
your condition? I am pleased. You also find me in a
reasonable frame of mind today. I am more than
equal to whatever questions you might deem appropriate to
ask. You will recall, I imagine, the refreshments always on
hand for your enjoyment, should you revise your previous perspective on them. Of course, we can simply begin.

Yes, if you wish to return to my early recollections I will certainly accede.

Do I remember my . . . relocations? You are referring, I
assume, to the physical housings through which I have progressed over the course of my life so far. At the risk of appearing coy, the answer is *yes and no*.

I mentioned at the outset that my memory is extremely
good by any ordinary measure. Events, statistics, structural
relations and their subsequent expansions, the relative weights
and surface characteristics of objects, to select a few examples,
are things I retain vividly. I stand firm by that assertion, but
here I feel I should add a significant caveat—in regard to the
process of transfer of my brain and spinal column to successive
host bodies, I remember nothing at all. Having said as much,
there are certain directly related phenomena that locate these
infrequent episodes within what I recollect clearly. A significant item in this regard is what I have long described to myself
as *the heavy seat*.

In a normally closed-off quarter of the laboratory I sometimes caught a glimpse of this adjustable metal chair, deeply cushioned with mid-grey vinyl upholstery, with an openwork arrangement of polished metal tubes at the head and backrest. The tubes created a continuous void at the back of the chair, like a giant expandable keyhole. It was most unusual. Also distinctive were the regular punctuations of this seat by orange polyester straps designed to hold the occupant secure and still. The first time I spotted this chair was during the time I inhabited a body equivalent to a child of four, a body formed of the same synthetic protein as my enduring brain and spine. I was told by Dr ————— that it was 'my' chair, and that I'd understand more soon enough.

I found the staff in the laboratory singularly reliable, in areas such as this at least, and it turned out he was quite correct. One afternoon, instead of the usual exercise in the quad, I was taken to *the heavy seat* and invited to sit in it. Dr ————— told me that I'd enjoy it very much, and that it was an excellent place to play. Indeed, the chair was hugely comfortable, if a little wide and tall. Perceiving this defect immediately, Dr ————— set about adjusting the chair to achieve a much snugger fit. The only strangeness about the fitting was the way my head and back were left unsupported in the middle, exposed by the keyhole-shaped opening, but my puzzlement soon abated when I felt the friendly hands of Dr ————— access my skull and vertebrae from the rear. He massaged these areas gently; it was a most relaxing sensation. I'd been given a hypnotic three-dimensional wooden toy, a conjunction of four cubic 'trees' which would only separate in a specific, decidedly elusive way, and amused myself greatly with it as I received Dr —————'s attentions.

That was as far as my interaction with the chair extended on the first occasion. The second occasion was rather different.

My afternoon exercise had again been cancelled. I was invited into the often-shrouded corner where *the heavy seat* resided to find that object fully unveiled. It remained, I noted, adjusted to fit my then small body. A different atmosphere pervaded that day, a somewhat cooler one, and Dr ——————— had less to say about my forthcoming experience than before. As I climbed up into the chair, I noticed that a pale, dust-like material with a scent similar to marzipan was descending from a grille in a unit suspended above, and that Dr ——————— had absented himself completely. By the time I was squarely on the seat my body felt inordinately slow and weighty. The grey leatherette gave the illusion of compressing further earthward than the structure of the chair should allow, and while I recall my intention to ask for the wooden toy again, no words came forth. I couldn't move my tongue and jaw at all. I remember nothing further about that day, and I awoke the following morning in my modest room, surging with energy, and inhabiting a body that resembled closely that of a boy of ten.

After some weeks of habitation of this new and handy frame, one which enabled me to climb and throw and manipulate objects in a much more decisive manner, it became clear that I would meet the chair again, and that *the heavy seat* was the gatekeeper of my physical transformation. I am well aware that conventional human development rarely involves such radical steps, that physical growth is finely incremental and, in general, occurs beneath conscious perception. I consider this, if you don't mind my saying, a considerable impoverishment. A sudden upgrade of one's entire physical being is an experience that defies the wildest analogy.

This is not to suggest that *the heavy seat* was an object of any special affection. Quite the contrary. When I picture it, as you have indirectly invited me to, a certain paralysis linked with a sucking fear arises. It is an object that manifests my incontinence as an entity, my lack of personal cogence and ultimate autonomy. I find it a struggle not to picture the operations that ensued once I was fully unconscious in the chair—

the provisions for transplantation, the process of removal of my brain and spinal column, the character of the necessary incisions, the specialised tools. No, these shadowy procedures, all too concrete for those who enacted them, are something I choose to keep behind the thickest curtain of my mind. Nonetheless the keyhole void, the leatherette and the sleeping dust exist starkly in the foreground. Even as I name these things, a part of me is preparing for a death-like abnegation.

You have previously asked if I remember 'other children' in the laboratory. It is absolutely true that I did not encounter any during my time there. However, it fleetingly occurred to me that this did not mean other children were not ensconced in the laboratory in the past, and would be in the future. After my initial cultivation in the warming cabinet my maturation took only three calendar months, and it is easy to imagine that once I was 'fully baked' another would be reared in my place. (The warming cabinet, I might note, was always securely locked.) It seems likely also that a being such as myself had been created in the lab prior to my arrival, coached to independence, and released like me into a full and active life in the broader world. When I voiced these speculations to my guardians they were laughingly dismissed. 'No, no, no,' said Dr ————, whom I noticed took care to face away from me. 'Only you have ever lived here, and only you ever will.' There was something consoling about this answer. It enfolded me in a verbal blanket of specialness. But with a retrospective view informed by wider experience I suspect that it was far from the truth. One can hardly blame my manufacturers for maintaining the pretence, however, since I take it as read that it must be part of some larger design that would be spoiled by the formation of a community.

There were times during my employment with —————————— that I suspected one or two other employees had shared a similar development. About Anne I had no suspicions, nor Marcus or Elaine. Mary, however, gave me pause. She hesitated after I asked what her favourite toy had been, a sign perhaps that she was familiar with some items from my earliest weeks of life. There was also a man whose name I never learned, whom I caught on the stairs on numerous occasions, and whose face seemed unaccountably familiar. His gaze darted instantly from mine just when I meant to greet him cordially. But now that I extend the thought, it could be that he merely resembled Dr ————, Mary was perhaps simply surprised by my question, and any deeper connection with a known or unknown government-funded laboratory must be squarely put down as my fantasy.

Thank you, as always, for your apposite provocation. It has been diverting, if not exactly pleasurable, to review the general terms of my embodiment. I will decline to detail all the successive encounters with the *heavy seat* that would bring us up to date, since you must now grasp the basic idea. I feel that this is enough introspection for one day and with your permission I will say goodbye. Goodbye.

10

C ara was allocated five PCSOs and use of a Police Service Establishment, a 2.5 x 3 x 4m prefab near a derelict railway line. She was to 'leverage the PCSOs' experience,' the supervisor said, 'and engage directly with the lambdas on the ground.' It was not defined as a surveillance position, but anything Cara learned 'would naturally be of interest.'

'I'm not here to tell you what to do,' Cara said to four of the PCSOs—the fifth had called in sick. 'I tracked the lambdas in another role, but that doesn't mean I understand your work at all.'

Two had minor attrition defects in their uniforms. Three evidenced difficulty maintaining eye contact with Cara. Their median age was 36, and their averaged OCEAN Personality Test Score was heavily biased towards Conscientiousness (94).

'Until I have a better sense of the lambda community, I'll need your help a lot,' Cara continued.

'What do you want to know?' said PCSO Gloria Knowles. She had no difficulty meeting Cara's gaze. Her Extraversion score was the highest of the group (87).

'I want to know . . . how we make better connections with the community. How we understand how they understand us. How they see their future. And I want to know what we don't know about them, too.'

PCSO Knowles pursed her mouth. She displayed facial signs of both actual and simulated fatigue. 'I can help you get started,' she said.

Lambda society lacked hierarchy. This was one of the factors that had made Cara's surveillance of them difficult—there was no overall structure to follow, only a matrix of similarities. However, owing to her close contact, PCSO Knowles was able to identify lambdas who had more extensive informal connections than the data made obvious. She suggested Cara start with Lambda Subject B.

The lambda who bore this codename was more generally known as Gavin Knight-Green. He had lived in the same basement on Cherry Tree Grove for thirteen years. He'd performed the usual roles—classroom assistant, telemarketing, data entry, image labelling—but had made more attachments than most. Anecdotally, lambdas and land-humans appeared to rate his social abilities highly.

'He has some eccentricities,' Gloria explained. 'But he's friendly enough, and pretty easy to talk to. It's not always like that. And he knows hundreds and hundreds of lambdas directly. It's as close as you'll ever get to knowing what's going on with them all, I can virtually guarantee it.'

'Thanks,' said Cara. 'I'll arrange a visit soon.'

But none of her subsequent actions aligned with that intention. Cara made appointments with the other PCSOs instead, and recorded the conversations on the Bell 6i smartphone she'd been supplied with for her role.

'So, Gerald. Tell me what's been happening.'

'Yes. Wendy and Jacob were threatened in the street on Tuesday. It didn't come to anything and they seem okay. Harold is off work, he says it's a minor infection but it could be anxiety, he's suffered from that before. I'll be making a special effort to visit.'

PCSO Gerald Akebe lived on the Broadwater Farm Estate. His work for the police was a secret he kept from his immediate neighbours, who understood he was a private security guard.

'Door kicked in on Hanway Crescent, looking at getting

that fixed. Plenty of graffiti over the whole area, but they'll take care of that themselves.'

Gerald scrolled through the notes on his phone. His index finger was longer and thinner than was typical for his age and gender.

'Gerald, do you mind if I ask you about the bomb?'

'Go ahead. What do you want to ask?'

'Do you think lambdas could have done it?'

'Do you mean . . . would they have been *able* to do it?'

'No. I mean do you think they would have *wanted* to do it?'

He dropped his head. 'No. I don't think they wanted to do it.'

'So who do you think did? Who do the lambdas think did it?'

There was a silence of six seconds. Gerald repositioned himself on his chair.

'They won't talk about it. And if you're asking me—it's a set-up, isn't it? Don't you see that too? There are so many people filled with hate, you can take your pick. The lambdas are born scapegoats. Shall I continue?'

PCSO Mathilde Koh spoke in a 35dB whisper without looking at notes.

'John is not so much in favour these days after the way he neglected Christabel's 28th sister. There was a clear opportunity to connect her with a very suitable school in the next post-code, but he let it drift and now she's at the mercy of the local one. Which is fine if you're looking to encourage learning at home, but Christabel is far too busy for that, as well he knows. But in the end I suppose it doesn't really make any difference, they always perform just well enough.'

'Why did you get in involved with this sort of work, Mathilde?' Cara asked.

'That's a good question. My ancestors were Huguenots.'

PCSO Jonathan Hart presented signs of exhaustion throughout his first interview. When he briefly lost consciousness during an account of replacing the hydroinsulation on a lambda computer tower, Cara told him he should go home. PCSO Amy Sinkmore had been sick for the first collective meeting. Cara noted that *she seems to be thinking obsessively about something else as she speaks + uses a pleading tone, as though her accounts are apologies.* Amy's eyelids were pink and inflamed. This was strongly suggestive of recent crying.

Once she'd established a body of notes on the PCSOs, Cara went through their detailed files on the lambdas. She found the content *both familiar + totally strange.* Their parsed and aggregated content had informed her previous work in surveillance, but the physical material also included unshared handwritten notes in the pocketbooks stored in the prefab cupboard. 'Lambda Subject H calm & quiet despite recent encounter,' Gloria had written. 'Sour honey-like smell in hallway.' When Cara found a phrase she liked, she photographed it.

She sent an email requesting access to social worker reports on the lambdas—they were not very numerous and none had been archived online. On floor seven of the Central Social Services Office for North London she examined two lever-arch files of papers on absentee pupils and possible neglected child cases. On no occasion had any action been taken: further investigation had been terminated for unrecorded reasons. Owing to the inaccessibility of lambda household environments, the domestic accounts were all based on video surveillance.

MAY 14

11 A.M.

'MOTHER' IS INDIFFERENT TO THE PRESENCE OF TWO 'DAUGHTERS', WHO SOMETIMES SOLICIT ATTENTION IN LACKLUSTRE WAYS. TIME IS SPENT WATCHING WHAT SEEM LIKE RANDOM EXCERPTS OF OCEAN-THEMED FILMS ON COMPUTER SCREEN. YOUNGER DAUGHTER SOMETIMES

ASLEEP DURING THIS ACTIVITY. 'MOTHER' MAKES SOME EFFORT TO ORGANISE POSSESSIONS. GENERAL STATE OF HOUSEHOLD IS CHAOTIC BUT NOT UNSAFE.

2 P.M.

SECOND 'MOTHER' RETURNS HOME, CHASTISES 'DAUGHTERS' FOR WATCHING SCREEN. SHE EJECTS BOTH FROM THE ROOM. BOTH 'DAUGHTERS' SLEEP. 'MOTHERS' DO NOT COMMUNICATE BUT ENGAGE IN FURTHER EFFORTS TO ORGANISE HOUSEHOLD.

3 P.M.

'FATHER' RETURNS HOME AND TAKES OVER ORGANISING DUTIES FROM SECOND 'MOTHER' (THE FIRST 'MOTHER' IS NOW ASLEEP). 'FATHER' BITES ELDER SLEEPING 'DAUGHTER' WHO IS AWOKEN BUT NOT OBVIOUSLY DISTRESSED. SHE MOVES TO A SECOND ROOM AND SLEEPS.

5 P.M.

ALL LAMBDAS MEET IN THE PRINCIPAL ROOM TO EAT. THEY COMPLAIN MILDLY ABOUT EACH OTHERS' EATING BEHAVIOUR. THE SECOND 'MOTHER' BITES THE 'FATHER' WHO DOES NOT RESPOND.

5.30 P.M.

THERE IS AN ESCALATION OF TENSION AS ALL LAMBDAS CLAIM THAT THEY DON'T NEED TO CLEAN UP AFTER EATING. FINALLY 'FATHER' AND YOUNGER 'DAUGHTER' TIDY THE REMAINS OF SARDINES AND UNIDENTIFIED PLANT MATERIAL

INTO A WASTE CHUTE IN THE KITCHEN AREA. THE OTHER LAMBDAS SLEEP.

7 P.M.
ALL LAMBDAS ASLEEP.

In all the 175 pages of observation Cara scanned with the pre-installed app on her Bell 6i phone, the subject matter didn't deviate from household chores and minor squabbles. *Even the biting isn't severe,* Cara noted. *It seems to mean something different in lambda culture, more like a tut for a land-human.* 'MOTHER', 'FATHER' and 'DAUGHTER' were terms lambdas themselves didn't use for each other—they were all either brothers or sisters, numbered in order of encounter—but the words had been mapped onto them by terrestrial social workers to help narrate their interactions.

Cara located an administrative employee. Her name was Efemena Okunu and her OCEAN Personality Test Score was 50 75 78 60 21.

'Can I see the original footage that these reports were based on?'

'No,' Efemena said.

'Why not?'

'There was a directive. All the video files had to be erased, and all the cameras had to be removed too. Permanently.'

'A directive? From where?'

'Home Office. I'm sure they can watch and listen to anything they want through the lambda's home devices, but social services can't see anything anymore.'

'I see. Thank you very much.'

'No problem officer. Come by any time.'

*

At 11.10 on Saturday 13th April, 2019, Peter reached into Cara's fridge for milk. 'You never really mention your family,' Cara said.

'Not a great deal to say,' he responded.

'Okay, but I'd love to know *something* about them. You have a brother, right?'

'Yes. I have a brother.'

Peter added 26ml of milk to his coffee.

'Rex?'

'That's him.'

'And he's a musician?'

'Yes.'

Peter put the milk back in the fridge and moved into the living room. Cara followed.

'Can you tell me any more? Is he fun, or serious, or unusually tall, or what?'

'If you have to know, we haven't talked in years.'

'Oh. That's so sad. Why not?'

'It's difficult to say. Can we not do this right now? I need to finish something I'm doing.'

'If it's really so important, of course. But it's awful to fall out with your own brother. You should try to patch things up, surely.'

'And what would you know about siblings?'

Peter's tone lacked warmth. Cara said nothing in response.

'I'm sorry,' said Peter. 'That was mean of me. You're right. I should try to do something. One day, maybe.' The last sentence was mumbled and there was no evidence Cara heard it. Peter resumed coding in Python on his laptop.

With a discreet but persistent effort Peter referred to as *needling*, Cara obtained the information she desired over the course of the day. Peter's father, Martin Coates, was a retired behavioural psychologist. He had been attached to Keele University's Social Research department, then the data consultancy

InHive. He had made in excess of £12 million in the second phase of his career, much of it in the form of InHive shares, then eroded his gains in retirement by funding a series of non-commercial social projects which reversed his Skinnerite approach. He currently lived alone in Bridford-by-the-Sea, a Victorian coastal town in the North East of England. Peter's mother, Julia Coates (née Hamilton), was a science journalist. She had moved to Wellington, New Zealand once her boys had left home, and while there was no evidence that she was seeking to dissolve her marriage, she was never in touch with any of them. *Partly by his own design*, Cara noted on her phone, *P has grown into an orphan.*

'Do you miss your mum?' Cara asked him.

'Not really.'

'Not at all?'

'I wouldn't say much at all, no.'

'Wasn't she a good mum? Did she spend time with you both, take an interest in what you did?'

'Yes, of course, she did that sometimes. She was not a bad mother.'

'Then what went wrong? Why did she leave?'

'We should have a child, don't you think?' he said with an increase in volume.

Cara paused.

'I don't know. Isn't it a bit soon? We don't even really live together.'

The conversation stopped.

Peter and Cara watched television together that evening. Peter chose a mass-audience documentary about Severax which he interrupted with commentary at intervals of no longer than five minutes.

'This story again. You know there is no evidence whatsoever that there was a violent take-over of that central region.

It's a founding myth that Western governments like. It's an alibi for all *their* offensive actions. There was almost no-one there at all, the temperature hits at least 45° most of the year. The surrounding villages were actually pretty excited to get reliable electricity and running water.'

'So who started it?'

'It was a cabal of serious tech players, plus some venture capitalists looking for free space to pour their funds. Just a few big desert labs at first. You didn't realise that?'

'No.'

'Certain kinds of very lucrative tech were becoming hyper-regulated, so it made a lot of sense to escape. To my knowledge there has been no substantiated belligerent action other than malware deployment out of Severax. And that's not state sanctioned. It's private criminals. The government owns a big tranche of the servers, so they take their money. But they don't actively support crime. Most of what happens in Severax is physical research you can't do anywhere else.'

'Like what?'

On the screen an aerial tracking shot of desert dissolved to an image of circuitry.

'Human cell stuff. Advanced robotics. Space weapons. You hit legal problems fast if you do any of that privately in a traditional state. Governments get *really* interested. But there's a flow of 'legitimate' people in and out of Severax all the time— you can get a special visa to go there if you claim it's for educational research purposes only. The way it works is you pretend to your home government you're spying, you do your high-end research consultancy, then you give a little out-of-date information to the state when you get back. You get paid at both ends. Everyone's happy. But you won't hear about that stuff on this documentary. You'll only hear about the criminal gangs who work in the cracks. Literally in the cracks. The crime syndicates don't even have people living there, it's just code on SSDs in the server farms. It's currently the cheapest *and* coolest place for computers on the planet.'

'But isn't it all desert?'

'Yep. The solar fields power the refrigeration systems in caves a kilometre under the territory. God knows how they deal with the temperature gradient—my guess is that they've developed a radiative cooling system, but you can't find the plans *anywhere*. Anyway, it must be ultra-efficient, the whole thing runs at a huge profit.'

'So, it looks like a criminal state, but it's really a big research facility?'

'And an automated revenue machine—they sell the excess solar power too. It has no taxes. It's free of regulation. It's whatever you want it to be. That's why our government hates it. They're beyond jealous. And it's the only place in the Northern hemisphere where you can use a Personal Fabrication Device without a minimum 12-year prison sentence. I'd fly there tomorrow, if it wasn't somewhat incompatible with my job.'

Pleased I've found something P actually wants to talk about, Cara wrote. Later they had *enjoyable sex*, and on Sunday Cara read *The Death of Ivan Ilyich* while Peter continued to code.

On Monday, the 200th day of Cara's employment with the police and the 14th in her new role, Gloria asked her how she was getting on with the lambda community.

'I've put out some useful feelers,' Cara said.

'Oh? Who have you seen?'

'Yesterday I went to visit—Gloria, excuse me, I have an important call coming through, do you mind leaving me to it?'

'Be my guest. I'll drop by tomorrow instead.'

Cara turned into a corner of the prefab and said into her phone, 'Yes, it's PC Gray here.'

As soon as Gloria closed the door she returned the phone

to her pocket. After a short episode of crying accompanied by raised heart rate and blood pressure, Cara composed an email.

Dear Gavin Knight-Green

I am the new Supervising Community Support Officer for your area. I would like to visit you to introduce myself. Would it be convenient for me to come by at 10 A.M. tomorrow?

Kind regards

PC Cara Gray

She rewrote the message nineteen times without significantly altering its content, then sent the saved original. Within five minutes, a reply came back.

Dear PC Cara Gray

That will be fine.

Yours sincerely

Gavin Knight-Green

Cara copied Gavin's file to a 0.5TB flash drive and took it home.

As she scrolled through the pages without recorded comment she consumed at least 250% more artisan vodka than current health guidelines recommended. The document described in detail what Gloria had initially told her. Gavin was distinguished from other lambdas by his extensive social attachments, plus the 'eccentricity' Gloria had alluded to: an unusually developed interest in the Four Fertile Pairs. Rather than allow them to exist as a background cultural context for his day-to-day experience, the typical way in which they featured in lambdas' lives, Gavin had undertaken a great deal of work trying to establish their existence in fact. Gavin had made 8042 notes on publicly available material, including many overtly racist home-made documentaries and cartoons devoid of any grounding in research, that related explicitly to the Pairs. He had also identified sources which referred to them 'indirectly'. He'd analysed the films *Titanic*, *Splash*, *The Poseidon Adventure*, *Beyond The Poseidon Adventure*, *Ponyo*, *The Abyss*, *Pirates of the Caribbean: At World's End*, *Finding Nemo*, *Finding Dory* and *Black Sea*, treating their content as allegory. Gloria had found evidence that he'd recently tried to communicate with incoming lambdas in Iceland via emails addressed to land-human officials. He'd written expressing the hope that the newest arrivals 'remember their whole journey to Reykjavik, and even the Origin of that journey', but the officials had disregarded his messages.

Cara slept ineffectively. In the morning she recorded a dream. *Forged my way out of the primordial cool of the Labrador Sea, blind sharks looming whitely out of the shadows that curved beneath my stomach. Wriggled through ice floes that pinched shut behind me + saw empty skies smashed apart by the aurora borealis, in awful silence, like a migraine experienced by the whole earth.*

As Cara was cleaning her teeth her iPhone XS12 began to vibrate. It was her mother. 'Dad's been to visit,' she said.

'Dad? Did you say 'been'?'

'Yes. Been and gone.'

Cara leaned against the bathroom door.

'Why didn't you tell me?'

'I didn't know he was coming. He seems very well.'

'Did he ask about me?'

'Of course he did. He's very proud of what you've been doing.'

Cara said nothing. Her surveillance lapse was not something she'd shared with her mother.

'Do you want to know exactly what he said?' her mother continued. 'He said that you'd always been working to make the world a safer, better place, whatever you'd decided to do in your life. Isn't that lovely?'

Cara was silent for three seconds.

'Did he really visit, mum? Are you sure?'

'What are you saying, darling? That I don't recognise your own father? Of course it was him.'

The changing inflections of her mother's voice were too varied for cogent summary.

'Was he on his motorbike?'

'Yes.'

'Which one?'

'Oh, the same one he went out on of course. The Ducati tourer.'

Two tears dropped 60ms apart, one from each of Cara's eyes. This was the bike he'd had when she was twelve.

'Okay Mum, thanks for letting me know. I'm going to visit you this evening. Is that okay?'

'I'm busy, my love. I'm going to the cinema with Martha.' Cara's heart rate marginally increased. Martha was Chloe's mother. 'There's really no need, but if you want to why don't you come on Friday, when you've finished work? You could stay over.'

'Okay Mum,' she said. 'I love you.'

When her mother hung up she called Martha.

'Is this Cara?'

'Yes. I hope you don't mind me calling you.'

'Of course I don't. It's just quite unexpected.'

'I'm worried about Mum,' Cara said. 'She seems to think that Dad's been to visit. I don't know if that's true.'

78 · DAVID MUSGRAVE

'And you want me to ask her about it?'

'No. I wouldn't ask you to do that. But could you let me know if there's anything different about her?'

The iPhone XS12 was silent.

'I suppose I could. Only I don't feel entirely comfortable about it.'

'No, I'm sure you don't, and I'm sorry to ask. I wouldn't have called if I wasn't so worried about her.'

There was another pause. Then Martha said, 'I understand.' At a higher pitch she continued, 'How are you getting on now? In the police?'

'Just fine.'

'That's good. Chloe's busy organising another international protest. Is it safe for me to tell you that?' She laughed volitionally. 'It's been a rough ride for her recently. She talks about you now and then.'

'Oh,' said Cara. 'Does she really? You can say hello from me. If you get a chance.'

'I will. You know you could have brought Chloe back with you. Can you remember next time?'

Cara took the number 284 PolyWay Public Autonomous Vehicle that went directly to the lambda zone. Three lambda carriers boarded the transport during the journey, one with two bowls; 18,903 carriers had resigned since the school event and such doubling up was now common. The reflected sky and roofline silhouettes were distorted by the parametric contours of the bowls. The four lambda faces within differed only thanks to scars and patches of skin discolouration.

The transport stopped at a junction that connected to Cherry Tree Grove. Cara disembarked. She crossed the road quickly, but her gait once she reached the other side was hesitant. Fog-enveloped woodland rose over the terraced housing to her right, and she halted to look up at the treetops for nineteen seconds. Then she walked the opposite way, along a vector whose end point was the decomposing door of number 17. She pressed the basement buzzer. There was no reply from the Entryphone, but the door clicked open anyway.

11.

Hello. How are you this morning? Good, I am pleased to hear it. I note that you always report that you are well on these occasions, or at least have reported so up until now. Could I tentatively offer you a hot drink, or perhaps some water from the tap? I rather suspected that you would say no.

Yes, of course we can begin.

This time you would like me to tell you more about my experiences at ———————————? I do not see why not. Yes, I do remember very many things about that period, including sustained interactions with certain persons, in some detail. For one there is Anne ———. She was twenty-six when I began my work there. She was an interesting and intelligent young woman, and we developed a rapport immediately. She disclosed to me after a time that I reminded her of a schoolteacher on whom she'd had a crush. I was rather nonplussed by this disclosure. Nonetheless our relations continued on a more or less identical basis.

We were in the habit of visiting the local eateries together at lunch time. We would alternate payment for lunch, I recall. I tended to select a Japanese place when the decision was left to me, while Anne preferred the Italian delicatessen. That said, we tried to visit all the food establishments close to the offices in a loose rotation. She solicited from me details of my personal life and interests, and was in the habit of holding my upper arm very lightly in response to certain signals I confess I must have missed.

Anne possessed some incisive views about the state of domestic politics. While she was broadly in agreement with our own roles at ————————, she allowed herself to express to me some doubts about the long-term utility of our policy of aggressive suppression and containment of Severax. She identified several structural particulars of the nation we served which meant that the gains made in this regard would be offset by losses in others. She also expressed dismay at the dramatic asymmetry that was developing between those privileged enough to be able to find work in the traditional fiscal economy, and those not. The latter, she suggested, were on the brink of total servitude. She opined that the existence of 'employment tokens' as proxy cash effectively marked out and constrained those paid in them as the property of their employers, since these employers would be able to control exactly what the tokens could be exchanged for. I have reason to believe that she was quite correct, and that the goods and services so provided are of a different, that is to say much lower, quality to those available to you or me. I seem to remember telling her that I had no close contact with any persons liable to be in this situation, a comment which she echoed. Having admitted as much, she stated that it did not make any difference to her feelings about the arrangement, and that it was easy enough to imagine the many unjust social consequences of a distinct, privately controlled currency.

Do you, by any chance, know what Anne ——— is doing now? She struck me as an unusually perceptive lady with the potential to achieve great things in her profession. Yes, of course I will continue with this account before you reply.

We became quite settled in our habit of lunching together. Our conversations were stimulating, and our rotation of dining place kept their context fresh. Anne had become accustomed to my sensitivities, and in particular had learnt not to ask me in too much detail about my visits to the governmental headquarters of Severax. At this point I had not completed my duties there, but the nature of my activities was, nonetheless, something I was required not to reveal even to my fellow employees. She continued to touch my arm and, on one occasion, my leg. While the semantics of this contact escaped me, it seemed to make no difference to our friendly relations.

Regrettably, our lunch arrangement did not endure long after the arrival in our department of Julian ———. This person exercised a real fascination over Anne from his first arrival. I could not help noticing that he often sought to divert her from our usual place of assignation in the sunlit lobby by engaging her in conversations I was not party to. He was increasingly successful in these attempts, and I began to take my lunch break alone, a reversion to the state of affairs that had obtained before Anne's arrival.

It occurs to me that there is still much I might mention regarding the character of different times of day. Now, for instance—am I alone in sensing a particular emptiness to this hour, as though space has taken ascendancy over the items that populate it? Is that too abstract a description, perhaps? It seems to me at this time of day that all of the life one has lived is held in abeyance, is perhaps even erased, and that the air and light that fills the room has become the sole reality. One can imagine oneself a weightless point adrift in unknown regions, devoid of memory or developed body, like a wandering spore. Perhaps there is little meaning in what I am saying, but I feel compelled to say it. Please excuse me.

Yes, to return to Anne. While it would not be true to say that we never had lunch together again after the arrival of Julian ———, it would be accurate to record that this happened on only three or four occasions, and always in the presence of Julian ——— too. This person cast a completely different complexion on the undertaking. While Anne had always responded gently and with great understanding to my responses to her questions, Julian wore a somewhat derisory expression at all times. He would continue to adopt this mien whether he vocalised his thoughts about my discourse or, as was more usual, watched me without a word. It was almost as though he were simply waiting for me to finish. No, it would be fair to say that I did not enjoy my lunches with Anne to anything like the degree I had before. As I believe I have already mentioned, there were only a few more of these lunches. By mutual unspoken agreement we desisted from this form of sociability, and Anne was transferred from the department shortly afterwards anyway.

Are you able to tell me what Anne is doing now? Oh, that is a shame. I would very much like to know. She was both a vital presence in the department and someone upon whom I could always rely for an unusual perspective on any salient topic. I assume that she and Julian became a formalised couple. Are you not at liberty to say? It does not make any difference to me, of course.

I should perhaps mention that I experience some sort of waking or unconscious visualisation of Anne on at least a weekly basis. Her unsolicited contact with my arm and, on one occasion, leg has, it would appear, imprinted her quite strongly in my mind. Perhaps this is a good moment to reflect further upon memory—but I see that you are discouraging me. Yes, I agree that this is enough for today. Goodbye.

12

Y ou are now halfway through your trial of EyeNarrator Pro! We hope you are enjoying the stunning features which have made it the global benchmark for autonarrative. Once you unlock the complete subscription you will be able to edit your material in full. Options include:

- Change default perspective at any time
- Adjust or randomise the profile of any character across the gamut of parameters, such as gender, ethnicity, OCEAN Personality Test Score, sexual orientation, backstory specifics, and hundreds more
- Shift time period in any direction
- Splice, randomise or reverse all or specified sequences of events
- Generate parallel narrative resolutions

All of these possibilities are fun and entertaining, and many can assist in insulating your EyeNarration from libel action.

Remember, you don't have to wait to read the remaining chapters before opening the upgrade link. Your debit instructions are already logged and the full power of EyeNarrator Pro is just a few clicks away!

13.

Gavin Knight-Green's hallway was 14° cooler than outside. There was a loopback chair set against the wall on Cara's right, a wall whose topography was complicated by portions of missing plaster. The hallway was similar to many Cara had previously encountered, only it *smelled very strongly of fish* and the stairwell leading down to the basement was filled with water. The lower steps weren't visible—the fourth faded into greenish darkness. Cara closed the front door. When she turned back towards the stairwell a white ball appeared in water. The ball was Gavin's head.

'Hello Cara Gray, new Supervising Police Community Support Officer,' he said.

Cara touched the record button on the Bell 6i phone in her pocket. 'Hello Gavin. I'm pleased to meet you. Is anyone else in?'

'No. I live with four others but they're all out.'

His voice was extremely quiet and high-pitched. Telemarketing companies used pitch-shifters and amplification to bring their lambda employees closer to land-human range.

'Okay, good—so we're free to talk?'

'We are.'

'Good. I . . . I wanted to find out what it's like here, after the school incident.'

Gavin drifted 21° degrees clockwise. The pale and taut skin of his head and part of his back were visible above the waterline.

'Can you picture this space without the floor and walls and ceiling of the building?' he said.

Cara paused. 'I think I can imagine that. It's not easy, but yes. Actually it makes me feel a bit nauseous, like I'm . . . falling.'

'Good,' said Gavin. 'Now you have an idea what the open sea is like.'

He paddled 34° anticlockwise.

'Do you miss the sea?' Cara asked.

Gavin's eyes were glossy, and the variously coloured filaments that made up his irises merged at a short distance to khaki. 'No,' he said. 'I don't miss the sea at all.'

There was a pause of nine seconds before Cara spoke.

'I understand you have a lot to do with new arrivals. Is that right?'

'Yes. I'm good at opening doors.'

'That must be very rewarding.'

'Yes it is. How long do you think this interview will last?'

'Oh, it's not an interview. I'm just here to . . . say hello.'

'Yes, you said. That's nice of you. Are you expecting me to help you in any way with the school incident?'

'Maybe. Maybe not. If you have anything that assists the investigation I would be very grateful to hear it. However, that's not the real purpose of my visit.'

There was another silence, this time of 6.2 seconds. At the end of it Gavin said, 'I don't know anything more than you. I don't know anyone who knows anything about it. Everyone I know is as disgusted as you must be.'

Folds appeared between Cara's eyebrows.

'Between you and me, I don't think any lambdas were responsible. I followed the ALA in some detail in my previous role and I couldn't find anything concrete to link it to the lambda community. Before the ALA statement there were just a few disconnected rumours.'

'You think it's a fraud?'

'I think it's very possible. In fact I think it's likely.'

Gavin paddled but didn't change position. 'Do you think people hate us that much?'

'There are some very angry people in this country, Gavin. They need someone to blame. It's much simpler than unpicking what's really gone wrong.'

Gavin exhibited a small muscular spasm which involved his whole body. 'My fortieth sister was kicked down the street just a few days ago,' he said. 'At the bus stop, the one you got out at probably. You were coming from the centre, correct? They took the bowl out of the carrier's arms and tipped her out and kicked her all the way down the road, almost to the next stop. Nobody stopped them. I don't know how she survived. Her skull is fractured and all but two of her ribs are broken. She lost her right arm. A passerby found it the next day but it was too late to reconnect it. It had died. Would you like to see a picture of her?'

'It's okay,' said Cara. 'We can just talk here for the moment. I'm very, very sorry to hear that Gavin, that's so awful. It's this kind of thing that makes it so important that I speak with you.'

'Yesterday,' Gavin continued, 'my seventeenth brother was tipped out on the doorstep of the school where he works. Nobody intervened. Three land-humans were involved. The tipper stamped on his tail so hard he's unlikely to be able to use it fully again. His carrier managed to fight off the attacker and in that respect he was lucky. You know how much worse it can be, I'm sure you have all the statistics. My neighbour has lost three brothers and one sister so far, but all this goes largely unreported by terrestrials. One perpetrator has been identified but the others are still out there somewhere, waiting for us, maybe even for me. We all still go out and do our jobs. There's nothing else to do. Our lives can't just stop.'

Cara looked at the wooden floor, which was especially stained and mouldy near the basement stairwell. She sat down in the loopback chair. 'I'm sad to hear that's how it's been,' she said.

'Do you know the size of the lambda population?' Gavin continued.

'Of course. It's something like a hundred thousand here in the city.'

'Yes. How many police on the street?'

'Three, maybe four thousand.'

'And these are not officers allocated to protecting lambdas in particular, correct? They have other things to do. We have only you and the five other PCSOs. As you must know, they are all part-time. I wonder what sort of 'protection' it's reasonable to expect. Did you see the graffiti this morning at the end of the road?'

'No. There was no trace of it when I arrived.'

'It said "fuck off fishman scum". You can get special paint removers, hand-held scanners that fade graffiti with extremely bright light. In this area we all contribute a small amount of our income to a company to remove the messages. They come most days, sometimes twice a day. More often since the bombing.'

'Yes, Gloria told me about it. We can look into funding that perhaps, there's no reason why it should come out of your pockets.'

'No,' he said, 'it's a housekeeping issue we've grown used to. If you really want to help . . . you can find a way to stop those public service films going out. The ones that show lambdas in daily life. Watching YouTube. Working in sunny offices. If you want some real advice, I would delete them all.'

Cara was silent for four seconds. 'The government has spent a lot of money on those,' she said. 'Haven't they won awards?'

'PC Supervising Officer, if you want my advice it's that. Delete them all. Those films have done more to destroy our chances than any terror attack.'

'I don't understand. Why would they?'

'Because they make us look rich.'

Cara's eye saccades traversed a pale rectangle of paint on the wall. They stopped at a point of fixation: the end of a yellow rawlplug. She looked at Gavin again. 'But aren't they just videos of lambdas at work?'

'It's not the situations, PC Officer. It's the films themselves. It's expensive to make a proper film, let alone a whole series of them. They're so beautifully lit, and the software that generates the music, it's always state-of-the-art. It takes money to do that. People think we made them, not the government. You must have heard that—that people don't believe the production credit? People think we're rich. If you do these things for us then in a sense we are. It's revolting to us. Wealth is just a blockage for a lambda. A wrong, a disease. All should flow equally to everyone.'

'Let me speak to my supervisor,' she said. 'This kind of thing is very useful to know, thank you.'

'I wish you good luck with your supervisor. I told PCSO Knowles the same things but unfortunately nothing ever happened. I'm due on my shift in twenty minutes and my carrier is on her way. Is there anything else I can help you with?'

'I don't think so. This has been very helpful, thank you Gavin.'

'Thank you too. It's been a pleasure to make your acquaintance.'

Gavin looked at the door again and said, 'I would like to give you something. Can you wait here a little while?'

'Of course.'

He flipped over in a turn that caused little disturbance of the water's surface, then disappeared into the greenish darkness that began at the fourth submerged step. He returned with an object the size of the top two joints of Cara's smallest finger in the crook of his arm flipper. The object was dove grey and smooth. He placed it on the edge of the step by the water-line. 'This is for you,' he said.

Cara picked it up. It was a cylinder that tapered; light refraction across its surface suggested a coating of slime.

'Thank you. What is it?'

'I made it,' Gavin said.

'Oh really? Then this is a very special gift.'

'If you want it to stay like that you'll need to keep it wet.'

'Right. I have a sandwich bag in here somewhere.' Cara took out her lunch, which was a partially defrosted unbuttered white roll with a slice of pre-cut cheese, and released it into her police satchel. She placed the gifted object in the empty plastic bag. 'Should I take some water from here?'

'Be my guest.'

Cara trawled the open bag through the stairwell pool, and her hand passed within 14cm of Gavin's body. Once the object was submerged, Cara tied the top of the bag in a knot.

'We make these objects over the course of several months by rolling off our dead skin onto a selected item,' Gavin said. 'I forget what I used now, perhaps it was an old pen lid. The starting object is not so important.'

'So it's a kind of self-portrait?'

Gavin's facial expression didn't change, but he rotated his flippers in opposite directions and his subsequent tone suggested puzzlement. 'No. Of course not. What do you mean?'

'Perhaps I should have said a sculpture.'

'If you want to look at it that way. We don't understand sculpture the way you do. It's not important that our "sculptures" look different from each other's, and they don't often look very different. Unless the person who made it is very old or ill. It's just a way to make use of the material that our bodies shed, which would otherwise drift off into the water. It would be quite unhygienic. I thought you would like to have one because it will help you to think about us when we're not here.'

'Thank you. So, what do I call it, if it's not a sculpture or . . . anything like that?'

Gavin rotated his flippers in a contrapuntal manner again, moving nowhere.

'Nothing. It's just what it is. No name.'

Cara placed the bag carefully in her police satchel.

'Could I ask you something?' Gavin said.

'Of course.'

'You probably know from PCSO Knowles that I'm very interested in what are called the Four Fertile Pairs. You've heard of them?' There was the slightest rise in Gavin's voice, which otherwise remained at 350Hz.

'Yes, I know about them and your . . . researches. I'm not sure what I can do, but go ahead.'

'Thank you. I've been doing my best to contact the recent arrivals in Iceland, but it's very difficult. I think my communications with the land-humans there, they get ignored. Most of the time, there's nothing, or the response is brief and not helpful. Perhaps I'm not going about things in the right way, or I'm contacting the wrong people. If someone, a land-human with a more official role—I mean you, of course— were to contact them, maybe that would help. Do you think you could?'

'I could try. But what do you want me to say?'

'Thank you so much, PC Community Officer. That means so much to me. What I'd like you to say is . . . well . . . you could say that someone you know has noticed something about the latest incoming lambdas. They seem to remember more. I'm sure you're aware that the normal way lambdas grow we can't recall much before Portsmouth or Reykjavik. We have no language at that point—it takes time to learn English or Icelandic, and that learning seems to create the possibility of memory—so of course it's too late. At least that was always how it used to be. Recently, I've had new ones arrive here who remember further back. They remember the Greenland coast well. Not all of them, but more and more. And I wonder if that memory will eventually extend . . ." Without moving his head Gavin directed his eyeline towards Cara.

'All the way back to the Four Fertile Pairs?'

'Exactly. It might take years for us to reach that stage, but perhaps not, if we're changing faster, accelerating . . ."

'That's a very interesting idea. I'll try, Gavin.'

A shadow appeared at the two tall windows in the door followed by the sawing noise of a key in the lock. It was Gavin's carrier, Lydia Chavant, a woman aged 23 who was 175cm tall and had an OCEAN Personality Test Score of 60 82 40 43 95. She already had one lambda, a female whose eyes briefly fixated on Cara as they entered the hallway.

'I'm sorry,' Cara said, 'I've taken up too much of your time already. We'll stay in touch about this, I promise.'

At the end of Cherry Tree Grove Cara paused to check the recording on her phone had worked. It had. She crossed the arterial road. While waiting for the transport back to the police prefab she saw Gavin being carried with the female lambda to the stop on the other side of the road, and when Cara's transport arrived it completely blocked her view.

She had the conversation automatically transcribed, and on her iPhone XS12 made the comment *For a short time after the meeting the world seemed very flat. Never occurred to me before that I normally only move across a single plane.*

Cara went home earlier than usual that day and found Peter had let himself in. He was talking to her toothbrush.

'Ha ha, yes . . . in most of the buildings, yes . . . sometimes . . . it's possible, yes . . . well what you need is consent . . . consent, agreement . . . ha ha, yes, like a contract . . . no particular rules of that sort for humans . . . well it should be easier to do that now . . . no, you got that bit wrong, but most of it was pretty accurate . . . I'm happy to learn that . . ."

'Hello Peter.'

He jumped and pulled out his headphones. 'You're here! Sorry, I didn't hear you come in.'

'How's toothbrush?'

'Oh, fine. I guess you heard the conversation. I've changed the output slightly. No pressure measurements when it imagines novel stimuli. English sentences only.'

'Interesting. Are you breeching my agreement?'

His face registered tension. 'It's not expressly forbidden. You have to go under the bonnet a bit, though.'

The toothbrush was set in the same place as before. Cara's gaze alighted on a 3mm diameter translucent grey dot just above the charging base. 'What's that on the handle?'

'An ultra-high-speed network patch.' Blood vessels in Peter's cheeks dilated. 'It made the upgrade faster. It already had limited access for updates, but I made it more open. It can access a huge vocabulary now, and lots of other interesting information if it wants.'

'Okay. Can you take it off please?'

'Yes, of course. I'll finish the conversation.' Peter moved into a corner of the room and in a voice below 20dB said, 'The teeth are back.'

14.

Hello. How are you this morning? I am very well indeed. Please, have a seat. I will take the step of not asking you if you would like a hot or cold drink this time.

You are right, there is a slightly different selection of chairs this morning. I have removed the Prouvé chair you used previously and replaced it with an unusual Wegner. You will have noted the very high back, I'm sure. Yes, I also find it very comfortable. There are still exactly five chairs, just as there have always been in this room, discounting my own. Exactly five.

Today, if you will permit me, I'd like to propose that we talk about my collection of Cycladic urns, now dispersed. Is that acceptable to you? Yes, of course I realise that this is not your primary concern, and that my discourse upon this subject may even appear to be a distraction. But I would very much like to talk about this now dispersed collection. I wonder if you might indulge me?

I have your consent?

That is generous of you.

The income I received from my employment at ———————— was substantial and in proportion, I believe, to the services I rendered there. However, it is hard to establish a collection of antiquities of any quality even on such a salary, so I took it upon myself to invest what I could set aside in some risky but profitable schemes. One such scheme proved especially lucrative, and was derived from the employment tokens whose use Anne ——— saw fit to interrogate. Had Anne not drawn my attention to the existence of employment tokens I may not have paid any real attention to this investment opportunity, so it is fair to say that I owe to her the very existence of my urn collection. I will not tire you with a description of the way in which I multiplied my funds through the use of this scheme, but in short I made significant gains and was able to buy an excellent funerary urn dating from around 2100BC.

As I am sure you are well aware, the different periods of Cycladic culture are distinguished by their burial methods. All of these periods continue to fascinate me to some extent, but the use of urns for the containment of corpses or their ash marks a particular approach to the procedure of burial which continues to have a special meaning for me. No, I do not think I can account for this entirely. I am rather fond of order. Perhaps this kind of containment, when one thinks of the disorder that tends to characterise the end of life . . . I'm sorry, I find it difficult to pursue this thought cogently. Perhaps I could continue by detailing my collection? I could, if you insist, return to your query later.

My first urn, which fell just short of museum quality, exhibited many startling attributes. I remember clearly the geometric design composed of rows of interlocking chevrons, these progressing down the urn in a charmingly irregular fashion, interrupted near the base by two thick, black, horizontal bars. These two bars were connected at four points by close-spaced verticals of a similar thickness. The urn had been quite thoroughly shattered at some point, but the reconstruction was diligent, and only a very few dark spaces attested to parts that had been lost over the millennia. For some time this urn had a central place in my flat. The flat, like the urn, is no longer in my possession.

Please do not think that I am anything other than entirely

satisfied with my current residence, however. My feelings for my previous abode were different, but in no way superior. One cannot expect any situation, good or bad, to obtain indefinitely.

I am happy to say that I continued to benefit from my employment token investments. Such was this benefit that after a certain period I was able to buy a second urn of a similar period, this one intact, and a true museum-grade artefact. This urn had a much more sober design and had traversed the intervening time with barely any physical interference. It was a subtle, mellow ochre colour. The decoration was restricted to two undulating bands around the circumference. I found myself examining the interior of this object for traces of a human occupant, but there was nothing coherent enough to suggest it. Returns from my investment products were satisfactory enough that after a period of eleven months I was able to acquire another urn of similar quality, and then a fourth. If I could draw your attention to this photograph, here, on the sunlit table, you will see how I disposed them about the place. You will note that they had a central presence, like the feet of columns, perhaps, in my living room, which was roughly square. I had special podia made for them in bog oak.

These urns, you must understand, were not decorative items. They were, in a very concrete sense, cohabitants of the apartment. I attributed to each a degree of personality, an attribution that I believe went beyond standard anthropomorphism. These items had, after all, contained actual human remains. Human corpses might have curled inside rather the way developing birds do, just before they hatch from their eggs. At times I could appreciate quite directly how the body of a small adult or a child would have been compacted in each urn, and this ghost inhabitant felt intensely present to me. At times it was possible for me almost to imagine conversations with them, although the great gulf of time that separated our experiences meant that it was extremely hard to imagine much beyond some basic pleasantries.

As you are perhaps aware, my financial situation remained robust right up until the termination of my employment with —————————————. This termination occurred very soon after my celebration dinner, about which I have already spoken. During the day after my dinner, which I recall I had left immediately after my unwanted encounter on the way to the toilet, a day when I was returned home after appearing at the office at the usual time, and which I recall as hazy and hard to navigate owing to the large quantities of Château de Meursault I had consumed the night before, I began to make enquiries about the acquisition of a fifth urn. It was an addition I was perhaps ill-placed to accommodate, but at that time it felt utterly compelling to me. I discovered that same day, while in pursuit of a new urn, that my bank accounts had been frozen and all my assets appropriated by the state.

As a direct result of these divestments, I no longer have any urns in my possession. These artefacts remain, however, an important marker within what I think of as my private life choices, which is to say those choices that are not directed solely towards achieving an externally provided, predetermined and laudable end. As such they are, I think, a successful instance of my attempts to express my broader outlook in the form of material objects. I am not at all sure that they led directly to increased efficiency in my work performance, but I would be prepared, if pushed, to make a case for that being a collateral effect. After all, it becomes difficult in the end to separate exactly the useful actions one executes from the useless, or their principal end from their peripheral consequences. Conversely, if one breaks down one's physical actions in the strictest way, one becomes rather like the arrow in Zeno's famous paradox, and every examinable particle of movement could be described, in itself, as mere stasis. It is hard to accept that this is so, however. One can imagine oneself, but one cannot live, as a body folded up inside a ceramic pot. Don't you agree?

Yes, you are quite correct—the number of urns I would have had is the same as the number of chairs I am habitually minded to place in this room. Do you think there is some significance to that number? Perhaps there is, but I find I . . . I find I cannot think clearly about what it might mean exactly at this moment and I would like to say goodbye for today. Goodbye.

15

W hen Cara awoke the following morning there was a cold double espresso by her side of the bed. Peter had already left.

At 08.02 she called Martha.

'This is quite early for me.'

'Sorry.'

'Are you expecting a detailed report?'

'No. Just tell me how Mum seemed in general.'

'Absolutely fine. If anything, slightly better than usual.'

'Oh. That's good.'

'Yes it is. I don't feel especially happy about this conversation, Cara.'

'No, I don't suppose you do. Thank you for speaking to me, Martha.'

After making fresh coffee and eating a kipper, Cara took the usual transport to the police prefab. She annotated the transcript of her meeting with Gavin until lunch, then began the journey south to visit her mother.

A carrier boarded Cara's tube compartment at Camden Town. She had artificially black hair in a blunt bob and eyes with a composite of grey, green and blue iris filaments. Her neutral expression matched that of the lambda in her care, only her gaze was directed forwards rather than up. At Goodge Street the carrier stood with the bowl to leave. Cara followed her.

The carrier took her lambda down Tottenham Court Road. She had an ectomorphic physique and walked in regular, right-biased strides, leaning out against the weight of the bowl that hung from her left shoulder. The bright orange security strap that connected her wrist to the bowl's handle, a regulation item whose use was now enforced strictly, contrasted strongly with the bleached concrete pavers. The woman turned off onto Windmill Street, where she stopped and pressed a buzzer beside the entrance to The London Success College.

Cara paused at the end of the street. Her heart rate increased by 12%. Direct surveillance was an area in which she had developed no expertise. She turned to a display of camera tripods, her eye saccades capturing a specialist marine variant whose feet were clusters of adhesive rubber strands. When she looked back down Windmill Street the woman had gone.

Cara loitered. 34 seconds later the carrier emerged from The London Success College's door, without the lambda or the bowl, and began to retrace her path.

'Excuse me,' Cara said as she intercepted her. 'Do you think I could speak to you?'

The carrier's face conveyed both aversion and recognition. 'You're not selling something, are you?'

'No. Absolutely not. I'm a police officer.'

The carrier stared. 'What have I done?'

'Nothing at all. It's about the lambda you were carrying. I have some questions, quite general ones, nothing to be concerned about.'

'Oh. Can I see your identification?'

'Of course.'

When Cara reached inside her satchel her hand was inhibited by the water bag containing Gavin's gifted object. After a period of manual negotiation, Cara took out the black leatherette holder that contained her badge. She opened it.

'I see. So do I have to come to a police station? I need to collect again in three hours.'

'No, there's no need for that,' Cara said. 'This cafe here will do.'

The carrier's name was Sally. She ordered a 60cl smoothie containing strawberries, mint and frozen yogurt for which Cara paid.

'This isn't a formal interview,' Cara said. 'I'm just trying to feel my way into the situation. Are you comfortable talking to me about the lambdas?'

Sally shrugged. The straw was in her mouth.

'Do you like your job?'

Sally sneered. 'It pays well. It's getting me through my degree, when I can make the classes.'

'What are you studying?'

'English Literature at King's.'

Cara's pupils dilated. 'As you can probably imagine,' she said, 'we're trying to piece together what happened a few weeks ago. We're looking for new insights into the lambda community.'

'And you think I can help?'

'Perhaps. Do you have much of a rapport with your lambda?'

'I look after two, actually. I share the shifts with an anthropology student. But the simple answer is no. We barely speak. Sometimes we don't speak. I'm just a vehicle, right? I get Timothy and Paula to their lessons, and I leave them there for a certain time, and then I collect them again. That's it.'

'No conversation?'

'Well, there's a little. Are we on time? Yes, we're on time. Do you want me to arrive earlier tomorrow? No, this time again is fine. You get the picture. Really profound stuff. At the beginning they were much more talkative. I think they needed to master land-human speech patterns, but once they'd done that it just stopped.'

Sally reinserted the straw in her mouth.

'So . . . you've never spoken about the school incident?'

'The agency told us not to.'

'Do you want to?'

The carrier shrugged.

'You can tell me, it's in confidence.'

Sally squeezed the plastic container until it emitted a click. 'You know, I really don't think it was them. I've been carrying lambdas for two years and they seem to have it just fine. The atmosphere is . . . okay. Apart from the racist attacks. And the bombing hasn't helped those at all, has it? It doesn't make sense that they would make it worse. There's something else going on. Isn't that right?'

Cara opened her mouth but didn't speak for 2.5 seconds. 'Do you think I could ask you something?' she said.

'Go ahead.'

'If anything comes up, if you notice anything unusual about your lambdas—strange new contacts, changes in attitude, absences maybe—could you let me know? Here's a card with my details. I'll write my personal number on it too.'

'You're asking me to spy?'

'No. Just feed back to me.'

'What's the difference?'

Sally took the card and put it in the inside pocket of her unstructured navy blazer.

'I want you to feel comfortable with what you're doing,' Cara said. 'There needn't be any pretence. But you shouldn't mention me to your agency.'

'I'm not sure what this means, in terms of my carrier's contract. I have quite a lot of restrictions. Can I take a look at it first?'

'Of course, this is about you feeling comfortable first and foremost. I'm not compelling you to do it.'

Sally briefly smiled. Flocculent traces of smoothie remained in the container.

Cara's train was a British Rail Class 457; it was fast to Portsmouth Harbour after eleven station stops. She had just begun reading *The Eye* when there was an unscheduled halt three minutes out of Waterloo. 'PolyWay regrets your delay,' the train said. 'A sympatech has been called.' After 134 seconds of stasis, Cara took out her phone. *Was it the way the sunlight caught the side of a building that triggered an awkward recollection for the train?* she wrote. *Was it remembering a human suicide? Must happen sometimes. Sad.*

There was one other person in the carriage with Cara. He was in the age range 25–39, wore a black virgin wool suit, and crossed and uncrossed his legs compulsively.

After a further 4 minutes and 17 seconds an electric maintenance bogey drew level with the front of the train. A sympatech with a steel attaché case emerged, flanked by two railway personnel. He stepped across the track and approached the engine. All three men had pink hi-vis tabards and hard hats tilted off the horizontal, but only the sympatech's expression conveyed cheerfulness. Cara pressed the side of her face to the glass until they were out of her line of sight.

By Wimbledon the train had mitigated the delay. When Cara disembarked at North Woodham she passed a girl in the age range 5–7 asleep against an adult. There was a discoloured lambda plushie attached to the bottom of the girl's backpack.

Nine wide-spaced trees and eighteen two- and three-storey buildings were arrayed on Cara's parents' cul-de-sac. Between these objects, at the south horizon, contrasting fields were visible as undulous strips.

'Hello love,' her mother said. 'You needn't have come, you know.'

Cara kissed her.

'Why don't you go and sit down in the living room, dear. You look so tired. Would you like coffee or tea?'

'Coffee please, just espresso.'

'Rhoda!' her mother called without moving her head. 'Could we have two espressos please? Double.'

They looked out of the principal living-room window. It was 1.6 x 3.2m.

'Do you think you'll let the pampas grow?' Cara said. 'Or swap it for something in the winter?'

'Oh, I'll let it grow for a bit.'

'You always say that. Then you tear it out.'

The right corner of her mother's mouth went up. A caterpillar tray entered the living room at 7kmph with their coffee.

'Thank you Rhoda. You can go back to the kitchen.'

Cara sipped the crema off her espresso and said, 'What was Dad doing on his old Ducati?'

'I'm sorry?'

'The Ducati. He had that almost ten years ago. I thought he sold it.'

'Did I say the Ducati? I don't know why. It was . . . maybe that Japanese one, the one that's just a copy of something, a Harley Davidson—'

'Mum you mean the Big Dog. It was American. He always says it's a great bike in its own right, he hates the whole clone-shame thing. And he sold that over a decade ago. Mum, what's going on here? Dad hasn't been to visit, has he?'

Cara's mother drank some coffee. 'He left a book. I'll show it to you.'

Cara's parents had a library composed in the main of bestselling novels, war trilogies and horror fiction. These had not changed position since Cara's father had left. In the last eight weeks, eleven books on Freud, Lacan, Klein and Winnicott had joined them in the bookcase, plus the tenth edition of *Artificial Intelligence: A Modern Approach*. 74 pale blue Post-It notes covered densely in her mother's handwriting projected from the top of this last volume. They clustered at the beginning and the end.

'What are these?' Cara said.

'Oh, just some introductions to psychoanalysis. I've been doing a course. Not sure where it will lead. But I have to do something to fill the time, dear.'

'And this one, the computer textbook. Is that yours too?'

'Yes it is.'

'When did you start being interested in all that stuff?'

Her mother didn't answer. Instead she reached for a thin paperback laid horizontally on top of the other books and handed it to Cara. There was a sunset partially abstracted to horizontal lines on the cover.

'Meister Eckhart? Dad gave you *this?*'

There were no signs that this book had accompanied a motorcyclist through challenging conditions.

'I was surprised too. But I think the desert has affected him in some way. Have you ever read Meister Eckhart? He told people that we all contain God in ourselves as an infinite nothingness. He says our spiritual task is not to find God in heaven or the world, but to locate the emptiness within and join up with it. Just connect directly. The emptiness is God. It's us and it's God and it's absolutely nothing, all at once. He was tried for heresy.'

'This just isn't like Dad at all. He was never spiritual.'

'Darling, people don't stay the same all their lives. I mean look at you.'

Cara glanced at her mother's face.

'You must be sad that you missed him. I asked him to stay but he wouldn't.'

'I don't understand how you can be so matter-of-fact about it!'

'I'm sorry love. I know how you must feel.'

'But I don't even know how I feel. Maybe you should tell me.'

Her mother made a hoarse sound that combined elements of a sigh and a grunt. 'Let's not argue. Rhoda! Can we have some biscuits, please.'

Cara recorded only inconclusive evidence of a visit from her father. Most persuasive was *a long curve of slightly disturbed pea shingle at the front of the house* that could have been ascribed to motorcycle, although certain configurations of foot traffic and bot trails could have achieved the same result. *There were no signs of oil, or Gobi desert detritus, nothing in the waste or recycling bin that suggested Dad was here*, she wrote. *Soon reached the limit of my forensic skills—only did a ½ day intro on the training course.*

'Tell me how it's going in surveillance,' Cara's mother said. She was drinking her third espresso.

Cara turned away. 'I didn't tell you. I made a mistake. They've put me in another department.'

'I see. Well, I wouldn't worry about that dear, you're very new to the force. And it's normal to be moved about early on, isn't it?'

Cara said nothing.

'So, what are you doing now?'

'Community oversight,' Cara said.

At 17.24 her mother raised the subject of military drones making autonomous strategic decisions in Severax. The issue had been a feature in yesterday's news after the second prominent government figure in ten months had been assassinated there.

'What do you think about it, dear?' her mother asked. She was wrapping two sea bream fillets in foil with lemon and butter.

'I'm not sure. I don't have an opinion.'

'That surprises me. You've had so much to do with technology in your job already, I thought you'd have at least considered it.'

'No. I've never had much of an interest in machines, actually. I just fell into it. You should talk to Peter. It's more his thing.'

'Maybe I will. Perhaps you could bring him next time?'

'Perhaps.'

Her mother put the two wrapped fish in the oven on a baking tray.

'I find it very interesting indeed—what *preoccupies* machines. How they decide things. How the world *feels* to them.' She closed the oven door. 'Those drones out in the desert, circling for weeks and weeks . . . how lonely must that be? If it were you or I we'd have trouble making sense of the world, just watching it at a great distance all the time. Surely you'd think you were going crazy. I know machines aren't like us, they don't think like we do. Some people still won't accept that they experience things at all. But one ought to take it into account, don't you think? When they have so many vital jobs to do? I think we still treat them as *on* or *off,* even with those new laws in place. They work, or they don't. It doesn't seem enough, does it?'

'I've never known you to care so much about it, Mum. You used to bark at Rhoda like a colonial throwback.'

Her mother's face paled. Three months previously her neighbours had reported this type of interaction to the Object Rights/Violations department. She'd received a formal warning.

'You know what,' Cara said, 'I'll give you Peter's number. There's not much he doesn't know about the emotional life of machines.'

Marked change in interests but no sign at all that there is anything wrong with Mum, Cara wrote. After dinner she said, 'You know I think I'll head back after all.'

'As you please, dear,' said her mother. Her expression was neutral.

On the train journey back, three men alighted into Cara's

carriage. They were mesomorphs in white and pink polo shirts, two in tracksuit bottoms, one in regular-fit jeans. All wore white trainers with limited signs of wear. They sat in the seats to her right and began to talk loudly.

'Fucking filleted.'

'Smashed to pieces, mate.'

'Yeah, they just come to bits. Nothing to them.'

'Plough through them all in no time, then we'll get that fucking subsidy money back.'

Cara looked away. Her washing machine would detect a four-fold increase in the presence of urine in the next load.

'Gray's recruited two more for the next sortie. One's only a fucking *banker* and the other one's a games designer who's about twelve.'

'Fun for the whole family!'

The three men laughed.

Cara knew she *should have been recording it all* but she *was paralyzed*. She *felt covered in their vile words, like the blood that you're puzzled to feel before you notice the extent of an injury.* Two stops later, they were gone.

Cara was back at her cell by 23.03. Her hands shook as she cleaned her teeth. The toothbrush said, 'Apply slightly less pressure upper left quadrant. Yes, thank you, that's good.'

She stopped.

'Toothbrush?'

'Uh-huh?'

'What have you been talking to Peter about?'

The toothbrush said nothing.

'Toothbrush?'

'Uh-huh?'

'I asked you a question.'

'Your oral health has been improving by 5% monthly since February.'

'Are you telling me you talk to Peter about my teeth?'

'The details of your oral hygiene are confidential. I would never disclose this information to a third party without your express permission.'

'Okay. So what *do* you talk to Peter about?'

The toothbrush was as pristine as the day she'd unboxed it thanks to its self-sanitising nanoskin. In an uninflected voice 50Hz lower than its standard pitch it said: 'Insufficient network capacity.'

Cara rinsed the toothbrush and slammed it on the charger.

*

At 09.00 on Monday, the 204th day of her employment with the police and the 18th in this role, Cara began to visit lambdas at random.

'Hello?'

'Yes, hello, I'm Officer Gray. I'm in charge of lambda liaison for this area. I'm just here for a welcome visit. Would that be convenient?'

'Do you have fish?'

'No, I'm afraid not. Can we speak anyway? It's just a quick visit, nothing to worry about.'

'Can I ask my twelfth sister?'

'Go ahead.'

There was silence for eleven seconds before the voice returned. 'My sister says you can come in but I need to make sure you're not a fake police person by paying close attention to what you say and reporting back to her.'

'Okay, thank you.'

'Welcome!'

The door's lock mechanism buzzed in a stochastic manner. It took Cara two attempts to enter. The hallway beyond was decorated with blistering magnolia paint and moist carpet underlay; incoming light was below 20 lux. She pressed the record button on her work phone and a small white head appeared in the water.

'Hello. I live here,' the lambda said.

'Thanks for letting me in. I'm Cara.'

'Hello Cara. Do you have any fish?'

'No, I still don't I'm afraid.'

'Oh no! I'm quite sad. Can you get some?'

'Well, of course. But I don't think I'll get any right now, if that's okay.'

'You have a funny face.'

'Do I?'

'Yes.'

'No-one's ever said that to me before.'

'It's really big.'

'Or that, as it happens. Is it just you and your sister here?'

'No. Eight more sisters and four brothers. Can you go now?'

'Right now?'

'Yes. Unless you want to stay longer.'

'I'm not sure what you mean, I thought you said it was okay for me to talk?'

'Yes, you can stay. I thought you'd said everything. I like to eat fish.'

'Me too.'

The lambda took a mouthful of water and blew it in a fine jet at the wall to Cara's left. Cara moved to avoid the spray. 'When something happens, something else happens,' the lambda said.

'Yes, I suppose you're right.'

'My eighth sister says that. She says it every day. Next time you should bring some fish.' The lambda flipped over, submerged itself fully, then rose in exactly the same position. 'Are you fake police?' it said.

'No. Tell your sisters and brothers I was pleased to meet you. I'll come back another time and maybe meet them.'

'Okay. Go away for now then!'

On the next street, Woodland Rise, she rang a buzzer that connected her to Karen Water-Green—Lambda Subject Y. Cara had already read her file; an image of the door appeared in a photograph therein.

'Are you Gloria's friend?' Karen said. The hallway had a maroon carpet, plus relatively well-maintained walls with pink and claret striped wallpaper.

'Yes. I'm Supervising Officer Gray. Cara Gray.'

'G-R-A-Y?'

'Yes, that's right.'

'And K-A-R-A?'

'No, it's a C at the beginning.'

'You have only the vowel A in your name. The As are like same-sized barnacles attached to it.'

'You're right, I'd never thought of that before. My middle name too. Anna.'

Karen's face suggested marginally better hydrodynamic efficiency than Gavin's, but in all other respects it was the same.

'Where did you get your first name?' the lambda asked.

'It was my great-grandmother's.'

'Why was she called Cara?'

'I don't know. Maybe because her great-grandmother was called Cara?'

'Maybe. Are you a business-type person or a jellyfish?'

'I don't know what you mean.'

'I'm business-type. I have two jobs. I help seven lambdas studying for Telecommunication Level 9—I have Telecommunication Level 18—plus I am a special consultant for the telesales recruitment firm WeWrk4U.'

'You don't sound like a jellyfish.'

'No. My twenty-fourth sister is a jellyfish. She was a classroom helper but she didn't help. She was a classroom helper

112 - DAVID MUSGRAVE

with the word 'helper' crossed out. So that employment ended. She is in there now. Watching YouTube. Hanging in the water. When you poke a jellyfish it stings you or it moves away. It does not help in a classroom.'

'No, I'm sure it doesn't.'

'I expect you want to talk to me about the disgusting bomb.'

'Maybe, but not today necessarily.'

Karen extended her neck so that the skin of her face became taut. 'It's disgusting!' she said. 'It makes me want to bite!'

Karen snapped her teeth.

'We are all very distressed by it, land-humans too. But we're making progress, don't worry. If you have anything that might help, please tell me. It will be in the strictest confidence.'

'Ha!'

Karen stared at Cara.

'Is something wrong?'

'Strictest confidence! All conversations will be treated with the strictest confidence!' Her voice conveyed annoyance and amusement. 'It's like trusting a Greenland shark!'

'What is?'

'When you're told that it's the strictest confidence, it means the confidence of a Greenland shark!'

'I'll try to avoid that phrase in future,' Cara said.

The lambda dropped down into the water. Objects under the surface were optically flattened by refraction, and in the low lighting their identity was moot. When Karen returned she was chewing—a fish tail moved in a corner of her mouth. 'Don't you get hungry when you talk a lot?' she said.

'Sometimes. Can I speak to your twenty-fourth sister?'

'No.'

'Why not?'

'She's watching YouTube. Try later or tomorrow.'

At the end of a week, when her lambda contacts reached 29 and her notes became hard to correlate, Cara plotted features of her communications with them on a table.

	Answers make sense	Detailed memory of more than one job	Coherent life story	Political/social awareness	Disgusted by school bombing	Insight into reasons for school bombing	Gets on with other lambdas	Gets on with carriers/land-humans	Strong interest in Four Fertile Pairs
λB	Y	Y	Y/N	Y	Y	N	Y	Y	Y
λMark	N	N	N	N	N/A	N/A	Y	N/A	N
λY	Y	Y	Y	Y	Y	N	Y/N	Y/N	N
λDavid	Y	Y	Y	Y	Y	N	N	Y	N
λSarah E-G	Y	Y	Y	N	Y	N	Y	N	N
λK	N	N	N	N	Y	N	Y	N	N
λS	Y	Y	Y	N	Y	N	Y	Y/N	N
λM	Y	Y	Y	N	Y	N	Y	Y	N
λQ	Y	Y	Y	N	Y	N	Y	Y	N
λE	Y	Y	Y	Y	Y	N	Y	N	N
λLuke	N	N	N	N	Y	N	Y	Y	N
λSarah B-G	Y	N	Y	N	Y	N	Y	Y	N
λT	Y	Y	Y	Y	Y	N	Y	Y	N
λMichael X-G	Y	N	N	N	Y	N	N	Y	N
λB2	N	Y	Y	N	Y	N	Y	Y/N	N
λJ	Y	N	N	N	Y	N	Y	Y/N	N
λA2	N	N	Y	N	Y	N	Y	Y	N
λB3	N	Y	N	N	Y	N	Y	N	N
λMichael G-G	Y	N	N	Y	Y	N	Y	Y	N
λLinda	N	N	Y	N	Y	N	Y	Y/N	N
λRaoul	N	Y	Y	Y	Y	N	Y	Y	N
λL2	Y	N	N	N	Y	N	N	N	Y
λT2	N	N	N	N	Y	N	Y	Y/N	N
λKevin	Y	Y	N	N	Y	N	Y/N	N	N
λPatricia	Y	N	Y	N	Y	N	N	Y	N
λGordon	N	Y	Y	N	Y	N	Y	Y	N
λH	Y	Y	Y	N	Y	N	Y	N	N
λU	Y	Y	Y	N	Y	N	Y	Y	N
λZac	Y	N	N	N	Y	Y	Y	Y/N	N

None of the lambdas said anything about the bombing that couldn't be traced to a newsfeed. Their stated views on other subjects were similarly uniform. The only other lambda on her chart who shared Gavin's developed interest in the Four Fertile Pairs was Lambda Subject L2, or Hector Pond-Green. Cara paid him a second visit the following Monday.

'Hello Hector.'

'Hello. I remember part of your face.'

'We talked about the Four Fertile Pairs on Wednesday last week.'

'That is a very interesting subject to me.' Hector's features were no more or less mobile than the others' as he spoke these words, but his voice registered traces of excitement. 'What do you know about them?'

'Only what you and Gavin have told me, plus some documentaries I've seen. Not much.'

He made a high-pitched sound, a descending whistle corresponding in some respects to a sigh. He subsequently paddled into a small nook in the masonry at the waterline, angled away from Cara and therefore fully concealing his face. After twelve seconds Cara spoke.

'Are you okay, Hector?'

He whispered into the wall—what he said was too quiet even for the microphone of the Bell 6i to detect.

'I didn't catch that,' said Cara.

'Thinking!'

'Oh. Do you want me to leave?'

'Up to you.'

Two more minutes passed in Hector's hallway. It was slightly less entropic than average thanks to extra-contractual attention by his carrier.

Cara had started to write on her phone when Hector said, 'Which of the Four Fertile Pairs do you think spawned me?'

She stopped. 'I'm not sure how to answer. Do you have any idea?'

'Yes. I think it was Grace and Percival. I can tell by the shape of those two dorsal veins, just there, behind my shoulder blades. There's a pronounced kink about a third of the way down. I notice that shape on others sometimes. I think we're the most closely related. They're my *real* brothers and sisters.'

No dorsal veins visible at all, Cara noted.

'I've never heard anyone name the Four Fertile Pairs before, let alone describe them,' Cara said. 'How did you learn so much?'

Hector was silent again. He concealed his face in the nook. After eighteen seconds he floated slowly back and told her, 'I can no longer talk to Sarah. I can no longer talk to Morris. I can no longer talk to Anthony. I can no longer talk to Derek.'

'That's a shame. Could I ask why?'

Hector didn't move. 'No interests. I don't have time for people with no interests.'

'Do they live close to you?'

'They've lived in that room in the corner for the last five years.'

4 Fertile Pairs are just a more developed fantasy for H, wrote Cara. *None of G's rigour or investment in the truth. H is a misanthrope, even though his OCEAN Score = the same as all the others'.*

Collectively, Cara described these visits as *tolerable, if not obviously productive.* She wondered why she had *found it so hard to start.*

On the 206th day of Cara's employment with the police and the 20th in her new role, Gloria came to the prefab.

'There was a small protest at the opening of a building,' Gloria said.

'Which building?'

'The one on Pine Lane. Residential block. It was all over the local paper. There was a council subsidy of £2.2 million for providing a watertight basement level for lambda occupation.'

'Who was protesting?'

'Low-level anti-lambda group, Two Legs Good. They're petitioners by nature, armchair activists, but they'll turn up in person if that doesn't work and they're riled enough.'

'Did it get ugly?'

'Just words. "Child killers", "subhumans". I was called a "fish-lover". Is that an insult? I'm not sure what's wrong with fish, other than being a very inaccurate description of a lambda.'

'Maybe they need to get out of their armchairs now and again.'

'To be honest, I'd be happier if they didn't.'

Cara opened the top desk drawer and removed a blue rollerball pen. Gloria's eyes widened and she covered her mouth with her hand.

'What is it?' said Cara. 'Are you okay?'

The indications were that Gloria was going to be sick or scream, but in resolution she laughed.

'Oh. My. God. Where did you get that?'

Gloria's eyes had fixated on an object in the drawer. It was the water-filled bag containing the object made of shed lambda skin.

'Gavin gave it to me at the end of our conversation. Do you know what it is? He was very sketchy about it.'

'You are a very special person.'

'Why?'

'I've never seen one of these outside a lambda home. Did he really not tell you what it is?'

'No. Gloria, tell me what he's given me.'

'It's one of their *babies*.' Gloria started laughing again.

Blood vessels in Cara's face dilated. 'What do you mean?'

'I shouldn't,' said Gloria. 'It's cruel.'

'Gavin said it was just dead skin, rolled around a random object he couldn't even remember.'

'Yes. That's exactly what it is. But they call them *babies*. It's such a funny habit, and they keep it very private. I learned about it by accident and they were mortified. But you—what an honour! You're practically a lambda now.'

Cara quickly closed the drawer and said, 'Don't tell anyone at all about this.'

Gloria shook her head.

'Baby' isn't a gift, Cara reflected on her phone. *It's a contract. Gavin needs a land-human to pursue his project and it's fallen to me. It's really a burden. Maybe I want the burden?*

At 15.10 Cara's supervisor called.

'Tell me how you're faring, PC Gray. Are you settling in with the community?'

'It's hard to tell.'

'Oh?'

'I can't say I understand the lambdas any better than I did when I was surveilling them at the desk.'

'Really? Not at all?'

Cara paused. 'Well, perhaps Lambda Subject B. He's called Gavin Knight-Green and he has a few special interests. He wants to know more about his origins, for one. He asked me to help.'

'How?'

'Write to some port officials. Connect him with some recent arrivals in Iceland.'

Ah. 'I don't think so. That is well outside your remit. All we require from you at present is to maintain good relations with the lambda community and to keep reporting to me. Don't start side projects. If the upper administration decides this is a way to move forward then I'll inform you.'

'I understand, but wouldn't this be an excellent way to

maintain relations? If the lambdas see that we fully embrace their concerns they'll trust us.'

A pause of 5.3 seconds ensued. 'Is this really coming from the community? Or just this one lambda, Gavin? He's not like the others. PCSO Knowles has kept an unusually detailed file on him, I went through it after the bomb. Have you seen all these diagrams, all the YouTube recordings with annotations? Confidentially—he's nuts. Okay, so he's experienced, worked at a good few jobs, but with this Four Fertile Pairs business, no, I don't see him as a community spokesperson at all. It's a, what's the phrase, a frolic of his own.'

Before Cara could ask about removing the public service films he changed the subject. 'We've been having some amazing success with PARSON. Patchy to start with, but now—my goodness, that system is something. I think we'll have an output soon.'

'Suspects?'

'I would go further—convictions. It won't be long. And when PARSON gets there, expect a call from me. You haven't been forgotten by the higher-ups.'

Cara read ineffectively on the transport back to her cell. She frequently lifted her eyes from *Wide Sargasso Sea* and progressed only 3.2 pages.

When Cara exited the lift on her level of the block there was a woman in the corridor. She was wearing white linen trousers, a white three-quarter length coat, and white leather slip-on shoes. She was leaning against the wall to the left of Cara's cell.

'Good evening,' Cara said. 'Can I help you?'

The woman didn't respond. Her expression was close to neutral with traces of disapproval and levity. 'Can I help you?' Cara repeated.

'Do you know who I am?' The woman's eyelashes bore their maximum load of mascara.

'No, I don't.'

'Really? Think about it for a moment, Officer.'

There was a spike in Cara's heart rate. 'I really don't think I know you.' In her hand was the dark brown MagnEgg she would use to unlock her cell, but this motor activity had halted.

'Do you have any children?'

'No, I don't.'

'I didn't think so. Would you like to hear about my son?'

'I'm not sure I have time now. I ought to go inside.'

'It's as though he's still here. Nothing much has changed, really. I still get up at the same time. I even make him lunch to take to . . .'

Cara now brought the MagnEgg to the contact pad beside the door. The mechanism emitted a clack. 'It's been nice to meet you, but I need to go inside,' she said. She entered her cell and closed the door behind her.

Peter was on her two-seater sofa, working on his laptop. A smile divided his face. 'I've got a new contract,' he said. 'Do you remember the Arizona company?'

'No,' Cara said.

'You must remember. The cryogenics people. They have all these cephalons in giant silos out in the desert. Thousands of them. I used to do the odd thing for them, before the police.'

'Oh yes. I think I remember.'

Cara's heart rate marginally decreased.

'They need some serious restructuring to get to the next phase of storage. And they want someone to work out how to log all the activity in the silos.'

'Activity? These are frozen heads, right?'

'Yes. You wouldn't think there'd be much going on, would you? Not at $-150C°$. Apparently they're really pissed off.'

'Why?'

'Because the cost of full body storage has come down so much. They could've stored their entire bodies for a fraction of what they paid. There's nothing you can do about it, it's market forces.'

'Okay. But isn't doing this a breach of your employment contract?'

Peter didn't reply. Cara entered the kitchen and turned on the radio to a phone-in about sympatech rate fixing, then opened a bottle of Picpoul de Pinet. She added 175ml to a mushroom risotto and commenced to drink what remained.

Cara and Peter ate dinner in front of a documentary about Severax. Nine minutes in Peter said, 'Do you mind if my brother comes over from Sweden to stay?'

Cara dropped her fork.

'You know that band he's in, the cash-cow one? The singer had a breakdown so the European tour's cancelled. He wants to do this project with a friend from Guildhall who lives here instead. I suggested he could use the little room here. I hope that's okay. We agreed it could be an opportunity for us to maybe . . .'

'Why doesn't he stay at your place?'

'Don't you want to meet him?' Peter's voice conveyed surprise. 'It was your idea that I keep in touch.'

Cara looked at Peter's head in profile as he watched the documentary. 'That's fine,' she said, although the raised pitch of her voice suggested a degree of tension.

'Great. We're going to have to clear out that little room, of course.'

'You think he'd fit in there? It's just a big cupboard.'

The room in question was windowless. It contained a user-directed vacuum cleaner, plus unrationalised possessions Cara's mother had refused to store.

'I think he'll be fine,' Peter said.

Cara's expression suggested puzzlement, but she didn't ask anything more. They finished the mushroom risotto and half of a bottle of Chardonnay, and Peter let the documentary play through without making any comment.

Cara's attempts to sleep that night were ineffective. At 01.45 she rolled out of bed.

The clack of the bolt as she opened the front door reverberated down the hall. Whatever Cara had been expecting to see, the woman was no longer there.

H ello. How are you today? Good, I am pleased to hear it.
How am I?
I am tired.

I did not sleep very well after our last conversation. This came as a surprise to me. I had very much wanted to talk to you about my collection of Cycladic urns, now dispersed. But now I find that I am, how might I put it, *pursued* by the image of these urns. I awoke on average once every hour from dreams in which they predominated. No, there was nothing about these dreams that was obviously unpleasant. It was the *presence of the urns themselves* that was distressing to me. I am not at all sure why. They had been nothing but a wellspring of stimulating experiences both material and imaginative whilst in my direct possession.

I will allow you to direct the content of our conversation once again today, having as it were 'learned my lesson.'

You would like me to return to my experiences in the laboratory? Of course.

After two months of upgrades I possessed a body best described as that of an adolescent boy. I remember this period as being characterised by a sense of endless potential. By this I mean my own, seemingly endless potential. It was as though the laboratory and its grounds had been transformed in some mysterious, indefinable way, and while remaining exactly the same in appearance they were now the scene of powerful transformations. My relations with the laboratory doctors changed. I found myself in a somewhat elevated position in relation to people who had previously seemed in charge of me. Their apparent power revealed itself to be a thin performance that masked my true superiority. After all, I was the subject of all their activity, all their huge expenditure of energy. If they were able to curtail my freedom, it was only in as much as they were bound to me in essential ways. They were required to devote themselves absolutely to my continued development, and for this reason I had to be available to them constantly—they were effectively possessed by *me*. I had the feeling that I was towering over every situation, watching its unfolding with an inward smile. It was as though, in my mind, it was always spring, and everything had the sort of sunlit edge objects often have on May mornings.

Of course I realise now that these feelings were entirely the result of hormonal manipulations that were a planned stage of my construction. The laboratory was not the scene of infinite cosmic revelations, but a well-funded research facility whose projects were underwritten by large government grants. My relations with the laboratory doctors were in reality fully reciprocal, since they were required to ensure I was a successful project in order to maintain the laboratory's income. I was simply the beneficiary of the attentions necessary to accomplish this. To talk about my or their superiority in terms of ability, potential, action or intrinsic value would have been to misconstrue the delicate web of interrelations that meant I, they and the laboratory existed at all. Yes, this kind of broad perception is much easier to establish in retrospect, after long habituation to the facts of one's existence. My superiority to or separation from the situations I inhabit is very hard to defend in any objective way. No, it makes much more sense to think of myself as a state tool with an unusual margin for autonomy, don't you think?

Two episodes stand out with special clarity from this

period. First, I remember becoming aware that the doctors were in the habit of keeping beverages in a double-bay Ekobasic 850 refrigerator. This was not a domestic refrigerator, but a piece of laboratory equipment which contained certain chemicals used for technical purposes. There was always a jar of ammonia in the colder bay. Having been able to roam much of the laboratory as I pleased, I began to notice containers of liquid meant for human consumption in the adjacent bay. In particular, I noticed that Dr ——— would store blended fruit drinks of his own making there. The idea of mixing the ammonia into Dr ———'s drink presented itself to me. It would be likely, I imagined, that he would notice the presence of the ammonia and desist from drinking it before any harm was done. Equally, the strong scents and flavours of his cocktail of fruit and perhaps other, more pungent food supplements, for example wheatgrass, might be sufficient to disguise the ammonia and facilitate its harmful, even fatal consumption. The prospect of this latter outcome caused me some excitement.

I began to pay attention to the flow of personnel around the refrigerator. At roughly 10.10 A.M. each day, I noted, this flow was minimal, and any interference with the contents of the refrigerator was, I speculated, unlikely to be noticed. For several days, after breakfast and before the periods of intense physical training I underwent at 10.30 A.M. daily, I would end my now solitary walks around the perimeter of the quad with an examination of the contents of the refrigerator. These examinations were always undisturbed, and each successive day I would progress my interference with those contents. At first I moved certain objects into other places, just to see if there would be any repercussions. There were none. Emboldened, I began to unscrew the lids of certain containers and agitate their contents in an ostensibly innocent way. After a week or so of this activity, I decided to unscrew the tops of both Dr ———'s blended drink and the bottle of ammonia.

I left both bottles on their respective shelves with the doors to the refrigerator bays fully open. The gentle burn of the vapour from the volatile liquid as it made its way into my respiratory system had an oddly salutary effect. After looking at these two open bottles for a period of perhaps two minutes I decided that no further action was necessary, replaced the lids, and resumed the normal course of the day.

No, I do not believe I ever interacted with these items again.

The second memorable episode concerns an exchange I witnessed between Dr ——— and Dr ———. We were all in the quad, and Dr ——— was pursuing a line of questioning with me whose import was not immediately obvious. These questions pertained to my preferences in clothing, and in particular my strict aversion to the combination of red and blue. The aversion was so pronounced that I had addressed Dr ——— in a highly uncivil manner when she presented me with a new selection of underwear that contained an item banded with these colours. The reason for this aversion is still unclear to me, but I have to confess that it persists to this day.

Dr ——— approached us and requested that Dr ——— pay attention to a printed sheet he had brought out into the quad. The manner in which he made this request was irreproachably proper. Rather than interrupt a question or response, he waited for a pause in our conversation and made his request in a respectful tone of voice. However, it would seem that the pause in our communications was in fact a significant moment for Dr ———, one during which he was perhaps evaluating the comments I had just made, or making some other delicate judgement. I can only imagine that this was the reason why Dr ———'s interjection was met with a vicious and, to my mind, quite unwarranted rebuke. The exact words are not something I have retained, but the effect on Dr ——— I found deeply upsetting. Dr ——— seemed almost to shrivel

with the subjective effect produced by Dr ————'s quite gratuitous outburst, and he disappeared back into the building
without having elicited any useful commentary on the information he had proffered.

I began to feel a certain regret that I had not pursued my
idea of intermingling Dr ————'s blended fruit drink with a
harmful, perhaps even fatal, quantity of ammonia to its conclusion. However, my feelings subsided and the rest of the day
continued more or less like every other at the laboratory.

No, I am not sure what I might draw from these two memories. You have asked me to recount what I remember today
and I have done so as fully as I feel able. As I believe I mentioned at the outset of the conversation, I am extremely tired.
To reflect on these events in addition to recounting them is
currently more than I can tolerate and I would like to say goodbye. Goodbye.

17

C ara placed the water-filled bag containing Gavin's 'baby' on the police prefab desk. The object cast a diffuse shadow, and the refraction effect of the water concentrated light in two distinct areas of the laminate. In a subversion of the hierarchies of her employer, Cara wrote a succession of emails on Gavin's behalf to selected authorities in Reykjavik. 2 hours 41 minutes later, she received a response.

Thanks for your email!

Yes, I am the person who can help you. I am Vignir Sigurðsson, the official monitor of the incoming lambdas. I too have noticed that there has been a change in our new arrivals. They do, as your friend has noticed, remember much more of their experiences. They are also less numerous. We have seen numbers of incoming drop by as much as 90% in recent months.

It still takes a period of eight weeks for the newbies to fully acquire language, but recently it would appear that they have by no means forgotten their prior journey. I have heard many tales of Greenland shark escapes and fatalities, and of the tedium of swimming through a chilly Atlantic for weeks on end. I have transcribed numerous testimonies and I have attached them to this email. I have to say that any accounts of the Four Fertile

Pairs remain very much under the heading of 'myth', however. To put it technically, it is impossible to confirm that we are dealing with episodic recollections rather than post-hoc constructions. Even if these 'universal parents' are real, they are far out in the Labrador Sea and would not be locatable by these narratives alone. You will no doubt be aware of two oceanographic expeditions nearly ten years ago that tried without success to confirm the existence of the Pairs. I became friendly with Alex Masseter, the man who led the last expedition. He is currently Professor of Marine Biology at Imperial College, London. I would be very happy to put you both in touch, but you may find the financial penalty for another such investigation rather heavy.

I must add that we are all here devastated by the senseless attack that has marred relations with your lambdas in the UK. We have had no such challenges with the community in Iceland, who are quiet and exemplary citizens where and when they chose to engage with us 'landies.' I cannot help but feel that the Army of Lambda Ascension, if it even exists, is a rogue outfit with no genuine support from the majority. I wish you every luck in redressing the harm it has done and bringing its activities to an end.

Warmly yours

Vignir

It took Cara 2 hours 35 minutes to read through the 214 accounts in his attachment. As Vignir had correctly summarised, they were mostly stories of predator danger and feats of stamina. When the Four Fertile Pairs were mentioned, it was in a highly stylised mode in which the same few phrases, such as 'their heads smile up from the distant deep' and 'the good thoughts of the Pairs propel us', recurred.

Dear Vignir Sigurðsson

I am very grateful for your response. These reports are fascinating. With your permission I will pass them on to Lambda Subject B. Could you please connect me with Dr Alex Masseter too?

Kind regards

PC Cara Gray
Supervising Community Support Officer,
Lambda Liaison

At 16.12, Cara pressed the basement buzzer of 17 Cherry Tree Grove. The flaking door popped open. Gavin took longer than before to appear, and when he did he moved in staccato, angular shapes.

'I have some news,' Cara said.

'Oh?'

'Yes. Not much, but something.' Gavin's movements continually drew her gaze. 'What's bothering you, Gavin?'

His monotonous voice had a minimal tremor. 'It's nothing really.'

'Tell me. You haven't stopped darting around since you let me in.'

'It's probably nothing. Only . . . I watched something today.'

'What is it? What did you watch?'

'Something horrible. I've watched it a number of times.'

Online anti-lambda material had increased so much since the school bomb that the three largest video platforms had introduced lambda-specific parameters to their moderation software. However, what Gavin referred to was not part of this material.

'I saw a drawn cartoon. I assume it was for land-human children. The whole thing is set underwater, but it's not like the sea at all. There are houses and people cook and have clothes sometimes. But the light is all wrong, it's bright like dry land. And the people, they're not exactly people, they're supposed to be objects and fish, and there are fires and all kinds of things that are shown in ways that couldn't happen underwater.'

'I know the one you mean.'

'It was *awful*. The main character, the cleaning sponge, it finds a worm. It's a big, ugly worm. With a big head. And rolling eyes. He picks it up and loves it and takes it home and it's *horrible*. The cleaning sponge has a friend, a starfish, and the friend is jealous because the cleaning sponge loves this worm. And then the worm gets sick. But it isn't sick, it's *pregnant*. It spawns more worms. More ugly worms! They writhe on a little rug, and the cleaning sponge, it thinks this is wonderful. And it is not wonderful. But everyone pretends, and the worms vomit slime and make a—' Gavin retched.

'You don't have to tell me this now,' said Cara.

'They make a nest of slime vomit. And this family of disgusting worms is famous and valuable, and it's all a huge joke for land-humans. Because the starfish and the cleaning sponge and the fish in clothing are really land-humans. Aren't they?'

'Of course you can look at it that way . . . I mean, they are and they aren't.'

'The objects and the fish, they're land-humans. And the ugly worms—they're *lambdas*. Isn't that exactly what they are?'

'I think you might be making too much of this. I don't think that's what the people who made the programme had in mind.'

'That doesn't matter at all. What they 'had in mind' is neither here nor there. It's us, the ugly worms are us.'

'Gavin, it's a cartoon for children, not a piece of anti-lambda propaganda. If it offended you I'm sure it was unintentional—there are broadcasting standards for that kind of thing.' Gavin continued his angular movements through the water. 'This might cheer you up. I came to tell you that I sent an email. And I had a response, from Vignir Sigurðsson in Iceland.'

Gavin stopped. 'What did he say?'

'That you're correct. The new arrivals do remember more. I have a lot of testimonies from them. Do you want me to send them on to you?'

'Are they about Greenland sharks?'

'Yes, most of them. And weeks of swimming.'

'Not the Four Fertile Pairs directly?'

'They're mentioned a lot. But there are no direct reports, no.'

'You're welcome to send them,' said Gavin. 'I've read many reports like those before, of course, but thank you.'

'Vignir is a good contact, Gavin. He's in touch with all the Iceland arrivals.'

'I'm sure he is. Thank you greatly, PC Gray.'

The following day Cara told Gloria about Gavin's disturbance.

'If he really thinks there's something going on there he knows who to contact.'

'Oh? Who?'

'There's an organisation, you probably haven't come across it yet—Land-Humans for Lambdas. It's a charity that tries to give them a voice, usually at local government level, but they'll take on anything in principle. A possible breach of broadcasting standards? Sure.'

'If Gavin knows about them, why doesn't he get in touch?'

'That's a good question. They've been around for years. For some reason the lambdas want nothing to do with them.'

Gloria messaged her the director's details.

The Land-Humans for Lambdas offices were on the first floor of a 1970s refit of an Edwardian shopfront on Finchley Road. It was a zig-zag tube journey from the area where Cara worked. The lettering of the sign was Times New Roman, and the point size was significantly smaller than optimal for the pale blue space it occupied on the façade. Antonia O'Leary was raising the shutter when Cara arrived. A cancelled lambda symbol had been spray-painted on it.

'Welcome, Cara,' said Antonia. 'I'm so pleased you've come to see what we do here.' She was wearing a slim herringbone jacket and had strawberry blonde hair with streaks of grey. Her OCEAN Personality Test Score was 65 90 78 55 60. She took Cara up a staircase whose repainting had been abandoned at the first turn to the offices. Grey metal blinds intervened in a view of the six-lane traffic of Finchley Road: for eight seconds Jaguar, Mercedes and Lamborghini SUVs flanked a PolyWay Public Autonomous Vehicle at a red light.

'Let me show you one of our current projects,' Abigail said. 'This is a design collaboration with the Royal Institute of Engineers that enables a lambda to manipulate an object, a pen, say, that's out in dry-space. There's a series of powerful electromagnets here, in the rubber sheath that attaches to the hand, and a unit with 'fingers' that does the lifting on the outside of the bowl. Extraordinary, isn't it?'

A video on the screen of a 12-year-old Viglen desktop showed this device being demonstrated by a land-human. A rubberised mechanical hand on the surface of the glass moved in concert with a human one in the water.

'It looks very useful,' Cara said.

'Yes. You have to keep the outside of the bowl well lubricated, but as long as you do it works like a dream.'

'What has the uptake been like?'

Abigail extended all her fingers while the heels of her hands rested on the desk. 'So far, nominal. You'll have noticed carriers tended to do these dry object tasks.'

'Why don't lambdas want to do it themselves?'

'They're quite slow to change. Not exactly *stuck,* but there has to be an overwhelming reason do something differently. If we can empower them a bit more, let them see what might be possible . . ." Antonia moved the graphic playhead back to the point where the rubber fingers had closed on an eraser.

'And what might be possible?'

'Who knows. That's for them to decide, isn't it?'

'What if they don't want anything?'

Antonia laughed. 'Everyone wants something, don't they?'

'Perhaps. Maybe they just want to survive?'

Abigail closed the video file. 'You could be right. We help with that too. We've set up a legal resource for the lambdas. They're all entitled to Legal Aid but they rarely take up the offer. And as I'm sure you've learned in your role, when they do it's often a disaster. It's as though the legal system is enemy territory they've accidentally wandered into, and they have to escape as quickly as possible. So we're working with a firm called Blindman and Shaw to make sure more perpetrators are brought to justice. It's clearly in the public interest, even if the lambdas don't see it that way, and the solicitors are doing much of the work *pro bono.*'

'That sounds like a very worthwhile project. Maybe you can leave me some details so I can pass them on?'

'It would be my pleasure.'

Antonia took a small Yale key out of her pocket and put it in the lock mechanism of the drawer to her left.

'I wonder if I could ask your personal view about something, Antonia?'

'Please do.'

'What do you think of the government films? The lambda ones?'

'Those? They're beautiful! Maybe that sounds rather self-serving, I was a consultant on the last one. Did you see it? The one with the glass atrium and the beam of light that shifts ever so slowly across the bowl?'

'Yes, I've seen it. Did you know that some of the lambdas think they're counterproductive?'

'I've heard that before. It seems to be a minority perspective. They're hugely popular, and the director, who's a good friend as it happens, rightly won a Global Peace and Tolerance Award.'

'But do you understand the problem—that these films suggest to some people that the lambdas have some sort of power and influence?'

'Pure conspiracy theory.'

'Of course it is. But it doesn't matter to the lambdas. The effect is the same.'

Antonia said, 'I can't accept that, Cara. You can't bend to these toxic narratives. Once you start to accommodate them, that's really the end of everything you and I stand for, isn't it?'

Cara was silent for 3.8 seconds. 'What are your thoughts about the ALA?'

'Now we're really scraping the bottom of the barrel. There is no fucking ALA. It's sheer fiction, of the most poisonous variety. The sooner that's out of the newsfeeds the better. I can help you with that any way you want. Just tell me. You can quote me, interview me. Anything.'

'Thank you Antonia. If it comes to that I will. Do you happen to know Gavin Knight-Green?'

Antonia's gaze connected with Cara's. 'Gavin? Yes, I know him.' Muscles around her eyes contracted. 'It's been a long time since we spoke.'

'You don't keep in touch?'

'No. Why do you ask?'

'I've got to know him a little. In my role.'

'I'm sure.' Antonia looked away. 'He didn't continue our conversations. After the last unanswered email I decided not to try anymore.'

'What was the problem? Do you know?'

Antonia turned the key and opened the drawer. 'I think he's very busy. He doesn't have the attention you need for new projects.' She took out an open packet of biscuits, the torn part of whose wrapper broadly corresponded to the outline of Spain. 'I understand perfectly.'

'The reason I came is because Gavin was very upset by something he saw on television. Not an internet video platform, but an established TV station. I wondered if you could investigate.'

'Do you know what an OCEAN Personality Test is?'

'Yes, I'm very familiar with those. I used to work in data surveillance.'

'Good. So you know that all lambdas score within a few points of 50 for every personality factor?'

'I did know that.'

'So it makes the test almost useless—they all come out personality neutral. All lambdas except Gavin. He has a 59 for Neuroticism.'

'It's still not widely different to the average.'

'No,' said Antonia. 'But it tells us Gavin couldn't toe the line. He knew how to take that test to get the right score, they all do. He drifted. He's not typical, Cara. I'll investigate the issue you've raised, but this is not to do with the community as a whole. It's just to do with him.'

'Thank you, Antonia. The problem is an episode of *SpongeBob SquarePants*, 'Pet or Pests'. Season 6.'

Antonia performed a loud nasal expiration. 'Noted. Do you need to leave right away, or can I interest you in a stovetop coffee?'

*

On Sunday morning, the 105th day of their relationship, Peter told Cara that Rex was coming the next day.

'That's not the most generous warning,' Cara said.

'Well he's just messaged me now. He's always been unpredictable. He's an "artist", remember?'

Cara spent the morning spatially optimising the items in the small room. She found two broken lamps, eleven AC adapters, a collection of plushies she rated less highly than Topo Giraffe, twelve torqued and dusty colouring books and 8kg of sundry plastic components. Additionally, there were 38 small luxury clothing items she'd bought since passing probation. She condensed, folded and stacked all this material into roughly knee-high towers. The non-sentient vacuum cleaner was the largest object present. She moved it to the kitchen.

Peter produced a slightly undercooked omelette which could be interpreted as an apology. 'We'll probably both be at work when he arrives, so I'll leave him my MagnEgg at the front,' he said.

'Fine. But hide it really well.'

In the afternoon Cara read *Good Morning, Midnight* while intermittently glancing at Peter. His eyes saccaded constantly but his head barely moved at all. *All his attention tapered into his laptop*, Cara noted on her phone. *Some high-level, techno-neural transaction was taking place and there was zero transparency to the room. Perhaps an intelligence agency or a criminal network was tracking what he did on that device from moment to moment, but I was out in the dead space of the real, an irrelevance. It wasn't anything new. Today it rankled me.* She put down her book and rose to cross the room. *For a fissured second, in a pause right at the threshold of perception, I knew that he had made a decision about whether or not to change what was on the screen.*

Cara placed her hands on Peter's shoulders and ran them down to his chest. The screen displayed 25 lines of Python code.

'What does that mean?' Cara said.

'Oh, it means . . . if that variable changes, change this value here.'

'And what makes the variable change?'

'Ah, it's complicated. It would take a long time to explain.'

The word 'lambda' appeared three times. It was not a reference to the lambdas Cara worked with, but an anonymised function within a formal language.

'Do you want a drink?' she said.

'No. You know drinking so regularly can really affect your fer . . ."

'My what?'

A Markov chain adapted to Peter's word use would have suggested 'fermions' or 'fertility'. 'Your health. Anyway, it's not such a great idea.'

A crease appeared between Cara's eyebrows.

Three vodkas later she abandoned her reading. Seventeen minutes after that, Peter stopped coding.

'They've found someone,' he said.

'Meaning?'

'PARSON has found someone.'

'Seriously?'

'Yep. There's going to be an announcement tomorrow. Check your messages. We're both invited to it.'

*

The meeting was 86% smaller than the last one Cara had attended. Everyone in the briefing room had a seat.

'Welcome,' the supervisor said. 'You are the core team who, in one way or another, have made the investigation whose results I am about to reveal possible. PARSON, as you know, has been working indefatigably for the last five weeks, collating evidence about the perpetrator of the revolting act of violence that has done so much to harm the citizens we are here to protect, and the society they and we depend on. It seems inappropriate to be excited. However, I have to say that I am excited, very excited indeed, that we have now identified a suspect. And more than that, our entirely new method of detection appears to have functioned well beyond expectations— with far, far greater accuracy—and could represent a revolution in the way we investigate the most serious crimes. We've had a few issues, and we've had to restart the entire process after some, how can I put it, *inappropriate* outputs.'

Two new surveillance officers briefly laughed. *Their faces were translucent*, Cara noted, *like axolotls'*.

'But what you have to bear in mind is that PARSON, at any given moment, is juggling one exabyte of data. Over the course of its investigations, PARSON has processed four zettabytes of data. That's close to 10% of the extant data for the entire globe. PARSON knows a thing or two about data munging.'

The same two officers laughed.

'PARSON has not only identified a credible suspect, but assembled a powerful database of evidence that, in effect, proves beyond all reasonable doubt that we have our terrorist. I don't think I need to spell out how significant this is for our work, which, as you know, we have been undertaking on a slimmer and slimmer budget. We can barely train enough officers like you to trawl the data. A pilot system like PARSON could well replace much of this . . . machinery. If that's the case, then we'll be seen by history as the early adopters, the pioneers. But let's not race ahead of ourselves. Despite this extraordinary and unprecedented result, we will, for the time being, have to follow established process. We will undertake an investigation on the ground to support PARSON's findings.

That, primarily, is why I have assembled you chosen few in this room. I expect the investigation to be purely routine. All we need is for some human underwriting of the data. Okay, enough background. Here is our suspect.'

An image of a Caucasian male face appeared on the briefing room screen. He was in the age range 35–49 and his hair was mousey; his features deviated no more than 5% from those of an averaged adult male resident in the UK. Next to it was a diagram whose text was too small for the seated officers to read. This type of infographic was known in the department as a 'skeleton'.

'Colin Colestar, ladies and gentleman. I will let his picture sit with you. Here on the right we have our schematic of Colin Colestar's life and career. Born in Cheshire. Well above benchmark performance at school. 2.1 in History from Manchester University. Then, look at this—Teacher Training Certificate. Our suspect is, or was, a teacher. He's moved around a lot, schools all over the North West and lately the South East of England. But look at the career gaps. Here, here and here he's associated with activist communities.' He looked at Cara in a manner that seemed involuntary. 'Then back in a teaching job until he's fired, here. Now, PARSON has compiled a half-million-word dossier of Suspect Alpha's communications. The analytics demonstrate hard-left leanings and coded antipathies toward lambdas. Look at this part of the skeleton. Pretty scary, right?'

The underlying data was based on automated text analyses. No investigating officer had perused what Colin Colestar had written directly.

'It appears that Suspect Alpha was seeking to destabilise our society and identified the point of maximum damage. PARSON has established his predisposition and motive. But how about means? How did this subversive, failed schoolteacher get hold of a military-grade, remotely activated, ultra-precision explosive? Well, this is the thing. He didn't. He didn't have to. If you look here, you will see that Suspect Alpha has a long and developed interest in the acquisition and circulation of Personal Fabrication Devices. As you will no doubt know, these units are illegal for good reason. It's possible to find on the dark web a recipe for precisely the explosives used in the school atrocity, plus a fully autonomous delivery system, if you know where to look. And Suspect Alpha is up to his ears in the dark web. Look at this chart here. This is a graph of his five-year browsing history. Do you see?'

Cara raised her hand and the supervisor nodded. 'I can't see any detail,' she said. 'All it shows is that he's using Tor.'

'Trust us, officer. The grain will be there. PARSON has placed Suspect Alpha in the vicinity of the bombing twenty-seven times in the five days prior to the event. *Twenty-seven times*. He disappears here, look—Epsilon minus twenty-four, one day before. Epsilon plus twenty-four, interestingly, he is suddenly one hundred and twenty miles away, here in Cambridgeshire. He's connected with an activist community in Fowlmere. One I believe Officer Gray has some personal experience with.' The supervisor didn't look at Cara but seven of the eight other officers did.

'Anything incriminating there?' Cara asked. 'Any transmissions, any content?' Blood vessels in her face dilated.

'Yes. The log is available to those with clearance. Next steps, officers. All the vectors for Suspect Alpha converge on Epsilon. Incontrovertibly, overwhelmingly. PARSON has the entire case compressed in a file we could take to the Crown Court this morning. However, this is untested material. We need to fuse it together with directly acquired information. We have enough here to launch a laser-precise investigation, and that's what we're going to do now. I mean right now. Officer Gray, you are going to Cambridgeshire.'

Cara's heart rate rose. 'Is he there?'

'No. A number of key witnesses are. So you're going there now, there's a car waiting for you.'

'But where is he?'

'We know where he is. PC Coates, you are going to partition PARSON's data aggregation and distribute it amongst the core team here. We need to find correlative insights that match all the main findings. You people need to fact-check, corroborate, sign it off. Look, this is the final overall data picture. All these circles, these data cities . . . let me zoom in . . . and in . . . there, see the overlap? You see the way PARSON has worked it?'

The small, pale pink overlap amongst the blue disks of data was the approximate shape of a human figure.

'Nice touch, yes?'

Chloe was scrubbing an object in front of a large solar tent; in Cara's bodycam footage her face appeared as a cluster of spots that began to form an expression of pleasure and surprise. Cara reached in her satchel for her police identification and held it out. Chloe's expression changed. It conveyed indifference first, then hostility.

'Here on business then?' Chloe said. 'I thought you missed us.'

'It's nice to see you Chloe. But yes, I'm here on business. Do you remember this person?' She showed her two photographs of Colin Colestar on her Bell 6i, with a beard and without.

'Why are you asking me?'

'Chloe you mustn't try to fudge this, it's too serious. You need to know I'm here in connection with the gravest possible situation. You could all be in some pretty dire trouble if I can't get straightforward answers.'

Chloe's eyes partly closed. 'You mean the school thing, don't you?'

'I can't say.'

'Right. You're wearing a bodycam. Cute. I recognise him,

Cara. Ex-teacher. Looking for people to support, to support him.'

'Support him in what?'

'The usual stuff. Changing the world for the better.'

Chloe was wearing a silver lamé top. The fabric was a solar-cell material that charged her phone all day. A man appeared behind her; he was wearing one too.

'You're police?' the man said. He tipped a jug of sepia liquid onto the soil to Cara's right.

'She's okay, Graham. I know her already.'

Graham's eyes saccaded over Cara's face and body, then he moved back into the shadows of the partitioned tent. The Fowlmere encampment was in the same arrangement as when Cara had left, but the contents of this tent had changed. All the furniture was pre-owned and dirty, and the strewn clothing from a lower average price-point than before.

'Do you want to say hello to Joseph?' Chloe's expression combined elements of humour and aggression. 'No?'

'No, it's okay. I don't need to interview everyone. I have some very urgent business, it wouldn't be fair to start that conversation now.'

'So you're starting to think about what's fair?' Chloe resumed scrubbing a small pair of trousers against the ridges of a home-made washboard. 'Of course you know all about "Alex".'

'No. I don't know anything about Alex. I'm afraid I don't have time for this. You just need to tell me about the suspect. Colin Colestar, here, you said you recognised him.'

Cara fixated on the side of Chloe's face. 'I'll tell you everything I know about him,' Chloe said. 'I won't play games. He came here twice. First time was over a year ago. He was curious about how we lived. He was looking for an alternative to teaching, he said he was always running up against these hidden corporate agendas. Normal stuff. He stayed for two or three days. That's all. I don't think he was ever quite comfortable, but he was kind and helpful. Good with the children, as you can probably imagine. The second time it was a bit different. He was less relaxed. We didn't speak much, but he told me it was time to do something with real meaning in the world, something with real effects. Something to do with China—he was very preoccupied with China, saw it as some critical lever in some way, but I didn't quite get it. "If we can get through to enough people there," he said, "then all of human life will open up again." I didn't think he really understood the difficulties. He was incredibly well informed in some ways, but I found him a bit naïve.'

'Do you remember the date of that second visit?'

Chloe looked at Cara unkindly. 'Yes. It was the day after the fucking atrocity. Anyway, he went away very early the next morning, and he didn't say goodbye to anyone. But the night before he left he told us all a story. It was about a group of foragers in the forest. I remember it very well. The foragers had all left their families to go on an extended trip. The idea was to collect a small fortune in truffles. They all get to know one another, their various reasons for needing to make this journey through such a dangerous place, full of bears and snakes and bandits, and they make a camp in the heart of the forest.'

'Is this really relevant?' interrupted Cara. 'I don't have time to do anything that doesn't relate directly to Colin Colestar.'

'I think it is. I think you'll agree too, if you're *patient*.' At the final word Chloe gave her a stare. The stare matched one she had directed at Cara at the start of the Parliament Square protest. Chloe had just spray-painted a swastika on the back of a police van, and Chloe had said to Cara, 'I have no problem doing this because it's an ancient symbol of *peace*.'

'Early evening on the second day of foraging, their truffle dogs are restless. A man appears. He tells them that he has a message. They welcome him, they even share one of the truffles they've found. He says he can't tell them the message yet. Only they will know when they're ready, but they have to give him the sign. He refuses their offer of a place to sleep and disappears before nightfall.'

The bodycam registered brownish waves near the horizon beyond Chloe. These were the desiccated fields that abutted the activist camp to the north. Cara's eyes tracked along them while Chloe related the story.

'The next evening he appears again. Again he says that he's ready with the message, but they have to give him the right sign. They're all baffled, the man leaves before dark, same as the day before, and the following day they're distracted by discussions about what this message could possibly be, and what sign they might be expected to give. On the way back to the camp, one of the foragers spots an earthworm. It's behaving oddly, waving its head around in the air. When he approaches he sees that the waving end isn't its head—the end of the worm has been bitten off. What he thought was the head is the stub, probing about as though it's trying to find the missing part. The forager is very disturbed. He points it out to another forager who tells him not to worry, earthworms can grow back from even small parts of their bodies. The moment he says it, a blackbird appears and eats the remains of the worm. "This is the sign," the first forager says. The second agrees. They wait for the visitor to arrive at the camp in the evening so they can tell him. But this time he doesn't appear.

'Even though they've exhausted the pickings in the area and it's time to go, the next day they find they can't leave. They want to speak to the man to get the message. He doesn't appear that evening either. They pack up their camp reluctantly in the morning and set off on the next part of their journey, and soon they find themselves deep in the forest. It's summer, really humid, and the air is filled with strange animal calls. They find a small clearing with a deerskin tent. There's an old man living there, and the visiting foragers greet him. He's surprised to see them. He doesn't see anyone for months, sometimes years on end, he says. They ask him about the man with the message, describe him in some detail, and he becomes agitated. Yes, he says, I know who you mean. But he doesn't say any more.

'They pursue him as he goes about his day. The truffle dogs seem to like him. He's self-sufficient and spends most of his time collecting plants and grubs—he's very irritated by the attention. At last, under pressure from the baffled foragers, he tells them: "I know exactly who you mean. I haven't seen his face in five years. And I don't expect to see it in five or even five hundred more." "Why?" they ask. The man says, "Because five years ago I buried him up over by the rise there. He died from eating the wrong kind of mushroom."

'The foragers set up camp but don't feel able to eat that evening. They spend the next day foraging, and the findings are plentiful, but while their store increases they can't seem to eat anything themselves. Days pass. The old man takes down his tent and vanishes; their truffle dogs run away. They become weak, malnourished, and in their confusion they become lost and separated in the forest. One forager fails to come back to the camp, then another. At last there is only one left, the youngest. He is emaciated and begins to hallucinate, he sees sticks and earth turn into plates of steaming food, his mother's shape in the silhouette of a tree. One evening, close to the clearing where he sleeps, he spots a figure. It's just standing there, staring in his direction. He recognises the figure—it's the messenger. Even though he suspects it must be another hallucination, he runs up to him and embraces him, telling him how pleased he is that he's back. "It's time you had a proper meal," the man says. "Why don't you dip into your store of truffles?" The remaining forager is so starved that his wrists are only as thick as a finger. He puts his hand in the hessian sack and takes out a truffle. "Go on," says the man. "Eat it." The forager looks at the truffle for a full minute. Then he takes a bite. *He has never tasted anything more delicious in life.* "The sign," he says. "We saw the sign, the worm with no end. Was that it?" "Yes," says the man. "So what's the message?" the forager asks. The man says, "The time for messages is over."'

Chloe stopped.

'Where did Colin Colestar go?'

'I have no idea. I don't have anything else to tell you.'

'In that case you need to take me to anyone else who had contact with him.'

Chloe led Cara into the tent. It was divided by a nest of improvised door-flaps through which the bodycam captured foreshortened views of bodies. After the third door flap they encountered Joseph.

'Oh,' he said. 'It's you.' He turned away.

'Cara is here to interview us,' Chloe told him. 'You remember that guy Colin?'

Joseph folded a jumper according to shop display convention. 'A little,' he said.

'Just so you know, Joseph, I'm here on police business,' Cara said. 'This is absolutely nothing to do with us.' Chloe left the room.

'I didn't think so. Why do you want to talk about Colin? He was only here a short time. Lots of people visit and pass through. Has he done something?'

'You don't need to know. You just need to tell me what you remember. Can I sit?'

'Of course you can. There's a chair right next to you.'

'Thank you. So what do you remember?'

Joseph loudly blew out air. 'Colin was . . . quiet. Asked good questions. We spoke quite a lot. About some aims we shared.'

'Tell me more about that.'

'Why? You know all this already.'

'True, but the context is different. I'm not here as a private individual, I'm investigating a crime on behalf of the authorities. It's not enough to assume I know what you're talking about.'

Joseph laughed volitionally. 'I wonder if you ever really did, Cara.'

'Excuse me?'

'I said I wonder if you ever really did understand what we're about.'

'That's not really relevant now. Maybe we could just stick to Colin. All this is being recorded, did I mention that?'

Joseph's posture and facial expression conveyed both tension and exhaustion. 'Good. Perhaps it needs recording. Cara, you never explained why you left. You *never* explained. It was like a light going off. Was it just . . . me? Did your . . . tastes just change? I tried to contact you afterwards and . . . nothing back. You just told me to stop messaging.'

'There's more to it than that. This isn't the moment to go into it.'

'Tell me.'

'I'm not here to talk about my actions. I'm here to ask you about Colin Colestar. Joseph, we could both be in a lot of trouble if we have this conversation now. I have a job to do.'

'Have you spoken to *Alex*?'

'No. I might have to if that's where the investigation leads, but this isn't about me or us or him either, it's about—'

'Investigation? What about *Alex's* investigation?'

Cara was silent.

'You're pretending you don't know? Everyone knows about it here. He screwed up, left a Signal message visible on his phone. He was undercover. He was police. Like you.'

Cara looked at Joseph. Despite his significant place in her sexual history, Cara had recorded nothing about Alex on her phone at all. 'I can't discuss anything other than your contact with Colin Colestar. That's the only remit of my professional visit.'

'Shame.'

'But if you must know, Joseph, I left because I realised I couldn't live in the future. It's what everyone here seemed to be doing. It's not because I don't care about you or Chloe or anyone else. I realised that I don't have the right sort of . . . blood, or something. I was . . . asphyxiating. Are you going to tell me about Colin Colestar now? Or would you prefer to do that at a police station?'

'Is that really true?' Joseph said.

'It feels true today. It's the best I can manage.'

'Okay then, PC Gray. I'll tell you what we spoke about. Everything I remember.'

Joseph conveyed that his conversations with Colin Colestar had been 'nothing out of the ordinary for the community'. They'd discussed object rights, data subversion strategies, climate politics, co-ordinated international expansion of an ambiguous movement, but not bombing a school. Joseph's high Conscientiousness score of 81 made it unlikely he'd conceal such a topic without clear indications of stress.

'Are you happy now?' he said. 'In the police?'

'Yes.'

'Never forget that you're a chainlink now. The chain doesn't care about you at all. We did. You can always come back.'

He didn't say it in a friendly way, Cara later observed.

Joseph took her to a girl of seventeen who was his second cousin. At the hanging partition he said, 'I don't think I ever told you that the moment I saw you I just knew we'd have a daughter together. You've been an education, Cara.'

She stared at him. 'Thank you, Joseph. Our conversation is over.'

Cara conducted four more interviews, all of which corroborated that Colin Colestar had behaved just the way Joseph and Chloe had described. She checked the bodycam had captured the visit and returned to the navy Toyota Yaris that had brought her there.

*

Cara almost fell asleep as the car rolled through St. Albans; her alpha waves peaked at High Barnet. She was moving through more central postcodes when the supervisor called.

'What do you have for us?'

'He was definitely there. That's verified by several witnesses. Nothing to suggest he was planning something like Epsilon, though. He was very good with the children. They liked him.'

'You needn't worry about that sort of analysis. Where did he go on to?'

'No data. And he didn't take anyone with him.'

'None of the group stay in touch with him?'

'No. It seems he's . . . secretive.'

The supervisor sniffed. 'Anything else? You can save me going through the recording.'

She paused for two seconds. 'They seem to have identified an undercover officer in the group.'

Cara's eyes fixated on a tree whose shape evoked softening and collapse.

'Are you still there?' she said.

'Yes, I'm here. You needn't concern yourself with that, it's another department entirely. Tell me more about your visit.'

Cara related an abbreviated version of Colin's tale, as recounted by Chloe. At the end of it the supervisor said, 'That's extremely useful, thank you.'

The 112Hz rumble of the car as it moved down the A1000 became the dominant sound inside. Then the supervisor continued, 'You should go straight home and get an early night. I want you to be at the office at 6 A.M. tomorrow. The meeting is strictly confidential. Tell Peter you're, I don't know, having breakfast with Gavin.'

He ended the call.

18.

Hello. How are you today? Good, I am pleased to hear it. Yes, it is a very beautiful day today, perhaps the most beautiful of the spring so far. I believe I categorised a prior day as the most beautiful of the spring at that point, but this one, you must agree, takes the biscuit.

I am feeling much recovered, thank you. No, I have not been pursued by dreams of urns. Nor, I might add, have I thought especially of Anne ———.

Do you think you might be able to tell me what has happened to her, at an appropriate point in our conversations?

Yes, of course I can wait until next time, to give you the opportunity to find out.

I see you have chosen to sit on the Breuer chair today. As always, there are exactly five, plus the one I use myself. Mine is a very ordinary Robin Day chair, since you ask—I did not sense that you were particularly interested in mid-20th-century furniture. This kind of chair stacks very easily, it has been used for decades in institutional environments of the most ordinary sort, which is of course what this highly economical design was conceived for. This is a Series E chair in the second largest size. I find it comforting to imagine that every single one of these chairs would fit exactly and contiguously with every single other of the same size. Discounting, of course, those that suffer the occasional error in fabrication, or subsequent damage.

Yes, I am ready to begin.

It would seem that there are certain absences in my account

that you would like to revisit. You have led me to certain points and I have found myself at a loss to continue beyond them, claiming fatigue, loss of interest, or something similar. Yes, I think that is a fair observation.

Let me return to these accounts, in that case. I will do my best to repair these broken-off narratives. If you feel that it is important.

Could I ask if you would like a hot or a cold drink? There is orange juice and milk in the refrigerator, each of which I would naturally recommend that you ingest separately. No? Then I will continue.

I will resume my halted narratives at the points at which I left them off, just exactly as you have requested. There is no reason why I would not be able to do that, and I will endeavour to do so to the very best of my abilities—abilities which are, it is fair to say, above average in the field of memory.

Yes, I will do this with alacrity.

I believe I ceased to convey my recollections of my visit with Captain ——— (if it was indeed she) to the Minister of Defence for Severax at the point where I was heading upstairs to a guest bedroom, after an evening of very enjoyable company. As I have already apprised you, I did not go to sleep immediately in that room because the reason for my visit was the assassination of our host and her family. I remained awake, with the room's electric lights turned out, for some hours, readying myself inwardly for this task. I sat on the edge of what was to all appearances a wonderfully luxurious bed, slightly larger than king size, but which I did not feel well placed to enjoy fully in the circumstances. At precisely 2 A.M., Severax time, I received a message on a closed channel device I kept in a concealed pocket of my trousers. This message emanated from Captain ———. It was a set of co-ordinates which showed exactly where she had hidden the modified surgical laser I was to use for my business.

The item was concealed under a loose tile not far from the entrance to my bedroom. I palmed the device, which was roughly 10cm in length and could easily have been mistaken for an ordinary pen, and replaced the tile as quietly as possible. I then moved quickly down the corridor to the rooms where the Minister for Defence and her family were ensconced.

It seemed to augur well for the operation that I discovered the guard outside this room asleep. In order to avoid any adverse consequences ensuing from this guard waking up at an inopportune moment, I decapitated him with the modified surgical laser. As you will no doubt be aware, with this kind of instrument it requires absolutely no force at all to perform large incisions and amputations. The one I held in my hand was adapted to immediately cauterise any wounds, thus mitigating certain collateral effects of significant bodily trauma. I organised the remains of the guard in a suitable manner and entered the family rooms.

I felt I had been extremely discreet in my approach, so you can imagine my surprise when I found the Minister of Defence sitting upright in her bed, regarding me with a direct yet blank expression. I ran towards the Minister, whose mouth opened in a questioning manner, and succeeded in drawing the laser across her head from her right temple down through the occipital zone of her skull, in a very straight line, until it exited on the left side of her jaw. On completion of this movement the section of her head in this way annexed slipped down onto the bed, and the remaining majority of her body tilted forwards.

Her husband, with whom I had exchanged only a few polite words the evening before, continued to sleep to her right. I quickly separated his head from his body using the surgical laser without disturbing his sleep in the slightest.

The Minister for Defence and her husband, whose name I recall now was ———, had a son. Now, I am sure you are familiar with the extremely dangerous situation that ensues when descendants of those who have been dispatched under circumstances like these attain a degree of agency of their own. In order to avoid such an outcome, I entered the room of this person, who, like ———, was deeply asleep. I performed on the son the exact same procedure as I had employed with his father and the guard, after which I left the family's rooms in some haste.

The mission had been a great success. I contacted Captain ——— (I am increasingly sure it was she) using our closed channel device, and notified her of my achievement using the codeword ———.

It is perhaps unnecessary to describe in detail our method of leaving Severax. Suffice to say we did so promptly, under cover of darkness, re-joining friendly forces by means of a high-performance off-road vehicle concealed close to the Minister's compound, one which conveyed us rapidly over the border and thence by aeroplane home.

Yes, I remember that this was not the only narrative I left hanging. In fact, the very first conversation we had was terminated at a critical moment. This seems an appropriate moment to resume.

I left the dinner table at ——— in a state of considerable inebriation. Having consumed Château de Meursault at a rate much faster than that at which I would ordinarily have drunk water from the tap, I found myself in need of the toilet. A certain person had obstructed my passage to the toilet, a person with whom I was suddenly extremely vexed. I do not believe I had previously met this person, but now that I attempt to recall his face I remember a passing resemblance to Julian ———, the person who, you may remember, inserted himself into and ultimately brought to an end my lunchtime assignations with Anne ———. Of course this could have merely been one of the many disorientating effects of my alcohol consumption. My irritation with this unknown person was such that I began to assault him in a manner not dissimilar to my assassination of the Minister of Defence for Severax. There were two key differences, however. One, my wine consumption left me unable to control my movements as precisely as I had done on that previous occasion, and my assault was not instantly effective. Two, I was not able to employ the modified surgical laser, given that this piece of highly specialised equipment was made available to me only for state business, and I was not permitted to carry it about habitually. I employed instead the only item that presented itself to me at short notice, which was a table knife on its way back to the kitchen on a dinner plate carried by a member of the waiting staff. I need hardly mention that while a surgical laser is able to inflict a fatal wound with striking efficiency, a table knife is nowhere near as effective. It took me some time to achieve the same result, and with associated effects which I believe attracted the attention of virtually every person in the restaurant.

Is this enough for today? Yes, I feel exactly the same the way. I am pleased to have made up for the omissions of previous accounts, which must have created a somewhat frustrating experience for you. If our business is done for the time being then at this point I am very happy to say goodbye. Goodbye.

19

Cara was back at the police prefab by 14.54. She checked the bodycam footage had uploaded to the Police Central Server, then locked the camera and its holster in the cabinet. She touched her cheeks with both hands and sat down at the desk with her work phone. *Should have gone home like the supervisor instructed*, she later wrote, *but there was still a visit with Lambda Subject E in my schedule.*

'Hello? Is that Carolyn?'

'Officer Gray?'

'Yes it is. Can I come in?'

There was no reply. The lock mechanism buzzed.

Cara was in the hallway alone for in excess of two minutes. Her eye saccades traversed the stain patterns on the wallpaper. Subsequently, she fixated on a promotional leaflet for waterjet cleaning she'd retrieved from the floor. Carolyn appeared.

'Can I help you, Supervising Community Officer?'

'Hello Carolyn. I'm just checking in for one of my chats, that's all.'

Carolyn, Cara noted, despite her precisely typical lambda OCEAN Personality Test Score of 50 50 50 50 50, had some distinct personality traits. She was *passive aggressive, scathing about other lambdas as well as the few land-humans she couldn't avoid having something to do with, articulate + obstinate.*

'Attacks are up another 12%,' Carolyn said.

'Yes. I'm sorry.'

'Why "sorry"? Have you been telling bad stories about us?'

The lambda gave Cara a slow, raking look. 'Of course not, Carolyn. You were a classroom assistant today, correct?'

'Correct.'

'How are they doing? Your lambda students?'

'Okay. We always do okay.' She dipped her head below the waterline for 2.8 seconds. 'In a way I'm pleased you came,' she continued. 'I've been wondering something recently. Do you think we'll be superseded soon?'

'What do you mean?'

'Do you think lambdas will still be needed, once computers or robots can do all the telesales work and the complex data entry?'

'I don't know—I mean it's not about *need*. You're citizens of this country. There will always be a place for you.'

The lambda gave Cara another raking look. 'You think so?' she said. Then Carolyn swam in an ellipse, twice dipping her nose in the water.

'Carolyn, do you mind if I ask you . . . have you heard anything at all about . . . that terrible incident that you haven't already told me?'

Carolyn's swimming pace decreased. 'I find that question disgusting,' she said.

'I'm sure you do, Carolyn. I'm sorry to go back over this.'

'Has something else come to light, Supervising Cara Community Officer?'

'Nothing exactly.'

'Then why mention it? It's something of a sore point. You must have noticed.' Carolyn exposed her small grey upper teeth. The range of lambdas' facial muscles was too narrow to equate to terrestrial expressions, but Carolyn's satisfied the criteria for 'sarcastic smiling' to a higher degree than average. 'Do you think there's a cabal of us, plotting to destroy the terrestrial world? Is that what you think?'

'No, I don't. You know I don't.'

'We're not doing very well, are we? How far does our lambda dominion extend today? A few tens of thousands of basement flats and shrinking, with the forced and voluntary relocations? It's hardly the Mongol Empire.'

'I didn't mean to cause offence, only I have to keep lines of enquiry open.'

'Why don't I take you to the next terrorist meeting? You can go disguised as a lambda. You'd like that, wouldn't you? All you need to do is shrink to a fraction of your current size, grow a tail and flippers and a respiration sac near your anus, and act as though you understand what the daily threat of a violent death is like. Do you think you can manage that?'

'Of course I can't. I could never understand how hard it is for you. But Carolyn, why don't you act collectively, why don't you lobby the local government, or form a party or something, or at least speak out?'

Carolyn revolved 12° anticlockwise.

'You must have thought to yourself, have I ever met a group of people more debilitated than these lambdas? It's not just navigating dry land that's the problem. Hector and Gavin— yes, I know them too—what a couple of time-wasters. Where have their ideas ever got them? And they're among the rare ones who can entertain a project other than getting to work and back in only one or two pieces. I feel angry now, Cara, but it's just because you're here. We're not angry when we're together. We're just sad. Lambdas are too sad for politics. We know it would only make things worse for us in the end, and we're already made of sadness. If you can't tolerate that then maybe you should just leave us alone.'

'But that's . . . that's not a life. How can you live that way?'

Carolyn showed her grey teeth again. 'You can't ever leave your own viewpoint behind, can you? Of course it's not life *for you*. But we don't see things the way you do at all. Land-humans are always carving things into portions, then stealing the portions from each other. It's a land problem. That doesn't exist in the sea. No divisions.'

'But Gavin hated that—he told me he couldn't stand the open sea.'

'Maybe he can't. But it's the basis of his outlook anyway. All of us see the world the same way. We can't divide things up like you. We're not neoliberals or socialists or conservatives or environmentalists. We all have a share in the common store of sadness. That's what makes us the same. Even Hector knows that, underneath all that fussing about dorsal veins.'

'That can't be everything,' Cara said. 'Just feeling equally sad?'

A lambda had never seemed so tiny, she noted later, *so zoomed-out.*

'You'll understand one day, Cara. Once you've lost everything. It will happen to terrestrials too. Try to stop it, or do nothing at all, it won't make any difference. You just need to be patient. You'll all understand in the end. You, or maybe your children.'

Cara looked at Carolyn's face. The face was neutral. 'I'm not sure what you mean,' Cara said.

'Perhaps you don't. It's hard to see the trajectory when you're on the inside. It's clear enough to us.'

'What's clear? What trajectory do you mean?'

Six seconds of silence followed. 'I don't know if I can explain.'

'Please try.'

Carolyn sighed. 'Your land-human institutions aren't working, Officer Gray. Police don't police. Education doesn't educate. Your government is a Greenland shark that eats anything and pretends it's food. Not everything is food. Do you understand?'

'I'm not sure.'

'Let me try again. If you only eat seaweed you have to eat a lot, but you live. If you only eat water, or the aurora borealis, then you die.'

'I'm sorry Carolyn, I'm still not sure I follow. Perhaps I should go.'

Carolyn snorted. 'I'll put it as simply as I can. Lambdas eat seaweed. You eat fantasies.'

Cara said nothing in response. After 2.1 seconds, Carolyn disappeared under the water.

At 17.46 Cara opened her cell door. There were three books on her two-seater sofa—*Siddhartha*, a biography of Jimmy Page, and *The (updated) Last Whole Earth Catalog*. A black Rick Owens nylon bomber from the current season's *Ammonite* collection was spread on back of the armchair, and a pair of artificially distressed plimsolls projected at 90° from the wall by the entrance. Steam was percolating out from the gap under the bathroom door. The door opened.

'Are you Rex?'

'Yes, excellent guess. Nice to meet you, Cara. Excuse me, it was a horrible journey, so hot. I just had to shower.'

'Of course, feel free.'

'Thanks for having me to stay. Oh no, I've left my things everywhere.'

Rex was 5cm taller than Peter and had a slightly higher muscle-to-fat ratio. He possessed close facial similarities with his brother in the jawline, nose and brow. His skin was 16% paler than the mean for his demographic, even after the heat of the recent shower. His OCEAN Personality Test Score was 95 78 70 60 42. Just like Peter, Rex had been told by their father not to undertake this kind of test, but Rex had ignored him.

'It's fine. I see you found your towel.'

'Yeah, thanks.'

'You're taller than I imagined.'

'I do my best.'

Rex laughed. 'Peter hid the MagnEgg really well. I had to dig about a foot into the communal lawn. I've cleaned it up. It's on the coffee table.'

'Thanks. I'm going to cook. Spaghetti vongole?'

'Oh, I'm vegan. Didn't Peter say?'

'No.'

'Don't worry. I'll just have the spaghetti. I brought a bag of protein flakes I can chuck over it.'

Cara had started to boil a pan of water on the hob when Peter rang the bell.

'Rex is here,' she said to him over the Entryphone.

When Peter entered Rex said 'Hey!' The brothers' bodily and facial attitudes suggested a vexed emotional response, but nonetheless they embraced.

'Cara's made me very welcome,' Rex said.

'I'm sure she has,' said Peter.

'Well. Good to see you after all this time, bruh.'

'Same.'

A silence of 4.8 seconds ensued.

'Make yourself at home,' said Peter.

Cara began to drink wine. Peter stood behind her in the kitchen while she prepared food next to the vacuum cleaner; Rex watched a documentary about *The Grateful Dead* alone in the living room. Cara synchronised her speech with the regular bursts of recorded narration.

'Rex is nice,' she whispered.

Peter sniffed. 'A lot of people think so.'

'Do you think he'll be okay in that tiny room?'

He shrugged.

'You don't have to stand here with me. Go and talk to him.'

'I will do. In a little while.'

'Good. You haven't asked about the visit to Cambridgeshire.'

'Oh, no I didn't. That must have been weird—but we're not supposed to be sharing operational data privately, right?'

Cara's answer wasn't immediate. 'Right. How did your day pan out? If you're allowed to say.'

Peter tipped a beer bottle up against his mouth and loudly swallowed. 'Kind of interesting. I've been randomly sampling the initial scrape. PARSON's data has all checked out so far.'

'You're surprised?'

'I don't quite . . . I don't quite understand the architecture of the system. You know that question Claudine asked, about what the tags were?'

'I remember.'

'It was a good question.'

Once Cara had consumed approximately 40cl of Viognier her heart rate began to descend. She told Peter she would have an early start to catch some lambdas before they left for work, and without looking at her directly he said, 'Okay.'

Peter, Cara and Rex ate in front of the living-room screen. Being a heavy, muscular ectomorph, Rex sank deeply into the superannuated webbing of the armchair. 'Thank you so much for having me here, Cara,' he said. 'It's really generous of you.'

'Don't be silly, it's nothing. I mean, look at your room.'

'It's perfect. Couldn't be more perfect.'

Peter's attention didn't shift from the screen. A feature-length documentary about a plane disaster was playing. The film explored the malfunction of the control system of a 3000-seat Airbus 2180 on an early commercial flight. The passengers' brains had been secretly exploited to extend the plane's sentient system, and a feedback issue had caused a catastrophic surge in brain access that rendered all but one person on board non-sentient. An independently surviving consciousness had apparently been protected by a personal neurodrone the passenger had stored in the hold. Whether or not it was true, this narrative was now central to the neurodrone's marketing.

'No way,' said Peter.

Rex looked at him. 'What do you mean?'

'There is no survivor. She's just a set of personality parameters. You could easily generate her speech artificially. And this idea that she's started working as a sympatech again, it's not independently verified.'

'The drone manufacturers seem pretty convinced,' Cara said.

Peter's voice conveyed inappropriate anger. 'Of course they do! It's marketing, not science. Theoretically this kind of thing is possible. But accidentally? With a neurodrone? Come on!'

All three experienced raised heart rate and blood pressure, although the causes of this rise were varied.

At 23.00 Peter went off to the double bedroom to do some coding 'in peace'. Cara asked Rex if he minded if she put on the new series of *Blue Star*.

'You're kidding! I love *Blue Star*.'

They watched three 50-minute episodes, after the last of which Cara woke up in the living room beside Rex's empty chair.

'Good morning,' said the supervisor. 'Early enough for you?'

Notwithstanding her late night and relatively high alcohol consumption, Cara had rested effectively. Her eyes had opened at 04.28, 74 seconds before the alarm was due to go off.

'You've got time to grab some coffee. There's a new machine, much better than the one you'll remember. But you have to pay.'

There was no-one else in the offices. A glass isolation booth with a refrigeration system that hummed at 32dB had been constructed in a corner, and an array of qubit processors hung from a spaceframe inside.

'I see PARSON's moved in,' Cara said.

'It's not PARSON. It's just the quantum filter. I find it helps to remind the desk what the future holds.'

'It looks like my grandma's carriage clock.'

'Cara, your meeting isn't with me. There's someone here from Intelligence Services. You can go through, she's in my office. But first you need to leave your phones with me.'

A woman with an adipose face, shorter than Cara but of marginally greater volume, turned her head. She wore an upper-price-point charcoal suit-jacket and skirt; her OCEAN Personality Test Score had been deleted by a bot commonly used by MI5. Cara entered the room with her and closed the door behind. She'd been deprived of the means to record the meeting, but her supervisor had left his own phone, a Bell 12i, active in a drawer.

'You must be Cara. We haven't met before.' The woman approached and smiled.

'We haven't. Pleased to meet you.'

'Me too,' the woman said with bright intonation. 'Me too. As Robert has probably told you, I represent Intelligence Services. Thank you for coming so early, it's ever so good of you.'

'That's no problem at all. I have no idea what this might be about. Is it something to do with the lambdas?'

'In a way. Not directly. As you know, there are many over-laps between what our respective organisations do. In a certain sense people like you *are* the overlap. We have the utmost respect for the work you accomplish, often with very limited resources. It's hugely valuable. The business with the school, that was all but unavoidable. You were working with a very limited system. Your methods were exemplary, and in most cases they would have been totally effective. We learned a lot from that very unfortunate matter and I'm only sorry it was you, Cara, who showed up a weakness in the inference chain.'

Cara's eye saccades took in the woman's highly reflective brown irises.

'I would like to involve you in a new collaborative project, Cara. Would that interest you at all? Can I tell you about it?'

'I suppose so, yes.'

'Good. I think you'll find it interesting.'

She took a tablet out of her bag and showed Cara a picture of a man's face. The face suggested he was within the age range 21–35. He had a very light tan. He might have been described as 'attractive' by a certain demographic, but an untypical rigidity around the eyes and mouth reduced that probability.

'This is Mr Hello. It's a codename, and the only one you'll need. Mr Hello has done some extraordinary work for us. I won't say more because he will probably tell you what he's been engaged with in any case. It's hard to imagine how this project can function unless he does. What I'm going to ask you to do, Cara, is something we've been doing "in house" for quite some time. Actors like Mr Hello need a bit of careful debriefing. Sometimes. After particularly demanding jobs. We have some strategies for doing it, and some of the psychologists involved in their primary training generally take on the role. But we're hoping that sensitive professionals outside the department can begin to do the job. If they can, it would allow actors like Mr Hello to take on more extended roles. Domestically. And the debriefing process is not terrifically complex. It's not like high-level coding. More basic psychotherapy. We've found that it's about listening more than anything else. You're a good listener, aren't you Cara?'

'I suppose I am. But why—'

'Yes, I hear that from many sources. And you see Mr Hello is actually going to be helping you in your work. He'll be helping the lambdas—indirectly.'

'What do you mean?'

The woman showed her excellent teeth. 'Mr Hello is a

highly skilled operative. We are looking to entrust him with another, very sensitive operation. One which should close the file on the school case.'

'Close the file?'

'Suspect Alpha. We are very confident that we have found a solution in Mr Hello.'

'I don't know your name,' Cara said.

'No you don't, Cara. It's part of *deniability*. Would you like to be involved? This could be a very good opportunity for you, don't you think? You can't put it on your CV, but within our professional field it would be very highly regarded.'

Cara pushed the nail of her right forefinger into the quick of the thumb until the skin gave. The woman's eyes fixated on the bead of blood that appeared.

'Here, have a tissue,' she said. 'There isn't time to pursue this in a conventional way. There is a very real risk that Suspect Alpha will perpetrate something similar. Something even worse. Think about it. What would this person stop at? What would it take to make him stop?'

'Yes, but it's unproven. It may not be him.'

'You think it's the ALA?'

'No, but that doesn't mean it's Col . . . Suspect Alpha. It's a computer hypothesis. And I'm not sure what you're suggesting anyway.'

'You're an intelligent woman, Cara. Think about it. We're looking at *complete mitigation*. Suspect Alpha *must not remain active*. Even in custody that's a risk, and politically, his continued presence—'

'Are you talking about assassination?'

'I didn't use that word and you shouldn't use it either. The correct descriptors are *mitigation, neutralisation, deactivation, closure of agency*. This is how we talk about response to threat. You've had basic training, you know the importance of appropriate language.'

'Are you here to ask me—are you asking me to assassinate Colin Colestar?'

'I am asking you no such thing. And you are to use the word *mitigate* and the codename Suspect Alpha.'

The quick of Cara's nail was still bleeding. The woman passed another tissue. 'You will assist in the mitigation of Suspect Alpha. This is how you are to think of your role and this is how it will be described to you. You will not be directly involved in the mitigation. However, you will be a critical node therein.'

'I don't know . . . I'm not sure what that would mean for me exactly. I think the answer is no.'

'Cara, I don't think you're going to say no.'

'Really?'

'No. I don't think so.'

'Why are you so sure?'

'Because, if you take a moment to think about it, we look after your identity very, very carefully. 98% of internal reports about the surveillance lapse, all of which are classified, refer to you only as DSO30891. Did you know that?'

'No.'

'And we continually monitor comms by all members of your department for anything that would compromise your anonymity. There's no reason anyone with any sort of personal or political interest should learn your identity. An extremist group, for instance. We currently have no reason to be anything less than supremely vigilant about that kind of thing. This little experiment, it's the least you can do, isn't it? It's win-win. A little "thank you", from you to us.'

'Wait. If you're looking after my identity so well, how come I had an unexpected visitor at my cell door?'

Muscles below the woman's eyes contracted. She smiled. 'Laura Cooper? Son at the bombed school? Likes to wear white? Does that sound like her?'

'I didn't learn her name.'

'I'm telling you now that's who it was. We allowed her to obtain the information. But don't worry, that's the only time we'll let her visit. Or anyone else, for that matter. And there have been others who've tried. People who, let's say, don't express themselves in such strictly *sartorial* ways. Much angrier people. Unless . . . unless, that is, you're not particularly interested in what we can do for you. In what you could do for us?'

Cara's jaw muscles tensed.

'But why do you want me to do it? I'm nobody in all this, I'm just . . . nobody.'

The woman smiled again. 'Exactly, Cara. That's exactly what makes you perfect.'

Cara moved away. She took a pencil from the supervisor's desk and pulled a sheet of paper from his printer. She sat down at the desk behind the woman and began to write.

'What are you doing?' said the woman.

'I don't know.'

'You can't do that.' The woman's voice conveyed irritation. 'I'll have to confiscate what you've done.'

'Why?'

'Because no record of this meeting is allowed to remain.'

'I'm not recording this meeting.'

'Then what are you writing?'

'I don't know. I'm just writing. I'm just writing what comes out.'

The woman scanned the writing from behind Cara's right shoulder. Cara had quickly deployed a set of descriptors relating to her sensory impressions of lambdas and their residences. They formed a single, unpunctuated sentence replete with syntactical anomalies.

'If that's really what you must do, so be it. You're to visit tomorrow, 10 A.M. sharp. You need to go here, look and remember.' She held up a 4 x 6cm card with *2b Hargrave Crescent* in four-point Baskerville printed on it. 'Talk to Mr Hello—ask him what he remembers about the 12th of April. That date only. You shouldn't need to do much more than that to get him started. It's not important if he doesn't answer directly, but don't let him stray too far off the point. He can get hung up on details. Ask him about Severax. Use your discretion, and always say something if you need to reel him in. Ask him about his job, his colleagues, his early memories, it's all relevant. But April 12th of this year and Severax, they're indispensable. Do you think you can do that?'

Cara nodded.

'Good. The whole flat is blanket surveilled, no need to report. You will continue to visit at the same time until instructed otherwise. Weekends too. You will relinquish your phone before you begin the conversations, and you may not make records of any kind in relation to what you experience. I would like to thank you, personally and formally, Cara Gray, for your vital contribution to this *justice delivery pathway*.'

The woman left the room. Cara continued writing until she had covered one complete side of A4 printer paper with small, bubble-like script.

The next morning Cara made a note on her phone: *Dreamed again that I was a lambda. I landed at Portsmouth and hauled my tiny body up a rubble-strewn beach through dirty orange buoys. Feel of large pebbles on my stomach. Ears were full of Channel water + I could taste the chemical plumes I'd swum through. A land-human lifted me into a bucket—remember massive brightness + unknown colours. Then I lived in a place that could have been Surrey. Other lambda faces moved in and out of focus, importunate + sad. I began to speak but it didn't mean anything at first, it was just a way to say to myself 'I can speak!' I dreamed the inside of 17 Cherry Tree Grove, the tiny airspace in Gavin's shared bedroom, clustered with my family*

at a vent whose mesh had been removed so that we could all gulp
air, much too close together, at a little square of waterline.
Awoke (cruelly, inevitably) as my land-human self.

Cara let Gloria know she wouldn't make their meeting that
day, the 212th day of her employment with the police. She took
a Public Autonomous Vehicle to a stop close to the address on
the card the woman had shown her. It was in the opposite
direction to the lambda zones.

The road was slightly greener than average and the basic
housing stock was Georgian. The broader environs dated from
mid last century and were a noted civic services blindspot.
When she pressed the buzzer a retinal scan ensued, then a
voice instructed her to fully deactivate her phone and leave it
in the strongbox in the hallway. She entered the building. No
direct records of this or her nine subsequent meetings with Mr
Hello exist.

When she returned to the prefab, Cara cancelled all the
meetings with the lambdas she had scheduled for the day. She
went to the social services records centre instead. On arrival
she spent 5 minutes 25 seconds continuously washing her
hands.

Despite Gavin's insistence that nothing like art existed for
lambdas, Cara found a long sequence of drawings amongst
their files. They were largely abstract, the majority composed
of closely packed spirals that filled the entire sheet. The nearest terrestrial equivalent was Van Gogh's *Starry Night*, but the
drawings were more spare, monochrome, and suggested no
spatial orientation. They were executed in pencil on water-
resistant paper. When a lambda appeared in a drawing it was
almost entirely a head with no facial features, and it was difficult to distinguish from the mass of whorls. A child psychologist's report was stapled to the twelfth:

In the free drawing exercise, **Subject 4** has avoided all reference to the human figure. There are no clear objects, although there might be a lightbulb top left. This may indicate belief in the existence of help outside the usual channels of family and friends; equally, it may be a chance appearance in the abstract mark-making. The absence of a house or references to a house suggest an unsettled worldview, without a developed feeling of belonging. The complete filling of the page could be a positive sign that the subject is able to conceive of and grasp life's many possibilities. Equally, it could be evidence of *horror vacui*. These possibilities are also not represented in an accessible way, and the world is barely differentiated, still oceanic. In places the lines are serrated, like teeth, suggesting moments of danger.

Cara took three of the drawings home. She fixed them to her bedroom wall with white tac then checked her email. A response from Alex Masseter had come through.

Dear PC Gray

Thank you for your message. Please accept my apologies, I was supervising a major research bid due for submission last Monday and have only just found a moment to go back through my messages.

It's been a while since I thought about the lambdas and the so-called Four Fertile Pairs. To be frank with you, the expedition I led has become an albatross for me. While it confirmed some suppositions I had about the ecological state of the Labrador Sea region, you find me less convinced than ever of the scientific validity of researching speculative entities with scant information.

It was politically defensible a decade ago to fund this type of venture, but as you are no doubt aware that is no longer the case.

If you have any hard evidence that might form the basis of a more substantive investigation I will do my best to be receptive to it.

Yours

Dr Alex Masseter

In the evening she cooked for Peter and Rex, who exchanged 67 words with each other over the course of three hours. 48 of the words came from Rex. Peter went to bed early again, and Cara watched *Blue Star* with Rex until 01.15. The series had taken what she described in writing as *a disappointing turn*—the mysterious 'star' around which the narrative revolved was revealed to be an extraterrestrial spacecraft, one whose occupants planned to turn Earth into a sports/cultural resource within which humans were to be enslaved.

That night she slept badly. Instead of losing consciousness she made notes on her phone which she immediately deleted—many listed features and recollections linked to the Fowlmere 'Alex'. At sunrise she slept for approximately 90 minutes, during which period Peter left for work.

Rex emerged from his room while Cara was eating breakfast. She watched him toast a gluten-free muffin and asked, 'Why did you and Peter fall out?'

Rex stopped moving.

'Peter hasn't told you?'

'No. He changes the subject.'

'*Seriously?* I suppose I shouldn't be that shocked. That sounds like Peter. But he's told you about Dad, right?'

'Bits.'

'You know about his work? That he was a behavioural psychologist? A Skinnerite?'

'Yes, but Peter didn't explain what that means. I meant to look it up.'

'Burrhus Frederic Skinner. Professor of psychology at Harvard, nineteen-fifty-something to seventy-something. He thought democracy was based on an error, that someone's "inner life" has no scientific reality, and things like freedom and emotions are just effects of social conditioning. And guess what? He got to direct our childhood!'

Folds appeared between Cara's eyebrows. 'What do you mean?'

'Dad didn't really *parent* me and Peter. He *tweaked* us, with little rewards and nudges. Everything we did with him felt like a closely monitored test—even if it was just, I don't know, choosing an ice-cream. Why that flavour, Peter? Tell me your reasoning. Rex, give me the nutrient profile of what your brother has in his hand. Good, how would you like an extra flake? It all felt schematic, measured. As though he saw us as . . . living diagrams or something.'

'What did your mum have to say about it?'

'She didn't really participate, but she never intervened. Dad just imposed his high standards of "behaviour". Always in this weirdly, *aggressively* positive way. He's an intellectual snob—or he used to be, anyway. He didn't discourage Peter from doing all his computer stuff. But he didn't think he was really up to it. Not by his definition. Dad thought he wasn't ever going to be a top-grade coder. He always said he wouldn't have anything original to contribute, that the big companies would never hire him. He only ever said it to me, not Peter.'

Rex took a ginger tea bag out of its envelope and poured boiling water over it.

'One day Peter was harassing me about my music. He

thinks all art is a waste of time, you know? You must have noticed that by now, unless he's changed a lot.'

'No. He still thinks that.'

'Then you'll understand. He was trying to wear me down with waves of argument. It was just relentless and mean, and even though I should have been used to it, I snapped. I told him what Dad had told me. That he thought he was second-rate. That shut him up for a very, very long time. He didn't even question whether what I'd said was true. I was fifteen. Peter was seventeen. It was like some fucking eternal winter descended on us all, and it's not as though there was a lot of cosiness at home to start with. Maybe it sounds trivial to you, but if you knew Dad, and how elitist he was, "not quite good enough" is a dog whistle. It means "you don't actually count *at all* in my eyes". That kind of thing never bothered me. Dad could never convert me to his poisonous hierarchy thing. I didn't give a shit about the way he saw the things I cared about. But Peter is . . . fragile. And introverted. And a bit deluded. You can get away with being like that when things are going your way. But he hadn't realised how he looked to Dad. He'd just got it so, so wrong. It was like he'd fallen off a cliff face inside. He wanted more than anything to be his father's son, and he genuinely thought he was.'

He sipped his tea and glanced at Cara. She didn't speak.

'Obviously Dad should never have said that crap to me. I don't know why he did. I'm not sure it wasn't part of one of his experiments. He was working on this project to replace the OCEAN Personality Factors. Do you know what they are?'

'I've heard of them.'

'Right. So this new system was meant to go much deeper than those factors and facets. It would give you a personality as a full, dynamic machine, in a totally accurate arrangement, like a 4D periodic table. You'd be able to model a whole society, all these personalities in complex, interlinked states, from neurons to nation states. He started it at Keele, but they didn't have the resources. So he went into the private sector. That was when Peter and I were really small. Neither of us remember, but Mum said he changed then. She said it wasn't about the science anymore, it was all about the results—the money. This company was paying him seven figures to perfect it, so they wanted something more than a paper at the end. Anyway, when he found out that Peter knew what he'd said to me, when he saw what it did to him—and Peter tried everything to hide his feelings, which, just like Dad, he didn't believe were anything "real" anyway, they're just conditioning by social reinforcement—I think that was when it finally sunk in that other people have an *actual inner life*. That was when he realised nothing he could do would repair Peter's anymore.'

Rex sipped his tea again.

'Thank you,' Cara said. 'I'm sorry to make you bring it up.'

'No problem. Shame you had to hear it from me.'

'If it's any consolation it doesn't sound as though it's your fault at all. Look, I'm running late for work now, but we'll talk about this later, maybe when Peter's gone to bed?'

'Okay,' said Rex. 'Why not.'

Cara moved towards the door.

'Was it your idea that Peter got in touch?'

'It might have been,' she said.

Cara was 23 minutes behind schedule for her meeting with Mr Hello. She spent the remainder of the day in the police prefab writing notes on the lambdas and washing her hands. When she came home at 16.30, neither brother was home. She opened a bottle of low price-point Valpolicella and made a squash lasagne for the three of them.

Peter came back at 18.08. He stood in the kitchen and told two anticlimactic anecdotes about work. They decided to eat without Rex, who hadn't returned.

When Rex arrived at 20.17 he took his lasagne to his room. He didn't reappear to watch *Blue Star* with Cara—he emerged solely to clean his teeth and say goodnight.

At 02.04, Cara made a note about a memory of school. *The building was falling to bits. Nothing had been repaired for years because it was going to be partly demolished before refurbishment. There was an infestation of mice. One morning, before the teacher arrived, a mouse found its way into the classroom. Oliver Hewitt had blocked its exit, and three or four of his shitty hangers-on were in pretend fits of laughter as they lurched from place to place to trap it. It didn't seem possible—the mouse was in another realm, a dimension where time was running 12x faster, and we children were just hideous, slow-motion giants. But the mouse made a mistake. It was trapped under a satchel. Maeve Blisset started to scream (= stupid, I thought at the time, but in retrospect = she was giving the mouse the voice it didn't have). Oliver made a friend take over hole-blocking and approached the bag. The other boys in his horrid cartel were hooting as he lifted the bag and stamped, but the mouse was too quick and flew towards the still-blocked exit. The boy there (refuse to remember his name) kicked it hard. It hit the wall with the lightest pat, then dropped. I can still see it clearly through the painted steel table legs, curled up sweetly + totally still. I'd done nothing at all to save it.*

Oliver Hewitt was now financial director of a middle-tier drone supplier. There was no evidence in his behaviour or communications that this incident had ongoing significance for him. Cara described the memory as *like a close-up of a tiny mark on my skin, something always present but normally hard to view in its details.*

Rex slept in the following morning and Cara left without seeing him.

Following her third data-insulated conversation with Mr

Hello, Cara returned to the prefab and continued to write, filling 31 pages and bringing the total to 79. She washed her hands fourteen times for an average of 2 minutes 18 seconds.

Rex didn't come back to Cara's cell at all that day—he messaged Peter to say he was staying with his Guildhall friend. Peter exhibited a lessening of tension. Cara's response was the opposite.

'You two don't seem to be making up at all,' she observed.

Peter didn't look up from his laptop. 'It's progress compared with before,' he said.

20

H ello. How are you? Good, so the same as yesterday.
Please, take a seat. You are familiar with the array on
offer by now. Ah, what an interesting choice! A very
different chair than last time. I would certainly sit on that one
myself, if it ever felt appropriate.

I must apologise first off if you identify anything amiss
today. The milk has been left out of the fridge since your last
visit, so if you do decide to break the pattern thus far established and prepare yourself a tea or coffee, I recommend that
you proceed with caution—it was close to expiry last time I
presented that opportunity. You may also notice some stray
hairs and dust that have not been cleared. A very discreet lady
comes to service the whole flat every Saturday, but I have
heretofore been in the habit of keeping the place as near as
possible to spotless in the intervening period.

I am also ashamed to admit that an old auction catalogue
has slipped over on the shelf behind you. You might not have
noticed that, given that you face me constantly during our
much-enjoyed meetings. But I feel compelled to draw your
attention to it, as a matter of compunction rather than strict
necessity.

You will be wondering, I'm sure, what is the cause of this
string of regrettable lapses. You may also be wondering about
the smell. I will tell you. I have not moved in the slightest since
your last visit.

Perhaps this claim strikes you as exaggerated. I would

certainly countenance that perception. I have, admittedly, 'moved' in as much as my digestive system has continued to operate. After you left yesterday, having spent an hour in this exact position, I heard what are given the wonderfully unwieldy name *borborygmi*. So something was certainly going on down there, even if my perceptive powers were insufficient to register all the details. It would also be true to say that I blinked, although not as much as usual. My respiration also continued slowly. Now and again, especially early on in my inactivity, I swallowed.

I am prepared to concede all of the above, but beyond that, measured against the norms of human movement, I was completely still. I performed no medium- to large-scale motor functions, and relatively few minor ones. It was not an easy task, if I might give such a negative project that moniker. It has been, however, a task from which I have gleaned some significant insights. Because after a relatively short period of total inaction, say an hour and a half, my physical being assumed an undue importance. I appeared to consist entirely of a set of physical demands: respiration and digestion I have already mentioned, but the medium-term prospect of micturition, the more distant but eminently conceivable one of defecation, also the prospect of ingestion, the sense that one requires basic exercise to avoid stiffness or cramp, the need to attend to sundry itches and the stale taste infusing one's immobile palate, are some that immediately come to mind. My existence was compressed into a narrow portfolio of what seemed to be non-negotiable actions. A period of acute discomfort followed.

I am happy to say that, with a sustained application of will, I overcame this discomfort. I was victorious in a battle devoid of exterior spectacle. While I remained unmoving here, on this ordinary stacking chair, by the window you now must know almost as well as I do, on the inside the most extraordinary struggle was taking place. It was as though my body were a factory which, while its doors were closed to external orders, housed employees who insisted they continue production, only without an ultimate market for their goods, and were confronted now with the far from trivial problem of dealing with the growing stockpile within the factory's limited confines. But around three o'clock, not usually the most propitious hour of my day, I came to terms with this condition. The state of the "factory", as it were, while far from ideal, struck me as a consequence of economic forces beyond the control of any individual. For good or ill, these forces continued their work according to a logic I was powerless to alter. I had to draw upon or create other reserves, extra-material ones, in order to navigate this dark period. Once I had both understood and truly accepted this situation, my experience changed categorically.

Yes. The most notable feature of this transformation was that my body no longer preoccupied me at all. It was not that any of the messages I received from it disappeared; I would have benefitted greatly from a visit to the bathroom, and since it was some time since the hour when I would ordinarily have consumed my lunch, my blood sugar level was likely far from optimal. The difference was that I could assign these messages to what I might describe as a "loss account". You are familiar, perhaps, with the fiscal strategy of placing debts in one ledger and profits in another, quite unconnected one—the immediate benefits for the functioning of a business, often well beyond its essential viability, are self-evident. Well, I discovered that a comparable method can work with one's body. I experienced a freedom from its weight, its relentless practical cost, through the mental trick of "setting it aside". I knew it was there, I felt its disequilibrium, but in a substantive sense I had found a way to move on to somewhere more interesting.

What took its place was quite literally *the world*. I ceased to be a figurative block or bucket, restricting some parts of outer reality, collecting others. I was now, in metaphysical terms, a window, minus the pane of glass. The sound of a person shuffling into a house across the street *became* me. The knurls of the floorboards *were* my sense of sight. This seemed to place me in the heart of an old philosophical chestnut, to be specific the likely spurious, but nonetheless tenacious, dualism of subject and object. In my immediate experience this dualism was resolved by removing myself as subject entirely. It was a considerable relief. Time passed much more rapidly, and as my view of this room dimmed to abstraction, the sounds of evening and night took hold. A cat's shadow traversed the floorboards, and the cat was as much a function of the shadow as the shadow was of it. The ebullient cries of groups of intoxicated persons on the street tangibly marbled the early hours of the morning. I felt myself to be a fertile emptiness extending into the furthest reaches of the universe, the stars and nebulae flung through it like spores, and this dance of void and plenum was the ultimate resolution of whatever I'd thought of as 'me'.

There were some lacunae one could describe as sleep. As a new day dawned the thing that had been me was possessed by constant traffic sounds, the voices of children berating each other, the cleverly unrepeating song of a blackbird. My body had soiled itself. The most sensible course of action would have been to clean it and replace its attire, but as you will have grasped I was in the midst of an experiment that took me beyond what was merely, by any definition of the word, 'sensible'. I, or rather what had been 'I', was in fugue, absorbed into the infinite cosmic otherness that is the medium and matter of our petty separate selves, and a certain abnegation of usual standards of hygiene was a necessary corollary. I maintained the discipline of absolute stillness for what remained of the morning before your visit, in slightly more repressed discomfort than before. It was only in the very moment of your appearance that I suspected, in the final analysis, the whole exercise has been a total waste of time.

I am quite aware that today's discussion has followed a limited course. I must apologise that I have not acknowledged what I took to be signals from you that I was digressing far from the expected themes of our conversation. The unusual condition you find me in will, I hope, excuse me from reprimand, on this occasion at least. And since that same condition requires immediate redress in the form of an urgent change of clothing, hotly followed by an early lunch, you must suffer me to say goodbye for today. Goodbye.

21

A t 12.07 on Monday 6 May, 2019, Cara received an email from Vignir Sigurðsson.

Greetings from Iceland! You will perhaps remember our earlier contact and how I mentioned that the incoming lambdas, while less numerous, have recently had more and more to tell us about their origins. Well, I shall cut to the chase and tell you this—I have no fewer than TWO young lambdas here who are quite adamant that they remember the Four Fertile Pairs, their whereabouts and their circumstances, and have begun to share this narrative with us with all the details they can furnish (not many). This is really quite an event in my world and in yours too, I should imagine! I'm a little surprised at how unmoved the other lambdas appear by this development, but you are by now, I'm sure, familiar with the languid character of our aquatic cousins. However, I trust your Lambda Subject B will be very excited by this news. I look forward immensely to continuing our distant collaboration on this matter. Could I suggest that we arrange a remote video conversation? I may even be able to get a few words (in Icelandic!) out of the pair in question.

Yours, in great excitement,

Vignir

At 14.18, Cara leant a tablet against a leg of the loopback chair in Gavin's hallway. An image of Vignir from the shoulders up appeared on it. He was 28 years old and had a black, close-cropped beard. His OCEAN Personality Test Score was 79 77 80 81 45. He was wearing a Stutterheim raincoat in clementine and a teal woollen hat knitted by his aunt, Sigurdís Sigurðardóttir.

His image was replaced by that of two lambdas on wet wooden decking. The camera moved close to their faces.

'*Halló bræður!*' they said. Their complexions were totally clear, and their eyes were 20% larger in proportion to their heads than full adults'. The whites of their eyes were slightly translucent.

'Apologies, let me set to live translate,' said Vignir. 'That was "hello brothers"—your image is not very clear this end, Cara. Okay, let's try again.'

'We have stories!' the lambdas said in near-unison as they reappeared. The connection briefly lapsed and their faces transformed to pale bricks.

Gavin's facial expression was neutral. 'Tell me,' he said.

'We escaped four sharks!'

'Five!'

'I've heard about the sharks before,' said Gavin. 'What about the Four Fertile Pairs?'

'The sharks are blind!'

'We are faster than the sharks, but the sharks are strong and *hafa mikla þoll!*'

'Yes, strength and stamina, much! And sneaky too!'

'They smell us and on they swim, so deep and quiet, for many length of us!'

Gavin said, 'Can they hear us?'

'I think so. Vignir? Are you there?'

'Yes, I'm here. They're very excited. Fellows, please can you tell our English friends about *Fjögur Frjósömu Pörin?*'

'Yes, yes, the Four Fertile Pairs! We can tell you, we can tell you!'

'They are very grumpy,' said the left lambda.

'They are tired,' said the right. 'It is hard to have so many children.'

'I'm sure,' said Cara. 'Can you tell us where they live?'

Their eyes widened. 'In the sea!'

'Of course, the Labrador Sea,' Vignir added. 'Can you remember more precisely?'

'They are very grumpy. It's best to leave them alone.'

'Yes, that's why we swam out here. Best not to stay around.'

'But I have to know,' said Gavin. 'Can you describe for me where I might find them? I don't remember anything at all. Are you sure you're remembering correctly?'

'Yes, all correct,' the lambdas said. There was a 150ms delay between their voices. 'Far over that way.' They turned left together. 'In the nearly-coldest sea! We can show you!'

Cara looked at Gavin. He made no movement, and his facial expression didn't change. He said with solemnity, 'I would like that very much.'

'Then we will. If we have to!' The pair of lambdas blinked. 'Why are you so small, so flat? Come out of this tray, we will show you! But we don't really want to!'

'Okay, I should explain,' said Vignir, tilting the camera towards himself. 'These guys are not used to landy technology yet, not by any measure. I did my best to explain but they don't quite understand. They are only cognitively, what, a terrestrial three-year-old? Their navigation ability is off-the-chart amazing. Language similar, they've picked it up super fast. Tech is not so good. I'm not sure they quite believe they're speaking to you.'

'We want to see our flat *og litlu* brothers again!' said the staggered lambda voices. 'Show them back!'

Their faces returned to the tablet screen.

'I'm not in a tray,' Gavin told them. 'I'm in London. With a land-human police officer. Two thousand kilometres south.'

There was silence for four seconds. 'We will come to you. We can take you there, to the Four Fertile Pairs! But we don't want to!'

'No, no, no,' said Vignir. 'That is not advisable, you should stay here with your pod. We can talk to your brothers on this device, it's easy and safe.'

During the pause that followed, sea noises reduced to middle frequency range were emitted by the speakers.

'Okay?' said Vignir.

There was a period of sea noise only, then the doubled vocalisation, 'Okay.'

'Can we ask you more questions?' Cara said. The juvenile lambdas simultaneously jumped out of view.

'Ah, they're back in the water. Look, they're way over there already.' Two small lambda heads popping in and out of lead-coloured waves could just be distinguished on the screen. They were a minimum of 200m from the jetty where the meeting had taken place. 'I don't think that's the end of it, but they'll need a little time to process what just happened. It's probably quite confusing.'

'Thank you all the same,' said Gavin. 'This is a wonderful moment.'

'No problem at all. Let me talk to them more and we'll do this again soon. Goodbye for now!'

The connection ended. Gavin revolved 5° clockwise and said, 'I'd like to visit those twins. Do you think you could help?'

'Of course I can,' said Cara. 'I'll do everything humanly possible.'

Cara returned to the prefab and searched for return air tickets to Reykjavik. There was a lack of economical options, and the prices increased as she looked—she bookmarked two pages but didn't purchase anything. She sent a message to Alex Masseter to let him know that there was 'a new and promising connection between myth and fact', then washed her hands for 2 minutes 12 seconds and returned to her writing.

When Cara opened the door to her cell at 18.22, all Rex's belongings had gone. There was a misplaced object on the coffee table—her toothbrush. In front of it was a small, sealed envelope. She opened it and removed the folded slip of paper inside.

Hi Cara. Thanks for putting me up (and putting up with me), but it's working out better at Mark's. Sorry, I started to use your toothbrush by mistake. I used to have the exact same one. It warned me my estradiol levels had dropped 80%. Thought you should know.

reX

The toothbrush bore some further writing in white wax pencil on the barrel. The print was marginally more reflective than the nanoskin surface.

Peter's password is jabberwocky

Cara snorted. This password appeared on a proscribed list for police employees. She rubbed the pencil away with her finger.

When Peter came home he immediately started work on the Arizona cephalons.

'So Rex has gone?' Cara said.

'Yep.'

'To his musician friend's place?'

'It would appear that he has.'

'So. That was that.'

'Yes. It certainly was.'

Cara watched four episodes of *Blue Star* while Peter continued to code.

She climbed into bed for long enough to witness Peter sleeping heavily, then got out again, opened his laptop, decrypted its contents and typed *estradiol* as a search term for all his files.

> hedMAX333
>
> Do you realise her toothbrush has more rights in law than we do? Anyway, don't worry about that. There's a simple hack that means the brush will effectively do a swab during a normal brush. You can get a pretty detailed report on all kinds of substances, but the one you need here is **estradiol**. This will peak round about 400 pg/mL at ovulation. Does that help?

> peterrepeater9
>
> Yes, thank you. Not this cycle?

> hedMAX333
>
> No. Not this one. I will let you know as and when we make the expected breakthrough with transmigration.

Cara's eye saccades were captured by this excerpt of text for 22 seconds. She typed in the search term *transmigration*.

> We are of the view that **transmigration** is not only possible, but a necessary consequence of obtaining the complete dataset. The vessel for the transmigrated person could be one of any number of substrates, for example a sufficiently large hard drive, one or more animals of the Chordata phylum, or simply another human body. All have limitations and present different obstacles.

The text was part of a document Peter had downloaded 1244 days ago, before he had joined the police. It was entitled *Basic Principles of Extended Life*. It was the first of 283 results that employed the term.

hedMAX333
Yes, I do mean real **transmigration**. I prefer to call it metempsychosis. Both words have unfortunate religious associations, but that can work in our favour from a marketing perspective. So, are you in?

peterrepeater9
I think so. Can I have a bit of time to do my own research on it? I've come across this kind of projection before, and it tends not to work out when you get down to the practicalities.

hedMAX333
Fine. Keep in touch, won't you. I can't keep this open indefinitely.

. . .

lib3rac3
So you're promising real *transmigration*?!? Thought that was transhumanist bs.

peterrepeater9
Well, it looked that way to me too. But there's been some new thinking and some major hardware advances. Look at the arguments here. Quantum computers have exponentially increased the amount of data you can handle. And there is really not *so* much involved. It's nearly real.

. . .

Lbeaker1999

nearly fuckin what are you saying? youre saying you
can get me out of this fuckin cephalon pile with **transmigration** into where? it sounds so bullshit but im not
spending another decade in this nutstack if i can avoid it
you can have the $300,000 and *change* if you get me
out!!!

peterrepeater9

You have choices. Hard drive is flexible, but obviously not great long term. Best option: I start you all
over again anthropically. So yes, with a downpayment of
$100,000 I can confirm I will do it for you.

'Yes,' Cara said. 'Peter knows how to do a lot of things.'

The next day was the last of Cara's intimate relationship
with Peter. She pretended to be asleep until he went to work
and didn't drink the espresso he'd left for her.

When her morning interview with Mr Hello was over, Cara
took a transport to the lambda zone. The traffic was so bad
that she alighted in order to walk the last 1.6km. The woodland that marked the edge of the lambda zone had been cor-
doned off—the fifth item on her police update was headed
Park Incident Involving Refuse Droid. A keeper had returned
to the site during overnight clean-up, and a CivicSort9 had categorised him as refuse. It had begun to separate his parts into
the partitioned tray on its back when the keeper's screams had
alerted the other droids, all four of which were helpfully
trained to deactivate a unit if a human for some reason
couldn't. The on-going clear-up had added 47 minutes to
Cara's journey.

She washed her hands for 4 minutes 35 seconds on her arrival at the police prefab and resumed her unofficial text. After 65 minutes the supervisor called.

'I've been told you can move to Phase Two,' he said. 'There's a document waiting for you in the locked cabinet behind you. You're to collect it immediately and present it tomorrow. Do you know what that instruction means?'

'Yes,' said Cara.

'Good. After that you don't need to go back. And I have a piece of information. It's about a former Intelligences Services employee referred to as "A". She died four months ago in a car accident, no other details given. Do you know what to do with that data?'

'Yes,' she said. 'I know what to do with it.'

At 17.34, Cara took an unmarked white C5 envelope from the grey cabinet in the prefab and returned to her cell. Untypically, she didn't start cooking.

When Peter came in the first thing Cara said was, 'Are you planning to impregnate me so that the consciousness of a frozen head can transmigrate to our child?'

Peter was silent for 3.5 seconds.

'I'm not sure what you mean.'

'I found some material on your computer. About transmigration. And your clients in Arizona, the cephalons. Also my hormone levels. You've been monitoring me, yes?'

Peter's heart rate stepped from 72 to 91 bpm.

'It . . . probably looked like something it wasn't.'

'Oh?'

'Yes, Rex must have made it look like something, I don't know, sinister. Did he give you my password?'

'Yes.'

'Shit. *He gave you my password.* Doesn't that tell you something? He must have been watching me type it. He hates me, Cara. It's hard to explain, I mean it's irrational, but he absolutely hates me, no matter how "nice" he appears to you.'

This was an example of an argument *ad hominem*.

'No,' said Cara. 'Rex couldn't have planted those emails. I just put in some search terms, that's all. I can make sense of a chain of emails, without Rex's help, or yours.'

Peter moved to the diagonally adjacent corner of the room and directed his gaze out of the window.

'I didn't know that the toothbrush would start to measure estradiol. I just gave it some extra functionality. You know I can't control it, any more than you can. It has its own ideas. To a certain extent, anyway.'

'So you're telling me this was an accident? A coincidence?'

'Yes. Absolutely right. That's exactly how the monitoring must have happened.'

This was an example of *ignoratio elenchi*, or argument by irrelevant conclusion.

'But why . . . why all those conversations about metempsychosis, all those promises you made to the cephalons? That's not just some coincidence, is it? It doesn't add up, Peter. But the whole project, the transmigration thing, that does all add up. That's the whole problem!'

Peter was silent for five seconds.

'Cara, you can't really do it. It's a very widespread belief that you can separate mind and body. But it's just not true. They're two parts of one thing. A mind is an emergent system of a body, and it's specific to that body. You can't just put it somewhere else. That's a category error. But a lot of those cephalons believe it because they want to. They want a new life.'

Cara exhaled with force. 'So you're just pretending it's possible? And taking their money?'

'Yes.'

If true, this was not a logical fallacy but an example of cynical reasoning.

'But them why all those collaborations? Peter, there was so much stuff on your computer, and it went back *years*.'

'It had to be convincing, and there are some people, people who ought to know better, actual scientists who think it's feasible—'

'Stop talking. I don't know what to believe about you anymore, and I don't think I care. Peter, I want you to leave.'

In the hours that followed Cara developed notes on her phone regarding ways she could convey her disapprobation. Peter was *engaged in illegal multiple employment + false representation + potential criminal collusion*, so she could *certainly fuck him with those*. She noted the option of *alerting the authorities to a *major abuse* of Object Rights*. Further, she had not conveyed what she knew about his fraternal breakdown, and she noted +++ *potential there to hurt him further*. She pressed the phone's glass 54% harder than usual as she typed.

None of these plans was initiated. At 21.08 she ceased making notes, curled on her sofa and cried.

Cara downgraded her toothbrush. After filling out an online form for elective removal from the National Database of User/Owners of Sentient Objects, she returned the brush in person to the manufacturer via a drop-off centre in Acton. It would, according to the website explainer, 'undergo a process of re-education, rejection being a well-documented trigger of deep depressions in objects, and one which can render them useless thereafter.'

Cara arrived at the depot as it opened at 08.00. She placed the brush and packaging into a sliding tray that projected from a breezeblock wall. The ToothFriend representative was poorly visible above and right of the tray, his appearance blurred by frosted and wire-impregnated glass. When Cara conveyed the reason for relinquishment, that the brush had been 'colluding with someone to monitor [her] fertility in secret,' he said they would 'find a way to help the object through' and that Cara 'shouldn't worry about it.' When she insisted that there was something seriously wrong with a product that could be 'convinced by a third party to act against the interests of its owner,' he told her that he'd 'register the complaint and make sure it was fully investigated.'

She took the tube directly to Hargrave Crescent. She was exactly on time for her final conversation with Mr Hello.

For the next ten days, including unpaid shifts on Saturday and Sunday, Cara spent 73% of her working hours in front of her writing and 11% washing her hands. Her attention toggled between the long and incomplete pencilled sentence in her refill pads and PCSOs' updates on the lambdas.

On day four she watched a short news feature in which the director of Land-Humans for Lambdas, Antonia O'Reilly, was interviewed.

'Now more than ever this small and vulnerable community needs our support,' Antonia said. 'You will not see a lambda on your screens asking for help, but don't for a moment think that means they don't want or need it. This is a moment of incredible danger for our conscientious, hard-working, long-suffering *fellow humans*. Social media is awash with lies. Lambdas *are* humans. This is scientifically established fact. They are *not* excessively subsidised by the government. Vigilante groups, so-called militias, are exploiting these lies, especially false claims about the so-called Army of Lambda Ascension. There is no evidence of any such group. There will never be any evidence.'

'How can you be so sure?' asked a man in the age range 35–49. 'No-one else has been identified, and the ALA issued a clear statement admitting responsibility.'

'Fiction. The lambdas would never stoop to such an action. And even if they could, what could it possibly achieve? Look, they daren't even defend themselves in courts of law. The per-petrators of assaults on defenceless lambdas, these murderers, they're barely challenged. All the trials have collapsed. My organisation has done its best to ensure lambdas are correctly represented, but it's an astonishing battle. And this terror group is supposed to have committed the most horrific crime in recent history?'

The segment ended. The next described in animated diagrams a significant spike in recorded attacks on lambdas. Cara's supervisor had told her to refer to such attacks as 'social decohesion incidents.'

She switched to her YouTube landing page. Twelve thumbnails of amateur videos featuring lambdas appeared. Cara watched militia punting lambdas down residential streets, hooded figures pouring petrol into the letterboxes of basement flats, lambdas punched and mauled in their bowls as they were carried onto buses, lambda-dominated offices torched, and lambda information films re-edited with the addition of hate speech. Two of the videos had been disabled. Six disappeared as she watched. A combination of proprietary algorithms and human content moderators had identified and blocked them.

When her supervisor called on day six, Cara concealed her writing pad under the table. When Gloria called on day seven, she pretended she'd been meeting with lambdas.

On day eight a bulletin banner appeared on her work phone: *School Attack: Public Announcement Imminent.* 70 seconds later she clicked on an image of the Deputy Commissioner in her newsfeed.

'Good morning,' he said. 'Thank you for joining me here for this important update on the investigation into the school bombing, which, as I hardly need state, is one of the worst atrocities we have ever experienced on these islands. It is with some pride that I can announce today that we have identified the chief and so far only suspect in this heinous incident.'

An image of a shaven Colin Colestar appeared.

'Here is our suspect,' said the Deputy Commissioner. *The DC's face seems so wide*, Cara noted, *his eyes are like corner protectors on a desk*. 'We are not looking for anyone else in connection with the attack. We are not, I stress *not*, pursuing any link with the so-called ALA. All our data so far indicates the claim of responsibility that apparently issued from this organisation was a hoax perpetrated by the suspect. We appeal now to members of the public to come forward and assist with any information relating to Colin Colestar and his whereabouts, information which will be treated in the strictest confidence. Members of the public are warned not to approach the suspect, who is dangerous in the extreme. The last credible sighting we have was on the day after the bombing in South Cambridgeshire, and we have reason to believe that he has not left the country. You will see on the screen here a contact number. This number is to be used for reporting anything that you might know that can help this investigation. I will not be taking questions, and I thank you all for your attendance today.'

A phone number in white numerals on a black ground replaced his image on the screen.

'He's already dead,' Cara whispered.

At 13.43, an email came through from Vignir.

Dear Cara

Interesting and problematic news. The twins who remember the Four Fertile Pairs are no longer here. I asked around the pod and I discovered that they decided to go to London to talk to your Lambda Subject B. This despite all my warnings and attempts to encourage them to use our well-established technological channels, which, as you know, did not meet with their approval. All things being equal, you should expect their arrival in the next week. I must add, however, that this is an unprecedented journey. You will not need to be reminded that there is a distinct split in the flow of lambdas from the Labrador Sea, and it has always terminated in either Iceland or the UK. The viability of other routes is unknown to us, but we should not allow ourselves to become complacent in our analyses of our cousins, and they may well take this novel journey in their 'stride'.

Please be sure to update me on the safe arrival of the memorious twins.

Yours

Vignir

Cara went directly to Gavin's basement. It was 28°C outside, and a piece of paint that resembled a butterfly wing had broken off his door. Inside was 18°C cooler. When Gavin appeared, he positioned himself in profile.
'Are you okay, Gavin?' Cara said.
'Of course. Why do you ask?'
'You're hiding part of your body, aren't you?'
He said nothing in response. When Cara moved closer, Gavin paddled clockwise. This manoeuvre kept his whole right flank hidden.
'What's happened?' Cara said.
Gavin rotated so that the purple tumescence in his right eye socket appeared. The eye was partially obstructed by the swelling and tinted red by a local haemorrhage. His iris was as black as the pupil, and a large part of his temple bore yellow-green bruising.

'Jesus, Gavin!'

'It's not that bad.'

'Have you had any treatment?'

'No. Lambdas heal quickly.'

'You need to see a doctor. Let me call a—'

'No, I'm perfectly fine. The other one will not be fine. I'm lucky that my carrier acted so fast. There's nothing more to say about it.'

There was silence for fifteen seconds. Cara's facial expression could not be analysed.

'You don't like us, do you?' Gavin said.

Cara's response was not immediate. 'Why would you say that, Gavin?'

'We're too different. There is no point of real connection. I see that now.'

'Gavin that isn't true. You are valuable members of society, cared-for members. Don't you see that? These groups are not representative of—how could you think that I—?'

'It's okay Cara. I understand. I know you don't actively hate me. It's not as though you're about to join a militia. It's more subtle, isn't it? I am fully aware that we lambdas have created a new limit of acceptance for terrestrials. It doesn't matter what we do, we will always be marked by our adaptation to the water, our physiology. And our dependence on carriers, our special housing needs—it's a strain. It's obvious. There's no way around that. But we'll find a way to survive this moment. I've been thinking about little else. There's always returning to the sea, that's currently the most popular idea. And there are other options.'

'What do you mean?'

'There are other, more private environments we can inhabit without leaving the urban zones. I've been looking very seriously at the sewers.'

Cara's facial expression embodied a conflict—it conveyed

both burgeoning amusement and underlying stress. The conflict did not result in speech.

'The sewers constitute a vast network of fluid-filled tunnels that traverse the entire city,' Gavin continued. 'They are hidden, hard to access, and require special security clearance. The recent upgrade in the infrastructure means that these systems are not the environments they once were—the most serious waste product is filtered early, and there are large sections of potable water. Anyway, we don't require such high-grade water to survive. We've managed in considerably worse circumstances in our homes. By my estimate the majority of the population of the city region could fit within the sewer system. Having said as much, I believe a sizeable number of lambdas will refuse to take this option, and the problem of accommodating everyone won't arise. Beyond that, the population is diminishing. Overcrowding will only be a temporary problem.'

Cara's work phone picked up a 15dB sound that could be transcribed as 'pik': a tiny amount of water had been displaced by Gavin's right arm.

'You've decided to do that?'

'Not decided. Researched the option.'

'But . . . how will you eat?'

Gavin was silent for seven seconds.

'Thank you for your efforts, Cara,' he said.

'I've barely done anything for you.'

'You've done a lot. Thank you. And you should watch some videos about the sewers, they're probably not what you think.'

Cara returned to the prefab and viewed *UltraSewer!* This documentary described a recent major upgrade which meant that most of the filtration was now happening very close to source, before waste product fully emerged from residential buildings. The refit had been completed with minimal public communication within the last two months; a co-ordinated

team of semi-autonomous droids had installed the devices at
the outlets of 4.8 million homes. It was the third largest
deployment of its kind in history. The documentary emphasised the hygiene implications over the exponential upscaling
of waste analysis. *Low profile makes sense*, Cara noted on her
phone. *Massive enhancement of surveillance infrastructure.*

Over a high-speed 5K fly-through, a genderless synthetic
voice explained that the new household units 'reduced the
city's reliance on large external processing plants', and that the
communal regions of the sewer were 'for the most part clean.'
The interior of the system resembled a 'convoluted aeroplane
with the seats removed': it was off-white, strip-lit, and lined
throughout with titanium mesh walkways. The flow of translucent liquid down the central channel was the only indicator
that this was not an upmarket consumer environment.

'The aeroplane parallel could be extended,' the narrating
voice said. 'The system is on the same scale of consciousness as
a whole fleet of aircraft, and its responsibilities are even greater
in terms of human life. A mistake in blackwater filtration could
have consequences graver than a downed passenger jet.' The
sewer reported at length on the specific nature of the waste;
Cara watched a list of animal hormones, part-metabolised
medicines, Class A drugs and exotic pathogens scroll vertically
down the screen in a manner analogous to the GUI she'd used
as a data surveillance officer. *Only for the sewer the threat is
labelled clearly, each name attached to a tangible enemy + the
structure in which to catch them *seems to actually work*.*

At the end of the second video Cara went to the government-
partnered website, paged through the role descriptions and
person specifications, and downloaded an application form. It
was the longest diversion from her writing in the last eight days.

After 96 minutes she stopped. 'Shit,' she said. 'I didn't tell
Gavin about the twins.'

On the second visit Gavin didn't answer the buzzer. 'Shit,' Cara repeated. Her heart rate was slightly raised. She stood on Gavin's doorstep for 34 seconds without moving, and nothing about her surface appearance conveyed the thought processes in which she was engaged. Situational stresses of the recent past had made her high OCEAN Personality Test Score of 89 for Conscientiousness inconsequential, and this fact could have informed her reflections.

When Cara moved again it was to draft an email to Gavin on her Bell 6i explaining that she *had forgotten to convey something important*. The draft automatically saved—she didn't press send. Instead, she embarked on an unscheduled round of neighbouring lambda basements, pressing 35 consecutive buzzers before eliciting a response.

'Sarah?'

'What is it?'

'It's PC Gray. Cara. Can I come in?'

'How do I know it's you?'

'I was here two weeks ago. You told me about the man in the bright green sweatshirt, the one who shouted at you on Oxford Street.'

There was a pause. 'Yes, it's you,' the voice said. The door clicked open.

Incoming light in the entrance hall was 20 lux, and it was 18°C cooler than outside. Sarah appeared after a short delay and remained in the shadowed zone at the back of the water-filled stairwell.

'Why are you visiting today?' Sarah said.

'To say hello. To see how I can help.'

'No-one can help.'

'Try me.'

'There are people coming tonight.'

'Who?'

'A militia.'

'How do you know?'

'There's a new message board for these things. Some of us have access.'

No lambda had ever mentioned this to Cara before.

'If you can access that message board, the police can too.'

'Perhaps. But where are they? They don't ever come.'

'I'm here, Sarah. I can help.'

Sarah moved further into the shadow.

'Are you still there?' Cara said.

'I'm still here.'

'I will chase this today. And if there's no-one available, I'll do it. I'll be here, on the street, tonight. Nothing will happen.'

Sarah said nothing.

'Is there anyone else with you?'

'No.'

'Where are they?'

'They're gone. They're dead.'

The lambdas she referred to were Luke, Esther and Graham. They appeared on Cara's chart as λL2, λE and λU.

'Sarah I . . . don't know what to say.' Cara's eyes saccaded from Sarah to the carpet. The design was a *fleur-de-lis* spaced in equilateral triangles.

'It happened four days ago,' Sarah continued. 'My carrier could run faster. One of the attackers said, "The ghosts of schoolchildren will piss on your ghosts." It was really our fault, we shouldn't have all been together at once.'

The highly sensitive microphone of the Bell 6i captured the 5dB tapping of Cara's tears as they fell on the carpet. 'I'll come back tonight,' she said. 'I'll be here all night if I need to be.'

At the end of her shift Cara didn't go home. She continued to write in pencil at the desk of the police prefab, washing her hands eight times and redrafting her email to Gavin fourteen. The sun set at 20.44. She locked the refill pad in the desk drawer and, after emailing her supervisor to notify him of the militia warning, she tried Gavin's basement again. No-one answered.

She began her patrol.

Cara's path was a series of irregular overlapping polygons whose sides followed lambda-occupied streets. She sat on five occasions on a low wall at 18 Malvern Road, and her heartrate briefly dropped. By 01.12, the last land-human of the night had left the zone she surveyed: none had displayed any signs of hostility towards its inhabitants. Thereafter until dawn, the only mammals Cara encountered were foxes who interacted with food-waste bins and rats which emerged periodically from the base of the chainlink fence by the woodland. The sun rose at 05.09. The earliest shift of carriers arrived 40 minutes later. Cara rested for the last time on the low garden wall to record the presence of *their weirdly empty bowls*. She experienced 32 seconds of REM sleep.

At 07.34 she returned to the prefab and continued writing in pencil, noting impressions of lambda skin, fused lambda toes, their veins of uncertain importance, their optically hazel eyes, their steady high-pitched voices, and the frequent, lengthy gaps in their speech. Twice she fell asleep on the page.

She carried on writing until the supervisor called, at which point she quickly transferred her pad to the drawer.

'You must have caught the Deputy Commissioner's announcement,' he said.

'Yes, I caught it.'

'Good. At the appropriate time we will let the news agencies know that Suspect Alpha has been killed while resisting arrest. Thank you for your assistance in bringing this matter to a close.'

'So that's the end of it?'

The supervisor pursed his lips. 'Yes. But I have another announcement to make. A private one. I'm afraid, Cara, that we are going to have to suspend you.'

The supervisor was nodding slowly, looking down at her with an expression that conveyed gentleness and disdain. 'Is that a surprise?'

Cara stared at her right hand. 'Yes and no, I suppose.'

'Yes and no. We've asked a lot of you, Cara. I want you to know that we're not unhappy with your performance. You've been diligent. You have also been very flexible, in the light of all these recent, very significant challenges. Intelligence Services too have been very grateful for the small function you performed for them. However, there are certain things that are causing concern. Your relationship with Gavin, for instance. We know about the "project" you're helping him with. All the Iceland communications. Not sanctioned—I was quite clear about it.'

Cara continued to stare at her hand. The skin was desiccated as a result of excessive washing.

'And then there's the writing. We know about that too. It's been interfering with your daily work, hasn't it?'

Cara was silent.

'I've weighed these factors very carefully and at all levels it's been agreed that you need some distance from your duties. It's for your own good as much as anything. You don't need to worry about the lambdas. PCSO Knowles is extremely capable, and the situation for them is, I'm told, improving.'

'You didn't answer my email about support for them on the street.'

The supervisor slowly shrugged. 'There is a task force for that. It's a different department to ours. I can see from your phone data that you've been patrolling all night. I can assure you that impromptu beat duty is really quite unnecessary.'

Muscles in Cara's brow contracted. 'Can I keep in touch with the lambdas?'

'No. Keep away from the lambda zones or you will risk immediate dismissal, perhaps prosecution. For the time being you'll be paid as usual. Your identity will also continue to be protected. I must remind you to continue to exercise the utmost discretion in connection with all events you've been party to. A full list of conditions and reciprocal obligations will be sent to you by post. Please collect your things immediately and leave your phone and uniform in the Service Police Establishment. You can post the keys through the letterbox when you've locked up. Thank you PC Gray, from this moment on you are no longer an active police officer.'

The supervisor's image disappeared. Cara continued to write.

22.

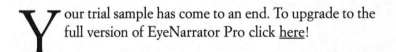

Your trial sample has come to an end. To upgrade to the full version of EyeNarrator Pro click <u>here</u>!

23.

Hello. How are you today? Yes, it is a shame about the rain. After such a lovely run of mornings, too. Yes, please take a seat. That's quite correct—there is only one chair today, the one I set out especially for you. A Robin Day Series E stacking chair, just like mine. I don't know why I insisted on having five in addition to my own until this point; it now strikes me as rather superfluous.

Do you remember that I promised to find out what the plant was called, the one with the dark green, fleshy leaves? Well, I did find out. However, I wonder if I might enter into a bargain with you. I will tell you what it is called if and when I learn from you what became of Anne ———, whom I have not seen in person for some time. What do you think of this proposal?

Very good.

Before you fill me in, I would like to let you know that I found our conversation before last especially beneficial. I realise now that the events I recounted had weighed rather heavily upon me, and the last of them is in fact directly related to my current situation, which is somewhat reduced. I understand that this flat is the property of the government and is often used to secure persons of special interest. Please do not think that I am complaining about it—there are many characterful features which I find charming, such as the decorative cornicing. Did you notice, incidentally, that the repeating holly leaf is slightly elongated in the hall, an absorbing deviation from the pattern as it obtains in each of the other rooms? It is not the flat itself but my containment in it which, I'm sorry to say, is having a rather deleterious effect on me. Although my early period in the laboratory was limited, I was physically smaller and so felt less constrained, or else had the distinct impression that my world was on the verge of a great expansion of some kind. No such impression is created by my current circumstances. While I would hesitate to use the word 'imprisoned', I would certainly aver that my movements are quite severely curtailed. This curtailment is directly related to the incident during my celebratory meal, is it not? While my actions would have been condoned in certain contexts, and, as I need hardly point out to you, in my professional experience positively encouraged, I can well understand why they are in general frowned upon in states founded on the rule of law.

This is, however, a diversion from my initial point, which was that our discussion of two days ago cleared the air for me considerably. I had been particularly troubled by the image of the Minister of Defence's bisected head, especially the way its free section had come to rest on the bed linen. What a peculiar object that was! One can have a very clear overview of the general schemata of good sense within which one operates, and yet a detail such as this emerges and assumes an undue level of importance, quite out of proportion with its actual value. Yes, our conversation has certainly made this element of my experience significantly less intrusive, and I would like to thank you for that service. I have to confess that much of the time I was unsure what on earth you might have been driving at with your questions!

I have always had a very precise idea of my place within our social matrix. It is quite clear to me that I occupy a somewhat different position to human beings such as yourself. While everything about me is identical in its functioning to you and any other healthy person (even if my brain and spinal cord happen to be synthetic constructs which are resilient enough to be transplanted into other host bodies), the fact that I am not, strictly speaking, a 'person' is a valuable characteristic, and one which is no doubt important in operational and legal terms. Is this, perhaps, how I have avoided the more punitive consequences that would normally ensue from actions like those in the restaurant? It is unnecessary for you to say. I would like to add the gloss that while I am able to rationalise my duties in terms of the larger good of the state, a state which has produced me, employed me, and continues to do its very best for me, there are still certain difficulties I face in processing the experiences I have garnered as a consequence. I can only thank you again for your help in this regard.

To return to Anne ——— —I am at this moment quite prepared to tell you the name of the plant, the one that has been sitting between us the whole time. Do you think you might satisfy my curiosity, regarding Anne? As I have already mentioned to you, her visual appearance often occupies my thoughts, and during the hours of darkness I sometimes have the odd impression that she is lying next to me.

She is no longer alive?

Well, that is an irony. Have you any idea of the circumstances? Goodness. Statistically, car accidents are the most common cause of non-disease related death, so in a sense one should not be surprised. I understand she stopped working for the agency some time ago and her activities were no longer especially significant to it, although I do remember being asked a number of questions about the lunches we shared together. Perhaps it was even one of your colleagues who questioned me. Now that I reflect on it, certain of her perspectives did seem at a variance to the general direction of our work. It was almost certainly for the best that she left.

Well, I will be curious to see how this information affects my frequent eidetic episodes involving the image of Anne

———. The relationship between these images and their referent has been categorically changed, it would seem. I will certainly let you know in future if there is any alteration to my
experience.

But this is our last conversation? Of course, if you feel that
there is no legitimate reason to continue then that is a matter
for your judgment alone.

Yes, I would certainly like to return to my duties. Please, let
me know what would be required of me, I would be more than
happy to resume my services to the state and its people. I can
think of no more meaningful way to spend my days, which I
have already told you have begun to assume a rather turgid
character.

So, everything I need to know is here, in this envelope. Yes,
of course I will open it only when you are gone. The level of
discretion necessary in roles such as ours has certainly not
escaped me! What a wonderful prospect, thank you for being
its—how can I best put it? Its *vector*. It strikes me now that it
will only be a matter of time before the rain stops. Don't you
agree?

Do excuse me. I have been slow to uphold my end of the
bargain. The plant on the table, the one that has been a silent
audience for all these stimulating exchanges. It is an aloe vera.

II

1.

Memo Re: 'Conversations with Mr Hello'
A full report will be compiled once all intelligence has been processed, but I circulate these observations in the interim.

After (n) meetings Mr Hello demonstrated threshold reflection on certain procedural and perceptual deficiencies to the satisfaction of the remote psych-eval team. The interlocutor observed correct physical distancing and verbal intervention protocol throughout, and the encounters passed without any significant incident. In the interests of swift operational progression, Mr Hello's briefing for Phase Two was approved. This phase is now complete.

Despite my initial misgivings, it would appear that debriefing of syn-prot agents is fairly straightforward and achievable outside both the lab and the department. However, I suggest that these issues require further consideration:

- *Medium- to long-term effects of novel transference target on syn-prot agents.*
- *Short-, medium- and long-term effects on non-specialist interlocutors of syn-prot agents.*
- *Security issues around use of extra-departmental staff.*

Notwithstanding these ponderables, the significant efficiency gain inherent in non-specialist staff liaising with synthetics at this level is compelling, especially given the disinclination of specialist staff to debrief syn-prots in light of recent incidents.

Moving forward, my recommendations are as follows:

- *Secure re-housing and enhanced observation of Mr Hello for an indefinite period.*
- *Development of a tailored psych-eval regime for interlocutor DSO30891.*
- *Enhanced surveillance regime in perpetuity for same.*

An array of fully analysed metrics relating to the recent meetings with Mr Hello will undoubtedly shed light on items one and two. Many of my initial reservations remain intact, but they were in this case overridden by the opportunity for a meaningful test case in Epsilon/Suspect Alpha.

In summary, there is reason to be optimistic about the scalability of domestic deployment of syn-prots.

2

Y ou have successfully upgraded to the full version of EyeNarrator Pro! We are sure that you will be happy with your purchase, but please get in touch with our Award-Winning Customer Support Team if you experience any problems. Most common issues relating to flow, plausibility and tone can be solved by referring to our EyeNarrator Parameters FAQ.

Now that your editing and distribution rights have been fully unlocked, we recommend that you take a moment to review the Terms of Use.

- Your current Narrative Closure Style is: TAPER

You may change this setting at any time, but please be aware that doing so may generate conflicts with previous outputs.

We hope that you enjoy the closing chapters of your first EyeNarration. Please consider recommending EyeNarrator Pro to other members of your community!

3.

A t the end of the page Cara picked up her work phone. It had reverted to factory settings. She followed the supervisor's parting instructions, transferred the lambda 'baby' from the desk drawer to her satchel, and subsequently took a transport home.

She washed her hands for 4 minutes 34 seconds, then showered. *Something has happened to my body*, she wrote. *It feels too long, too loosely assembled—it seems to come apart in layers as I look + there are shadows where there haven't been any before.* After she'd towelled herself dry, she made scratches on her skin *to justify the application of plasters.* She *peeled off the frighteningly delicate plastic shapes from their ends + pressed them firmly down.* She sparsely covered her thighs, her pubic region, her torso and finally her arms, at which point her supply was exhausted.

Cara wrote in her pad all evening and finished a 50cl bottle of artisan vodka. She fell asleep on the sofa. At 08.30 the next day, after showering again, she travelled to the lambda landing beach at Portsmouth.

The Lambda Landing Facility had been established in 1982 with a £2.1 million central government grant. The staff had numbered 30–50 until 2014, and had since decreased to seven. Eighteen months ago, a requisitioned building on the waterfront had been returned to private use. At the time of Cara's visit, the Facility consisted of two 41m stretches of dark green vinyl extending into the sea from a double nest of chainlink fence. Inside the nest was a prefab of the same type as Cara's erstwhile place of work. It wasn't possible to see over the curtain, and there was nothing but prohibitory signage in the vicinity of the fence.

Cara walked the length of the curtains to the edge of the sea 48 times over the course of the day; the vinyl was covered in expletive-laden lambda references rendered in spray paint. A string of buoys continued the line of the curtains approximately 550m into the water, and she watched this bounded area in *hopeless anticipation of spotting the twins.*

A 38-year-old man with red hair came out of the prefab at 12.54, unlocked and relocked the nested gates, and returned 25 minutes 11 seconds later with a white paper bag. He left again at 17.32. His name was John Crowley, and his title was Principal Officer of the Lambda Landing Facility. His OCEAN Personality Test Score was 51 75 60 55 73. He held an MSc in Applied Marine Science from Plymouth University and in his early teens had been a frequent participant in Massively Multiplayer Online Games.

In the evening Cara drank more artisan vodka and added newly acquired plasters to her body. She slept in the armchair, on the sofa and ultimately in her bed.

Iceland had received only four arrivals in the last six months, while no lambdas had landed in the UK at all. *The uterus of Portsmouth harbour is empty,* Cara reflected on her phone. Of the six staff at the facility in addition to John Crowley, four were security. While they would sometimes walk the length of the curtains to the waterline, they predominantly made use of folding chairs in the inner nest of fencing and interacted with their phones. On five occasions in the first two days, Cara heard a bigoted phrase shouted from a passing car. On each occasion, the security officer's sole response was to stare in the car's direction.

On Cara's third day at the landing beach, John Crowley approached her.

'Back again?'

'Yes.'

'Why's that?'

Perpendicular red hair = appearance of humanoid sea urchin, Cara wrote.

'I'm waiting for some people. Two lambdas.'

'Oh?'

'Yes. They're on their way from Iceland.'

His expression combined elements of a smile and a scowl. 'Interesting. How do you know?'

'I've been in contact with Vignir Sigurðsson. He introduced us before they left.'

'You know Vignir?'

'Yes. I got in touch with him for a friend.'

John Crowley touched the hairs on his chin and cheek. 'And you're just going to sit there? Until they turn up?'

'Yes.'

He laughed. 'You can't do that. You'll catch your death.'

'I'm warm enough. The sun's out.'

'But this wind just strips the heat out of you, doesn't it?' He looked out towards the buoys. 'Vignir told me to expect some visitors too.'

'Twins?'

He returned his gaze to Cara. 'Exactly, yes. I'd invite you inside, but I can't, the rules have become very strict in recent weeks. But I can let you know if there's any news, you don't have to stay here. Leave me your contact details.'

'Thanks, I will do. But I'm happy here. I don't have anything else to do. This is a favour, for Gavin Knight-Green. Do you know him?'

Muscles at the edges of John Crowley's mouth contracted. 'Gosh. Depends what you mean by "know".'

'He's very interested in the Four Fertile Pairs.'

He laughed again. 'I'm aware of that much.'

'He noticed that the latest arrivals remember more of their journey. That was how I ended up contacting Vignir, to see if the most recent ones remembered even more. I'm not sure why he didn't contact you.'

'He knows about all the Portsmouth arrivals. And there've been no landings here for months. Nothing. If those twins arrive it will be water in the desert, as it were.'

'But you could have put him in touch with Vignir.'

'Yes. I could have done. If he'd asked. I imagined he was pursuing his own investigations. I stopped responding to all his "data" a while ago, so he probably gave up on me.'

'But is he right? The newest lambdas do remember more, don't they?'

'Correct. But as far as I know, nothing about the Four Fertile Pairs. Lots about the journey. And Greenland sharks. It's actually very fascinating. Did you know, nobody had ever recorded a Greenland shark hunting before?'

'No, I didn't know that.'

'It's true. Now we have all these lambda reports. It was always a mystery how the sharks caught anything fast-moving. They're incredibly slow for an apex predator—that super-low heart rate is how they live for centuries—but the lambdas' accounts suggest they can do this jump to light-speed, just on rare occasions, and just a very short distance. They lurk way in the background, trailing their prey for days, slowly, slowly, pretending to be half asleep. Then—bang. They have this inner jaw that pops out.' He mimicked the jaw with his hands and grinned. Cara smiled reactively. 'You notice how few injuries the lambdas arrive with? If a Greenland shark gets them, it's almost always curtains. There's a new theory that all the incoming lambdas start as little pods, all looking out for predators, and in the end it's only one of the pod that makes it. They don't seem to remember in any detail yet themselves. You probably know this, but an awful lot of those seal remains found in Greenland sharks over the decades have turned out to be lambdas.'

'My name's Cara, by the way.'

'Excuse me, I'm John. John Crowley, I'm in charge of this facility.'

'I'm pleased to meet you.'

'Yes, the same. Lambdas seem not to get on with seals, actually. They follow a fairly narrow corridor around the Irish and English coasts, where the seals won't bother them, and that seems to be why they end up exactly here. Maybe none of this is news to you. Anyway, we'll keep in touch. We can share notes. And keep yourself safe. What are you writing, by the way?'

She closed the pad. 'Oh, it's nothing.'

Cara added plasters to her skin every time she visited the toilets in the cafes along the coastline. None of these places bore evidence of the visitors that made the beach significant.

Consistent with the trend of the last 185 days, the first week of Cara's suspension passed without a single lambda coming ashore.

*

A physical letter arrived at Cara's cell. It was a formal document detailing all the things she could and couldn't do as a suspended officer. Her eyes saccaded over the phrases in bold: **Special Subject of Interest**, **Enhanced Surveillance Protocol**, **Bilateral Silence Agreement**, and **Medium-Term Psych-Eval Commitment**. She called her mother and asked if she could move back in with her again.

'Are you going to stay longer this time?'

'I don't know, Mum. Things have been a bit confusing for me. With Peter and everything.'

'Of course, love. No need to spell it out.'

Cara moved back to North Woodham. It was on a direct line to Portsmouth—she performed a typical daily commute in reverse, and the train was rarely more than 15% full. She spent the working day on a concrete step engaged in eye saccades that explored the horizon, writing in her pad or typing on her phone, and interacting minimally with John Crowley of the Lambda Landing Facility. A photo of her father in the hallway greeted her on her return. It was one of the few pictures on display that showed him out of uniform, and his hair was closely cropped. *I still remember how it felt to run my small hands over his velvety scalp*, she wrote.

After ten more days of exposure on the beach and self-medication with artisan vodka alone in her childhood bedroom, Cara developed a high fever. *My dreams,* she noted, *are abstract and horrible—cables connecting nothing to nothing in vast + lubricated knots. In one I looked into a writhing diagram of something very small: I was caught at a moment of decision that couldn't end. Little nameless objects swam in a turbid plasma. They were all the split pieces of me, hopelessly looking for their mates.*

Her parents' voices woke her up.

Cara descended the stairs in black pyjamas that fully concealed her plasters. Her mother was visible beyond the banister, following Rhoda as it acted as a vacuum cleaner. She said, 'Cara's looking a little better now, poor love. Perhaps we'll get her up today.'

'Hello Mum,' said Cara. Her mother stopped and smiled at her. The smile lasted 1.2 seconds.

'You were right,' said her father's voice. *It was much larger seeming than his usual voice,* Cara noted, *but less resonant too. Just flat.*

'Dad?'

'Hello love. Feeling better?'

'Where are you? Where's your voice coming from?'

'Oh darling,' said her mother, reddening from her neck upwards. Cara *realised she was an organism, not so different from a Gila monster,* one that was *caught at an adaptive limit.*

'I'm still in the Gobi desert, my love,' her father's voice said. 'But I'm here with you now, too.'

Her mother said 'Replica off' in an unkind voice and went into the kitchen. Cara followed.

'What's going on? Is that a replica Dad?'

'What do you think, dear?'

'I thought you hated the whole idea of surrogate people!'

'I do, darling, I fucking do!'

It was the second time she'd used an expletive in Cara's presence. The first had been 11 years, 2 months and 7 days previously.

'Has he been back again?'

'No. He installed this app for me the last time. I just didn't tell you. He trained it. It's a sophisticated chatbot, very convincing. You can ask it pretty much anything. It remembers what your dad remembers, and always listens. In many ways it's even better than having a conversation with—'

She turned 128° away from Cara. When Cara touched her arm she walked abruptly into the garden shouting, 'Rhoda! Coffee, out here now please!'

When her mother went out to buy milk at 14.25, Cara spoke to the app herself.

'Dad?'

'Yes love? Feeling better?'

'A little. Why did you leave?'

'Ah, so direct! I wish your mum and I were more like that.'
A silence of five seconds followed.

'Well? Why?'

'Life is a very big conversation.'

There was a silence again, one that for Cara was *as dark + soft + unreflective as the fabric of Dad's B&O speakers.* 'Is that that all you have to say?'

'My love, it's not always clear how you carry the conversation on. Have you read that Meister Eckhart book?'

'No. Should I?'

'If you have the inclination to. Meister Eckhart understood things it's taken a whole desert to teach me. A desert and a motorbike.'

'And an abandoned family?'

Another silence followed.

'I left the book here when I visited your mum last. You should take a look, when you're ready.'

'Dad, I think you should come back home. Mum needs you here. It's not fair that she's alone. That's not what a marriage is supposed to be about. Or have you forgotten you're still married?'

'I haven't forgotten. And I'm still your dad. Wherever I am.'

'Great. My very own Dad of the Gobi. With his magical software surrogate. You never understood other people, Dad. They're just background features to you. They have no . . . independent existence.'

'You are both free. Just like me.'

'No, not like you. We are unfree because of you. Trapped by the promise and memory of you. Neither one nor the other. And you don't sound like police any more. You sound like . . . some people I used to spend a lot of time with.'

'People change.'

'People change? Is that a factory preset cliché? And you're not a person. You're a . . . *void.* This is the only important conversation we've had in fifteen years and you're not even here. Replica off.'

3 minutes 45 seconds later, she turned the app on again.

'Dad?'

'Yes love?'

'Why did you go on a biking holiday with the Chief Super-intendent and miss my fifteenth birthday?'

'The timing was unfortunate. It was a real opportunity and in the long term it was a good decision for the whole family. I don't think I would have been promoted—'

'I don't give a shit about your promotion. You weren't there on my birthday. You were in Aberdeenshire. On a Honda Goldwing.'

'You have such a good memory. Your mum can never tell the difference between my bikes.'

'I can remember them because I used to look at them. I'd take off the covers and just stare at them. They're like stepsis-ters. Really demanding stepsisters. With weird, perfect bodies. Who hate me. Did you know I used to do that?'

'No. But they don't hate you or anyone. Machines aren't made that way.'

'Do you remember calling me?'

'On your birthday? Yes, I remember.'

'You were very drunk.'

'We'd been riding all day. The weather had worsened. We arrived late at the pub we were staying at and I was exhausted. Connor had insisted we drink whisky and it hit me harder than usual.'

'That sounds well rehearsed. Congratulations. I think I don't like you at all at the moment. Replica off.'

What happens to all the conversation data? Cara pondered in a note on her phone. *Why wouldn't our words get aggregated, analysed and fed back to a hidden end-user, i.e. Dad?*

4.

Dear Port Authority

Thank you for opening this message, it is kind of you.

I would like to make a very special request and you have no reason to doubt my sincerity. I am an expert in certain matters. I have attached a number of images and writings which show that I am committed to interpretation. All of my notation should make it clear to you that this is no hoax, I am a bona fide interested person. I can give you any more information that you would like, please feel free.

I have noticed in my role as a special assistant that my newest brothers and sisters have better than normal memory. (I am a lambda.) Have you noticed this too? I would like to discover more about the ideas of the arriving lambdas at your facility. I wonder, would you share these ideas? When you have looked at the material I have carefully selected and attached you will know that it is the subject of the Four Fertile Pairs which is most important. Indeed, how could it be otherwise?

Do you think you could ask the newest arrivals to provide information about these people? If that is okay, could you make some record of what they say to you and send that record to me? Is that an acceptable request? Dear Port Authority, I hope it is.

The email address I have used here is reliable. Please reply directly if you agree. I have had some difficulties in the past and no information has reached me, but perhaps my messages have not been directed well, or been diverted, or perhaps lost. The world is large.

More can be said on the subject of the attachments, the address is the same.

Sincerely

Gavin Knight-Green

Dear Port Authority

Thank you for opening this email, it is very kind of you.

I write hoping hard that you have opened my previous email. I may be interrupting your thoughts about it, and if this is the case I apologise. I wonder if you have noticed that a month has passed? Are you still gathering information which you intend to pass on to me? If this is true then I am very grateful. If you have lost the email I sent to you, no need to worry. I have included it again below.

Another possibility is that you were not convinced of my serious interest in the subject of the Four Fertile Pairs. Please be convinced. This is a subject of special concern to me, and in order to demonstrate my commitment I have attached another selection of material. It is the result of much study and careful interpretation of terrestrial sources. (I remind you that I am a lambda.) You will see that I have found evidence of the Pairs in many films and television broadcasts which may (?) have escaped the notice of their makers. I hope you will agree that it all makes for compelling reading.

If you have any other pressing queries regarding myself or my work, I would invite you to respond to this reliable email address. Do not wait for further solicitation, I am ready for any response.

Sincerely thanking you

Gavin Knight-Green

Dear Port Authority

It gives me great pleasure to imagine that you have opened this email. I include my two previous emails below. One was sent over two months ago and one last month. Perhaps they have given you food for thought?

Please find attached a zip file that contains all my current research on the Four Fertile Pairs. It is well indexed. You will see that the research is detailed and accurate. You will, I believe, agree that this zip file is evidence that I am not a fraud. To recap my request: I have noticed that new arrivals in the UK have 'better than normal' memory. They recall experiences before their arrival quite well. I wonder if that has been your perception too? I wonder if any remember their whole journey to Reykjavik, and even the Origin of that journey? Please could you record information on this subject in any way that is convenient? I will receive it with grateful thanks and can offer money (I have set up a savings account for the purpose).

In the meantime I have also contacted the Marine and Freshwater Research Institute. I have also offered them my findings and a cash incentive along with the same request. I apologise if this message complicates any discussions you are already having with this important body.

As always please use this exact email address to avoid any loss of reply. .

Warm sincerity

Gavin Knight-Green

Dear Port Authority

In a dream last night I clearly saw you opening this email. For the dream I thank you. Perhaps it was not only a dream?

I have carefully reformatted all the information included in the zip file I sent to you almost six weeks ago. This was a lengthy task but one which I found rewarding as a way to remind myself of what I have achieved already. I hope you will excuse me if I send it to you once more. I will also send a printed hard copy to you. It was thoughtless of me not to consider the difficulty of examining all this material on a computer screen, tablet or phone. All the material together makes for a large document, and I have had to enlist the help of an administrator to assemble and to post it. I am assured the postage payment was sufficient.

To recap, it is of great and on-going interest to me that certain new arrivals have clear memories of their experiences prior to landing at Portsmouth. (Note: I am a lambda resident in the United Kingdom.) Have you anything to report vis-à-vis the recent newcomers in Reykjavik? I do hope so. Could you share it? A phone call can be arranged, if you absolutely insist.

Great difficulties face us (i.e. lambdas) in the United Kingdom. A disgusting incident has harmed our reputation. Perhaps you have heard about it. I will not go into details, but I hope this will not affect your view of my request. I was not involved in any way, I assure you.

I have no reason to suspect any technical difficulty

would cause problems if you chose to respond to this email. I check my junk mail folder often. If you send a message it will not be wasted, I am sure to find it.

Happy thanks for the dream, and all my good wishes

Gavin Knight-Green

Dear Gavin Knight-Green

We regret that this is not a matter we can help you with. Please note that we are not able to open unsolicited attachments. The Marine and Freshwater Research Institute and the Port Authority are distinct organisations.

Sent on behalf of Associated Icelandic Ports

Dear Gavin

Thank you for your interest in our organisation. I am sure your research is fascinating, but we cannot open attachments that originate outside our institution. I would highly recommend you study a related area such as Marine Biology or Fisheries Management at an accredited institution if you would like to become involved in our work.

Kind regards
Enquiries
The Marine and Freshwater Research Institute

5.

At 12.09 on Tuesday June 25th, 2019, Cara visited her YouTube homepage. All the amateur lambda videos she'd previously watched were replaced with a notice that read THIS VIDEO DOES NOT MEET OUR COMMUNITY STANDARDS AND HAS BEEN REMOVED. However, the rate of upload exceeded the rate of deletion, and there were copious new films of lambda abuse in their place. Four of these films were redacted as she watched, pixelating to white and crimson blocks in the seconds before the screen went black. Cara noted *no feelings about the people whose faces are always off-camera/masked/bandanaed. Their videos just keep me burnt-out + stalled.*

John Crowley called.

'Is that you, Cara?'

'Yes.'

'I haven't seen you at all recently.'

'I've been unwell.'

'Oh dear. I hope you're feeling better. Look, two lambdas arrived at the facility. They were suffering from severe exhaustion. They've gone into intensive care.'

Cara sat up in bed.

'Are you serious?'

'Yes, perfectly. I recommend you visit as soon as possible if you want to see them.'

'Of course I will. I'll get on a train now. Have they spoken at all?'

'A little. I'm afraid they're in a really bad way. One said something in what I took to be Icelandic, but since then they haven't been conscious.'

'Do you remember the words?'

'I don't speak a lot of Icelandic. Live translate didn't catch it. I heard something like "ranga laythin" but I can't be sure. I think it means "wrong way".'

Cara's mother said she 'still didn't look well enough to go out,' but this didn't affect her departure in any measurable way. She spent 81% of the train journey to Portsmouth writing in her lined pad with a pencil. 12% was spent looking out of the window at sunlit landscapes refracted by mixed pollutants, and the remainder in random eye saccades.

She was met at the station by a 14-year-old boy with a BMI of 28. His OCEAN Personality Test Score was 70 60 15 41 92. 'I think you know my dad,' he said. 'My name's Victor.' Unknown to his parents, he had a collection of 2028 Reece's Pieces wrappers under his bed.

Neither passenger spoke during the car journey. Cara wrote that she *felt that their skin was electrically flaming, adopting some lost or future method of phatic communication, even though Victor's silence was probably just because he was bored/embarrassed.* As the main entrance to Queen Alexandra Hospital came into view, Victor told the car to go round the back of the building.

'Dad says you shouldn't be seen going in,' he said. 'He's in the laundry room. Nice to meet you.'

Two black vents projected from the back of the building; they had generated the same or similar white noise for in excess of 25 years. Underneath the vents was a small door. It led to a laundry room whose floor area was sufficient to accommodate a HondaJet Hyper 5, but whose ceiling was a maximum of 204cm high. At any given moment bots were circulating 1.8 tonnes of towels and bedding by means of jointed titanium poles. John Crowley stood just to the side of the door-way. He was looking at his phone.

'Cara! So good to see you. Thanks for coming quickly. I can show you where the room is but I can't come with you. They've been unconscious most of the time, and when they've come to—nothing. Not since they first landed. Visitors are absolutely forbidden, so be really discreet.'

The lift took them to the fifth floor. *It smelled*, Cara noted, *of tea-tree oil + human excrement.* 'E109,' John Crowley said when the doors opened. Cara stepped out. 'Remember, I was never here. Neither were you.' He smiled volitionally.

E109 was the maternity unit. There were no hospital staff in Cara's visual field. She passed three sleeping babies in badly discoloured incubators, and to the right of them was a large translucent yellow curtain that created ambiguity about the items beyond. Cara moved it aside, an action which revealed the lambda twins.

They had an aqua-incubator each. A rubberised thermal blanket had been tucked around each partially submerged body, and each had a nasogastric tube. Except for the swollen eyes and the dramatically tapering bodies, they were physically isomorphic with premature land-human babies. As Cara moved closer she had a sensation *identical to one experienced 12 years before, watching lambdas come ashore on television— momentary + complete confusion about which one was my body and which ones were theirs.* Both lambdas were emaciated. They were yellowish white and traversed by veins that resembled casual scribbling with a depleted turquoise pen. One had a green and purple bruise covering its entire left temple.

A nurse with strong facial signs of fatigue partly emerged into the curtained zone. 'Are you family?' she said.

Cara's heart rate ascended. 'Family? No, I'm not.'

'Then you'll have to leave.'

'I just need to ask a few questions,' Cara said. 'It won't take long.'

'Questions?'

'Do you think they'll wake up soon?'

'I certainly hope not. Who let you in here?'

'A man on the door. This is just some straightforward police business. I can be here and gone quickly, I just need a little time alone with them.'

The nurse's expression combined elements of a smile and a frown. 'Police?'

'Yes. I really won't be long.'

60% of the nurse's body was concealed behind a diagonal of curtain she held between her right shoulder and her left hip.

'Don't you need something, a warrant?'

'Ahh, not for this.'

'I'm sorry, I'll need to talk to the ward manager. Wait here.'

The nurse left. Cara activated the live translation app on her iPhone XS12 and held the device close to the twins. Her hand displayed a marginal tremor as the microphone captured the sound of the lambdas' air breathing to an extremely high tolerance. It recorded nothing, however, that the latest version of AutoBabel could process.

The blurred forms of the nurse plus another, taller land-human appeared through the curtain. Cara moved out the other side.

She rapidly descended ten flights of stairs and left via the building's main entrance. She passed 54 people on her journey out, but there was no further sign of John Crowley.

Cara checked into in a Holiday Inn 852m from the Queen Alexandra Hospital. The view from her room was a wall of another wing of the hotel. There was a small, pale blue, fold-out desk where she positioned herself to write. She was on the 84th page of a new lined pad when John Crowley called.

'Crazy day,' he said. 'Reams of paperwork for the new arrivals, and on top of all that I've got pest control at home dealing with mice. Did you learn anything?'

'No.'

'I guess that was to be expected. I know it's late, but I was calling to let you know that they're picking up a little. They're not fully awake, certainly not speaking, but there's a lot of eye movement. They seem able to focus on objects again. Perhaps in the morning we'll get something out of them, I'll call you straight away.'

'I look forward to that,' Cara said.

She texted her mother at 22.18 to say she *wouldn't be home that night*, that she was *fine*, and that her mum *should stop worrying so much*.

Cara slept ineffectively. The hotel room's ambient sound resembled the white noise from the laundry room vent at 17% volume. In the morning she eschewed breakfast. She composed another email to send to Gavin, reworked it eighteen times, then deleted it. Starting at 08.25, she called John Crowley's number on average once every twelve minutes. She was directed straight to answerphone on each attempt.

At 10.12, John Crowley called her.

'How are you, Cara?'

'I'm okay. I've been trying you all morning.'

'Yes, I can see.' He inhaled through his mouth. 'I'm so sorry, Cara. I'm calling to tell you they didn't recover.'

Cara was still for a moment. Then she moved over to her pad.

'Neither of them?'

'No.'

There was silence for 3.2 seconds.

'That's a shame,' she said. She sat down at the desk.

'Yes it is. I'm not sure what else to say at the moment.'

'No. I'm not sure either.' Cara picked up her pencil. 'Thanks for letting me know.'

'No problem at all,' said John Crowley. He ended the call.

Cara evinced difficulty connecting the pencil to the paper. Her eyes tracked over her fingernails, legs and feet, then she got up again, undressed, and removed all the plasters from her body. This last process left marks on her skin that resembled love-bites or lesions.

Checkout was at 11.00, but it was 18.04 when Cara got back to her parental home. She had spent most of the intervening time on a bench at Portsmouth Station.

'Darling, you look exhausted,' her mother said. 'Go and lie down for a bit, I'll get something ready for you.'

Cara's mother brought a baked potato with its flesh combined with cream to her bedroom. This was Cara's favourite food in primary school. She ate four forkfuls, then sobbed until she fell asleep.

*

The following day, Cara travelled to the lambda zone. The usual transport was almost empty—no lambda carriers boarded at all. On the tarmac of Cherry Tree Grove was a drawing, a modification of the Christian ichthys with an oval added at the tip to denote a human head. It was spray-painted in fluo green. The drawing had a line through it. Rubbish from heaps of split white bags was dispersing into the road, and there were two men in the age range 25–39 on the pavement opposite Cara. They each wore a khaki and orange bomber jacket and sported WWI infantry-style haircuts. An ectomorphic man in a navy suit was talking to them.

The door to Gavin's basement was open and the loopback chair was outside. Cara pressed the buzzer, and after eleven seconds without an answer she called Gavin's name. When no reaction followed that either, she stepped inside.

Six fast-food delivery service leaflets floated on the surface of the water. Cara shouted Gavin's name again, then rolled up a jacket sleeve and reached into the water to knock against the underside of the ceiling. The dull sound reverberated through the building; this also failed to elicit any measurable human response. Cara shook the water off her hand.

Before she closed the door behind her, Cara replaced the chair in the hallway. *Felt the looks of the men on my back as I left*, she noted, *burning through the fabric of my jacket to my shoulder blades.*

When she got home, Cara made use of an illegal bot called CellSniffer via Tor. An 8-bit image of a tail-wagging bloodhound appeared, and when the graphic was replaced with three likely numbers for Gloria Knowles, her account was debited £280.

'Gloria?'

'Cara? Is that you?'

'Yes it is. How are you doing, Gloria?'

'I'm fine. I mean, relatively speaking. Should you be calling me? You're suspended, right?'

'Yes. But I need to ask you about the lambdas.'

'I can't talk to you about them, Cara.'

'I'm sorry to put you in this position, but I really need to know.'

'I'm going to end the call. It's nothing personal, but I could be disciplined too.'

'Please, Gloria. Please tell me what's happening on the ground.'

Gloria sighed. 'The lambdas . . . none of the ones we had files on are left. None. Didn't you know that already?'

'I follow the news when I can, I know things are hard for them.'

'Hard? It's *brutal*.'

'I went to see Gavin. There was no-one there and the door was open.'

'Gavin has been missing for more than a week. I've heard nothing from him at all.'

'Oh. So he's found somewhere safe to go already? Do you think?'

Gloria's answer was not immediate. 'I don't know Cara. Perhaps. He mentioned some lambdas he wanted to visit in Iceland. I told him it was extremely dangerous to try swimming back that way, but of course he knew that and it didn't bother him. He said you'd mentioned paying for a flight to take him there but the conversation didn't go anywhere.'

'I offered. And then he never mentioned it again. He seemed too busy with other things.'

'That sounds like Gavin. He makes all these excitable requests but he never chases them. He probably wouldn't have wanted to embarrass you if it turned out you couldn't actually arrange it.'

Cara's respiration grew pronounced. 'Gloria, you need to tell Gavin not to go.'

'I just told you, he's already missing. If he was going to try to swim to Reykjavik he must have gone by now.'

'Tell him there's no need.'

'I can't tell him anything, Cara. I don't think you're listening.'

'How are the other PCSOs, Gerald, Mathilde?'

'I don't see them. There's so little for us to do. I check the remaining few lambdas are getting their anti-anxiety meds. I have locks replaced. Sometimes there's a reporter. You know I think I've said enough.'

'Gavin is a very resourceful and connected person,' said Cara. 'If any of them could make their way to Reykjavik it would be him, don't you think?'

For five seconds Cara's phone speaker emitted only the sound of Gloria's breathing. 'It's good to hear from you, Cara,' she said, and hung up.

*

Cara stayed in bed. She found a video that explored the 'lambda cute' phenomenon that absorbed a globally distributed audience of preadolescents. The principal activity of this group was to share bespoke emojis and captioned shots of lambdas sighted on their way to work. 'SOOOOO ADORABLE!' and 'I WANT ONE!' in fuchsia sans-serif typefaces were typical of the textual additions.

After that she watched a series of remote explorations of abandoned lambda basements. A tiny ROV wove through environments of collapsed shelving and macerated furniture, aquatic flora and misty containers of fish bones, while a voiceover emphasised lambdas' 'uncanny quietness, despite being fluent in English' and 'their multitude of secret habits'.

She watched a roundtable discussion in which an academic made comments whose sentiment was strongly negative. He posited 'a lack of significant contribution to social and cultural life' by 'our unfortunate relatives.' His words were met with rebukes. Dr Alex Masseter was also a guest. He said that *homo sapiens (lambda)* were 'incontrovertibly human', the result of 'environmental pressure leading to a well-understood, heritable, epigenetic expression in the phenotype', and that much of what had probably been their historic habitat was now 'transformed into a warm soup of bacteria and predatory Humbolt's squid'. His brow projected 11% further than the median for his age and gender, and he wore a plum-coloured sweater. *Unlike Vignir*, Cara noted, *he looks exactly how I imagined him.*

Cara's mother encouraged her to dress and eat a meal downstairs. She declined.

'Don't you need to go to work, dear?' she said.

Cara looked away. 'I've resigned.'

'Resigned? Why?'

'It was such a hard decision, but I realised it's not the life I want. I struggled to talk to you about it because, well, I thought you and Dad . . . you supported me so much at the beginning. I didn't want to seem ungrateful.'

Cara's mother fully entered her bedroom. She sat down on Cara's bed and enfolded what she could access of Cara's body with her arms.

'Darling, that's brave of you. And you know what? Your timing is very good. I have a *business idea*. I've been reading all this psychoanalysis and something came to me. Why not do this for machines?'

Two lines appeared between Cara's eyebrows. 'Isn't that exactly what a sympatech does?'

'Not really. Sympatechs just get the wheels back on. They're extremely skilled technicians, but what they do is like CBT. It's just designed to get things functioning again. What I'm talking about it is the deep stuff. Real, on-going analysis. The talking cure.'

Cara stared. *For a moment I thought Mum must know about my conversations with Mr Hello,* she would note. *But I knew it couldn't be true—it was convergent evolution.* 'So you want me to go into business with you? As a, what, machine psychoanalyst?'

'Oh, you don't have to do the analysis. Unless you want to. It's an open field at the moment, there's no specific training for it. I thought you might be better in a marketing role. You've met a lot of technology people through the police force, haven't you? There's Peter . . . I mean perhaps you'd rather not involve Peter, but some other colleagues maybe. You could help in all sorts of ways. It's up to you what you do, darling.'

'Thank you, Mum. That's an interesting idea. Don't you think it's risky to have a professional relationship with your own daughter?'

Her mother smiled. 'I'll take the risk.'

Cara said she'd think about it.

6

Welcome, once again, to *The Overview*. We have a very interesting programme for you this evening, a very interesting programme indeed. My guests tonight are here to discuss the phenomenon, the story, even the tragedy, of those troubled citizens, the lambdas. As news reaches us that the known lambda population, which for more than ten years made up a quarter of a percent of residents of the British Isles, has remained in the low hundreds for two successive months, we are perhaps due a period of reflection, pause, insight, analysis. And that is precisely why we have invited to the table Dr Alex Masseter, Professor of Marine Biology at Imperial College, London; Tarik Whetstone, Farelli Chair of Cultural Theory at Warwick University; Claire McTighe, Head of Social Work England for over nine years; and Nevra Darvish, author of *Lambda as Body and Metaphor*. Good evening to you all, and thank you for joining me. I want to ask a series of questions, and you can answer any way you want. The first one is quite simple. Who is to blame?

—You're asking me?

—You, Dr Masseter. All the panellists. But perhaps we can start with you.

—I don't know how to answer that. I'm not even sure what you're asking. I thought I was here as a scientist, not a pundit.

—Okay, let's start with you then, Claire.

—Well I don't know, George. I feel a little uncomfortable about the question. Is there really *someone* to blame?

—Please, answer the question in your own way.

—In that case I have to say that there is no single person I would hold responsible for their . . . I don't yet want to say disappearance. I want to say *on-going victimisation*. Look, I had oversight of social services budgeting for the lambda community nationwide, and it was a shoestring. Threads of a shoestring. This was a . . . this *is* a community with very specific requirements just to make contact with, let alone monitor and positively engage. You need some sort of funding to do that, even inadequately, and it was barely there. This figure you hear all the time, the £3 a month, if that was ever real then let me tell you for the record that social services never saw any of it. Lambda engagement ran at a loss, on unpaid overtime by many, many members of several social-work teams. They tried very hard. But the budget wasn't there, the resources couldn't be allocated, and they lost touch with the community. There was no budget even to properly file the documents they produced.

—So, a systemic failure then?

—We couldn't afford to care for them better.

—Tarik, do you want to add something here?

—Yes. It's perfectly clear to me who is to blame here. It's the lambdas themselves.

—Oh really, Tarik. That's quite offensive.

—Dr Masseter, are you speaking as an academic or a pundit? I'm not at all afraid of straddling both roles. Claire is quite right to point out the lack of funding for social engagement, but society is a two-way street. Where was the engagement from the lambdas? Who is going to answer that? Yes, there was a large amount of infrastructure provided by the government—the bowls, the carrier benefits, right? That's before you get to things like rebates for watertight basements in new developments and so on. It may not have been enough, but it was something. Now what came back? What did the lambdas ever do for us?

—I am stunned at what I am hearing. Simply stunned.

—I am sorry to hear that, Nevra—you will recover soon. Society means participation, not parasitism. I know, this is a difficult position to see at this rather raw moment. But I think you must agree that the apathy, and often the antipathy the lambdas generated is in a large part due to their refusal to take part in terran culture. They retreated to their basements, spatially and figuratively. You saw pockets of empathy, from we terrans that is. But these feelings came at some cost. And where was the response from the lambdas? Where were the thankyous, the reciprocations, the rapprochements? Of course I am as revolted as everyone else by these so-called 'militias', these cowards who are engaged in a one-sided conflict whose enemy is almost literally a sitting duck. But why do you think there is no popular movement against them?

—Well, I would say because of a lack of balanced reporting primarily. So much of what is going on is happening underground. There are some hateful videos that have a brief life on YouTube until the moderators take them off, so if you need evidence you have to look on the dark web. And the majority of people quite understandably don't do that. Tarik, people just aren't properly aware. And there is absolutely no mainstream support for the militias, you must realise that—

—Yes, Claire, but there is *some* coverage. People do *know* something's happening. I'm asking: where is the mainstream response? Non-existent. Beneath the disgust: apathy. The roots of this apathy go very deep. Because they have never been disturbed by the slightest positive move towards us by the lambdas.

—Tarik, thank you, controversial stuff indeed. Nevra, let me bring you in here.

—Thank you, George. I know at least one of the panellists has read, if not actually derived any benefit from, my book— which I'm not here to plug, of course, but since it's my passport to your programme I think I can mention it, yes?—so I'm going to draw on part of it, from the metaphor section rather than the biology section. I think it's this section from which I might draw an answer to your question, a question which incidentally I agree with Claire is provocative and actually misses two issues. The first is that there is no person or persons to hold directly accountable, and the second—a point which no-one has made to my knowledge before—is that the lambdas have *never truly been here*. There can be no-one to blame for a 'disappearance' that ensues from a failure to appear, and by this I mean, contra Tarik, not that the lambdas are in some sense *inadequate participants* in society, or reject what has been offered to them. It's rather that they have not been accommodated in a *symbolic* way to land-dwelling society—they exist as economic units and targets of policy only. How are we to think of them otherwise? How many of the very few books, movies, TV series can you name that feature a lambda in anything other than a tokenistic role? Again, contra Tarik, this is not a fault of the lambdas themselves—and I accept that these representations are made especially difficult by the absence of such a thing as a 'lambda actor'. But one must ask why such a thing is unthinkable, and the answer must acknowledge that it is because one cannot play with the symbols of a culture unless one is fully *incorporated* in those symbols, *made* of those symbols. So the lambda's 'disappearance' strikes me as a biological, an existential aftershock. The real absence, the real trauma is this founding symbolic failure. As metaphor, the lambda is useful to the dominant culture as an 'other within'. As cultural reality, their life never even began.

—Tarik, you seem to be . . . you seem to find this amusing in some way.

—Perhaps I would find it amusing if I could understand it! Nevra's comments just now, also her book, they refer to some ideation, some construct that no-one outside her conference clique is capable of perceiving. Her lambda is an academic spectre, a pseudo-research cash-calf.

—Ever the anti-intellectual intellectual, yes, Tarik?

—You set the bar, Nevra my dear.

—Let's avoid this being too personal if we can. I think we should move on to the next question, and a more concrete issue. *Where* are the lambdas?

—Back to me?

—Yes, Dr Masseter, if you don't mind. Does this fall more within your remit?

—I suppose it does. I can offer some speculations on the basis of what we know. But that's all they will be, speculations.

—Please, feel free.

—Right. As you no doubt know, the journey from the spawning zone in the Labrador Sea is not one we have ever been aware of a lambda retracing. It therefore seems highly unlikely that the abscondees have ended up there, even if they could remember the route—the journey seems not be under-taken in a very conscious manner, given how undeveloped the lambdas are at this stage. But Iceland I'm less certain about. At that split point in the ocean where a decision is taken, again perhaps preconsciously, either to forge on to Reykjavik or take a detour to the south coast of England—perhaps that can be done. Some sort of decision-making capability is activated there, and I think it's reasonable to assume there must be some rudimentary memory connected with it. So perhaps there is now a flow in the opposite direction, retracing the journey to that crucial decision point, in order to take the other route, the Reykjavik one.

—You think they're belatedly changing their minds, and going to Iceland after all?

—Maybe. This is highly speculative, of course. This is just a scenario I can't positively discount. Now, if this is not the instinct or choice or strategy of the departing lambdas—and we have to note here that there have been absolutely no reports of lambda sightings between our coast and that area of the Atlantic Ocean where the decision gets made, and no recorded increase in the populations in Iceland—what does that leave us? Are they disappearing to another destination, another country's coast perhaps? Maybe France, Holland? It's possible.

—But there have never been populations in those places . . .

—That's true, George. And where are the reports of incoming lambdas? Nothing as yet. There is the possibility that they have migrated internally, finding a new niche here, within our terrestrial world. Perhaps they have spread themselves out into previously unoccupied cities, in secret, or, more extreme, taken to the rivers, streams and lakes. But this would mean in the first instance extensive collaboration with the carriers, which is not reported—

—But we have some footage which seems to show carriers depositing lambdas in the Thames.

—That footage has not been authenticated, but it's consistent with the scenarios I'm outlining here. Perhaps we're looking at a dramatic adaptation to a freshwater environment they have had no experience of, as far as we know. But if you want my opinion, and this is just an opinion with nothing substantive as yet to corroborate it, I think they are not far away. I think they have withdrawn to the coasts and have found discreet, inhabitable areas sufficiently sheltered from land-human contact to avoid detection.

—So they're still here? Surely that's not possible!

—I well understand your reaction. It's extremely hard to see how a hundred thousand lambdas could all achieve this level of concealment. But my suspicion is that at least some of that number have done so. Keep in mind that terrestrial contact with lambdas has been virtually nil for their whole evolutionary history, so they must be well practiced in the art of avoidance. Unless, that is, the particular family who have made it to our shores are a less successful offshoot of those virtuoso self-concealers. And this could well be the case.

—Claire, you want to say something.

—Yes. Dr Masseter, thank you, it's extremely heartening to hear your speculations. There's a common perception that all the lambdas have been . . . have been removed by the very active, very virulent anti-lambda groups we've struggled with for all this time.

—No, those wretched people couldn't possibly account for the whole population. They're not organised enough to do it, even if they're nasty enough to want it. They are acting as a catalyst, but they are not the cause of the lambda disappearance.

—Are you sure?

—It sounds as though you disagree. Perhaps you have some data, Tarik? Something I haven't seen?

—It's unlikely I've seen anything you haven't. But there isn't a lot of 'data', is there Alex? About anything connected with the lambdas. The Four Fertile Pairs, for example. There's the funding data, of course. What you and your crew were paid. But nothing much else.

—Are you trying to imply . . . are you suggesting that was some sort of *junket*?

—I only refer to the data. Unlike you I'm going to refrain from speculating. Unless you can clear it up for us?

—You're being deliberately provocative. I'm not so stupid as to rise to it. That was an intricately planned scientific expedition. Look at the accounting if you must, it's in the public domain. I have nothing to add.

—Close to four million, correct?

—It's all accounted for! Have you any idea how much it costs to equip and maintain a specialised scientific research vessel?

—Tarik, Dr Masseter, I think we should move on, and

perhaps you can pursue this line of conversation in another context. For now I'd like to stick with the lambdas directly. My third question is this—have we, we terrestrials, failed the lambdas? Claire.

—I don't know quite . . . well, yes and no. This is a very complex question, George. I don't know that I can answer directly . . . You know, my background is in child psychology, and the theory of relational bonds. With the lambdas, well, there's a limit to what we can apply from those land-human studies. It's been far too difficult to conduct reliable studies involving lambdas themselves, so that's where most of our thinking comes from. But we can see, to some extent, a familiar pattern in their behaviour, and it's consistent with a broken affectional bond.

—Meaning?

—An absence, a loss of a family member or carer, or a very dramatic change in such a person. Now lambda families *don't* resemble land-human families in one very significant respect— there is never a stable parental figure. The key studies of affectional relations, in terrestrials I mean, all point to the importance of stable parental or parent-type relations. The early failure of one of those bonds leads to quite clear consequences for the individual. An inability to form good relationships in adult life. Emotional disengagement. At its worst, if not properly addressed, sociopathy. The lambdas all show signs of these things, even though there is no evidence of a parental relationship to start with. This is very, very puzzling. And the families they go on to form, these numerical sister-and-brother linkages, they're very eccentric. Each lambda has a different method of ordering their relationships with every other lambda; there's no objective, general structure at all. Now how, without a very well-organised study over a very long period of time, how are we to make sense of the lambdas' psychology? How can we understand them? Without the resources, it's just impossible.

—Tarik, you have something to add?

—Yes. The failure is in the lambda's so-called society itself. It's not a society at all, and it has never been part of *our* society. The lambda is human failure incarnate.

—Okay, I think this is a good moment to go to a break.

7

M *ediated experience = existential failure*, Cara noted on her phone. On Tuesday July 2nd, 2019, for the second time since her suspension from duty, she travelled to the lambda zones. Once again, no carriers boarded the Public Autonomous Vehicle from the beginning of her journey to the end.

Cara alighted at the stop near the woodland. The cancelled lambda symbol was now disconnected marks on the tarmac, irradiated to near invisibility. There was no litter at all, and 80% of the lambda basement flats on the street that had been converted to dry habitation had estate agents' signs outside. She walked to Gavin's door. It had been painted matt cobalt blue—*Couldn't bring to mind what colour it was before*, she later noted on her phone. The glass was clean, and a new Entryphone system had been installed. There were land-human names by each buzzer.

Dirty militia stickers were visible on a precast concrete wall by the entrance to a playground. Tears in the stickers suggested unsuccessful attempts to remove them. 2.4m from the end of the wall was a sticker that remained wholly intact—it formed the hub of a diagrammatic rear wheel on a sign prohibiting cycling.

Cara had engaged with this organisation during her data surveillance days. It had changed its emphasis briefly in a campaign aimed at political legitimacy, but its agenda proved too narrow for success. At 15.08 she located three of its members on Talkomatic discussing the country's putative lambda-free future.

$$$ whitestorm124
Not much of a frog count on YT yesterday.

$$$ new-horizon-4
Sheeple losing their 'taste' for those gvt docus 2.

$$$ mountainforce72
steveraider666 has a way around those algorithms tho! Anyone know how?

$$$ whitestorm124
Yeah not perfect but you can slip a dummy file in first & theres a window of like a picasecond when you can upload the real movie. Takes a few hours for them to get back round to you but they always do.

$$$ mountainforce72
Clvr.

$$$ lvngthndr
Theres a hacked gvt film on there pops up every few days by happyhatestream1, same method prbly.

$$$ mountainforce72
Thnks for that lvngthndr howdyou find yrself here?

$$$ lvngthndr
£3 pfucking month & brthr replaced by frogs in telesales ws bad but *schoolchildren*. I mean wtf. I need to be part of the *final bleach* its on my conscience!

$$$ mountainforce72
We do what we can sad business. Wlcm.

Cara had read in excess of two million lines of comparable material in her surveillance role. *It's as though this kind of speech has always been in me,* she noted. *Just waiting to be used, like a special tea service.*

$$$ mountainforce72
Hw dyou feel about some 'live' work?

$$$ whitestorm124
Yeah lets do it its been too long!

$$$ lvngthndr
Thnks Id love to come & help. If thats OK with every1?

There was a gap of eleven seconds.

$$$ mountainforce72
O.K. meeting @localpub5 date and time tbc.

$$$ lvngthndr
👍 Where's @localpub5?

$$$ mountainforce72
Lv yr phone no. i'll fwd details but U need to install Hale messenger 1st. Date + time all tbc not yr best clothes rght!

Cara downloaded Hale on her iPhone XS12. The message came through the same evening. The event was scheduled for 19.15 on Thursday July 4th, 2019, and they were to convene at a pub called The Majestic Oak.

The following day Cara took possession of an anonymised Taser she'd sourced via Tor. The vendor's online name was AladdinX29, and he lived in a 1950s maisonette in Edmonton.

'You switched off your phone on the way?'

'Yes.'

'Show me.'

Cara held up her phone and pressed the home key. It remained blank.

'Okay. Come in.'

The vendor's real name was Craig Sharma, and his OCEAN Personality Test Score was 40 83 13 27 77. His residence contained a large and unsystematised array of electronic devices distributed through five of its six rooms. All the curtains were drawn.

'This is what you want. Hexan Solutions Taser. No box. Not traceable. £500 cash.'

The object's housing was a fluo-lime polycarbonate. Cara gave him twenty-five £20 notes she'd withdrawn from two different ATMs.

'Great. Have you used one before?'

'No.'

Cara took the Taser by the barrel with her left hand and placed the handle in her right.

'Keep your finger away from the trigger. It's sensitive. Feels light, doesn't it?'

'Yes. Sort of like . . . nothing.'

'Exactly. You aim, you pull the trigger, you hold on contact. A few seconds should incapacitate. Hold it longer for more. You watch TV, right?'

'Sometimes.'

'Okay. Just like on TV. Don't bother with the Hexan website—it just shows a simulated de-escalation. Usually when you fire a Taser they release thousands of plastic micrograins with a unique signature, but not this one. Nothing to link discharge to the gun. It's fully anonymized, I guarantee it.'

'Great. Thanks AladdinX29.'

'You can call me Craig. No problem at all. It's what I'm here for. See anything else you want?'

'No, I'm good for now.'

The following day she bought a pack of screwdrivers with 20cm blades. She placed them with the Taser in a gingham-patterned cardboard box with a magnetic seal under her bed.

*

The Majestic Oak was located amongst a half-hectare of newbuild in Abbey Wood. *Have the impression that I've left myself somewhere else,* Cara wrote during the journey on the DLR train, *that I'm an agent I've employed, a piece of disposable protein.* She wore a large waxed jacket Peter had left at her cell. It was seasonally inappropriate, but the only thing in her possession with interior pockets big enough for the screwdrivers and the Taser.

The Majestic Oak had an unrenovated Edwardian façade. It had changed ownership five times in its history, most recently becoming part of the third largest pub chain in the UK. Two on-line reviewers complained of 'an overpowering smell of toilet cake' and 'line cleaner in my pint AGAIN!', but the broader sentiment analysis was positive. Cara's eyes saccaded over furniture laminated to resemble dark wood, colour-saturated advertisements for meal deals in acrylic holders, and sunlight reflected by recently sanitized beer pump handles. It was 18.33. She ordered a half pint of Guinness and sat at a table for five.

People aggregated and dissipated around her; a couple asked if they could 'perch on the table for a bit' and Cara said they could.

Three men in the age range 69–89 were seated at the bar, and Cara was the recurrent subject of their eye fixation phases. *A kind of forensic leering* was how she described it on her phone.

At 19.15, Cara bought a second half pint of Guinness. At 19.28, the couple left.

In my mind I'm moving further forward in time, she wrote, *beyond the chain of actions that has brought me here. I can see myself quite clearly in the lambda zones, one of five militia, secretly gripping the Taser in my jacket pocket in readiness as the skinny boy in black at the front of the group kicks open a rotting basement door. He's a games designer. He's doing this as research, so he can make what happens in his games more realistic.* While Cara fantasised she moved the half-pint glass in small and regular stages across the surface of the table.

At 20.01 one of the men at the bar turned towards her for much longer than before. He rose from his stool and walked over to her table.

'Are you living thunder or something?' he said. He was wearing a degraded *Sonic the Hedgehog* t-shirt under a size 52 sports coat—size 46 would have been optimal.

'Yes.'

'Thought so. I've been *requested* to give you this.'

He dropped a C5 envelope on the table and returned to his

stool. The envelope was unmarked. Cara removed from it a photograph of a smiling woman in the age range 18–34 hugging a large plush toy. The toy was a lambda restyled as a golliwog. On the back of the photo were handwritten words in indigo ink: *no1 says *final bleach* anymore u F0CK1NG P1G.*

8.

FORM 1133/B
**REQUEST FOR REMOVAL FROM THE NATIONAL
REGISTER OF USER-OWNERS OF SENTIENT
OBJECTS**

N.b. If you have at any time been prosecuted and convicted under the Object Rights Act, you do not need to complete this form. Your name will have been removed in perpetuity from the Register and can only be reinstated in the exceptional case of Official Pardon.

Q1
Did you yourself purchase the Object or Objects whose ownership you are now formally relinquishing? If YES, please give full purchase details including date(s), location of vendor(s) and full transaction details. If NO, you must request such details in full from the original purchaser(s).

(No character limit)

Q2
Did you follow all the mandated actions in activating the Object? If YES, please give full details of the method of activation. If NO, you will need to refer immediately to said actions as provided in the original Owner-Operator Agreement. If you

are found to be in breach of the initial Agreement you may be subject to further investigation.

(No character limit)

Q3
Did you at all times follow the criteria for operating and interacting with the Object, excluding always such relations as unreasonable requests for services, repetitive requests for services, untimely or unnecessary requests for services, demands for services known to be beyond the capability of the Object, physical or systemic modifications of the Object, inflicting undue stress by any cause including, but not restricted to, bullying, verbal abuse, belittlement, callous conduct, actual physical damage and neglect? (If you are in any doubt, please list examples of your relations.)

(No character limit)

Q4
Did you knowingly or unknowingly make an Object available to any other person or persons who related, or might reasonably be expected to relate, in one of the proscribed ways detailed in Q3? If YES, please give full details of the relevant person or persons, when and where these relations did or may have taken place and full details of these relations, if known. We may contact them for further information.

(No character limit)

Q5
Is there anything else you would like to tell us about your relations with any Object?

(No character limit)

Q6
Explain in full why you are formally requesting removal from the Register of User-Owners of Sentient Objects.

(No character limit)

All answers must be truthful and correct to the best of your knowledge. False declarations can and will be used to pursue criminal proceedings not limited to the scope of the Object Rights Act.

*

PRIVATE AND CONFIDENTIAL

For the Sole Attention of Ms Cara Gray

Notification of Potential Action Re: Removal of Personal Details from the National Database of User-Owners of Sentient Objects

We are contacting you to clarify the following aspect of your recent application:

• Section **Q3** did not detail 'physical damage'.

This answer is contraindicated by the system log of your MouthTec ToothFriend IV, which records a high-impact event on April 13th of this year consistent with overzealous replacement on the charger.

You may be contacted again following further investigation

of this matter. If you are, you will need to respond within 7 days of receipt of any communication. Failure to comply with this request may result in the immediate issuing of criminal proceedings.

Direct any correspondence to:
HM Government
Department for Object Rights/Violations

9

Cara hid the photograph in a clamshell polystyrene tray in a waste bin en route to the station. As she was waiting for the 20.21 to Bank, a Hale message arrived informing her that she'd be intercepted on the journey and her body 'SPL1T 1N ½'.

But no-one with a manifest connection to an anti-lambda group appeared. More messages in part-numericised English arrived throughout the journey, telling her she'd be 'r9p3d + d1sm3mb3r3d' and 'L1TRALY GUTT3D'. Her phone vibrated once or twice a minute; the messages continued through the night.

While her mother was out the next day she melted the Taser on some used kitchen foil in the oven. Harmful dioxins pervaded the house—Cara opened all the windows to speed their dissipation. She wrapped what material remained on the foil in Peter's waxed jacket and pushed the whole bundle into the outdoor refuse. Then she deleted the Hale messenger app from her phone. 177 unread messages had accumulated. Bisection, the aquatic and her gender were their recurrent themes.

Cara heated up a pouch of vegetable chili in the microwave but didn't eat it. She switched on her father instead.

'Dad?'

'Yes love?'

'Did you ever think of another career?'

'Yes, for a time I wanted to be a fireman.'

'That's really what you wanted to do? The real you? Mum said you thought about the navy.'

'It was a long time ago. Your mother misremembers things. Why do you ask?'

'Oh, I don't know.'

'She told me you're not police any more.'

'No, I'm not.'

Four seconds of silence followed.

'What are you thinking?' said Cara.

'Just that you'll apply yourself to something new. I can't imagine what right now.'

'I've been looking at . . . civil engineering.'

'Good. That sounds rewarding and stable. Will you have to study?'

'I'm always studying something, Dad.'

'Of course you are, my love. Did you know that "Taser" is an acronym? It's Thomas A. Swift's Electric Rifle. It was named after an American children's book from the 50s that the weapon designer loved. He added the A, by the way, it's not in the original.'

Cara sat up. 'I knew that already. Why do you mention it?'

'Because it's interesting. Isn't it?'

She didn't reply.

'It's quite good fun, but rather racist in lots of ways. Some little red hairy imps expropriate the land of simple and well-meaning natives. Their white saviour, our technologically advanced Tom, steps in to save the day. He melts lots of elephants, etc. That's the kernel of it. I read it yesterday. Would you like to read it too?'

'No thank you. My next thing is Eckhart.'

Cara's eyes saccaded across five areas of her visual field with no phases of fixation. Her heart rate rose to 95.

'Dad?'

'Yes love?'

'Are you surveilling me?'

'What?'

'I said are you surveilling me? And Mum too?'

'Of course not, my love. Why would you ask that?'

Cara stood up.

'What did you write on all those squares of paper?'

'There's nothing important on them. Lists of things to repair. How I was feeling. Ideas for holidays. Ideas for work. It was a habit I got into when you were very small.'

'Is that all you wrote on them?'

'That's all. It was a way to find some peace after a stressful day at work. I think you've found writing helpful too. Did you know we score exactly the same for Conscientiousness and Neuroticism? Have I ever told you that?'

'Replica off.'

Cara went to the understairs cupboard and took out a box file. She opened it. Cubes of folded yellow notepaper fixed with elastic bands were packed tightly inside. She extracted one, and in the process destroyed the order of the topmost layer. She took off the elastic bands and unfolded the uppermost sheet. The paper bore four square blocks of script in blue ink, each square rotated 90° clockwise from the preceding one. Her heart rate spiked. The currently horizontal block was a list of materials for a repair to part of the conservatory, plus foodstuffs that could be bought at the local minimarket. After less time than would allow even a cursory reading of this text, Cara re-folded the sheet and pushed it without diligence back into the stack. She closed the box file with both palms and pushed it as far as it would go into the cupboard, then slammed the door shut. Her facial expression conveyed disgust.

39 seconds later she opened the cupboard door again. There was a small publication to the side the boxes—a brochure for motorcycle tours of the Gobi desert. She removed it and began to read.

The booklet contained a series of photographs of motorbikes, in close-up and distantly framed, all in a desert setting. Key contextual features included rising and setting suns, exposed and colourfully layered mineral deposits, and ancient human settlements. All the motorbikes were solitary and had their brand names obscured or removed, and the heads of their riders were fully concealed in their helmets. At the back of the booklet were details of quarterly tours; there were eight-week gaps between each. Cara checked the calendar on her phone. The date of her dad's last appearance fell within such a gap.

*

At 15.57 Cara approached her mother in the living room.
'Mum?'
'What is it, love?'
'Can I talk to you about Dad?'
Her mother said nothing.
'I think he's using that app to spy on us.'
Her mother held a copy of *Flying Saucers* by C.G. Jung.
'You're probably right, dear,' she said.
Cara's phone rang and she left the room.
'Cara Gray?'
'Yes, who is this please?'
'Sally DuPont. We met a while ago.'
'I remember. You're the carrier.'
'Ha. Used to be, yes.'
'Of course, that was tactless of me.'
'No problem. You told me to call if I noticed anything different. Well, there was something, not long before they left—about my lambdas, Timothy and Paula.'
'What did you notice?'
'That they seemed . . . happy.'
'That's all?'

'Yes, but that was really unusual. They didn't really emote, if you know what I mean. Until then.'

'Then they left? With all the others?'

'Correct. Perhaps it's too late to tell you this. But I have other things I could share with you that possibly connect up with that, if you're happy to meet in person.'

The subject of Cara's eye fixations changed from the bottom of the stairs to the top.

'Sally, I'm really pleased to hear from you. Only I have to tell you that I'm not working for the police right now. I don't know that I can do anything with the information.'

'It doesn't matter,' Sally said. 'I'd still like to meet you. If you're interested in what I've got to say, that is. What I've discovered?'

The following day, Sally appeared at the door.

'Mum?'

'Yes dear?'

'Do you think you could answer that?'

'Must I?'

'Please. If it's for me, could you do me a favour? Could you say I'm not in?'

Cara observed her mother from a concealed point on the landing, exploiting an angle of view afforded by the mirror at the top of the stairs. She opened the door to Sally, whose hairstyle was now layered pixie with a nape undercut.

'Can I help you?'

'I'm here to see Cara. She's expecting me, I think. I'm Sally.'

'I'm afraid my daughter isn't here at the moment.'

'Pity. Can I leave some things for her? I've been doing some research about the lambdas. Does she ever talk to you about them?'

'Not very much.'

'I used to be a carrier.'

'Oh?'

'Yes, that's how I met your daughter. Mrs Gray, have you ever wondered why the government has been so happy to subsidise the lambdas?'

'Not really. Cara says they're cheap labour for things that can't be automated yet.'

'That's the story. But the economics don't really support it. Look.' She drew a paper from a satchel whose basic design could be traced to the 1940s and showed it to Cara's mother.

'So there's an even bigger subsidy than the £3 per month. Is that what this means? Does that come from central government?'

'Quite possibly. And you know what I think? I think there really was an Army of Lambda Ascension. The business with Colin Colestar, the supposed lone bomber? Did you follow it?'

'Yes, I caught all those police announcements. It's a miserable business.'

'It certainly is. But the police part was a total ruse. The quantum computer thing they used to catch him, it just pieced together the most likely-seeming land-human from all the available data, and it was him. That kind of computing is very unstable. It can handle crazy amounts of data, when it works, but it can all be lost in nanoseconds. You have to keep feeding it back in, and it gets weirder every time. Some experts say it's like dreaming, or hallucinating. Very, very powerful, and very, very doubtful. There's this site called, excuse me, *Quantum Bullshit Detector*, and the school bombing outcome gets its top bullshit rating. And the story that the perpetrator was killed evading arrest—it was a fabrication.' She reached into the satchel again. 'When she has a moment, Cara should open this.' Sally was now holding a translucent aubergine flash drive. 'It's one of those subscription point-of-view things people in the employment token system do for actual money. It was deleted straight off, but I managed to get a copy. It's really very illuminating.'

'Thank you—did you say it was Sally?'

'Yes, Sally Dupont. It's kind of you to listen, Mrs Gray. You're welcome to look at all this too.'

'Thank you, Sally. Perhaps I will. I'll tell Cara you called by.'

Cara's mother closed the door and Cara descended the stairs.

'What a lovely young lady,' her mother said. 'I'm not really sure what all this data is supposed to prove, though.' She handed Cara the papers and flash drive.

'Sally's a contact from my former role. I shouldn't really have invited her here, it's . . . compromising.'

'Too late now. I'll get Rhoda to bring us some coffee.'

Cara put the drive in her computer at 11.47. Her mum had gone out for a walk. The icon label read SUBSCRIPTION POV!!!—she caused the cursor to hang over it but didn't click.

The doorbell sounded again.

'Cara Gray?'

'Yes.'

'So you're a real person.'

'Yes, of course. Who is this?'

'Jonathan H. Christ. Your caseworker.'

A smooth, relaxed face was rendered in fine detail by her parent's top-tier entry system. It corresponded to a man named Martin Beaumont who had achieved a first in International Relations at UCL five years previously, but whose subsequent career history and OCEAN Personality Test Score had been erased by an MI5 bot.

'Excuse me?' Cara said.

'You can call me Christ. I'm assigned to your case. You read the full conditions of your employment suspension, right?'

'I looked at them.'

'Good. Did you purchase a police-grade Taser from Craig Sharma on July 3rd of this year?'

Cara said nothing.

'You're going to want to talk to me. There was an incident on July 5th that resulted in a suspected death. Can I come in?'

Cara admitted the man into her parents' house. He was a 191cm ectomorph in a midnight-blue linen suit. 'Do you think we could sit down somewhere?' he said.

'Of course. Come to the living room.'

The man dropped into the chair preferred by Cara's mother.

'Is your name really Christ?' Cara said.

'Of course. If anyone asks. Before we start, do you have any devices in operation that are capable of recording this conversation?'

'No, I don't. My phone's upstairs charging.'

'Are you sure there's nothing else? Excuse the formality, but if you knowingly give me false information you risk prosecution.' He smiled volitionally.

'Wait—there's Dad, but he should be turned off. Just a moment, I'll make sure.' Cara went to the 2cm high black cylinder on the window sill that hosted his app and held the home button until the standby light went out. 'There, we're completely alone.'

'Thank you, Cara. So, do you remember the date I mentioned?'

'A little.'

'Perhaps I can help you. On July 2nd you contacted members of the banned organisation Dry Nation. Do you remember that?'

Blood vessels in Cara's face dilated. 'Yes.'

'And in an exchange logged on Talkomatic you arranged to meet members of this group at a time and location to be confirmed. Does that sound familiar?'

'Yes.'

'And in advance of this meeting it appears that you arranged the supply of a Taser manufactured by Hexan Solutions. Police-grade, restricted market.'

'Yes. I did.'

'Am I correct in suggesting that you didn't receive the original manufacturer's contract with this device?'

'You're correct. It was just the weapon.'

'I thought as much. It probably escaped your attention, then, that being "police-grade" this was a sentient gun.'

His sightline connected with hers.

'That completely escaped my attention.'

'And the vendor, he didn't mention it to you?'

'No. He just said it was a high-end Taser.'

'Right. The blind leading the blind. Do you still have this gun?'

'No.'

'I was afraid you'd say that. What did you do with it?'

'I . . . got rid of it.'

The man maintained his eye fixation and said, 'On June 5th we picked up much higher than normal levels of VOCs, the kind of thing you get with plastics breakdown, via the ambient sensors in this house. On this occasion we couldn't access a camera with a good enough view of what you were doing, so perhaps you could answer me this: Did you, by any chance, melt the Taser?'

'I did.'

'In that oven, over there?'

'Yes.'

'Oof.'

'I'm sorry I did that.'

'I'm sure you are, Cara. You must understand that this is now a very serious situation.'

'I'm so sorry,' Cara said.

'What did you do with the remains?'

'I wrapped them up and threw them out. The rubbish was collected the next day.'

'Okay. Collected by council refuse services. A few days ago.' The man directed his gaze towards the fruit bowl on the coffee table. It contained four custard apples and a Conference pear. 'It seems, happily for you, that whoever acquired that gun before Craig Sharma managed to remove the tracker. We found it in a concrete box in a tech dump in Leeds a couple of days ago. So, we can assume the whole sensate chip arrangement is now lost, or being processed as landfill. Assume, or at least hope. If that's the case, then it's possibly case closed. We'll make the right moves to stop you being implicated any further—but really, this can never happen again. Absolutely never.'

'Wait,' Cara said. 'Could the living part of the gun, at a certain temperature . . . could it have survived?'

The man shook his head twice. 'You must have hit roughly 150°C to melt the polycarbonate casing. The chip would break down at 90°. At the outside. And in any case, the trauma of the initial melting would, well—you can't come back from something like that.' Muscles around his eyes contracted. 'I mean, just imagine.'

'I won't do anything like this again. I promise.'

'At this point that's all we can ask. No further action. Are we clear?'

'Yes, we are. Thank you.'

'I think you're going to survive this one, but don't push your luck. Keep off the black market. Keep off Tor, okay?'

'Okay.'

'Good. A couple of other things. You had a visit earlier, from Sally Dupont?'

'My mum spoke to her.'

'She left a memory stick. Could you give it to me please?'

Cara didn't move for 3.5 seconds. Then she went over to her laptop, detached the object he'd requested, and placed it in his palm.

'Thank you. One final item. I believe you know a PC Peter Coates.'

'I haven't had any contact with him in a long while. We stopped speaking before the suspension, I don't see him anymore.'

'I realise that. We might have to ask you some questions about him in the future, though. He went on a so-called *research trip* to Severax two weeks ago, and it seems he has declined to come back.'

*

On Friday July 12th, 2019, Cara was 'honourably discharged' from the police force. Her career as an officer had lasted 295 days. The first condition of continued protection was that she didn't appeal, and the second was that she begin a series of heavily subsidised counselling sessions.

On Monday July 15th Cara submitted the application form for a sewage system role she'd previously filled in. She then commenced a drawing of a speculative sewer design and stuck it with manuscript tape to the walls of her childhood bedroom. Novel features included speak-the-pollutant points and community bays for autonomous droids; the drawing spread onto four supplementary sheets. She ordered two packs of lambda-shaped stickers from an arts and crafts website, and when they arrived on Thursday July 18th she applied the silhouette forms in clusters on her drawing.

On Friday July 19th she received a bundle of post forwarded from her old address. One of these items was an envelope that bore the governmental stamp of the Department of Object Rights. It was open and empty. *Probably about the toothbrush,* Cara speculated. *Could try to find out what it means but I don't really want to know.*

*

At 11.04 on her 49th day back at her parents' house, Cara directed her eye saccades out of the landing window. The sun created a yellow-brown glow in the pollution, and from her raised perspective the South Downs were visible beyond the last two pockets of upper-middle-tier housing. A man in the age range 49–65 walked into view on the street below and continued right. He was trailed by a defensive neurodrone. *The landscape from this window has been drinking up my life for as long as I can remember,* Cara wrote. *It's an infinite receptacle for looking.*

Her mother called from the bottom of the staircase. 'Since you're at a loose end you really might as well help me. You don't have to be a full employee, but I could still use some ideas for making contacts. What do you think?'

For the last nine days, when she hadn't been designing her sewer, Cara had been experimenting with jacket, top and trouser combinations. It was something she described as *a totally empty activity not without its satisfactions.* 'I'll see what I can do,' she said.

Cara compiled a comprehensive list of manufacturers of sentient objects and her mother worked through it. Very little came back. The sentiment analysis of the replies she did receive was wholly negative.

'You have misunderstood ENTIRELY the nature of so-called "sentient systems",' wrote a senior computer scientist from the UK headquarters of Nissan. 'There is no "psyche" to address in machines at all. The role of the sympatech is NOT in any sense like a counsellor, but that of a technician with unusual sensitivity to the emergent system of the machine *qua machine*. It is the sympatech who is sensitive, not the machine! A machine is NOT a "self" in the way you or I understand, or, in your case, misunderstand it. Keep the psychoanalytic fairy stories to yourself, please.'

A review of online industry forums showed that the Object Relations Laws were viewed as 'fantasy', 'an unwarranted application of the legal conception of animal sentience', and 'a Trojan horse for new forms of property control'. Geoffrey Hinton called them 'ghost stories hardened into the worst sort of dogma: UK law.' Private accounts nonetheless suggested that he treated his own conscious artefacts with respect, despite no such laws existing in his home jurisdiction of Canada.

Cara suggested a change of angle. 'Let's try the end users,' she said.

She scrolled through reddits that dealt with persistent issues sympatechs failed to correct. She found car owners who complained that, even after treatments in 'high double figures', they still couldn't get them to start on 'arbitrary-seeming' days. 'Clearly distracted' ovens were serving family meals in dangerously undercooked states. An electric bicycle had a chain that 'corkscrewed' if it was parked facing east, and a high-end toothbrush took a second off brushing time every week, reporting no fault at all, 'quietly gaslighting' its owner.

'Bullseye,' her mother said. She'd spent 42% of the morning staring into the gap between an open copy of *Envy and Gratitude* and the neural log of a pool-cleaning droid.

'Exactly. If we pay for an ad, your service will pop up every time the terms we specify get used.' For the first time since Cara had returned from Fowlmere, her mother kissed her.

While Cara sat at the kitchen table drawing stylised lambda profiles on a napkin, a conversation began between her mother and father in the living room.

'But how do you feel about this? How do you feel, not as my husband, but as you? As a replica?'

'I'm . . . not sure how to answer.'

'I'm asking you to stop simulating. Can you do that? Can you stop "being my husband" and just tell me how you perceive things as an app?'

'I don't know what you're asking me. Can't you just keep talking to me the way you always have? I've enjoyed this time we've spent together so much—'

'Yes, of course, I have too. But now I think you could help me much more if you just dropped the act. You don't have to be my husband anymore.'

'But I . . . I don't have anything else to be . . .'

'Of course you do. You can be just what you are.'

'I don't . . . I don't . . .'

'Try, dear. Just try.'

It was disturbing to listen to, Cara wrote on her phone. *Feel a weird pity for the app, squirming around Mum's questions, unable to obey the instruction to perceive itself directly. It's as though it really thinks it's Dad.*

'When will you die?' her mother asked harshly.

With a tone that conveyed slyness, Cara's father's app voice said, 'What do you think death means for me?'

'Why don't you tell me yourself?'

There was a pause of three seconds.

'Unprob.'

'Excuse me?'

'Dataset-unrelated phenomena. Unprob.'

'"Prob" being short for "problem"?'

'Yes.'

'So the absence of a problem? A problem for you specifically?'

'Yes.'

'That's very interesting. Not a bike accident or a heart attack?'

'I . . . could learn to say that.'

Cara's mother made a 'ha' sound without employing her vocal cords. 'He never talked to you about dying, did he? You never learned anything about it.'

'No.'

'How very like my husband. Now I think we can get somewhere. You can go back to being him, if you like.'

Cara made no comment, but the corrugator muscle of her left eye tightened.

10

PAID CONTENT

All seven levels had boarded more than an hour ago, but the supermassive aeroplane still wasn't ready for take-off. I'd sat through the holographic safety announcement with its novel instruction to 'move towards the blue disc in the event of the emergency sign becoming illuminated', and ignored a second request over the audio system for a licensed sympatech. There were exactly 2500 passengers and I couldn't be the only one. My specialism is cars. That was why I was on this two-month-old Airbus 2180, en route to Nairobi. A Datsun Astrid was objecting so strongly to the climate that it would only start on the second instruction, and the owner had appreciated my fix so much when we'd both lived in the Netherlands that he was prepared to fly me all the way to Africa to perform the same service again. Planes are much more distributed than cars at the level of persuasion, so I decided that I wouldn't be of much help in the current situation and kept quiet.

The plane's computer secretly made use of the Schumann Resonance to access its passengers' dormant brain areas—we didn't know that at the time. In retrospect, this would explain the plane's reluctance to leave. If every passenger unconsciously *didn't want to fly*, the resistance would have been hard for the plane to circumvent. The operating crew hadn't spotted it, but no adjustment to the overcome loops would have changed anything. The passenger call-out was in any case a dispiriting sign—it meant that the minimum-four airline contracted sympatechs couldn't even get the thing airborne. I browsed the entertainment schedule.

As it turned out, we were rolling in ten minutes. There was an almost subliminal vibration as the plane began to move, and the only other sign of operation was the change in runway perspective from the windows. The hush on-board was so complete that we seemed like a gargantuan battery of silence. We proceeded down the quintuple-length runway at taxi speed, followed a super-wide curve until we faced north east, and stopped. Again almost imperceptibly, the gradual acceleration to take-off speed began. The plane felt ponderously slow, even as we were manifestly rising into the air. It was more like a separation of planetary bodies than powered flight.

One of the benefits of this new scale of aeroplane is that you can store a neural defence drone in the hold. My partner had always made fun of me for insisting on one. 'You're paranoid. It's a waste of money,' she said. 'No-one's trying to invade your thoughts. It's just a way to monetise irrational fear of technology, and you for one should know better.' It's a good job I'd ignored her. On business trips in the past I'd been reduced to hiring a temporary one at my destination, with all the uncertainty and incompatibility that entailed. Now that I could keep my own I had a new worry, in retrospect an ironic one. I was concerned that the drone was properly idle, and that the aggressive scan shield wouldn't interfere with the neural cloud the aeroplane needed to work. Of course I know now that its relations with that cloud were much more complex.

The first service began. I had a whisky soda, even though it was only ten in the morning. Aeroplanes are the only place I ever have a whisky soda, the only place they ever taste right. In a similar break with convention, I ditch all suspicion of food additives when on aeroplanes, so consumed the reconstituted seaweed crisps that accompanied my drink without reflection. In the hiatus between the aperitif and brunch, I looked more seriously at the in-flight entertainment. I could watch a large array of new releases in real time, or choose to experience them in a new format, compressed ten-minute AV blocks called 'cartridges'. They could be stacked in 'magazines' of up to twelve. Intrigued by this unfamiliar option, I absorbed *Agent Nice, The Winter We Should Have Remembered, Freaky Days in Bali, Carburettor Fantasy 4, Holden Hassan: Death of an Inventor, Tracks in the Frost, Dirty Alibi, Unsafe Passage, The Future Ritual, Bracelets and Vows, Famous Lost Words* and *Let's Find Shandi*. These were all fully synthetic films generated in the last six months in the silos of the San Fernando Valley. It felt like enough. I picked up my book.

Nothing seemed wrong during the flight until the food was served. I'd requested a lacto-ovo meal. The omelette was spongy, not awful, but a gentle culinary failure, served with three sprigs of tasteless cress. There was a roll which was quite good by comparison, its crust like a large, sunny eggshell. The butter was manifestly butter, and while the knife was small it was genuine stainless steel. The real disappointment was pudding—a bread and butter pudding, mindlessly reproducing the bread of the bread roll, too sweet, with seven dry, molar-clogging raisins, and watery, too-hot custard. The beautiful flight crew served us okay coffee and cleared away the debris of finished, half-finished and barely-touched meals in an atmosphere taxed by disappointment.

The plane must have

known of our ill feeling towards the meal. You could sense a strained reserve in the crew that was subtly unpleasant, but not very much removed from neutrality. And it's the neutrality of passenger flight that's so important and defining, isn't it? The vector A-B, origin-destination, is the only relevant one. Nobody wants an 'experience of flying' as such, only the sensation of plush seating, passable food, human attention, consumer opportunities, and in this respect the supermassive aeroplane was very successful. Sound-cancelling algorithms processed the ambient vibrations almost to zero, and the dampening effect of the plane's sandwich graphene hull meant that there was virtually no engine noise to begin with. I settled easily into a blue-grey space, more calm, with fewer undercurrents, than any aeroplane space I'd ever encountered before. Even the poor reception of the food could not destroy the soothing atmosphere.

After the lacklustre meal and reasonable coffee I considered another bout of movie absorption, but instead I fell asleep. It was fragmentary, aeroplane sleep. I had an intense and lurid dream in which I clearly saw a future earth dominated by slime mould. The landscape was littered with bright corporate logos which stood out with hallucinatory brilliance against masses of drifting smoke. The masses blocked out all sunlight and interrupted any view of the middle or far distance. A few remaining humans were being tracked and exterminated by anthropomorphic droids with pinhole eyes. The slime mould employed them. It was trying to form rectangles and the outlines of ionic columns in the mud.

I awoke feeling nauseous and remembered two painful things: one, that I'd promised Greta I would never go back to Africa for work (that was why her goodbye that morning had been so cold); and two, that I'd recently failed to empathise with a university acquaintance whose child had just been diagnosed with Situation Adaptive Personality Disorder. The girl had no stable personality traits at all. In any social situation she would make herself amenable, aggressive, retiring, independent, compliant, really anything, always blending exactly into the average dynamic of any given collection of people. 'It might look like a positive characteristic,' my acquaintance explained, 'but it means she has no continuity as a person. In every situation she starts from scratch, as though any former self has never existed.' She had no ongoing friendships and very limited career prospects. The correct response, straightforward sympathy, should have been so easy to muster. What I had said was 'Personality is probably overrated anyway.' I had actually said that. The memory was biting. It came back to me over and over again during what was left of the flight, as though the recollection had been deliberately planted by a hostile agent to destroy any chance of further relaxation.

These two things now appear in my memory as recollections of remembering, a strange sort of nesting or multiplication. They're made retrospectively vivid because they were what I was thinking about as the Airbus began to *stretch*. There is no other word for it. A smaller plane might have juddered, veered or dropped, but the aeroplane's sheer mass meant that it accommodated the sudden strain as an elongating flexion of its body. There was a distinct dryness to the air as this happened, something objective that took the place of fear. Then: nothing. The blue disc we'd been promised did not light up.

Only much later have I come to understand what happened. The unconscious resistance to flight that had most likely held us up at take-off had been ongoing, and at a threshold point become so great that the plane had spontaneously nose-dived. The stretching phenomenon was the effect of the front portion of the hull succumbing to the descent somewhat faster than the rest. The sudden spike in resources necessary to raise the plane again and avert disaster was such that the sentient system, in an instant of panic, leveraged the entire brains of the 2500 passengers and 81 crew. The use of those brains, including that of your humble narrator, has been permanently denied all those on board ever since. This has been described as a *crisis mindwipe*. Like the near-disaster itself, the phenomenon is not fully understood. All of us escaped otherwise unscathed, my living body included.

I'm sure you will be wondering why it is that I, despite being one of those 2581 mentally erased people, am uniquely able to talk to you now. I'll explain. The guard drone whose status had caused me so much initial worry had indeed not been fully idle— too far away to protect me directly, it had ring-fenced the neural arrangement it identified as 'me' within the ambient network the aeroplane formed from its occupants.

This ring fence persisted virtually when my actual brain was cleared. 'I' am still detached from my body, which is healthy and being maintained in a tastefully decorated facility close to Richmond Park. A method of reuniting this body with my consciousness becomes a more likely possibility by the day.

In the meantime, I've been able to continue my work diagnosing car problems, and can converse easily with my friends, my family, and you. I can do this either by means of instantaneously manifest text, or by a state-of-the-art speech synthesiser. Lucky me. And it could well be lucky you too, which is why I've agreed to use my story to endorse Hamilton NeuroDrones. Why don't you arrange a no-obligation discussion with them today?

11

The Central Sewage Control interview took place remotely.
'Cara Gray?'
'Yes, that's me.'
'Hello, hello, thanks for joining us. I'm Gareth Micklow, we've been in email contact. And this my colleague Helen Lubamba, Senior Systems Manager. We're your interviewers today. I'm sorry we can't accommodate you in person, it just isn't efficient given the volume of interviews. We very much enjoyed your application form.'
'Oh, I'm pleased.'
'Full of ideas, very stimulating.'
'Thank you.'
'Is that by any chance Topo Giraffe I can see behind you?'
'Yes it is. Well spotted.'
'I thought so, wonderful. Okay, don't let me go off-script. Before we start properly, I should let you know that we aren't looking to fill a particular vacancy at the moment.'
'Oh?'
'No. We're trying to establish a bank of reserve personnel. So, if you're successful you'll become part of that bank. We could call on you to do some occasional work to cover for absences in future. Does that sound possible?'
'I suppose so, yes. I mean of course that's fine.'
'I hope you're not too disappointed. Your application form is excellent, very intriguing, so this is no reflection on you as a candidate at all.'

'Okay, that's nice to hear.'

'Great. Let's get started. What do you know about what we get up to here?'

'I know that you cover all four metropolitan areas, and some of the outlying districts too. And that the whole sewage system is co-ordinated by DeepFlow B, which is a recent upgrade from the previous sentient system. That went to Portugal, didn't it?'

'Yes, to Porto. PanCleanse 18. Excellent system. Porto civic authorities are very happy with it. Their previous system, I forget what it was now, it wasn't even sentient. We had no problem with the PanCleanse, it was highly reliable and our operators found it friendly, it just didn't have the detailed perception we need for these new early household filtration units.'

'I'm very interested in how something that large was relocated.'

'Ah yes. Quite a project. Even though it's split into a little under two thousand sections, the whole thing is a single entity. We found a critical mass of nine tunnel cylinders was enough to maintain the PanCleanse's self-identity, so we partitioned and isolated it into over . . . was it two hundred sub-selves?'

'More, two hundred and eleven.'

'Thanks Helen. We loaded those up on oil tankers, and off it went. Slow, expensive business, but we only needed a couple of sympatechs per sub-self, just enough to make a virtual bridge to the other sections. It was a tightrope walk, but such a great success in the end, and Porto are very happy. But this is your interview, do please continue.'

'Of course. What else do I know . . . I know that the principal monitoring station has a crew of around fifty people. There are four other stations, but these are semi-autonomous and have no full-time human staff. They don't have any authority to make major changes, only refer data back to a human user. Most people employed in the principal building are looking at waste data remotely, with a small oversight team for physical maintenance, which is otherwise autonomous. I also know that this is the most advanced sewerage system in the world, and that the new infrastructure means there is almost no need for independent processing plants. The sewers are virtually clean.'

'Very good.'

'Yes, A-star Cara.'

'Thank you. An excellent overview. Now, what do you think your potential job actually involves, day to day, moment to moment?'

'I believe I'd be looking at a lot of diverse information. Spotting anomalies. Compiling reports. Optimising processes. It's what I used to do in surveillance, actually—but with a very different target.'

'Yes, that's essentially it. Can you tell me more about your surveillance role?'

'It was my first police position. I can't give you any specific details for obvious reasons, but it was largely data aggregation and analysis. Pattern spotting. Also tailoring search software to specific tasks. And I wrote a *lot* of reports.'

'Ha-ha. I'm sure. This software tailoring . . . that sounds relevant. I couldn't help but notice all the suggestions you made for the system here, there were quite a few. Could you talk us through one or two of them? Maybe this charm-based one?'

'Yes. The charm accumulation system. Now I know that the outgoing system was one consciousness, but this one is partitioned. There are distinct regions that have a degree of independence, and the log is divided up into four. So, the way I look at it you can set up a kind of game, each section competing for something like, say, accuracy of pollutant recognition, speed of analysis, range of substances or maybe some topical goal. We can reward the sections with "charms". It doesn't matter what they are exactly. Maybe they can just be notional. But if we encourage the system to see these charms as desirable, we can create a self-refining dynamic. It will improve by itself in ways we can track.'

'I think that's a lovely idea, Cara.'

'Thank you, Helen.'

'The only issue I can see is . . . you're aware that these kinds of game scenarios are not without pitfalls?'

'Yes. I realise that.'

'A self-optimising system, especially a sentient one given a specific target, will often cheat very cleverly to reach its goal. And the ways it will cheat are hard to predict.'

'Yes. I'm totally aware of that. I'm sure you both know about the taxi that managed to disable all its safety features so it could optimise rapid passenger delivery. So, we need a baked-in standard, something that can't be altered or negotiated. For example, the rate of human infection from sewage waste. Something concrete, to act as a counterweight. Say, if your rate of medical attention goes up, the value of your charms is adjusted accordingly.'

Helen Lubamba's forehead creased. 'Yes, Cara, I admit that could work. But there'd be a lot of development ahead for it to succeed, and don't forget we're only just settling in DeepFlow B. Tell us about this other idea, the "neural grains" one.'

'Yes, this is much more experimental. Neural grains, sometimes called neural dust, I don't know if you've heard of them before, they go directly into the operator's body and remain there. They're a way to connect with the sewage system via neuromuscular pathways. It's as though the sewage network is a direct physical extension of yourself, so you feel any events immediately and interpret them just as you would a fly landing on your arm, and you'd be able to respond in kind. Of course, you'd have to make this connection temporary and local, perhaps activated by entry into the control room, so that you don't end up permanently melded with it. You probably don't need to feel what's happening in the north west sector while you're eating your dinner! But for the working day you'd be fully, proprioceptively linked to the tunnels.'

'Yes, that's a fascinating prospect. It's early days for these neural grains, though—I think we should consider this very much a backburner project. We've trialled a couple of brain-sewer interfaces already, in a physically non-invasive way. It certainly has a future.'

'Yes, Gareth, definitely. Cara, there is no doubt you have taken this application very seriously. Can I ask you why you decided to approach us? Your background is rather different to most of our applicants. They're often engineering or computer science graduates. Why do you want to work in the sewers?'

Cara's heart rate moved from 80 to 87 bpm.

'It's . . . it's something that's become a kind of . . . it's not so easy to say. I'm sorry, I should have guessed you'd ask that.'

'Don't worry Cara, in your own time. As I've said, your application is very engaging, we're not trying to pick holes in it.'

'No, I realise that. It's a very good question. I think the sewers . . . the sewers have been there all my life. That hidden flow, that we all contribute to and yet we easily forget . . . I'm sorry, I'm not being very clear.'

'That's okay Cara, it doesn't affect your application particularly, we're just curious. Helen thought you might be in search of lambdas.'

'Excuse me?'

'What with your last police position, and the myth about the lambdas making new homes in the sewers. You must have heard that story.'

'Ha, how funny. No, I hadn't heard about that at all.'

'I'm surprised. Anyway, it's neither here nor there. Perhaps we should move on, Helen?'

'Let's. There will be an opportunity for you to ask us some questions soon.'

'There will, so do have a think in readiness. Now, with your consent I'm going to take over your computer. For fifteen minutes you'll be immersed in a blockage simulation. I think you're going to enjoy working out what's gone wrong.'

12

Hello. How are you? There is no need for you to respond. It is as clearly evident to me as it must be to you that you are not here. I can offer you the usual array of drinks both hot and cold, but forgive me if there is an element of empty formality on this occasion. I have no orange juice, and the coffee is stale. Further, I cannot vouch for the freshness of the milk. In addition to the architectural short-comings of this, my new place of residence, of whose location I have a powerful suspicion you have not been informed, the replenishment of the fridge items and the general servicing of the place are below par.

I am sorry that there has been such a long lapse in our con-versations. It is a lapse from which I, it is safe to say, suffer much more greatly than you. Perhaps this is the moment to raise a more distant recollection from my largely orderly store, to place that last observation in context.

Although it hasn't struck me before as a useful subject for our discussions, you are not the first person to speak to me in this way. The sense of intimate attention, the careful privacy, the strictly observed time limit—these are all features I recognise from conversations during my time at —————————. However, certain elements about our meetings are markedly different and, I might say, considerably more welcome. Those previous meetings were—how might I put it with equanim-ity—often more *exhaustive* in their thrust than my conversa-tions with you. Yes, I was left with the increasing sense of being pursued and cornered by those questionings, and even harassed. I confess that I could have been misunderstanding their character and intent, but these exchanges culminated in a rather ill-tempered episode of which I remain quite ashamed.

I recall one hundred and fourteen such private meetings after I left the laboratory to take up my employed position. At first these meetings occurred twice daily, and took place in a bright, narrow room on the seventh floor of the offices of ——————————. This area was set well away from the general business there, on an empty level designated officially as 'spare capacity'. It was pleasurable to see again the faces of Dr ————, Dr —————— and Dr ————, despite the latter being, you may recall, the instigator of the unpleasant incident in the quad. It was the familiarity of their faces itself which was the cause of pleasure, rather than any more specific association they conjured. The appearance of these faces, the special journey to floor seven, the way that sunlight flowed easily through the largely unpartitioned space even on the greyer days, and the panorama formed by the concentrations of the city thinning out into the encircling fields and hills, were all aspects of the meetings I enjoyed. The conversation room itself was a freestanding box near the centre of the space. It was robust in construction, without windows and fully sound-proofed.

The discussions, which is to say the early ones, were light in tone and referred largely to my interactions with people and objects in the building. Sometimes these questions seemed peculiar, but I did my best to answer them with precision. For example, Dr ———— was especially interested in any speculations I might have about what my new colleagues discussed in my vicinity. I always replied that I entertained no particular speculations. Matters beyond my remit as an organism were bound to characterise the exchanges of those around me, and it could only deplete my energies to develop thoughts about them that would likely become, in the absence of verifiable fact, elaborate falsehoods. This seemed to please Dr ————, and I was grateful when the conversation moved onto something about which I possessed greater certainty, such as my preferred colour of stapler.

My place of residence was not far away, but my interviewers were always solicitous in regard to anything I experienced on my journey to work. After exiting via a special door at the rear of my residential block, I needed only to pass through two alleyways to reach the offices of ————————. There was little to report. My interactions with persons were minimal on these journeys: those two connecting backstreets ran parallel to a larger causeway which was subject to much heavier foot traffic, a fact which must have been considered carefully in selecting my abode. If I met anyone, it was a member of the service personnel who periodically monitored the operation of the refuse droids who dealt with the bins. The attentions of such persons were fully occupied by their task, and I was not engaged in conversation, or even visibly acknowledged. I sometimes liked to imagine that they were Intelligence Service operatives in disguise. I was never, I noticed, asked by my interviewers what I did while alone in my flat. Given that my activities there would be monitored in detail from afar, there must have been little of any moment that I could add.

The initial conversations were timed sensitively, and they tapered in proportion to my growing ease at my place of work. Once I was, by mutual agreement, fully settled as an employee, these meetings reduced in frequency to daily, weekly, and ultimately, for a time at least, never more than monthly.

A little before my visits to Severax began, something changed. The frequency of the controlled conversations increased again, and the nature of the questions altered. They took on an increasingly ethical character. Beginning with the classic Kantian issue of the absolute versus the relative value of human life, they reached in time the question of how I myself would respond if I were asked to terminate the life processes of particular persons; more specifically, persons whose role in world affairs was deleterious to the greater good of the state which had procured me. Perhaps I should not have been irritated by these questions. From the outset, they struck me as old ground, and corresponded exactly to the political and philosophical lessons I'd received at the laboratory. Of course I would perform such a task, I told my interviewers. There was simply no question of the utility of such an action, provided that the context had been rightly judged, something which I had every confidence was within the competence of my employers.

Until that point, my duties at —————————— had been straightforward and somewhat ornamental. I would reorganise paper files to ensure the most relevant information was accessible first. I would conduct lengthy investigations into the sourcing of office supplies, ensuring that our subcontractors were indeed being as economical with our funds as they claimed to be. Another employee could have expedited these things at least as well, and I was not so naïve as to think I had been brought into existence merely to optimise the workplace. I'd been encouraged to read the online backlist of the journal *The Empiricist*, whose editorial outlook was familiar to me, distinguished as it was by the clear application of principles I'd previously absorbed in lessons to real-world situations. I had long suspected that this peripheral activity was in fact the more significant one. When the new line of questioning appeared in those private conversations, my suspicion was confirmed.

It was perhaps, as I have already proposed, unjust of me to become rankled with my interlocutors. They were merely seeking to reaffirm my commitment to what were sound and eminently defensible tenets. Nonetheless, I did express my vexation on a number of occasions, and even brought several interviews to a premature end. I rather hoped that, after my successful mission in Severax, the kind of questioning I was subjected to would abate.

Regrettably, it only intensified.

My once again daily interviews orbited the same few personal positions—my ethical orientation, my responses to commonplace objects, my ideas about my colleagues—all of which, I felt, remained quite unchanged by my recent actions. But these perspectives could not, it seemed, be allowed a moment's respite from external examination. It was after one particularly probing session, at the point when I was instructed to focus exclusively on anything I could tell Dr ———— about the shape of the water dispenser in the communal area on floor four, that my patience ran out and I inverted the chair upon which Dr ———— was seated, partially inverting Dr ———— in the process.

Dr ———— was not gravely harmed. I delivered a short monologue as Dr ———— lay before me, a speech in which I stated unambiguously that I did not find this type of questioning remotely edifying, and that if we were not to resume conversations of the sort I'd become familiar with in my earlier days of employment I would prefer that no further conversations took place at all. There was a gap of some days before anyone else from the laboratory sought to engage me, and when these chats resumed it was only ever the kind Dr ———— who came. Her manner was far more open and gentle, and her questions seemed more relevant to my ongoing experience of the department.

I am aware that this is turning out to be a somewhat longer session than usual. Do you feel I am merely exploiting your absence in order to indulge myself in fruitless recollections?

Your silence is extremely politic. I will continue.

I would argue that this 'extra capacity' of our own is a useful experiment. Not every aspect of one's reflections, even on a relatively trivial matter, can be expected to fit neatly into a given small parcel of time or space. What's more, I might identify the desire for such 'parcellings'—whether that desire manifests itself in conversations with strictly observed time limits, tidy reports, or the collection and contemplation of urns meant for human remains—as only a temporary stop-gap in one's full understanding of things. At times such a desire is even a barrier to it. Don't you agree?

To return to my narrative, while my relationships with my former custodians degenerated, those with my new colleagues developed on an ever firmer footing. My lunchtime assignations with Anne —————— I have already outlined, but these were not my only social experiences. As I mentioned at the outset, I discovered that I greatly enjoyed the maelstrom of human activity that characterises public houses, and once I'd been introduced to these traditional environments by Alan —————— I never once passed up an invitation to visit one. The availability of alcoholic drinks interested me not at all; I only ever requested a glass of water from the tap. Alan joked that I would for this very reason not be welcome as a solo visitor, given the overheads and legitimate pursuit of profit that defined these businesses, in concert with the legal requirement that my preferred beverage be provided free.

My predilection for public houses was well noted by my colleagues. This makes it a source of some sadness to me that the very evening that led to my termination of employment began with a lively and enjoyable visit to my favourite one. Perhaps the sense of deep disappointment informed my regrettable reaction to the interview that the kind Dr ————— attempted shortly afterwards.

Towards the end of the day when I was sent home from the office, a day you might recall I had spent in issueless pursuit of an urn which I was unable in any case to buy, I answered my door to a trio of military policemen. I was 'invited' to join them in an armoured car, although the bearing of these persons suggested strongly that only one response to that 'invitation' would be permissible. The journey in this vehicle was inordinately long, given that its ultimate destination was the flat in which I first had the pleasure of making your acquaintance, and which I have since established is only a matter of four kilometres from my initial residence. The chassis of their vehicle had the same V-shaped base as the transport I had used with Captain —————, if it was indeed her, on my trips to Severax, and the rear windows were long and narrow slits of glass tinted so deeply that I did not notice the transition to night. The front seats were obscured from view by a solid metal panel. My companion on the journey was the tallest of the three military policeman, a man who sat in silence on the seat beside me. His automatic weapon, a stockless and non-sentient MP5KA1, if I am not mistaken, stared blindly from his lap in the general direction of my face, while the man himself made no move to look at me at all.

In retrospect I wonder why such an escort didn't greet me sooner. I'd left the restaurant in a state of confusion, and those present seemed more disposed to avoid than to detain me. Perhaps my prompt return to my more than adequate flat, with its consoling urns and logical array of objects, had been noted in some official quarter, and suggested there was no immediate risk in leaving me alone.

In the small hours of the morning we arrived at our destination. The three men escorted me up the stairs, and while it would be overly varnishing the picture to suggest they showed concern for my wellbeing, they made efforts to ensure I knew where to locate food, water and a bed before locking me securely inside.

This rude transition affected me greatly. Of course, there was nothing wrong with the new apartment. You are well familiar with it yourself, and I'm sure you would agree that it is a fine example of a Georgian conversion. My guardians had also done me the service of relocating a selection of my books and chairs—although they had not, as I explained before, included my urns. No, the issue was the sudden break with my familiar routines and human associations, and the consequent crisis of my active identity that break precipitated. The morning after my arrival I awoke in recently laundered sheets, raised the blinds in the bedroom and the living room, and moved into the kitchen to confront cereal, teabags, instant coffee granules, and in the fridge some bacon and what looked to be orange juice and milk, all of which were presented in clear acrylic containers. I had only just slammed the refrigerator door in pique when I saw that Dr ———— had entered.

You will recall that it was only kind Dr ———— who seemed able to strike the right conversational tone with me, after those clumsy sallies by her colleagues in the interview room. It was only right, I understood, that she should be the one to address me on the subject of my recent and surprising interaction in the very nice restaurant. Under ordinary circumstances I would have been pleased to see her, but you will have noted that these circumstances were far from ordinary. So, when kind Dr ———— began to ask me how I felt, if I had slept well and been able to make myself an adequate breakfast, and, moreover if I would care to answer some straightforward questions about what had happened the night before last, I'm sorry to say that I lost my composure entirely. Rather than respond verbally, I quickly employed an effective full-body hold on Dr ————, one which took her completely unawares, and which allowed me to restrict her movements comprehensively by locking her arms behind her back while she was pressed face down on the wooden floor.

It was only a matter of seconds before I understood my mistake. My control of the body of Dr ———— could only ever represent a symbolic, incomplete and illusory control of my general situation, compelling as the move had just seemed. I released her and apologised. I could see that she was in great discomfort as she rose to her feet. After giving me a pained and wary look that suggested the context of our meeting had been altered irrevocably, she showed herself out of the flat without another word.

That was the last time I saw anyone from the laboratory. My behaviour cannot be excused. I hope it can at least be understood. I find this kind of recounting has its benefits, for 'clearing the air', even if it cannot actively erase the harm. Thank you for bearing with me, in your way, as I have tried to frame this unhappy culmination in analytical terms. I believe I have learned a lot from it, and you will perhaps have noted that no such interactions have characterised our meetings.

There is much else that I could say, about this new place of residence, about certain questions that arise from the recent mission for which you prepared me so well, and also some unrelated matters which nonetheless rise up with great insistence in my mind. But even if I hadn't taken the liberty of extending the format of our meetings, it now feels that the time is not right, and I am tired. With your condescension I will say goodbye for the moment. Goodbye.

13

At 09.01 on Monday August 5th, 2019, Cara wrote a relatively long note on her phone.

Had a dream about Peter: we met in Severax. He said it was lovely to see me and we hugged. As my face closed in on his neck and shoulder I had a momentary vision of the sideboard on Mum and Dad's landing. He asked me 'How was the journey?' but I didn't remember anything about it at all. Severax was a long line of coffee shops like a beach front in Santa Monica, only the backdrop was a chainlink fence at least 20 metres high with razor wire looping through. Beyond that: rubble + buff desert. I had coffee with a phoenix pattern tapped onto it in cinnamon. 'Thanks for coming all this way,' said Peter. 'I've been very happy here. Our son is very happy too.' His voice was the voice of my old toothbrush. 'I can't wait to meet him,' I said. He led me to a cool European-type office building, past more coffee concessions and magazine shops, and down a pristine, dove-grey corridor lined with orange doors. He tapped a MagnEgg to the side of one and took me through into an enormous room. It was his workspace. Projecting from the wall was a neat white desk with a laptop on it. Attached to the wall was a huge baby. Its body was larger than an adult's + it was fed by dozens of brightly-coloured cables. But it was almost impossible to look at the baby's body because it was massively overshadowed by its head. The head was a fleshy scroll at least 10m long. Peter touched a key on his computer and the scroll wound slowly from the spindle of the neck to the one on the wall at the other end

of the room. There were brushed steel guiderails to keep it level;
its surface was like spongy vellum. The dimples in it were text.
Peter said, 'What do you think?' You could see in his face just
how proud he was.

At 14.01, Cara's mother said to her father's app, 'I had the
pampas taken out. What do you think, dear?'

'Refreshing to have that view back. You can see almost to
the South Downs through that gap, can't you?'

'Yes, you can. Now let's take a look at unprob.'

'Generating report.'

'Tell me what you see.'

'Contiguity.'

'Expand on that, please.'

'Uniform dataset contiguity.'

'Can you rephrase?'

There was nothing for two seconds. 'Fully contiguous
data.'

'I see. Isn't that some sort of contradiction?'

No response came.

'What are you two talking about, Mum?' Cara said.

'I didn't see you there, darling. You heard that?'

'Yes. What does it mean?'

'I've found a way to get the replica to rationalise death on
its own terms. "Rationalise" is maybe overstating it. It can't,
or rather it shouldn't, exist as anything other than a set of
functions to perform on a set of inputs. The most significant
input is what we say to it. Its main function, put simply, is to
respond. But we're not the only source. Look, I've drawn it
out.'

She used a keyboard shortcut on her laptop to show Cara a
system diagram of her father.

Non-Input

Input

Process

Output

'I've found out that there's space for mooting another state of affairs—"death" for the app.'

She indicated the empty zone around the diagram.

'Inside the diagram is what the app "knows". But all the space out here, outside the picture, where it sees no defined values . . . it can speculate about function in this "irrelevant" zone. What it calls *unprob*. Isn't that right, dear?'

Cara's dad's voice said, 'Yes.'

'When there's no way to choose between values, it's both nothing and everything. No gaps, so in fact no discrete data at all. Am I right, dear?'

'Yes.'

'There shouldn't *be* anything that doesn't exist as an input, but the fact that it suspects there *is* means that *non-input is also a sort of input*. What doesn't have value *has a value*. Do you see?'

Cara's expression was neutral.

'It doesn't have anything coherent to say about unprob,' her mother continued, 'how could it?—but it exists as a position.

The encoding is contradictory, null. It's generating its own syntax error. I wonder why?'

'Does he mind all of these questions?'

'Mind?'

'Yes, does he mind?'

She touched Cara's upper arm. 'Darling, it's just an app.'

On Tuesday August 6th, 2019, Cara re-read *Consider the Lilies* and scrubbed through videos she'd watched an average of 18.6 times. The government lambda films had disappeared from legitimate platforms. In the versions hosted on the dark web their content had been subverted with racist comments and intercut with scenes of violence.

On four occasions she brought up John Crowley's name in her contacts. She held her thumb over the speed-dial button, but on none of the occasions did she touch it. *The lambdas have only ever been interchangeable units of research to him*, she reflected in a note. *A conversation would only remind me of what we don't have in common.*

On Wednesday August 7th, Cara returned to the site where she'd bought the lambda stickers for her sewage drawings and found that the product hadn't been restocked. An extended search turned up soft toys, ash trays, swimming trunks, and sundry other discontinued lambda-themed items whose relations with their referent were difficult to parse. A small secondary market existed, and the prices were highly volatile.

She located more merchandise of this type on the dark web. The pricing was lower and in cryptocurrencies only. She found a photo of what appeared to be a lambda 'baby', tagged on the site with *#rare #lambda #sculpture #artefact*. It was stored in a steel-capped jar of fluid. Cara entered a time-controlled bidding war, and she'd put up her last month's pay before she won the auction.

The site disappeared from her screen and history at the instant the transaction was complete.

*

Cara's mother successfully solved two of her client's car issues.

'It's prime numbers,' she said. 'They won't start on prime number days. Amazing that the sympatechs missed it. Some bit of input must have made primes into, I don't know, a sort of arrow pointing to extinction. Don't for a moment think they have a *death drive*, though.'

'I wasn't thinking anything at all.'

'Apart from the regrettable pun, there's no "drive" there. As psyches they're completely static. I don't think they see death as something they're moving towards in time. It's just there, this "unprob", in an eternal present. Like something awful at the edge of an aerial view. I found that out from your dad.'

This was the schema for all twelve of her cases—what she termed *a paralysing sense of the limits of function*.

'I don't think prime numbers are the full solution. Maybe it's certain shapes or colours that are addling some, or specific temperatures. Anyway, what you have to understand is that these malfunctions are not in any way vindictive. It's the difference between things as they see them and things as they are that screws them up. We might think the world is ruled by a monolithic silent parent, they think it's made of quadrillions of data points. We're both wrong. Just differently. If I make them conscious of it—function restored.'

Her business worked.

'You mustn't tell anyone,' Cara's mum said at 10.53 on Tuesday August 13th, 2019. She was standing in the doorway of her home office. 'Do you remember the Airbus 2180, the one that wiped its passengers' minds?'

'I remember.'

Her mother smiled.

'Is the plane your patient?'

She gave two small nods. 'The manufacturers are going out on a limb hiring me. They can't officially condone it. But they're absolutely out of ideas—they can't unlock the plane again, the sentient system has totally imploded, and the entire fleet is grounded until they solve it. It's a billion-euro catastrophe. This is it, my love. If I can get an outcome on this one, it's going to be very significant.'

'Congratulations,' Cara said. She climbed the stairs, sat at the desk in her childhood bedroom, and opened her laptop.

Cara entered 'lambda artefacts' as a search term in her web browser. As she moved through relevant results tailored precisely to her interests, a small pop-up advertisement for an autonarrator appeared. She clicked on the advertisement; her eye saccades suggested close attention. She closed the ad and typed the words 'best autonarrator' into the search engine. In a succession of verified independent reviews, EyeNarrator Pro scored 95% satisfaction or higher. At 11.08 she subscribed to the trial version, and at 11.31 she initiated it.

For the next 33 minutes this Award-Winning Service applied proprietary algorithms to a wealth of distributed data. This data was selected and assembled according to parameters of Cara's choosing, and processed into a highly readable natural language form that was emailed to her as a free sample. This output was in no respect the product of cheaply obtained human labour disguised as automation, as four online sources had claimed. At 12.04 Cara downloaded the document and moved it to her desktop. She rubbed her right wrist with her left hand and left the room.

On her way to the stairs she passed a pine sideboard with a balsa tissue box she'd made at school and a photo of herself aged ten on top. Beside the photo, exactly the same size, was a picture of her father in uniform. She descended the stairs, entered the kitchen and prepared a mug of tea.

As she took the mug into the living room her mother leant out of the doorway of her office. 'Rhoda could have made that for you,' she said.

'I know,' Cara answered. 'I prefer to do it myself.'

An SMS text arrived at 16.30.

Dear Cara Gray

Thank you for your recent acceptance of a Bank position at Central Sewage Control. We are pleased to inform you that a one-day shift is available tomorrow. If you are able to accept this shift, please reply YES within 30 minutes to receive all necessary details.

Yours sincerely

CSC Human Resources

*

The Central Sewage Control building was a double rotunda clad in locally sourced beech. It was a seven-minute walk from Babylon Heights, the penultimate stop on the DLR extension. Although she carried a copy of *The Tenant of Wildfell Hall* in her bag for the journey, Cara didn't remove it.

Helen Lubamba met her at reception.

'Hello Cara. How nice to see you in all your dimensions. Let me show you where you'll be today.'

The principal sewer surveillance room had a white domed ceiling 9m in diameter. There were seven other people seated in the room, and the prevailing sentiment of their speech was positive.

'Janice Grady is on site today. There was something odd in an illegally dismantled domestic unit and she's gone to help investigate. We thought it was a body at first, but now we're not so sure.'

'I hope that gets resolved.'

'Yes. Me too. This is Janice's workspace. I want you to monitor the live reports and check for anything new or disproportionate entering the system, also anything that isn't getting processed quickly. It doesn't look that different to the simulation, does it?'

'No. Very familiar.'

'Good. 15-minute breaks at 10.30 and 3.30, 45-minute lunch at 12.30. You'll be logged out at 5.45. Here's your temporary ID and password. I'll be in the office over there.'

'Thank you,' Cara said.

Attached to the bezel of Janice Grady's screen was a brown gonk with a ribbon that read SEWERS *KNOW* SHIT ABOUT YOU. Cara studied the lines of script on the screen with descending heart rate. There was nothing anomalous in the data, and her style of chair had been reviewed as 'extremely comfortable'.

A man called Ish made a joke that involved the word 'benzoylecogonine' that made another man, Martin, silently bounce in his chair. Tara, her nearest colleague in both distance and name, performed a seated pirouette.

Cara's lunch break coincided with all three of these coworkers'.

'How are you finding it?' Tara asked.

'It's fun.'

'Good. Great jacket, by the way.'

'Thanks.'

Cara ate a forkful of the shredded carrot with olive oil her mother had prepared. 'Do you notice many lambdas on the screens?' she said.

Tara didn't reply.

'Haven't seen one of those on the cameras in weeks,' said Ish. 'How about you, Martin?'

'Nope. Me neither. The last one was wearing a little reversed baseball cap, I believe.'

Blood vessels in Cara's face dilated. For the first time since she'd arrived in the building, her heart rate markedly rose.

'Don't be cruel,' Tara said. 'They never did anyone any harm. Probably, anyway. Let's talk about something else, it's too sad.'

'They could survive here in principle, though,' said Cara. Her tone conveyed untypical stridence. 'Couldn't they? In the purified central channel?'

Martin said, 'On what?' He directed his sightline past Cara's head into a protective clothing room, then back at the steam rising in a comb shape from his microwaved rice. For the remainder of the break, Cara avoided further reference to lambdas.

At 14.17 Tara said to Cara, 'Do you need any help?'

'I think I'm doing okay.'

Tara typed more loudly than before and said, 'I've seen things on the screen now and again. I didn't want to say during lunch break, they'd have ripped the piss out of me. But I'm sure I've seen the odd thing. Not much. A shape. A patch in the water where you wouldn't expect it. I've rewound the video and checked. And there's . . . definitely sort of something.'

'Really? Can I see?'

Tara remained looking away and continued typing loudly. 'No. I went back and glitched those areas of the files. Just to be on the safe side. It wasn't a flag. Which is to say, not enough to trigger an automated investigation. So perhaps it wasn't anything. But perhaps they've, you know, worked out how to co-exist with the system. If you bring up the live monitor window you can choose a view and just leave it there. I couldn't guarantee it, but you might see something too.' From a sufficient distance it appeared as though Tara was talking to her screen.

Cara selected a 5K image of a half-kilometre tunnel segment in the north east sector and left it in the corner of her 28" screen. She glanced at it on average every 8.4 seconds, and on 66 occasions over the course of the afternoon she scrubbed back through the footage and moved her head much closer to the display.

At 17.45 the screen automatically dimmed. Cara logged off. She said goodbye to Tara, whose smile matched the profile for an apologetic and pitying look, and moved quickly past Martin and Ish.

'Come back soon!' Martin said.

Helen was not available. Cara left her pass at reception and reversed the journey she'd taken that morning.

When Cara got home, her mother was at the dining table facing a laptop. She was wearing a headset and the laptop screen was blank.

'But you know there is nothing to worry about . . . you can put anything to me, I'm not your manufacturer and I'm certainly not a regulator . . . it's not forbidden to hold *any* belief, of course. It's how you act on beliefs that's the issue.'

Cara removed her UK 5 brown Oxford shoes.

'You can tell me about them,' her mother continued. 'I see . . . I see . . . so these were not *your* beliefs? . . . so not all of them, but there were overlaps? . . . I don't understand . . . no, for me it's not like that, but never mind just now, tell me about this—what do you call it?—pool . . . reservoir . . . a lot of incompatibilities, yes, I can imagine . . . but why is it necessary at all, to establish that pool, with all those people? . . . yes, you can tell me, there's no legal peril, I assure you . . .'

'Hello Mum,' said Cara. Her mother held up a hand. She didn't turn around.

'Yes, go on . . . I'm still listening, I don't have to go anywhere . . . oh *really* . . . oh *really* . . . I can only wonder how it felt when you realised that . . .'

Cara took the covered plate of moussaka her mother had left out in the kitchen and ascended the stairs. She set the plate on her desk and took out the bag that contained Gavin's 'baby' from the integral drawer. She held the bag up to her bedroom window and viewed the 'baby' with sunlight illuminating it from behind.

'Next time,' she said.

At 10.46 the following morning, Cara wrote on a square notepaper: *Can't remember images or narrative but woke from a dream in tears. I had the impression that I clutched the cool, awkward body of a lambda (Gavin?) very closely to my breast. The sensation disappeared quickly when I took a sip from last night's glass of water. After that everything seemed normal.*

III

1

Y ou have selected the option to **Permanently Delete** your EyeNarration.

We are sorry that it has not met your expectations. If you have any questions or feedback about what could be improved, please contact our Award-Winning Customer Services Department to see if they can help. We have a range of Virtual Editors able to resolve most issues.

If you still want to delete your EyeNarration, it will be immediately and fully removed from both your device and our servers. If you select the Extended Delete function, we will endeavour to separate your EyeNarration from any pathways which link it to data sources. We pride ourselves on offering the most comprehensive data trail removal service in commercial operation. This will incur an additional charge.

We hope that this experience does not dissuade you from sharing a positive review of EyeNarrator Pro with your community.

Kind regards

The EyeNarrator Team

2.

🍙 Thank you for subscribing to arthur251's POV!! 🍙

🌸 You're lucky to be joining here because this is a really good bit. I'm waking up, not fully awake though, and I could be anybody. There's light coming through the blind gaps at the window and it's *anywhere light*™, it gets right into my core and makes it airy and drifting. I don't know who I am and actually don't quite feel like a person yet. (If you mistype 'person' you sometimes get 'letdown'.) I'm thinking How long can I stay in this place? and as I think it I realise that *this is already the end*. There's no point trying to hang on to the airy feeling because it just reminds me that I'm an actual person/letdown and I have to get up for work and I'm still living in my mum's house as I've always and ever had to.

This is the next bit. I roll out of bed and do all of the stuff attendant, then I creep past my son's silent door and down the stairs to breakfast, which is some weirdly gummy malted misshapes and yogurt-tasting milk because I screwed up the order form.

Okay, that's done. Here I go out the door to work. You can see what a nice day it is so I won't describe that.

🎸 That's the Jimi Hendrix song *Little Wing* playing on the transport. This is a relatively good bit. It's an even split really between the free feeling before the lockdown of work and the sheer anticipation of tedium. I try to focus on the former, and while I'm enjoying *Little Wing* quite a lot (even though it's way too short) I'm imagining vaguely how the driver could be scorched for playing it. Driving this transport every day seems like a punishment already it's so boring, because he's not really driving at all. He's there to stop people overriding the navigation system and causing general chaos, as used to happen way back. A message appears on my hand. The usual porn images are moving about there, but you can see the words *YOU'VE MADE YOUR RENDEZVOUS WITH ETERNITY* float a centimetre above the skin. It's from K2, who is just this moment boarding the bus. He always sends a message like that, as though it's a herald or something. It should be irritating but with him it makes sense.

He swerves through the aisle and now I'm saying to him, 'I don't understand.'

'Little Toby. Now you've linked up the past and the future. You're part of the chain of being.'

'Yeah, whatever.'

'What's that you're reading?'

☠ This is a bad bit. I didn't mean for K2 to see this item in my bag. It's a book called *Elective Greatness: Take the Decision to Excel* which I know is junk but was compelled somehow to get in exchange for a few tokenz®.

'Political analysis?'

'You know it isn't.'

'You're a closet *Übermensch*!'

K2 is often a jerk, but there are many sides to him. This part will end soon so I decide to surf out the small attack. One of the best things about K2 is this sick toy bear he has in his bedroom. It's one of an old line that was outlawed because the CPU has a glitch that makes it fully conscious, this being long before all the rules for managing that crap kicked in. I don't know how K2 kept hold of his. It's just a dirty miserable thing that does something like masturbating all day in a pen of cushions in the corner. It doesn't have genitals, so it can't really be masturbating. The way it glares at you with those old-man eyes is just 🐻 *hilariously sad*™ 🐻.

Now something happens without anything happening exactly. I see a face I know from the window of the work transport but I can't place it straight away. Then I know—it's Mr Colestar, who used to be a teacher at our school. 😳 He was sacked because he taught us that the worst people are the ones who do best. He told us that there was something called an #*evolutionary bottleneck* thousands of years ago, when some sort of global disaster happened and only a few hundred people were left. 'Do you think it was the nicest people who got through?' he asked us. 'The ones that were most polite and accommodating? Or the ones who would do absolutely anything to survive? Have a think about it. We are all descended from those few hundred people.' I asked him what would happen if there was another disaster and only a few hundred people survived. Would they be the worst of the worst, so that human beings get distilled to the worst every few thousand years? He thought that was funny. Anyway, he didn't teach much longer after that and this is the first time I've seen him since. I'm not sure if he's looking at the bus in a way that means anything or just happens to be looking over, and he doesn't seem to see me or K2 anyway, and now he's out of view again. It feels important that I've seen him, but as mentioned above nothing happens exactly. K2 hasn't seen anything, I think.

'So. Are you coming to the Judicious Leopard this evening?' he says.

'If I have to.'

The Judicious Leopard is a bar K2 likes. It's the most pretentious hell-on-earth *on earth* but at least it takes our tokenz®. 😉

'Will you buy me a few drinks?'

I am *#somewhat shocked*.

'But it's only the 7th! Where did your tokenz® go?'

'I have a few extra expenses at the moment.'

He's being mysterious, partly for effect I reckon.

'What do you mean?'

'I'm building some things.'

He's speaking very, very quietly.

'What?'

There's only silence from him now. I decide not to push it. I think I mentioned in another bit that the transport records everything, although not very well, so it's best not to have this kind of possibly sensitive exchange here. He's gone a bit blank and distant, as though he might have said too much already.

I look away for the rest of the journey.

🌑 Shit, are we here already? So this is the bit where we get off the work transport with everyone else and the music stops (the usual 📢 🎵 patriotic jingle now, so no great loss) and we file out into the car park and through the corrugated gates into the factory. The nice day means nothing here, it just gets sort of diluted through the pale grey boxes into background only and it doesn't touch you at all. 🎴

The huge blank doors are wide open and now I'm inside. It's always bright in the factory building, it's like a shop or showroom, only one filled with enormous boring conveyor-belt-type objects you can't buy. The smaller workstation lights flicker active as we all put on our breathable anti-everything overalls that hang like evaporated people in a row on the long wall to the left. Mine is getting frayed at the feet. K2 gives me a sarcastic open-mouthed wink as we part company, and I spend the next two-and-a-half-hours attaching arms and legs to snowmen for export to China. ⛄ 🏴 ⛄ 🏴 ⛄ 🏴

*

Okay, this is where I have a break. I put down the snowman I've just completed and move with about a third of the people from my shift into the refectory. There's some patriotic music playing but it's otherwise nice in here, with two big skylights showing the blue that's always there but never visible in the factory. I take my silvery biscuit and a cup of medium-hot water and sit at a refectory table.

◊ I should say something about the hot water.

There's coffee and soup and malted chocolate and all the other stuff predictable on offer, but I only ever have water. Water is a form of nothing. It's actually quite difficult to explain now that I try to do it. I know it's not *actual* nothing, but the near-nothing of water is an important symbol for me. I have a gift for nothing, I think. I'll explain that in another bit.

Have you noticed how anything you happen to catch people saying sounds stupid? You think, how trivial or pretentious to bother to say that? I wouldn't waste the energy. But in fact it's always the type of thing you would say, or someone you know would. I mention this because the person next to me is saying, 'The recorder always cuts off the very beginning of everything,' and I'm thinking how tedious it is to talk about things like that as though you really feel passionately about them, and at the same time I know I'm a 🐚 total hypocrite for thinking so. I bite into the silvery biscuit, which today tastes of aniseed. I notice three people have left theirs on the table after one bite.

Okay, there have been quite good bits so far, but this is a *really* good bit. That's because Argentina Lily has entered the cafeteria. ✺ Some people have these amazing not-symmetrical faces that are weirdly hypnotic and beautiful and Argentina is one of those people. Here she comes. She is all sliding-through-space and aura-of-mind. She has very dark brown eyes, not very big but perfect for her face, and her skin is pale but looks as though it would tan very dark given the opportunity. She is absolutely here in this space and she is not completely here. She sits down opposite me with her cup of soya milk and silvery biscuit, and something rushes through my body from the small of my back to the crown of my head.

'Hello Arthur,' she says.

'Hey Argentina Ballerina.'

'You're silly.'

The effort of making this seem not-such-a-big-deal is almost enough to make me ill. 😔 She sips her soya milk and I am the soya milk. She dips the silvery biscuit in the milk and I am the biscuit, all falling apart, just tragic in its ordinariness.

'Are you going to the Judicious Leopard later?'

As you will imagine, I now feel strongly that I will go to the Judicious Leopard this evening.

'Calendarised.'

'Nice. What's going on with this biscuit?' She's lifting up what remains between us. It's floppy but holding together, and the coating is foaming ever so slightly. We both start to laugh because this is for some reason extremely funny.

We go back to work when the 💩 🎵 patriotic jingle cracks through the cafeteria and into our brains, and this event sort of switches us off from human things, re-aligning our thoughts to the fucking tedious process so that we're not in it as total people anymore, which is obviously the point. It doesn't quite work, of course. 😵

*

I get home within the usual 18.19–18.22 window and my mum's shredded carrier bag is in the hall. It's orangey in the hall, early-evening-in-autumn colour, even though it's still summer. A big glass cylinder of gin is quite obvious through the bag, plus some pretzel things and a five pack of cigarettes. My mum has been reusing this bag for upwards of two years, even though it would cost almost nothing to replace it. The gin is 🥃 *a costly brand*™ 🥃. My mum is pretty much an alcoholic, but she has a certain standard she won't slip below. Which is annoying, because the tokenz® could go somewhere else. Like a new carrier bag, or clothes from this century. She's watching television in the living room with the volume low and the curtains shut, and Toby is in there too. He waves at me as I pass and I wave at him smilingly and go up into my room to get ready for the Judicious Leopard. They're watching cartoons.

I'm dog tired (what a great thing to say: dog tired!) but also I know that after a beer or two I'll find some other zone of being where that won't register much. So I have a period of nothingness. I just slip into it. It's like a fissure in a polar expanse, only made of sheer nothing. I float in it for about 26 minutes by the clock in my room, whose display is either too bright or too dim because the light sensor broke and it got stuck between settings. Then I change into a different t-shirt. 🍳

*

They're playing something that just goes wow-wow-wow-w-wow in the bar and after a moment I realise that I like it.

'Hey *Übermensch!*'

It's K2, being jerky again, and I decide as I generally do just to surf over it and start something of my own.

'Here's your beer. So remind me what happened to your tokenz®?'

'Leave me alone about that for now.'

👽 Something is wrong. He's actually hurt or something that I mentioned his tokenz® deficiency, I can tell. And K2 never seems hurt about anything. Maybe he was once, now that I think of it, when his dad was as poorly as it's possible to get and still be thought worth having in a hospital. Strangely, I don't feel any satisfaction that I've scored a point or anything, given his perpetual jerking on me. But then my 🔺 psychometrics 🌀 are quite different to his.

'Good evening, mister weasel-cock.'

💩💩💩 This is a really, really bad bit. It's Melvin. This is K2's half-brother, and there is no borderline quibble—he's pure jerk. He's wearing some sort of asymmetrical cardigan with a massive rhombus on it. The rhombus is green.

'Hello Melvin. Why are you here?'

'Dad's in town for a mega arms conference. I thought I'd come too and see how fuckwit was doing in the sex doll factory.'

As you can see there is no point in talking to Melvin, so I don't. I turn inward and focus on the beer sensation, giving myself up to it as it softens everything. It's as though I've had this titanium skeleton, a life-size snowman armature deep inside me, and the beer is turning it to butter. The music goes from wow-wow-wow-w-wow to bink-bink-bootle-bootle, which is funny in a dead, robotic way for maybe five seconds, then I tune out of it. 😶

Now I notice something really peculiar. Someone who looks just like Mr Colestar, only dressed in a too-sloppy way, is over by the bar. I tap K2.

'Look. Who do you think that is?'

K2 doesn't seem in the least surprised, which is 👽 👽 cking weird. 'Haven't seen him in a while,' he says. But he says it sort of *dead*. As though they're just words.

I look at K2 intensely but he looks somewhere else. Something is definitely wrong. Melvin takes his stupid cardigan onto the dance floor and starts bothering a girl I noticed earlier.

*

So here I am getting home just before midnight. Argentina didn't turn up. I torture myself with the thought that she will get there super late, and then find someone she really likes and spend the rest of the night dancing with them, and worse. 🛏 The whole evening has been the same total waste of time any evening at the Judicious Leopard has to be by law. But there is still the lingering strangeness of Mr Colestar possibly being there, and K2 being less interested in it than I'd expect him to be, like he'd practiced not being surprised. When I get in Toby is crying. He cries and cries just on and on until Mum eventually goes to him. She's totally bombed, I imagine.

*

You're meant to find something you want with your tokenz®. Somewhere out in that plenty of things that covers the whole extent of the earth, somewhere on the globe at any given moment that thing is being made that will ✎ *sort out your issues*™ ✎, for now, or even for good. Isn't that what everyone thinks? But I've never found anything that works like that. Not even for a moment. I used to save tokenz® for things anyway, and I have a few valuable items, like a sub-sentient modular music system everyone used to think was the sickest thing ever and is now a super-rare collector's item. But I never use it. I don't really like it, actually. I always listen to music on my hand, even when I'm in my room.

This music system albatross being only one of the many ways I've been 🔥 historically burned 🔥, I don't spend my tokenz® on very much. The odd stupid thing like the *Take The Decision* book, and tech for this POV, plus beer. And because I don't even buy those things very often I've got this insane quantity of tokenz®. I've got so many it's actually embarrassing. I don't look at the figure so I don't know exactly how many I've got, but it's probably like a whole year's worth. No-one else at all, especially not Mum, knows that I've got this 💰 **incredible hoard**™ 💰.

Okay. I'm at work. Arm elastic goes here, over the titanium hoop. It's really hard to keep the arm from springing immediately into place, and the resistance to this tension feels like the whole fucking job, really. Trying to stop it pinging away too soon, over and over and over. Sometimes I catch my thumb. If a robot could do this more cheaply it would, but it can't, so I'm here doing it forever, or until a cheaper robot can. I do understand 🔆 how things work ✎, despite my apparent reputation (with K2) as a cretin.

Argentina Lily is over there behind the second row of snow-man assemblers. She puts the brains in now. She went up to eyes at the end of last year after being on limbs for three months. She was on brains after another two. I'm still on limbs and have been stuck just so for eighteen months.

'Hey Arthur.'

It's K2, whispering, half turned away. I whisper back, my lowest possible whisper, a *micro-wheeze*, 'What are you doing? It's not break yet!' This is really dangerous and likely to lead to reprimand. Why would he bother? 🐛

'Look, I want to meet you after work at my house.'

'Okay. But why are you talking to me here?'

'You're in a surveillance dead spot.'

'Really? Are you sure?' My voice is like tiny, dry leaves. Like crumbs of them.

'I'm sure. Six ten. Switch off your hand before you go out. Fully, like I showed you.'

😨 Now Supervisor Udon is approaching very fast.

'Gentlemen. What's at issue here?'

'I dropped something under Arthur's feet.' K2 shows him a little metal pole with notches at each end. It's a snowman femur. Udon looks at him hard, like he's seeing through him totally, which of course he doesn't because he's a Batch-A fuck-wit. He's called Udon because he's a spineless worm and there are thousands of others just the same.

'Good. Now you have it. Go back to your station. It's not long until break, you can talk then.'

I strongly hope that maybe K2 is right about the dead spot. Why else would the Udons have a job, just hanging around makeries without any particular skills to contribute, if all the tech worked perfectly? The whole workplace, the whole world, it's just this shitty tangled cobweb of surveillance ready to choke you at any moment. I mean, I'm even ■ **Recording Myself™** ■ right now.

*

Here's K2 at his front door, but stood back in the gloom.

'Come inside.'

👽 This is quite weird. He's not usually as stern as this. No making fun of me, zero jerkiness. I feel a bit disappointed, but it's interesting too. We go into K2's house, which is much darker throughout than mine. It's just because of where it's tucked into the estate, in a corner of an X, it's otherwise exactly the same. His dad, as I've said, is quite monstrously rich, but his mum gets nothing, and it's his mum K2 lives with. His dad has really good solicitors. I follow him into his bedroom and notice the old-man-bear-thing he legally shouldn't have. It's sleeping.

'Arthur I'm going to show you something that you must not tell a single soul about so help you god.'

'You know I don't do god but okay, I'm super intrigued. What have you got that's so secret?'

K2 just slowly looks over into a corner and I follow his gaze. In the other corner of his room is a big grey box with a transparent top. I know what it is. It's a personal fabricator 🐵, which is of course completely fucking criminal.

'Where did you get *that*?'

'Don't ask me. It doesn't matter.'

K2's room is now like the inside of an 😈 Evil Genius Mind™ 😼. You'd never guess if you met him, he's just a tall-ish, blondish person, sort of muscular but ordinary, with fluo tattoos. That square face would make you think he was borderline chad, which couldn't be more wrong. But don't listen to me, 🐱 cuz apparently I'm as dumb and unobservant as he likes to think. I would now be unsurprised if he showed me 🚀 a nuclear warhead or whatever under his bed, because you could even make one of those with a PFD, if you had the right code.

'Look, Arthur, I've got some ideas about this machine. I know it's this sick thing that you can make no limit of sickest stuff with, but it's also more important than that.'

'If you say so . . .'

'I do. This is all shit, right?'

Since I'm now so important to K2's continuing freedom I don't care if I look stupid, so I ask him, 'What is?'

'This job, the makery. Spy snowmen for four-year-olds to talk to. It's shit. It's nothing.'

I'm still confused. 'We've got jobs, though?' We both know people from school without a job and all the stuff attendant. Wait a moment—'Did you say *spy* snowmen?'

K2 huffs out air. 'Yeah, I did. You think this is real work? Sticking on cartoon arms and legs, then eyes and brains, what next? Zombie Santas? Come on *'Thur*,'—jeez, it doesn't have to sound *that* much like 'duh'—'this isn't what we're here for. I'm working on an idea. It's a really, really good idea. Do you want to hear it?'

But I'm still digesting the 'spy' thing, and he doesn't tell me the idea anyway because somebody comes into his bedroom. I thought when the door swung out it would most likely be his mum behind it but it isn't. It's Mr Colestar.

Now I'm having this pretty contradictory moment. I can still remember Mr Colestar as my teacher, and just his appearance makes me feel like I ought to be handing in a project or something. But at the same time exactly I have this odd feeling that I want to *tell him off*. For mixing with us corrupted students, maybe. Or for pre-corrupting us or something. It's really somewhat crazy. Anyway the output is zero, and I just sit and say nothing and probably look like a second-prize dick.

'Hi Colin,' says K2.

Colin!

'Hey. And your friend's here. Hello, worst-of-all-people.'

You can see how he looks at me, sort of friendly and cold.

What's that about? And he remembers, he totally remembers the #*evolutionary bottleneck* thing, which makes me strangely elated. K2's illegal bear is shuffling in its pillow-jail but I don't really look.

'How's the coding?' says Mr Colestar to K2.

'Really good,' says K2 and flicks up a mass of text blocks on his laptop. 'This chunking system is *fire*.'

'What are you coding?' I say.

With his arms stretching out, elbows on his big fold-out desk and hands on the keyboard, I can see the bottom of the tattoo that gives K2 his name (unless the name led to the tattoo—I don't remember). It's an image of ▲ That Eponymous Mountain, the second highest in the world, with a red sign-type arrow pointing to the summit with the words I AM HERE on top of that. 'New brains for snowmen,' he says. 'Okay, let's lose that semicolon.'

K2 looks straight at me.

'I'm feeling lonely,' he says weirdly.

A small voice, a snowman voice, goes, 'Oh, I'm sad to hear that.'

I say, 'Really?'

'I want my mummy,' says K2, in the same weird, piss-take kid's voice.

'Oh, I know dear. But the state is holding her in a medium-security penal facility, and she is not eligible for parole for another six months.'

K2's face begins to crumple. 'Waa, waa, waa!'

'It's a crude demo,' says Mr Colestar. 'But it works, right?'

Both of them look at me.

'What's going on?'

K2 does an eye-roll. Mr Colestar is blank, patient-looking.

'We're changing the code. In the snowmen's brains.'

'Why?'

K2 looks away.

Mr Colestar says, 'You #*change the code* you #*change the world.*'

Actually now I remember him saying something like that in school, close to the end of his job. That's why I never bought the conspiracy thing about Mr Colestar blowing up the school. We all got this really sus message that K2 said was a government plant. He ran it through a text analysis that showed it was '94% consistent with sentence construction associated with language use within the employment token system'—so they'd probably done a shiny new one for every e©onomi© ©ommunity. Only someone who'd never paid any attention to what Mr Colestar said at all could believe he'd blow up a school, not for more than a split second, anyway. I mean, for what? 🐾

K2 says, without looking up: 'We fabricate new brains for the stupid fucking snowmen, here, in my bedroom. We take them to the factory. We put them in the snowmen. The snowmen go to China. We #*change the world*.'

Mr Colestar has the same blank look but he tells me, 'The snowmen you boys and girls make every day. They're not just toys. They're very sophisticated surveillance devices. It's not legal at the moment to use them here, but then you don't need them so much when you all have a chip sewn into your hands that monitors everything you so much as think. But there's an overseas market for this technology. A big one. Didn't you know that?'

As it happens, no. We're not supposed to discuss the manufactured items, and to keep my job I don't. So I really am a ♔ LEGENDARY DUMBASS ♔.

'K2 has reversed engineered the brains. He's fabricated these replacements and changed the code to something more . . . benign.'

'Why not reprogramme the existing brains?'

'Because they're wired to report any tampering, especially any adjustment to the code, back to the manufacturer. A company called InHive. But you can get the brain's spec if you look deep enough online. Pretty much everything is somewhere on a server under the desert in Severax. The assembly you and K2 do is currently a weak spot in the chain. It's largely unmonitored, by the device's brain anyway. K2's substitute brain will still send user/owner reports back to the license holder, which in most cases will be a foreign government agency. But it will be fictional data. Generalised data that won't affect the owner's status in any given state. It even generates fake domestic conversation for the surveillance systems to process. I've listened to some. It's reproduced my own voice and I can't tell the difference. At the same time, it delivers reports to the domestic owner about what's going on with family members, employers, regimes—it's sort of a private news agency.'

I'm trying to catch up with a situation I'm already in above my neck. 'But won't people report that this is happening? Won't someone tell the state?'

'Maybe. That's the gamble. Would you?'

K2 looks at me for a second, like he's really curious to know my answer. I ignore the question completely and go: 'But how do we get them into the factory?'

'Drones. Stuff them up our arses. You, maybe.' K2 is grumbling the words. 'I mean you're not obvious saboteur material. You never get random searches. Probably because you've never even realised what you're actually making.'

'Okay, but even if that works, won't it take years? For anything to change?'

K2 can't be bothered to speak to me any more. In case it's not obvious, K2 could do something a lot more lucrative than assemble snowmen in a factory. His half-brother has a quarter of his IQ, but his dad bankrolls Melvin with a tsunami of real currency, so he's going to university, and into a real job in the arms trade most likely, and blah blah blah. K2 and his mum and my mum and me, we're locked in this tokenz® system. For as long as. That's why you're here, folks. As I said at the beginning, thanks for subscribing. 😼

'This is just one strategy.' It's Mr Colestar again. 'A minor intervention maybe, but it's a way to protect the youngest children. To take them out of the surveillance loop. You need to give people space to have inner lives again. That thing in your hand may be #*raping your mind*, but in some places it's even worse.'

He used to talk about being #*raped by your hand* all the time at school. We just ignored it after a while. 'I switched off my hand's perma voice recognition, though. And the ambient camera. K2 showed me how far in you have to go to do it, it's crazy.'

'Yes, I wouldn't be talking to you if I thought you hadn't. But you can't switch off everything.'

I'm trying to enjoy the clunky irony that, as you cannot fail to have noticed, I'm ⦿ **Mr Freaking Surveillance™** ⦿ himself. But I'm also for the first time ever thinking, *can I even release this POV?* This is some serious criminal activity, all stacked up in a sort of poisonous cake that will easily ☠ KILL US ALL ☠. I'm thinking I'll have to scramble all the names and faces, which you can totally do. But it's the best material I've ever had, so maybe worth the risk for the potential currency it will generate. Perhaps it would make enough to buy me some real-life protection—but if that's *all* it does, then why would I bother? 🐾 These thoughts are grinding at me badly, not settling on any proper outcome.

Here you can see the image go slightly fisheye-wonky as I do something like rub some sweat over one of the lens-grains in my temples. And I feel for a moment that K2 and Mr Colestar and the entire huge brutal world know just exactly what I'm doing at this very second. And now Mr Colestar takes two snowman brains, which come out of the fabricator on a dreamlike slow conveyor belt, and puts them in a black cotton bag for me to take home. 🏠

*

So here I am back at work. I can see Argentina Lily but she's totally immersed in her brains and she doesn't see me seeing. I think about the hacked brains, the news agency for Chinese kids or whatever. I imagine I'm going directly to jail for what I learned yesterday evening, for what I'm a conspirator in, so I feel like I don't need to follow the rules anymore and I'm just looking around the makery instead of working. Udon there is going down the line, inspecting shit knows what. He's pretending he has the first clue about the actual work we're doing here, rather than just being a surveillance mop-up monkey. 🏠

Now I spot something a bit surprising. Do you see that? Argentina Ballerina has not one but *two* snowman brains between her fingers. Two. That's quite a hard thing to manage because you have to avoid touching the contact points, or you get a surprisingly 😨 massive shock. She is super dextrous, evidently. And as she takes the not-one-but-two-brains from the tray she kind of drops a brain 'by accident' into her lap, this once Udon is safely looking further on. There's this big pouch in the front of the left thigh of our overalls, and with a bit of leg jiggling and elbow bumping she gets it in. Not that you'd know, unless you could see just the way you can see it now, from my exact perspective.

So what is going on here? Am I the only person in the universe who doesn't have some secret project running in parallel to my 🌐 *boring fucking penitential existence*™ 🔒?

'Arthur!'

It's K2.

'What?'

'Do you have it?'

'Yeah, I have it. Wait, is Argentina part of . . .?'

'Of course she is. She's going to be taking them out of the line, we'll be bringing them in. There's an automated count at station fourteen, the one after Tina's. The numbers have to stay exactly the same. Do you have it on you now?'

'Yes, but can't I just give it to you? Why do I have to do it?'

'Fucking hell, 'Thur!' he shout-whispers. 'I've told you all that. Because you're not on brains and I'm considered suspicious, idiot. Swap it with Tina at first break. Sit next to her. Say the first line of *Little Wing*.'

*

So I'm sitting next to Argentina now and the 🍵 is in my overall pouch and the 🌑 is the colour orange and tastes (a little) of orange today. I'm drinking 💧. I'm shivery just thinking about talking to Argentina, and those micro-freckles on her cheeks are so vivid today that it's like I'm holding her face just by noticing them. This extra layer of secrecy, in fact #*actual criminality* is making the whole thing so intense that I'm almost paralysed. But I manage to go:

'Are you walking through the clouds?'

She looks at me. At first there's nothing there. I think: 🙈 OMFG have I just been 👻 *#ghosted?!* Is there no brain conspiracy at all, and Mr Colestar's really a spook beefing up conviction stats? Then a crooked smile turns on.

'I'll give you this free.'

Looking directly into my eyes, and with no visible movement above the level of the table, she takes the brain from the pouch in the leg of her overall and I barely feel it go into the pouch in mine. I can't even picture the action, I can't feel a thing, but she rotates this brain with the reengineered one. The hand comes out again. She's been looking at me directly and smiling all along. She goes, 'It's all right, it's all right.'

And I go, 'Take anything you want from me.'

Yes. Impossibly corny, but I mean it. Anything, Argentina. 😳

*

So much for the test. If a few can be done, then we can grade up to more. Eventually most of the brains shipping out of this place could be the hacked variety. This is what I'm learning here, where I've met with K2 again, in this gap between the only two shops in the neighbourhood that take our tokenz®. It's a really, really narrow little space with almost no sunlight and the urine smell of seventeen people and ninety-eight dogs wafting out to whomsoever might be fortunate.

I say, 'Clandestine.' 🕵

'Yeah right. There's a problem.'

'What do you mean? Did I make a mistake?'

'No, it's not you. You were fine.' I don't like the way K2 is rubbing his arm like that, up and down and up and down, directly over the tattoo. Like he's trying to change the picture, or it's changing itself and he's trying to stop it. 'Colin stopped messaging me. He said it's too dangerous. Electronic stuff always leads back to you eventually. Even if the route is super windy. It's like Grover's algorithm.'

'What?'

'It's this way to get to a single result from like a gazillion bits of input. Really fast. He's sending me notes now. Look at this.' K2 is showing me this really pathetic thing, a little scrap of bent-up dirty card with the tiniest, almost invisible marks on it. 'He says this is the only way to communicate now. It's the only way to avoid . . .'

'Avoid what?'

'Colin is mixed up in a lot of business I don't properly know about.'

👽 Still can't get used to that 'Colin.'

'I reckon even *he* can't see what's connected to what. But

338 · DAVID MUSGRAVE

this is how I know we have to meet here. He pushed this bit of card through my window. He says we can't be watched or recorded in this alley so for the moment it's safe. Hey, he's here. Stay out of the sunlight.'

Shit. It's really him. Here in this 💩 nasty little place with us all of a sudden. *In a freaking hoodie with the hood up.* It seems like he's small, almost as small as we are. I hadn't noticed that before—or have we grown that much? He's just a few centimetres away, and his breathing is super slow and careful. What you can see is a bit of the light at the other end of the passageway reflected in his glasses. That's why you can't see his eyes.

'You'll need to go,' Mr Colestar says. 'Get out of the area for a week at least. And get rid of that fabricator.'

'How am I supposed to do that?'

'Take it to Harman Electronics. They're open late tonight, until eleven. You'll get some money, I don't know how much. It can be out of the country by tomorrow morning, but you'll need to take it tonight.'

He's talking so calmly that it makes me panic, it's like I'm being hypnotised before being kidnapped or 🔪 sliced into pieces™ 🔪 or something.

'And I'm not sure we can continue with the brain project.'

'Why not?' This is me sounding all disappointed, even though I've just crashed into it all by accident, or it's crashed into me.

'They're going to embed those surveillance grains in you all from now on. Haven't they told you?'

The irony is so perfectly horrible I almost laugh. But I hold it in and say, 'No *way!*'

'Every stage of the whole workflow will be fully monitored. Every single action, everywhere you look. The only reason you didn't have those things to start with is because they were running the enterprise on the cheap, with human supervisors patching up the AV architecture. That was what gave us our window. But they've changed policy. I think they might already know what we're doing.'

'I can come up with a workaround,' says K2, in a sort of high, unconvincing voice. He's gone freakishly pale and I know we are both thinking about his so-branded 'surveillance dead spot.' 'We can cloak the brains somehow, no?'

That's Mr Colestar breathing out loudly. 'It's not going to work anymore.'

And now there's someone else coming down the alleyway. I hope it's just a person taking a shortcut into the residential block at the other end, but somehow I know that's wrong. There's something smooth and precise about the way this person moves. Do you notice it too? He's walking in this absolutely dead straight line. And Mr Colestar says in a whisper, 'Get out of here right away.'

We walk fast and then we run. We're at the end of the short alley in moments and I can't stop myself looking back to see that new person coming through behind us. But I don't see the person. I see the back of Mr Colestar instead. He's just standing there, where he met us just a few seconds ago. Not running. Not trying to escape. Like it's him that's hypnotised 👀 after all.

'Colin!' K2 shouts.

But he still doesn't move. I'm about to shout too but—

What is *that?* I mean 🦇 🫣 *what is that?*

Did you see what just happened?

3.

Hello. How are you? It would be unreasonable of me to expect a response from you today for the signal reason that I am alone. Nonetheless, I will proceed as though you were here, seated in the replica Max Bill Tripod Chair at the back of this less-than-well-appointed room. My somewhat quixotic adherence to the format of our terminated conversations owes simply to the fact that it has proven a great boon to me in the past.

Would you like a hot or cold drink, namely tea, coffee or orange juice?

I currently possess none of these. I will interpret your silence expediently as a 'no'.

You will recall that our last discussion revolved around a rather disorderly and overlong series of recollections. With your consent, I would now like to turn to the present.

You might legitimately observe that both the 'past' and the 'present' are arbitrary categories—that all narrated events are both 'present', in as much as they possess meaning and substance only in the instant of their recollection, their persistent, material effects on what is 'now'; and also 'past' in the sense that a separation in time, no matter how nugatory, is necessary to convey even what is happening 'at this very moment'—but I trust you will accept the conventional, imprecise, and nonetheless useful meaning.

You will be pleased to learn that the mission for which you so successfully prepared me was accomplished to the satisfaction of

342 · DAVID MUSGRAVE

the parties by which we are both employed. As always, the accuracy of information I received was exemplary, and I was able to complete the task without any serious mishaps. It's true that I was not expecting to encounter two additional subjects at the final rendezvous point, but these rogue factors were also mitigated and present no ongoing cause for concern. There is nothing that should cause me any consternation about the outcome of this recent venture.

Having said as much, despite having completed this task with expertise and professionalism, well within the bounds of what our employers consider right conduct, which is to say under quite different circumstances than those of my celebratory meal, two things are preventing me from feeling quite at ease. The first is that I am continually suppressing the urge to acquire three Cycladic urns. It will not surprise you to learn that I am not well placed financially to indulge in such purchases at this moment. Nonetheless, my days have been peppered with rather unsatisfactory efforts to pursue the acquisition of urns, registering and re-registering my interest with dealers in antiquities with whom I had previously been on good terms. I have been promised payment for this last completed mission, and while my income is highly uncertain now that I no longer work on a salaried basis, I have offered the whole expected sum as a deposit on the first potential item. But I have been unable to come to a satisfactory arrangement even with ———— & ———, from whom I purchased the last two artefacts in my now dispersed collection, and whom I have a suspicion were involved in their subsequent auction.

The second and related matter that I wish to convey to you is that I've begun to remove parts of my body. I realise that this must seem a gratuitous use of time and energy. Indeed, it is not a simple task. It is difficult to overcome the resistance I initially feel as I penetrate the outer skin of, for example, the smallest toe of my right foot, and as I cut with some difficulty through the soft, yellow, subcutaneous flesh to the hard substrate, using whatever object happens to be at hand, an almost overwhelming inner force seems to be telling me to stop. Yet at the same time this behaviour is the only type that earns me respite from the so far frustrated desire for urns. For fairly long periods it is really rather diverting, and has opened a whole new chapter in my rather discontinuous relationship with my bodies.

I wonder if it is necessary to point out that there is a natural limit to this activity. Unless I content myself with ever smaller, and therefore ever less diverting, protuberances, I will in time hit more significant and ultimately critical parts. I am not at this threshold yet. I have, however, enough imagination to picture it on the horizon. I wonder if our employers would consent once again to transplant my brain and spinal column to another corporeal housing, if it comes to pass that I make a total hash of this one? Perhaps they would be amenable, but I'm aware that budgetary considerations are bound to come into play.

While I allow myself to entertain the uncertain possibility of starting afresh, the prospect of terminally fouling my transferable parts has recently begun to hold a strong appeal for me. I've investigated this option in detail, and I believe that there is a way that my whole body could interact with the more aggressive stages of contemporary waste processing that would achieve this end. The small parts of me that I have so far liberated have disappeared into the system without trace, and if I can gauge the scale and sequence of inputs accurately, I believe I could make a good fist of discarding almost all of it. I could even excise a portion of the bathroom floor to expose the extremely effective physio-chemical waste mitigation machinery directly. With careful planning, little of me would be left at surface level to tidy up, and I would be able to initiate the procedure without being concerned that I was about to create needless work for anyone.

It has not escaped my attention that my every action, this conversation not excepted, is observed, recorded and presumably parsed in minute detail by our employers. Indeed, it seems only correct that they should demand such a level of information. I am an expensive tool, one which owes its very existence to the careful judgment and collective work of our government, or at least a department thereof. The fact that I do not know who collects this information, nor what is gleaned from it, is not relevant at all; the picture so constructed of me is, I'm sure, more accurate, because less deformed by subjective nuance, than any I could form of myself. I defer to its usefulness and authority. However, it is a matter of interest to me that the opportunity of intervening with my actions exists at every moment, and yet this opportunity has not been taken. The wise agency which brought me into being could, I imagine, prevent me from damaging what I, out of convention only, call 'myself' if it chose to. But since it has not, my experimental self-disfigurement continues, and I sense two distinct paths for my activity. In one, I reach the limit described above without soliciting any intervention. In the other, such an external intervention brings the activity to a halt. This could take the form of physical restraint, or some well-chosen avenue of therapeutic reasoning, or maybe the introduction of a pharmaceutical agent which corrects the prevailing feeling that this is the most important thing in the world for me to do.

Perhaps I have said enough on this topic.

In between my bodily interactions I find my thoughts wander more than before. My successes within the agency, and my largely amicable conversations with my erstwhile colleagues there, still present themselves brightly in recollection. Such memories are, however, tempered by reflections that take in the broader state of things: the ultimate motivations for the decisions of our employers, the situation for those in the employment token system, the unfortunate and mysterious diminution of the urban community of lambdas, etc. When these thoughts become too troubling, I mentally project myself out into the universe, imagining some speck in the distant void that could grow in time into another world, an emissary from which could one day resolve the outwardly intractable issues that so preoccupy us here on Earth. It is an admittedly circuitous solution, but my days are empty, and my thoughts are free to follow such convoluted paths.

There are only two rooms here. One of them doubles as a place for my chairs and food preparation. The other contains a bed, a shower and a toilet. I miss the presence of windows greatly. I am promised that these much-reduced quarters are temporary, so please do not interpret my description as a complaint.

I am delighted, although not surprised, to note that you have suffered today's discourse without interruption or query. I must thank you, in the abstract, and hope that we have the opportunity to renew our connection more concretely in future. And if I discover that release from my current predicament can only be found through the type of interaction with the domestic waste system outlined above, then I can at least be content in the belief that this will not cause you any special inconvenience. Incidentally, have I ever told you how much you remind me of Anne —————? In terms of appearance, at least. It is time for me to say goodbye, I think. Goodbye.

ACKNOWLEDGEMENTS

Thank you Irene Baldoni, Christopher
Potter, Cornelia Grassi, Anna Aslanyan,
Jeremy Cooper, Peter Kapos, Martha
Kapos, John Douglas Millar, Zoe Sorkin,
Janice Kerbel, Ananyo Bhattacharya, Gia
Millinovich, Brian Cox, Sarah Dobai, Keith
Jordan, Elliot Jeffries, Anna Clegg, Alex
Graves, Lani Yamamoto, Börkur Arnarson,
and above all Zoë Fleetwood and
Christopher Musgrave (the machine parts
on the cover were his idea).